U0080731

凱信企管

用對的方法充實自己，
讓人生變得更美好！

凱信企管

用對的方法充實自己，
讓人生變得更美好！

精準

7000單字

滿分版

中高級程度
Level 5 & Level 6

4201～7000單字

使用說明

7000 單字以「完美六邊型緊扣式學習架構」來
學習，能精準記憶單字，不論是學測、多益、
全民英檢中高級都能輕鬆過關，英語力大躍進。

1 收錄單字完整多義，學習滴水不漏

記住拼字的同時，單字的多重意思
及不同詞性收錄詳盡，不論怎麼考
都不怕，精準答題不誤用，滿分必
備因素一次掌握。

ac·ces·so·ry

[æk`sɛsərɪ]

名 附件、零件、幫兇、
配件
形 附屬的

2 英英解釋，協助更精準理解單字

中文直譯常常無法精準地翻譯英文
單字的字義。全書每一單字用英英
解釋再次完整說明字義，用字能更
準確，也能加強單字的深刻記憶。

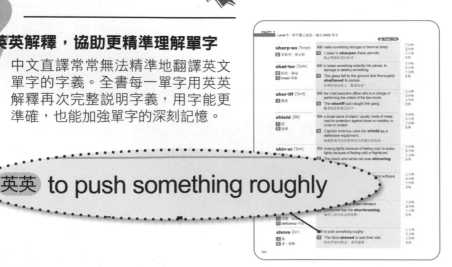

英英 to push something roughly

3 生活例句營造感官情境，強化單字記憶

善用感官讓單字自然記憶。利用例句營造情境，完美地理解單字並加深記憶，除能跟上出題方向，同時也能自然地提升生活口語能力。

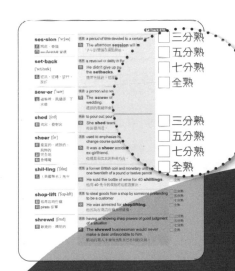

...or a series of events

例 I watched all the ten **episodes** of the Japanese drama in one day.
我在一天之內看完這部十集的日劇。

4 特別設計：「熟悉度評量表」，掌握學習成效

單字到底是記得三分熟、七分熟，還是滾瓜爛熟，用評量表檢測最準確。除了促進自我學習動力，還能在考試前，快速針對不熟悉的單字加強複習。

5 單字／例句音檔全收錄，學習隨時都可以

全書單字／例句音檔 MP3 收錄，QR Code 隨手一掃，藉由頻繁地用聲音刷腦記憶，刺激聽覺，單字一定記得住。

🎧 Track 118

...o down quickly

...lumped

全書音檔雲端連結

因各家手機系統不同，若無法直接掃描，仍可以至以下電腦雲端連結下載收聽。
(https://tinyurl.com/49wytdrx)

PREFACE
前言

　　你還再用「死背」的方式來背英文單字？！腦容量真的很有限，若用老方法來記單字，可能會讓你越背越忘，進入單字煉獄的痛苦輪迴中！

　　每回聽到學生們談到記單字的痛苦經驗，都忍不住替他們覺得辛苦！但英文單字又是考試拿分最重要的關鍵，不背又不行，到底該怎麼辦呢？

　　其實市面上 7000 單字的學習輔助教材已經相當多了，「如何選擇最好、最適合的」也常是學習者們最頭痛的問題；這亦是我們在一開始撰寫這本 7000 單字時，不斷在思量的。如何能有別與市面上的 7000 單字書，我們著實想了很久，於是決定讓台灣有許多教學經驗的 Michael 老師和從小在美國唸書的 Tong 老師聯手撰寫，結合對台灣考情的了解與在地生活英語的應用，讓 7000 單字的選字、例句的編寫，不僅能精準的符合 108 年新課綱注重英文與生活結合，徹底地讓學習者有效記憶單字，更能明確地理解單字及片語如何應用在句子裡，還能同步實際在日常裡發揮口說功能，齊步提升英語力，跨大步朝大考滿分邁進。

　　《精準 7000 單字滿分版》，我們特別著重三大部分：

　　一、收錄單字完整多義及不同詞性

　　單字的多重意思及不同詞性收錄詳盡，不論考題怎麼變化都不怕！答題能更精準，口說不誤用，單字一次學好學滿。

　　二、用感官情境法學單字

　　帶你用五感去感受單字。搭配生活例句及英英解釋，在腦海裡營造視覺畫面、創造英文環境，助你強化單字記憶；再利用音檔，刺激聽覺，考試沒問題，溝通也 OK。

　　三、單字評量表掌握學習成效

　　單字是三分熟、五分熟還是滾瓜爛熟，用評量檢測最準確！每一個單字特別設計「評量表」，除了掌握學習效果，亦能在考試前，快速複習拿高分。

　　期待這一本《精準 7000 單字滿分版：中高級程度 Level 5&Level 6》，能有效並無痛的幫助大家完勝 7000 單字，不論是學測、多益、全民英檢中高級都能輕易過關，輕鬆攻克任何大考。。

CONTENTS
目錄

Part 1

Part 2

Level 5 音檔雲端連結

因各家手機系統不同，若無法直接掃描，
仍可以至以下電腦雲端連結下載收聽。
（https://tinyurl.com/45e8e2mb）

Level 5

單字量
三級跳

邁向
5400單字

Aa

a·bide [əˈbaɪd]

動 容忍、忍耐
同 tolerate 容忍

英英 to accept or tolerate something or someone; to endure something painful or difficult
例 Mrs. Su can't **abide** her daughter's laziness.
蘇太太無法忍受自己女兒的懶惰。

☐ 三分熟
☐ 五分熟
☐ 七分熟
☐ 全熟

---

a·bol·ish [əˈbɑlɪʃ]

動 廢止、革除
反 establish 建立

英英 formally to put an end to an activity
例 Slavery was **abolished** in the 19th century.
奴隸制在十九世紀便被廢除。

☐ 三分熟
☐ 五分熟
☐ 七分熟
☐ 全熟

---

a·bor·tion

[əˈbɔrʃən]

名 流產、墮胎

英英 the intentional ending of a human pregnancy
例 **Abortion** is still a controversial issue.
墮胎仍然是個有爭議性的議題。

☐ 三分熟
☐ 五分熟
☐ 七分熟
☐ 全熟

---

a·brupt [əˈbrʌpt]

形 突然的
同 sudden 突然的
片 come to an abrupt halt
突然停下來

英英 describes something that is sudden and unexpected
例 The **abrupt** visit of a teacher surprised everyone.
老師的突然造訪讓大家感到驚訝不已。

☐ 三分熟
☐ 五分熟
☐ 七分熟
☐ 全熟

---

ab·surd [əbˈsɝd]

形 不合理的、荒謬的

英英 completely unreasonable, illogical, or ridiculous
例 Samuel Becketts is famous for the **absurd** play Waiting for Godot.
薩繆爾‧貝克特以其荒謬劇《等待果陀》著稱。

☐ 三分熟
☐ 五分熟
☐ 七分熟
☐ 全熟

---

a·bun·dant

[əˈbʌndənt]

形 豐富的
反 scarce 稀少的

英英 describes something existing or available in large quantities; something plentiful
例 Smart students tend to use **abundant** online resources to learn.
聰明的學生傾向於使用豐富的線上資源做學習。

☐ 三分熟
☐ 五分熟
☐ 七分熟
☐ 全熟

A

a·cad·e·my
[ə`kædəmɪ]

名 學院、專科院校

英英 a place of study or training in a special field, such as science, language, etc.

例 Emily plans to apply for the Royal **Academy** of Music.
愛蜜麗計畫要申請皇家音樂學院。

☐ 三分熟
☐ 五分熟
☐ 七分熟
☐ 全熟

ac·cus·tom
[ə`kʌstəm]

動 使習慣於

英英 to make used to something or doing something

例 You need to **accustom** yourself to all the school rules.
你必需適應所有的學校規定才行。

☐ 三分熟
☐ 五分熟
☐ 七分熟
☐ 全熟

ace [es]

名 傑出人才
形 一流的、熟練的

英英 a person who is very good at something or very skilled at something; very good at something or very skilled at something

例 Rachel is a swimming **ace**.
瑞秋是游泳方面的傑出人才。

☐ 三分熟
☐ 五分熟
☐ 七分熟
☐ 全熟

ac·knowl·edge
[ək`nɑlɪdʒ]

動 承認、供認
反 deny 否認

英英 to accept or admit the existence or truth of something

例 Sometimes people just don't like to **acknowledge** their mistakes.
有時候人們就是不想承認他們的錯誤。

☐ 三分熟
☐ 五分熟
☐ 七分熟
☐ 全熟

ac·knowl·edge·ment
[ək`nɑlɪdʒmənt]

名 承認、坦白、自白
反 denial 否認

英英 the action or fact of accepting or admitting the existence or truth of something

例 They want an **acknowledgement** of the existence of the problem of ocean wastes.
他們想要海洋廢棄物問題的存在能夠得到承認。

☐ 三分熟
☐ 五分熟
☐ 七分熟
☐ 全熟

ac·ne [`æknɪ]

名 粉刺、面皰

英英 a skin problem common in teenagers or young people, in which usually small red spots appear on the face

例 The **acne** is a kind of skin problem.
粉刺是種皮膚問題。

☐ 三分熟
☐ 五分熟
☐ 七分熟
☐ 全熟

ad·mi·ral
[`ædmərəl]

名 海軍上將

英英 the most senior commander in the navy

例 Nobody dared to disobey the **admiral**'s commands.
沒有人膽敢違抗海軍上將的命令。

☐ 三分熟
☐ 五分熟
☐ 七分熟
☐ 全熟

🎧 Track 003

ad·o·les·cence

[ˌædlˈɛsn̩s]

名 青春期

英英 in the process of developing into an adult from a child

例 Jack was impulsive when he was in his **adolescence**.
青春期的傑克是衝動的。

☐ 三分熟
☐ 五分熟
☐ 七分熟
☐ 全熟

---

ad·o·les·cent

[ˌædlˈɛsn̩t]

名 青少年
形 青春期的、青少年的
同 teenage 青少年的

英英 a young person who is developing into an adult

例 This program focuses on the study of **adolescent** literature.
這個計畫著重在青少年文學的研究。

☐ 三分熟
☐ 五分熟
☐ 七分熟
☐ 全熟

---

a·dore [əˈdor]

動 崇拜、敬愛、崇敬、寵愛

英英 to love, respect and admire deeply

例 Your grandfather **adores** you, Heidi.
海蒂，你是爺爺的心肝寶貝。

☐ 三分熟
☐ 五分熟
☐ 七分熟
☐ 全熟

---

adult·hood

[əˈdʌltˌhʊd]

名 成年期

英英 a person who is fully developed into an adult

例 When you reach **adulthood**, you understand more about life.
當你進入成年期，你對人生有更多的瞭解。

☐ 三分熟
☐ 五分熟
☐ 七分熟
☐ 全熟

---

ad·ver·tis·er

[ˈædvɚˌtaɪzɚ]

名 廣告客戶

英英 a company or a person who pays money for promoting sales

例 The **advertiser** asked the radio host to introduce their products.
廣告客戶要求電臺主持人介紹他們的產品。

☐ 三分熟
☐ 五分熟
☐ 七分熟
☐ 全熟

---

af·fec·tion

[əˈfɛkʃən]

名 親情、情愛、愛慕
反 hate 仇恨

英英 a feeling of admiration or liking

例 The famous actor's father didn't show him much **affection**.
知名演員的父親對他並沒有表現出太多的慈愛。

☐ 三分熟
☐ 五分熟
☐ 七分熟
☐ 全熟

---

a·gen·da

[əˈdʒɛndə]

名 議程、節目單

英英 a list of items of business or event to be discussed at a meeting

例 The **agenda** of tomorrow's meeting is listed on the notice.
明天會議的議程列在公告上。

☐ 三分熟
☐ 五分熟
☐ 七分熟
☐ 全熟

---

ag·o·ny [ˈægənɪ]

名 痛苦、折磨
同 torment 痛苦

英英 extreme suffering; pain or torture

例 The **agony** of the woman is shown on her face.
女人的臉龐顯露出她的痛苦。

☐ 三分熟
☐ 五分熟
☐ 七分熟
☐ 全熟

A

---

ag·ri·cul·tur·al

[ˌægrɪˈkʌltʃərəl]

名 農業的

英英 relating to the practice of farming, or farming

例 **Agricultural** economy has become a hot issue recently.
農業經濟學最近成為一個很熱門的話題。

☐ 三分熟
☐ 五分熟
☐ 七分熟
☐ 全熟

AI/ar·ti·fi·cial in·tel·li·gence

[ˌɑrtəˈfɪʃəl ɪnˈtɛlədʒəns]

名 人工智慧

英英 artificial intelligence

例 **AI** is a study about how to produce machines which have some human qualities.
人工智慧是關於如何製造有人類特質的機器的一門學問。

☐ 三分熟
☐ 五分熟
☐ 七分熟
☐ 全熟

---

air·tight [ˈɛrˌtaɪt]

形 密閉的、氣密的

英英 completely tight and closed so that no air can get in or out

例 Some chocolate cookies are kept in an **airtight** jar.
有些巧克力餅乾保存在密閉式的罐子裡。

☐ 三分熟
☐ 五分熟
☐ 七分熟
☐ 全熟

---

air·way [ˈɛrˌwe]

名 空中航線

英英 a designated route which airplanes fly from airport to airport

例 The **airway** is the area of the sky used by airplanes.
空中航線是飛機所使用的飛航區域。

☐ 三分熟
☐ 五分熟
☐ 七分熟
☐ 全熟

---

aisle [aɪl]

名 教堂的側廊、通道
片 walk down the aisle
　 步入結婚禮堂
　 （非正式用法）

英英 a passage between rows of seats on the bus or in an aircraft

例 Your grandma needs an **aisle** seat.
你的奶奶需要走道旁的位置。

☐ 三分熟
☐ 五分熟
☐ 七分熟
☐ 全熟

---

al·ge·bra

[ˈældʒəbrə]

名 代數

英英 a part of math in which symbols and letters represent numbers

例 **Algebra** is about using signs and letters to represent numbers.
代數與使用符號和字母來代表數字有關。

☐ 三分熟
☐ 五分熟
☐ 七分熟
☐ 全熟

---

a·li·en [ˈelɪən]

形 外國的、外星球的
名 外國人、外星人
同 foreign 外國人

英英 belonging to a foreign country or other planet

例 The government of this country was not friendly to **aliens** from Asian countries.
此國的政府對來自亞洲國家的外國人並不很友善。

☐ 三分熟
☐ 五分熟
☐ 七分熟
☐ 全熟

---

al·ler·gic [əˈlɝdʒɪk]

形 過敏的、厭惡的

英英 caused by or relating to an allergy

例 Sam is **allergic** to flowers.
山姆對花過敏。

☐ 三分熟
☐ 五分熟
☐ 七分熟
☐ 全熟

---

al·ler·gy [ˈælədʒɪ]

名 反感、食物過敏

英英 a condition that causes a person become ill or develop skin problems because they've eaten particular foods

例 My younger brother has an **allergy** to seafood.
我弟弟對海鮮過敏。

☐ 三分熟
☐ 五分熟
☐ 七分熟
☐ 全熟

---

al·li·ga·tor

[ˈæləˌgetə]

名 鱷魚

英英 a large semiaquatic reptile similar to a crocodile but with a broader and shorter head

例 The **alligator** eats fish and birds.
鱷魚吃魚類和鳥類。

☐ 三分熟
☐ 五分熟
☐ 七分熟
☐ 全熟

---

al·ly [əˈlaɪ]

名 同盟者
動 使結盟
反 enemy 敵人

英英 a person, organization, or country that agrees to cooperate with another; agree to cooperate with a person, organization or a country

例 In the Twilight series, the werewolf turned out to be the vampire family's **ally**.
在暮光之城系列中，狼人變成吸血鬼家族的盟友。

☐ 三分熟
☐ 五分熟
☐ 七分熟
☐ 全熟

---

al·ter [ˈɔltə]

動 更改、改變
同 vary 變更

英英 to change in character, appearance, direction, etc.

例 We reserve the right to **alter** the traveling schedule.
我們保留更改旅遊行程的權利。

☐ 三分熟
☐ 五分熟
☐ 七分熟
☐ 全熟

---

al·ter·nate

[ˈɔltəˌnet]/[ˈɔltɝnɪt]

動 輪流、交替
形 交替的、間隔的

英英 to have something happen one after the other repeatedly; every other

例 The actress **alternated** between rage and sadness.
這名女演員時而憤怒，時而悲傷。

☐ 三分熟
☐ 五分熟
☐ 七分熟
☐ 全熟

---

al·ti·tude

[ˈæltəˌtjud]

名 高度、海拔
同 height 高度

英英 the height above sea level or ground level

例 The **altitude** of Jade Mountain is 3,952 meters.
玉山的海拔高度是 3,952 公尺。

☐ 三分熟
☐ 五分熟
☐ 七分熟
☐ 全熟

am·ple [ˋæmpl̩]

形 充分的、廣闊的
同 enough 充足的

英英 enough or more than enough
例 You'll have **ample** time to think about this matter.
你會有充分的時間來思考這件事。

☐三分熟 ☐五分熟 ☐七分熟 ☐全熟

A

an·chor [ˋæŋkɚ]

名 錨、錨狀物
動 停泊、使穩固
片 weigh anchor 起錨

英英 an object used to moor a ship or boat by the coast or at the port; to lower an anchor into the water for stopping a boat by the coast or at the port
例 It's time to drop the **anchor**.
該是拋下錨的時候了。

☐三分熟 ☐五分熟 ☐七分熟 ☐全熟

an·them [ˋænθəm]

名 讚美詩、聖歌
片 national anthem 國歌

英英 an uplifting song which has special importance for a group or an organization, usually sung on a special occasion
例 A group of children are singing the **anthem**.
一群小孩正在唱聖歌。

☐三分熟 ☐五分熟 ☐七分熟 ☐全熟

an·tique [ænˋtik]

名 古玩、古董
形 古舊的、古董的
同 ancient 古代的

英英 a decorative object which is valuable because of its age; valuable because of its age; out of fashion
例 These **antiques** are the rich men's toys.
這些古玩是有錢人的玩具。

☐三分熟 ☐五分熟 ☐七分熟 ☐全熟

ap·plaud [əˋplɔd]

動 鼓掌、喝采、誇讚

英英 to show approval by clapping hands
例 The students **applauded** loudly.
學生大聲的鼓掌。

☐三分熟 ☐五分熟 ☐七分熟 ☐全熟

ap·plause [əˋplɔz]

名 鼓掌歡迎、喝采
同 praise 稱讚

英英 when people clap their hands repeatedly to show approval
例 The singer got a loud **applause**.
這名歌手獲得如雷般的掌聲。

☐三分熟 ☐五分熟 ☐七分熟 ☐全熟

apt [æpt]

形 貼切的、恰當的
同 suitable 適當的

英英 appropriate or suitable
例 "Nice" may not be an **apt** description of her kindness.
「好」這個字或許不足以形容她的善良。

☐三分熟 ☐五分熟 ☐七分熟 ☐全熟

ar·chi·tect [ˋɑrkəˌtɛkt]

名 建築師

英英 a person who designs new buildings
例 The **architect** on TV explained the structure of the house.
電視上那名建築師說明這棟房子的結構。

☐三分熟 ☐五分熟 ☐七分熟 ☐全熟

🎧 Track 007

ar·chi·tec·ture

[`ɑrkətɛktʃɚ]

名 建築、建築學、建築物
同 building 建築物

英英 the art or practice of designing and constructing buildings

例 The **architecture** of the garden was completely destroyed in the war.
這座花園建築在戰時被完全破壞。

☐ 三分熟
☐ 五分熟
☐ 七分熟
☐ 全熟

a·re·na [ə`rinə]

名 競技場
同 stadium 競技場

英英 a level area surrounded by seats, in which public events and entertainments are held

例 The Olympic **arena** needed a new designing.
奧林匹克競技場需要新的設計。

☐ 三分熟
☐ 五分熟
☐ 七分熟
☐ 全熟

ar·mor [`ɑrmɚ]

名 盔甲
動 裝甲

英英 the metal coverings which is worn to protect the body in battle; to prepare for fighting

例 The **armor** of the knight shines under the sun.
武士的盔甲在陽光下閃閃發亮。

☐ 三分熟
☐ 五分熟
☐ 七分熟
☐ 全熟

as·cend [ə`sɛnd]

動 上升、登

英英 to move up; climb or rise

例 Mr. Brown **ascends** the stairs slowly.
布朗先生慢慢地登樓。

☐ 三分熟
☐ 五分熟
☐ 七分熟
☐ 全熟

ass [æs]

名 驢子、笨蛋、傻瓜
片 make an ass of yourself 讓自己出糗

英英 a donkey or similar horse-like animal; describes someone acts like a fool

例 You don't need to care about what the dumb **ass** said.
你不需要在意那個蠢蛋說了什麼。

☐ 三分熟
☐ 五分熟
☐ 七分熟
☐ 全熟

as·sault [ə`sɔlt]

名 攻擊
動 攻擊
同 attack 攻擊

英英 to violently attack someone

例 The movie reveals the problem of sexual **assault** of women in the poor countries.
這部電影揭露了在貧窮國家的女性遭受性攻擊的問題。

☐ 三分熟
☐ 五分熟
☐ 七分熟
☐ 全熟

as·set [`æsɛt]

名 財產、資產
同 property 財產

英英 a useful or valuable thing or person

例 It touched me that Miss Chen donated 1/3 of her **asset** to the orphanage.
讓我感動的是陳小姐捐了三分之一的財產給孤兒院。

☐ 三分熟
☐ 五分熟
☐ 七分熟
☐ 全熟

as·ton·ish

[ə`stɑnɪʃ]

動 使……吃驚

英英 to surprise or impress someone greatly

例 Tim was **astonished** by how rich the beggar had been.
這名乞丐竟然如此有錢，這讓提姆很吃驚。

☐ 三分熟
☐ 五分熟
☐ 七分熟
☐ 全熟

A

as·ton·ish·ment
[əˋstɑnɪʃmənt]

名 吃驚

英英 the feeling of being surprised or impressed

例 To his father's **astonishment**, Bart chose to marry a girl from Vietnam.
讓伯特的父親吃驚的是，他竟然選擇娶一名來自越南的女孩。

☐ 三分熟
☐ 五分熟
☐ 七分熟
☐ 全熟

a·stray [əˋstre]

副 迷途地、墮落地
形 迷途的、墮落的

英英 away from the correct path or direction or correct way of doing something

例 The poor doggie seemed to go **astray**.
可憐的小狗似乎迷路了。

☐ 三分熟
☐ 五分熟
☐ 七分熟
☐ 全熟

as·tro·naut
[ˋæstrəˌnɔt]

名 太空人

英英 a person who is trained to travel in a spacecraft

例 Are you sure you'd like to be an **astronaut**?
你確定你想成為太空人？

☐ 三分熟
☐ 五分熟
☐ 七分熟
☐ 全熟

as·tron·o·my
[əsˋtrɑnəmɪ]

名 天文學

英英 the study of celestial objects, space, and the physical universe

例 **Astronomy** is a scientific field that focuses on the research of universe.
天文學是一門專注研究宇宙的科學領域。

☐ 三分熟
☐ 五分熟
☐ 七分熟
☐ 全熟

at·ten·dance
[əˋtɛndəns]

名 出席、參加
反 absence 缺席

英英 the action of presenting in an activity or event

例 Amy's **attendance** of the wedding delighted Jessie.
愛咪參加婚禮這件事讓傑西很高興。

☐ 三分熟
☐ 五分熟
☐ 七分熟
☐ 全熟

au·di·to·ri·um
[ˌɔdəˋtorɪəm]

名 禮堂、演講廳
同 hall 會堂

英英 the part of a theatre or hall in which holds the shows or performance

例 Doesn't the **auditorium** in our school look magnificent?
我們學校的禮堂看起來不是很富麗堂皇嗎？

☐ 三分熟
☐ 五分熟
☐ 七分熟
☐ 全熟

aux·il·ia·ry
[ɔgˋzɪljərɪ]

形 輔助的

英英 giving help of support to someone or something

例 My cousin works in the hospital as an **auxiliary** staff.
我表姐在醫院擔任輔助人員。

☐ 三分熟
☐ 五分熟
☐ 七分熟
☐ 全熟

awe [ɔ]

名 敬畏
動 使敬畏
同 respect 尊敬

英英 a feeling of great respect mixed with fear; to make a feeling of great respect mixed with fear

例 The people of the tribe look at the dawn in **awe**.
這個部落的人帶著敬畏的心看著黎明。

☐ 三分熟
☐ 五分熟
☐ 七分熟
☐ 全熟

a·while [əˋhwaɪl]

副 暫時、片刻
反 forever 永遠

英英 for a short time or for a moment

例 Kevin's daughter waited **awhile** and decided to call the police.
凱文的女兒等了一會兒，決定要打電話給警察。

☐ 三分熟
☐ 五分熟
☐ 七分熟
☐ 全熟

Bb

bach·e·lor

[ˋbætʃələ]

名 單身漢、學士
同 single 單身男女

英英 a man who is single

例 Jeff attended a **bachelor** party before marriage.
傑夫參加了婚前的單身漢派對。

☐ 三分熟
☐ 五分熟
☐ 七分熟
☐ 全熟

back·bone

[ˋbækˏbon]

名 脊骨、脊柱
同 spine 脊柱

英英 the spine on the back, which supports your body

例 After the examination, Judy found that her **backbone** needed to undergo an operation.
檢查之後，茱蒂發現她的脊椎必需要動手術。

☐ 三分熟
☐ 五分熟
☐ 七分熟
☐ 全熟

badge [bædʒ]

名 徽章

英英 a small flat object worn to show a person's identity, such as name, rank, job, or membership

例 The **badge** on the retired general reminds him of his past glory.
這名退休將軍的徽章提醒了他過去的光榮事蹟。

☐ 三分熟
☐ 五分熟
☐ 七分熟
☐ 全熟

bal·lot [ˋbælət]

名 選票
動 投票
同 vote 投票

英英 an occasion of voting secretly; to vote secretly by a group of people for finding out their views on a particular issue

例 The **ballot** stands for the voters' trust on the candidate.
選票代表了投票人對候選人的信任。

☐ 三分熟
☐ 五分熟
☐ 七分熟
☐ 全熟

ban [bæn]

動 禁止
名 禁令、查禁
片 call for a ban 呼籲

英英 to officially forbid

例 Religious beliefs are **banned** in this country.
在這個國家裡宗教信仰是被禁止的。

☐ 三分熟
☐ 五分熟
☐ 七分熟
☐ 全熟

ban·dit [ˋbændɪt]

名 強盜、劫匪
同 robber 強盜

英英 a thief or a robber that attacks people travelling through the countryside

例 The **bandits** were scared and ran for their life.
強盜害怕極了，逃命去了。

☐ 三分熟
☐ 五分熟
☐ 七分熟
☐ 全熟

B

ban·ner [ˈbænɚ]

名 旗幟、橫幅
同 flag 旗幟

英英 a long strip of cloth, which is with a slogan or design, hung up or carried on poles

例 In the parade, a group of students carried the **banner**.
遊行中，有一群學生舉著一面旗幟。

☐ 三分熟
☐ 五分熟
☐ 七分熟
☐ 全熟

ban·quet
[ˈbæŋkwɪt]

名 宴會
動 宴客
同 feast 宴會

英英 a formal meal for many people, often followed by speeches; to organize a formal meal for many people

例 My father was invited to the **banquet**.
我的父親受邀到宴會。

☐ 三分熟
☐ 五分熟
☐ 七分熟
☐ 全熟

bar·bar·i·an
[barˈbɛrɪən]

名 野蠻人
形 野蠻的

英英 a member of a people from different countries or culture, not belonging to any Christian civilizations; very cruel

例 Those **barbarians** attacked Robinson Crusoe.
那些野蠻人攻擊魯賓遜‧克魯索。

☐ 三分熟
☐ 五分熟
☐ 七分熟
☐ 全熟

bar·ber·shop
[ˈbarbɚʃap]

名 理髮店

英英 a shop that cuts or styles men's hair

例 The **barbershop** of this village is not far.
村裡的理髮店不太遠。

☐ 三分熟
☐ 五分熟
☐ 七分熟
☐ 全熟

bare·foot [ˈbɛrˌfʊt]

形 赤足的
副 赤足地

英英 without wearing shoes or socks

例 The **barefoot** farmer plants rice under the hot sun.
赤足農夫頂著大太陽種稻米。

☐ 三分熟
☐ 五分熟
☐ 七分熟
☐ 全熟

bar·ren [ˈbærən]

形 不毛的、土地貧瘠的
反 fertile 肥沃的

英英 of land too poor to produce plants or fruits

例 The land is **barren**.
土地一片貧瘠。

☐ 三分熟
☐ 五分熟
☐ 七分熟
☐ 全熟

bass [bes]

名 低音樂器、男低音歌手
形 低音的

英英 playing or singing in the lowest voice or musical notes; the lowest adult male singing voice

例 The **bass** in the musical sounds extremely beautiful.
音樂劇的低音樂器聽起來極為悅耳。

☐ 三分熟
☐ 五分熟
☐ 七分熟
☐ 全熟

🎧 Track 011

batch [bætʃ]

英英 a quantity of goods produced at the same time

名 一批、一群、一組

同 cluster 群、組

例 The **batch** of skates are from France.

這一批的溜冰鞋來自法國。

☐ 三分熟
☐ 五分熟
☐ 七分熟
☐ 全熟

---

bat·ter [ˈbætɚ]

英英 to strike repeatedly and violently with heavy blows

動 連擊、重擊

同 beat 打擊

例 Those houses were **battered** by the giant waves.

那些房子被巨浪連續重擊。

☐ 三分熟
☐ 五分熟
☐ 七分熟
☐ 全熟

---

ba·zaar [bəˈzɑr]

英英 a market with small shops for people to sell their things in a Middle-Eastern country

名 市場、義賣會

例 Irene bought a colorful umbrella from an Indian **bazaar**.

艾琳從印度的市場裡買了一把色彩鮮艷的雨傘。

☐ 三分熟
☐ 五分熟
☐ 七分熟
☐ 全熟

---

beau·ti·fy

[ˈbjutəˌfaɪ]

動 美化

英英 to make more beautiful

例 Why don't we place a Christmas tree here to **beautify** the school hall?

我們為什麼不在這裡放聖誕樹來美化學校的走廊？

☐ 三分熟
☐ 五分熟
☐ 七分熟
☐ 全熟

---

before·hand

[bɪˈforˌhænd]

副 事前、預先

反 afterward 之後、後來

英英 in advance; ahead of

例 You'd better prepare some vitamin pills **beforehand**.

你最好預先準備一些維他命藥丸。

☐ 三分熟
☐ 五分熟
☐ 七分熟
☐ 全熟

---

be·half [bɪˈhæf]

名 代表

英英 representing; instead of

例 On **behalf** of the school, Tiffany joined the table tennis competition.

蒂芬妮代表學校參加桌球比賽。

☐ 三分熟
☐ 五分熟
☐ 七分熟
☐ 全熟

---

be·long·ings

[bəˈlɔŋɪŋz]

名 所有物、財產

同 possession 財產

英英 a person's movable possessions or property

例 In the earthquake, Ho lost all his **belongings**.

在地震中，何失去了所有的財產。

☐ 三分熟
☐ 五分熟
☐ 七分熟
☐ 全熟

---

be·lov·ed [bɪˈlʌvɪd]

形 鍾愛的、心愛的

同 darling 親愛的

英英 a much loved person

例 Oh, my **beloved**, how can you be so cruel to me?

喔，親愛的，你怎麼能對我如此殘忍？

☐ 三分熟
☐ 五分熟
☐ 七分熟
☐ 全熟

B

ben·e·fi·cial

[͵bɛnə`fɪʃəl]

形 有益的、有利的
反 harmful 有害的

英英 advantageous or helpful

例 Drinking black tea is **beneficial** to you as well.
喝紅茶對你而言也是有益的。

□三分熟
□五分熟
□七分熟
□全熟

---

be·ware [bɪ`wɛr]

動 當心、小心提防

英英 to be cautious to risks or dangers

例 **Beware** of the dog.
當心惡犬。

□三分熟
□五分熟
□七分熟
□全熟

---

bid [bɪd]

名 投標價
動 投標、出價

英英 an offer of a particular price for something which is for sale; to offer a particular price to buy something

例 Jerry made a **bid** for the pottery plate.
傑瑞出價買下這個瓷盤。

□三分熟
□五分熟
□七分熟
□全熟

---

black·smith

[`blæk͵smɪθ]

名 鐵匠、鐵工

英英 a person who makes and repairs iron things by hand

例 Vulcon is the **blacksmith** of the gods in Greek and Roman mythology.
在希臘羅馬神話中兀兒肯是諸神的鐵匠。

□三分熟
□五分熟
□七分熟
□全熟

---

blast [blæst]

名 強風、風力
動 損害
反 breeze 微風

英英 an explosion; to destroy or damage something or someone

例 The garden was **blasted**.
這座花園遭受強風損害。

□三分熟
□五分熟
□七分熟
□全熟

---

blaze [blez]

名 火焰、爆發

英英 a very large burning fire

例 The **blaze** of the explosion looks terrifying.
這場爆炸中的火焰看起來很可怕。

□三分熟
□五分熟
□七分熟
□全熟

---

bleach [blitʃ]

名 漂白劑
動 漂白、脫色
反 dye 染色

英英 a liquid chemical substance which is used to make things white or lighter; to make things white or lighter by a chemical process or by exposure to sunlight

例 Mike's roommate asked him to buy a bottle of **bleach**.
麥克的室友要求他買一瓶漂白劑。

□三分熟
□五分熟
□七分熟
□全熟

---

bliz·zard [`blɪzəd]

名 暴風雪

英英 a heavy snowstorm with high winds

例 The giant snowman is flying high in the **blizzard** with the little boy.
巨大的雪人帶著這名男孩在暴風雪中高飛。

□三分熟
□五分熟
□七分熟
□全熟

🎧 Track 013

blond/blonde

[blɑnd]

名 金髮的人
形 金髮的

英英 a person with pale yellow hair

例 Is it true that the **blond** lady over there is your girlfriend?
在那裡的那名金髮女士真的是你的女朋友嗎？

☐ 三分熟
☐ 五分熟
☐ 七分熟
☐ 全熟

---

blot/stain

[blɑt]/[sten]

名 污痕、污漬
動 弄髒、使蒙恥（羞）

英英 a dark mark usually made by ink; to make something dirty by ink

例 The ink **blot** on the T-shirt is hard to wash.
T 恤上的污漬很難洗的掉。

☐ 三分熟
☐ 五分熟
☐ 七分熟
☐ 全熟

---

blues [bluz]

名 憂鬱、藍調

英英 melancholic music of black American folk origin

例 B.B. King was an American **blues** singer.
比・比・金是美國的藍調歌手。

☐ 三分熟
☐ 五分熟
☐ 七分熟
☐ 全熟

---

blur [blɝ]

名 模糊、朦朧
動 變得模糊

英英 something that cannot be seen clearly; to make or become unclear

例 The boy put off his glasses and everything turned out to be a **blur**.
男孩拿掉眼鏡，每件東西都變得模糊。

☐ 三分熟
☐ 五分熟
☐ 七分熟
☐ 全熟

---

bod·i·ly [ˈbɑdɪlɪ]

形 身體上的
副 親自、親身
反 spiritual 精神的

英英 relating to the body or physical; relating to the human body

例 The writer put up with the **bodily** pain and continued to write the novel.
他忍受身體上的病痛，繼續寫這本小說。

☐ 三分熟
☐ 五分熟
☐ 七分熟
☐ 全熟

---

body·guard

[ˈbɑdɪˌgɑrd]

名 護衛隊、保鑣

英英 a person employed to protect someone rich or famous

例 The **bodyguard**'s motorcycle crashed on an old lady.
重機上的保鑣撞上了一名老婦人。

☐ 三分熟
☐ 五分熟
☐ 七分熟
☐ 全熟

---

bog [bɑg]

名 濕地、沼澤
動 陷於泥沼

英英 a soft, wet, muddy area or ground; cause to stuck in a soft, wet mud

例 Take some photos of some rare crabs in this **bog**.
拍一些在這處沼澤裡稀有螃蟹的照片。

☐ 三分熟
☐ 五分熟
☐ 七分熟
☐ 全熟

B

bolt [bolt]
名 門閂
動 閂上、吞嚥

英英 a long metal pin on the door or window, which is used to lock it closed; to lock a door or window closed with a long metal pin

例 When the **bolt** is loosen, you can push the door open easily.
當門閂鬆開時，你可以輕易地推開這扇門。

☐ 三分熟
☐ 五分熟
☐ 七分熟
☐ 全熟

bo·nus [ˋbonəs]
名 獎金、分紅、紅利

英英 a sum of money given to a person as reward for good performance

例 Most employees expect to get year-end **bonus**.
多數的員工期待拿年終獎金。

☐ 三分熟
☐ 五分熟
☐ 七分熟
☐ 全熟

boom [bum]
名 隆隆聲、繁榮
動 發出低沉的隆隆聲、急速發展
同 thunder 隆隆聲

英英 a loud, deep, resonant sound; to make a loud, deep sound

例 The **boom** of the thunder scared the sleeping baby.
打雷的隆隆聲嚇壞了睡夢中的寶寶。

☐ 三分熟
☐ 五分熟
☐ 七分熟
☐ 全熟

booth [buθ]
名 棚子、攤子

英英 a small temporary structure like a box, which is used for selling goods

例 Some mountain climbers take a rest in the **booth**.
有些登山客就在棚子裡歇歇腿。

☐ 三分熟
☐ 五分熟
☐ 七分熟
☐ 全熟

bore·dom
[ˋbordəm]
名 乏味、無聊

英英 the state of feeling bored

例 Jogging alone is such a **boredom**.
自己一個人跑步真是件無聊的事。

☐ 三分熟
☐ 五分熟
☐ 七分熟
☐ 全熟

bos·om [ˋbuzəm]
名 胸懷、懷中
同 breast 胸部

英英 a woman's breast or chest

例 A red spot is on the **bosom** of the lovely bird.
這隻可愛小鳥的胸部有紅色的斑點。

☐ 三分熟
☐ 五分熟
☐ 七分熟
☐ 全熟

bot·a·ny [ˋbɑtənɪ]
名 植物學

英英 the study on the field of plants

例 Burnett visited the library to find some data related to the **botany**.
伯奈特造訪圖書館，要找些跟植物學有關的資料。

☐ 三分熟
☐ 五分熟
☐ 七分熟
☐ 全熟

🎧 Track 015

bou·le·vard

[ˈbuləˌvɑrd]

名 林蔭大道
同 avenue （林蔭）大道

英英 a wide street in a city, typically one lined with trees

例 When you walk through the **boulevard**, you feel quite relaxed.
當你散步通過這個林蔭大道時，你會感到很放鬆的。

☐ 三分熟
☐ 五分熟
☐ 七分熟
☐ 全熟

bound [baʊnd]

名 彈跳
動 跳躍

英英 to jump over something

例 The giant panda can leap several houses in a single **bound**.
巨大貓熊一個彈跳就跳過好幾間屋子。

☐ 三分熟
☐ 五分熟
☐ 七分熟
☐ 全熟

bound·a·ry

[ˈbaʊndərɪ]

名 邊界
同 border 邊界

英英 a line marking the limits or edge of an area

例 Some artists tend to cross the **boundary** of forms while creating artworks.
有些藝術家傾向在創作作品時跨越形式的邊界。

☐ 三分熟
☐ 五分熟
☐ 七分熟
☐ 全熟

bow·el [ˈbaʊəl]

名 腸子、惻隱之心

英英 the intestine; a sense of compassion or sympathy

例 The fruits can get your **bowels** moving.
這些水果可以讓你的腸子蠕動。

☐ 三分熟
☐ 五分熟
☐ 七分熟
☐ 全熟

box·er [ˈbɑksə]

名 拳擊手

英英 a person who boxes as a sport

例 Ali is a famous **boxer**.
阿里是個有名的拳擊手。

☐ 三分熟
☐ 五分熟
☐ 七分熟
☐ 全熟

box·ing [ˈbɑksɪŋ]

名 拳擊

英英 a sport in which two boxers fight by hitting each other with their hands

例 Hand your brother a pair of **boxing** gloves.
把這副拳擊手套拿給你哥哥。

☐ 三分熟
☐ 五分熟
☐ 七分熟
☐ 全熟

boy·hood [ˈbɔɪhʊd]

名 少年期、童年

英英 the state of being a male child or youth

例 We went to the nearby river to catch crabs and shrimps at our **boyhood**.
童年時，我們到附近的河流去抓螃蟹和蝦子。

☐ 三分熟
☐ 五分熟
☐ 七分熟
☐ 全熟

brace [bres]

名 支架、鉗子
動 支撐、鼓起勇氣
同 prop 支撐物

英英 supporting a part or piece of something; to support something

例 The dental **brace** could be removed next week.
牙套下星期就可以拿掉。

☐ 三分熟
☐ 五分熟
☐ 七分熟
☐ 全熟

B

braid [bred]

名 髮辮、辮子
動 編結辮帶或辮子

英英 a hair style which three pieces of hair are joined by putting them over each other in a special pattern; to join three pieces of hair by putting them over each other in a special pattern

例 Some little girls like to **braid** the hair of their barbie dolls.
有些小女孩喜歡幫芭比娃娃編辮了。

☐三分熟
☐五分熟
☐七分熟
☐全熟

---

breadth [brɛdθ]

名 寬度、幅度
反 length 長度

英英 the distance or measurement from one side to another

例 What's the **breadth** of your box?
你的箱子寬度是多少？

☐三分熟
☐五分熟
☐七分熟
☐全熟

---

bribe [braɪb]

名 賄賂
動 行賄

英英 to make a person do something for you by giving them something what they want

例 **Bribing** is illegal.
賄賂是不合法的。

☐三分熟
☐五分熟
☐七分熟
☐全熟

---

brief·case [ˈbrifˌkes]

名 公事包、公文袋

英英 a flat rectangular, which is used for carrying books and documents

例 Carry your **briefcase** and follow me.
帶著公事包，跟著我來。

☐三分熟
☐五分熟
☐七分熟
☐全熟

---

broad·en [ˈbrɔdn]

動 加寬
同 widen 加寬

英英 to make or become broader

例 The road was **broadened** last month.
這條路上個月就拓寬了。

☐三分熟
☐五分熟
☐七分熟
☐全熟

---

bronze [brɑnz]

名 青銅
形 青銅製的

英英 a yellowish-brown alloy made of copper and tin; made by the metal bronze

例 The **bronze** sculpture of Taichi was crafted by Ju Ming.
這個太極銅製雕刻是朱銘所製作的。

☐三分熟
☐五分熟
☐七分熟
☐全熟

---

brooch [brotʃ]

名 別針、胸針

英英 a small piece of jewellery with a pin fastened to clothing as a decoration

例 Why don't you buy the carnation **brooch** for your mother?
你為什麼不幫你媽買這個康乃馨胸針呢？

☐三分熟
☐五分熟
☐七分熟
☐全熟

---

brood [brud]

名 同一窩孵出的幼鳥
動 孵蛋、擔憂

英英 a family of young birds produced at one hatching or birth; to sit on eggs to hatch them

例 How lovely are the **brood** of swallows!
這一窩燕子的幼鳥好可愛啊！

☐三分熟
☐五分熟
☐七分熟
☐全熟

broth [brɔθ]

名 湯、清湯
同 soup 湯

英英 a thin soup consisting of meat or vegetable cooked in stock

例 Grandpa is good at making beef **broth**.
爺爺擅長於熬煮牛肉清湯。

☐ 三分熟
☐ 五分熟
☐ 七分熟
☐ 全熟

---

broth·er·hood
[ˋbrʌðɚ͵hʊd]

名 兄弟關係、手足之情

英英 the relationship between brothers

例 The news reporters are curious about the **brotherhood** of Chen family.
新聞記者對陳氏家族的兄弟關係感到好奇。

☐ 三分熟
☐ 五分熟
☐ 七分熟
☐ 全熟

---

browse [braʊz]

名 瀏覽
動 瀏覽、翻閱

英英 to view a text in a leisurely way or very quickly

例 Daphne **browsed** the picture book when her sister played violin.
當黛芬妮的姊姊演奏小提琴時，她瀏覽繪本。

☐ 三分熟
☐ 五分熟
☐ 七分熟
☐ 全熟

---

bruise [bruz]

名 青腫、瘀傷
動 使……青腫、
使……瘀傷

英英 an injury appearing on the skin of the body, which is caused by a blow rupturing underlying blood vessels

例 The **bruises** are all over the little boy's body.
這個小男孩的身上滿是瘀傷。

☐ 三分熟
☐ 五分熟
☐ 七分熟
☐ 全熟

---

bulge [bʌldʒ]

名 腫脹
動 鼓脹、凸出
同 swell 腫脹

英英 to stick out in a round shape

例 The round gift box made a **bulge** under her jacket.
圓形禮物盒在她的夾克下方凸了出來。

☐ 三分熟
☐ 五分熟
☐ 七分熟
☐ 全熟

---

bulk [bʌlk]

名 容量、龐然大物

英英 something is the mass or large in size or amount

例 It's possible that the footprint belongs to a big **bulk** creature.
這個腳印有可能屬於某隻體型龐大的生物。

☐ 三分熟
☐ 五分熟
☐ 七分熟
☐ 全熟

---

bul·ly [ˋbʊlɪ]

名 暴徒
動 脅迫

英英 a person who hurts or frightens those who are weaker; to threat someone who is weaker to do something

例 The **bully** should learn his lesson.
這個暴徒應該要學到教訓。

☐ 三分熟
☐ 五分熟
☐ 七分熟
☐ 全熟

---

bu·reau [ˋbjʊro]

名 政府機關、辦公處
同 agency 行政機關

英英 an organization or business that collects or offers information

例 The **bureau** on the 2nd floor can help you deal with the application of passport.
二樓的辦公處可以幫你處理護照的申請。

☐ 三分熟
☐ 五分熟
☐ 七分熟
☐ 全熟

C

butch·er [ˋbʊtʃɚ]

名 屠夫
動 屠殺、殘害
同 slaughter 屠殺

英英 a person who cuts up and sells meat in a shop; to kill something brutally

例 The murder was committed by a **butcher**.
這樁謀殺案是一名屠夫犯下的。

☐ 三分熟
☐ 五分熟
☐ 七分熟
☐ 全熟

Cc

cac·tus [ˋkæktəs]

名 仙人掌

英英 a dessert plant with a thick fleshy stem for storing water

例 A little water will be enough for the **cactus**.
對仙人掌來說，一些水就夠了。

☐ 三分熟
☐ 五分熟
☐ 七分熟
☐ 全熟

calf [kæf]

名 小牛

英英 a young cow

例 The **calf** followed the cow.
小牛跟著母牛走。

☐ 三分熟
☐ 五分熟
☐ 七分熟
☐ 全熟

cal·lig·ra·phy
[kəˋlɪgrəfɪ]

名 筆跡、書法

英英 decorative handwriting often created with a special pen or brush; handwritten lettering

例 Wang Xizhi is famous for the art of **calligraphy**.
王羲之以書法藝術聞名。

☐ 三分熟
☐ 五分熟
☐ 七分熟
☐ 全熟

ca·nal [kəˋnæl]

名 運河、人工渠道
同 ditch 管道

英英 an artificial waterway allowing boats to travel along

例 It's quite relaxing while we were taking the boat on the **canal**.
當我們搭乘運河上的小船時，感覺滿愜意的。

☐ 三分熟
☐ 五分熟
☐ 七分熟
☐ 全熟

can·non [ˋkænən]

名 大砲
動 用砲轟

英英 a large, heavy gun fixed with wheels, which fires heavy stone or metal balls; to collide with cannon forcefully

例 The **cannon** is placed on top of the castle.
大砲置放在城堡的上方。

☐ 三分熟
☐ 五分熟
☐ 七分熟
☐ 全熟

car·bon [ˋkɑrbən]

名 碳、碳棒

英英 a non-metallic chemical substance which has two main forms

例 **Carbon** emissions should be regulated.
碳排放應該要被規範。

☐ 三分熟
☐ 五分熟
☐ 七分熟
☐ 全熟

Track 019

card·board

[ˈkɑrd͵bɔrd]

名 卡紙、薄紙板

英英 very thick stiff paper, which is usually used for making boxes

例 You may cut off the **cardboard** and make a telescope.

你可以剪開這張卡紙，製作望遠鏡。

□三分熟
□五分熟
□七分熟
□全熟

---

care·free [ˈkɛr͵fri]

形 無憂無慮的
反 anxious 憂慮的

英英 free from anxiety or worry

例 Jack won't enjoy this kind of **carefree** life on vacation.

傑克不會喜歡度假時無憂無慮的生活。

□三分熟
□五分熟
□七分熟
□全熟

---

care·tak·er

[ˈkɛr͵tekɚ]

名 看管人、照顧者

英英 a person whose job is to look after a public building or people

例 Mothers are the major **caretakers** of the baby.

媽媽是嬰兒的主要照顧者。

□三分熟
□五分熟
□七分熟
□全熟

---

car·na·tion

[kɑrˈneʃən]

名 康乃馨

英英 a small flower with grey-green leaves and a sweet smell, which is usually pink, white, or red

例 The **carnation** is commonly seen on Mother's Day.

在母親節常見康乃馨。

□三分熟
□五分熟
□七分熟
□全熟

---

car·ni·val

[ˈkɑrnəvl̩]

名 狂歡節慶
同 festival 節日

英英 an annual period of public event involving processions, music, and dancing

例 In the Brazilian **carnival**, people dance with great passion.

在巴西的狂歡節慶中，人們以極大的熱情跳舞。

□三分熟
□五分熟
□七分熟
□全熟

---

carp [kɑrp]

名 鯉魚
動 吹毛求疵

英英 a large deep-bodied fish, often kept in ponds, which can be cooked; to complain continually

例 The **carps** serve as a common motif in Chinese painting.

鯉魚在國畫中是常見的主題。

□三分熟
□五分熟
□七分熟
□全熟

---

car·ton [ˈkɑrtn̩]

名 紙板盒、紙板

英英 a box or container made from thick cardboard

例 The milk **carton** should be thrown into the blue trash box.

紙板盒應該要被丟進藍色垃圾箱。

□三分熟
□五分熟
□七分熟
□全熟

C

cat·e·go·ry

[ˈkætəˌgorɪ]

名 分類、種類
同 classification 分類

英英 a class or division of people or things having some features that are the same

例 Miller knows the **category** of butterflies well.
米勒很清楚蝴蝶的分類。

☐ 三分熟
☐ 五分熟
☐ 七分熟
☐ 全熟

ca·the·dral

[kəˈθidrəl]

名 主教的教堂、大教堂
同 church 教堂

英英 the principal church of a diocese

例 The **cathedral** is decorated by colored windows.
這個大教堂用彩色窗戶做裝飾。

☐ 三分熟
☐ 五分熟
☐ 七分熟
☐ 全熟

cau·tion [ˈkɔʃən]

名 謹慎
動 小心
同 warn 小心、警告

英英 great care or attention taken to avoid danger or mistakes

例 You should handle the crystal glasses with **caution**.
你應該要謹慎處理水晶杯。

☐ 三分熟
☐ 五分熟
☐ 七分熟
☐ 全熟

cau·tious [ˈkɔʃəs]

形 謹慎的、小心的
同 wary 小心的

英英 careful to avoid problems or dangers

例 Be **cautious** of the wet and slippery floor.
小心溼滑的地板。

☐ 三分熟
☐ 五分熟
☐ 七分熟
☐ 全熟

ce·leb·ri·ty

[səˈlɛbrətɪ]

名 名聲、名人

英英 a famous person

例 Leonardo DiCaprio is a **celebrity** who cares about environmental issues.
李奧納多・狄卡皮歐是個關心環保議題的名人。

☐ 三分熟
☐ 五分熟
☐ 七分熟
☐ 全熟

cel·er·y [ˈsɛlərɪ]

名 芹菜

英英 a vegetable with crisp juicy stalks, used in salads

例 Add some **celery** to the bowl of soup.
在這碗湯裡放一些芹菜。

☐ 三分熟
☐ 五分熟
☐ 七分熟
☐ 全熟

cel·lar [ˈsɛlə]

名 地窖、地下室
動 貯存於
同 basement 地下室

英英 a storage space or room for storing things under ground in a house; to store something in somewhere

例 The old couple stored some bottles of wine in the **cellar**.
這對老夫婦把一些瓶裝酒藏在地窖。

☐ 三分熟
☐ 五分熟
☐ 七分熟
☐ 全熟

🎧 **Track 021**

---

cel·lo [ˈtʃɛlo]

名 大提琴

英英 a wood-made musical instrument with four strings, held upright on the floor between the legs of the seated player

例 The **cello** made of high-quality wood is expensive.
這把用高品質木頭製成的大提琴是昂貴的。

☐ 三分熟
☐ 五分熟
☐ 七分熟
☐ 全熟

**cell·phone/
cel·lu·lar phone/
mo·bile phone**

[sɛl fon]/[ˈsɛljʊlə fon]/
[ˈmobɪl fon]

名 行動電話

英英 a hand-held protable mobile radiotelephone

例 The bill of the **cellphone** this month is over $400.
這個月的手機帳單超過四百元。

☐ 三分熟
☐ 五分熟
☐ 七分熟
☐ 全熟

**Cel·si·us/
Cen·ti·grade**

[ˈsɛlsɪəs]/[ˈsɛntəˌgred]

形 攝氏溫度的
名 攝氏溫度

英英 a measurement of temperature on which water freezes at 0° and boils at 100°

例 In some areas of Russia, the temperature drops to below -20 **centigrade**.
在俄國的某些區域，氣溫可以降到攝氏零下 20 度。

☐ 三分熟
☐ 五分熟
☐ 七分熟
☐ 全熟

---

cer·e·mo·ny

[ˈsɛrəˌmoni]

名 慶典、儀式
同 celebration 慶祝

英英 a formal occasion, usually celebrating a particular event or anniversary

例 The Mazu religious **ceremony** was held in March.
媽祖的宗教慶典在三月舉行。

☐ 三分熟
☐ 五分熟
☐ 七分熟
☐ 全熟

---

cer·tif·i·cate

[səˈtɪfəkɪt]

名 證書、憑證
動 發證書
　 [səˈtɪfəket]

英英 an official document which records a particular fact, event, or level of achievement; to give or provide certificate

例 The **certificates** will be mailed to all the participants of the workshop.
證書會郵寄給這個工作坊的所有參與者。

☐ 三分熟
☐ 五分熟
☐ 七分熟
☐ 全熟

**chair·per·son/
chair/chair·man**

[ˈtʃɛrˌpɝsn̩]/[tʃɛr]/
[ˈtʃɛrmən]

名 主席

英英 a person in charge of a meeting or event

例 Professor Huang was the **chairperson** of the Taiwanese Literature Association.
黃教授是臺灣文學協會的主席。

☐ 三分熟
☐ 五分熟
☐ 七分熟
☐ 全熟

chair·wom·an

[ˈtʃɛrˌwʊmən]

名 女主席

英英 a female person in charge of a meeting or organization

例 The **chairwoman** will give a talk at the beginning of the exhibition.
這個女主席會在展覽開始前發表談話。

☐ 三分熟
☐ 五分熟
☐ 七分熟
☐ 全熟

---

chant [tʃænt]

名 讚美詩、歌
動 吟唱
同 hymn 讚美詩

英英 a repeated rhythmic phrase, usually sung in unison by a group; to sing a repeated rhythmic phrase in a group

例 The **chant** of the cherry blossom is really beautiful.
櫻花的讚美詩真的好美。

☐ 三分熟
☐ 五分熟
☐ 七分熟
☐ 全熟

---

chat·ter [ˈtʃætɚ]

動 喋喋不休、嘮叨

英英 talk at length about things that are unimportant

例 Lisa kept **chattering** with her friends all morning.
麗莎一整個早上都在跟朋友聊天。

☐ 三分熟
☐ 五分熟
☐ 七分熟
☐ 全熟

---

check·book

[ˈtʃɛkˌbʊk]

名 支票簿

英英 a booklet of blank checks with your name printed on them, which is issued by a bank

例 The **checkbook** was stolen.
支票簿被偷了。

☐ 三分熟
☐ 五分熟
☐ 七分熟
☐ 全熟

---

check-in [tʃɛkˌɪn]

名 報到、登記

英英 showing your ticket or reservation number at the counter of an airport or hotel so that you can be told where you will be sitting or the room you are going to staying

例 Annie will complete the **check-in** for us.
安妮會幫我們完成報到手續。

☐ 三分熟
☐ 五分熟
☐ 七分熟
☐ 全熟

---

check out

[ˈtʃɛkˌaʊt]

動 檢查、結帳離開

英英 to leave a hotel after paying and returning the key of room you stayed

例 We need to **check out** before 11 A.M.
我們需要在早上 11 點前結帳離開。

☐ 三分熟
☐ 五分熟
☐ 七分熟
☐ 全熟

---

check·up

[ˈtʃɛkˌʌp]

名 核對

英英 a medical or dental examination to detect any problems of your body

例 Regular financial **checkup** work is part of Fanny's job.
定期的財務核對工作是芬妮的工作之一。

☐ 三分熟
☐ 五分熟
☐ 七分熟
☐ 全熟

C

🎧Track 023

chef [ʃɛf]

名 廚師
同 cook 廚師

英英 a professional cook, especially the main cook in a restaurant or hotel

例 Paul, a French **chef**, is quite humorous.
法國主廚師保羅滿幽默的。

☐ 三分熟
☐ 五分熟
☐ 七分熟
☐ 全熟

---

chem·ist [ˈkɛmɪst]

名 化學家、藥商

英英 a person who sells medicinal drugs

例 The **chemist** specializes in researching the poison of snakes.
這個化學家擅長於蛇毒的研究。

☐ 三分熟
☐ 五分熟
☐ 七分熟
☐ 全熟

---

chest·nut

[ˈtʃɛsnət]

名 栗子
形 紅棕栗色的

英英 a hard reddish-brown nut which grows within a bristly case and can be roasted and eaten; having the color of hard reddish-brown

例 Some squirrels love to gather the **chestnuts**.
有些松鼠喜歡蒐集栗子。

☐ 三分熟
☐ 五分熟
☐ 七分熟
☐ 全熟

---

chill [tʃɪl]

動 使變冷
名 寒冷
形 冷的
同 cold 冷

英英 to become cold; feeling of coldness

例 We could feel the **chill** in the mountain.
我們可以感受到山裡的那股寒冷。

☐ 三分熟
☐ 五分熟
☐ 七分熟
☐ 全熟

---

chim·pan·zee

[ˌtʃɪmpænˈzi]

名 黑猩猩

英英 a black ape native to the west and central Africa

例 Jane Goodall is fond of researching the **chimpanzee**.
珍古德喜愛研究黑猩猩。

☐ 三分熟
☐ 五分熟
☐ 七分熟
☐ 全熟

---

choir [kwaɪr]

名 唱詩班
同 chorus 合唱隊

英英 a group of singers that takes part in church services

例 The **choir** is singing my favorite song.
唱詩班正唱著我最喜歡的歌曲。

☐ 三分熟
☐ 五分熟
☐ 七分熟
☐ 全熟

---

chord [kɔrd]

名 琴弦

英英 a group of three or more notes played together at the same time

例 Let's learn how to play **chords** on a guitar.
讓我們學習如何彈奏出吉他和弦。

☐ 三分熟
☐ 五分熟
☐ 七分熟
☐ 全熟

---

chub·by [ˈtʃʌbɪ]

形 圓胖的、豐滿的

英英 fat in an attractive way

例 The angel looks **chubby**.
天使看起來圓圓胖胖的。

☐ 三分熟
☐ 五分熟
☐ 七分熟
☐ 全熟

cir·cuit [ˈsɝkɪt]

名 電路、線路

英英 a roughly circular line, route, or movement

例 The electric **circuit** is broken, so there's no electricity.
電路斷了，所以沒電了。

---

cite [saɪt]

動 例證、引用
同 quote 引用

英英 to give an example as a proof to explain why something happened

例 Remember to **cite** the sources of data when you write your thesis.
寫論文時要記得引用資料。

---

civ·ic [ˈsɪvɪk]

形 城市的、公民的
同 urban 城市的

英英 relating to a city or citizen

例 To obey the traffic rule is the **civic** duty.
遵守交通規則是公民的責任。

---

clam [klæm]

名 蛤、蚌

英英 a large sea creature with shells of equal size

例 Lily kept the family secret like a **clam**.
莉莉像蛤一般的保守家族祕密。

---

clan [klæn]

名 宗族、部落
同 tribe 部落

英英 a group of interrelated families, that usually came from the same family and have the same last name, especially in the Scottish Highlands

例 Angus is our relative from the same **clan**.
安格斯是來自同一宗族的親戚。

---

clasp [klæsp]

名 釦子、鉤子
動 緊抱、扣緊
同 buckle 釦子、扣緊

英英 a hook or buckle; to grasp or hold tightly with one's hand

例 The blouse features the gold **clasp**.
這件女性上衣以金釦子為其特色。

---

clause [klɔz]

名 子句、條款

英英 A group of words that contains a subject and a predicate

例 This **clause** said you have to pay the damaged furniture to your landlord.
這個條款說明你必須付損壞家具的錢給房東。

---

cling [klɪŋ]

動 抓牢、附著
同 grasp 抓牢

英英 to hold on very tightly; to stick to

例 **Clinging** of the tree branch saves the mountain climber's life.
抓牢樹枝可以拯救登山者的生命。

C

Track 025

clock·wise

[ˈklɑk͵waɪz]

形 順時針方向的
副 順時針方向地

英英 to move in the direction of the hands of a clock moves

例 Move along the circle **clockwise** three times and jump into circle.
順時針沿著圓繞三圈，然後跳到圈裡。

☐三分熟 ☐五分熟 ☐七分熟 ☐全熟

clo·ver [ˈklovɚ]

名 苜蓿、三葉草

英英 a plant with three-lobed leaves on each stem, often fed to cows

例 Four-leaf **clover** is said to bring people luck.
四葉草據說能帶給人們好運。

☐三分熟 ☐五分熟 ☐七分熟 ☐全熟

clus·ter [ˈklʌstɚ]

名 簇、串、群
動 使生長、使成串
同 batch 組、群

英英 a group of similar things occurring closely together; to make as a group

例 A **cluster** of fans screamed when they saw the Korean star.
當一大群粉絲們看到那個韓星，他們放聲尖叫。

☐三分熟 ☐五分熟 ☐七分熟 ☐全熟

clutch [klʌtʃ]

名 抓握
動 緊握、緊抓
同 hold 抓握

英英 a tight grasp; to hold or grasp tightly

例 The baby **clutches** the toy tightly.
小寶寶緊握玩具。

☐三分熟 ☐五分熟 ☐七分熟 ☐全熟

coast·line

[ˈkost͵laɪn]

名 海岸線

英英 a length of coast

例 Walk along the **coastline** of the ocean and you'll see the old ship.
沿著海岸線散步，你就會看到那艘老舊的船。

☐三分熟 ☐五分熟 ☐七分熟 ☐全熟

co·coon [kəˈkun]

名 繭
動 用防水布遮蓋
把……包住、保護

英英 a silky case spun by the larvae of many insects for protection during the pupa stage; to protect something or someone from pain or dangerous situation

例 The moth emerged from the **cocoon**.
蛾從繭中出現。

☐三分熟 ☐五分熟 ☐七分熟 ☐全熟

coil [kɔɪl]

名 線圈、捲
動 捲、盤繞
同 curl 捲

英英 a length of something which is arranged into a series of circles, one above another; to arrange into a coil

例 A **coil** of rope is placed in the basement.
一圈繩子置放在地下室。

☐三分熟 ☐五分熟 ☐七分熟 ☐全熟

C

col·league
[`kɑlig]

名 同僚、同事

英英 an associate in office, or in a profession

例 Jennifer is the most admired **colleague** for me.
珍妮佛是我最為欣賞的同事。

colo·nel [`kɝnḷ]

名 陸軍上校

英英 a officer of high rank in the army and in the US air force

例 The **colonel** is giving a lecture in the hall.
陸軍上校在大廳演講。

co·lo·ni·al
[kə`lonɪəl]

名 殖民地的居民
形 殖民地的

英英 relating to or characteristic of a colony; a person who lives in a colony

例 In the 18th century, the British Empire governed some **colonies** in North America.
在十八世紀，大英帝國治理北美洲殖民地的居民。

com·bat [`kɑmbæt]

名 戰鬥、格鬥
動 戰鬥、抵抗
同 battle 戰鬥

英英 fighting, especially between armed forces

例 The **combat** between the white and black angels got intense.
黑白天使間的戰鬥越來越劇烈了。

co·me·di·an
[kə`midɪən]

名 喜劇演員

英英 an entertainer whose act is intended to make people laugh

例 Robin Williams is my favorite **comedian**.
羅賓・威廉斯是我最喜愛的喜劇演員。

com·et [`kɑmɪt]

名 彗星

英英 a celestial object moving around the sun, that is very rare can be seen

例 Halley's **Comet** could be observed from Earth.
哈雷彗星可以從地球觀察到。

com·men·ta·tor
[`kɑmən͵tetɚ]

名 時事評論家
同 critic 評論家

英英 a person who comments on events or issues in the media

例 The sports **commentator** has a sense of humor while reporting the game.
運動類的時事評論家在報導球賽時有其幽默感。

com·mis·sion
[kə`mɪʃən]

名 委任狀、委託
動 委託做某事

英英 an instruction, command, or duty; to bring into working order

例 Helen **commissioned** the lawyer to reduce the criminal responsibility of her brother.
海倫委託律師減輕其刑責。

🎧 **Track 027**

---

com·mod·i·ty

[kəˋmɑdətɪ]

名 商品、物產
同 product 產品

英英 a substance or agricultural product that can be bought and sold

例 The most valuable **commodity** in Saudia Arabia is oil.
沙烏地阿拉伯最有價值的商品就是石油。

☐ 三分熟
☐ 五分熟
☐ 七分熟
☐ 全熟

---

com·mon·place

[ˋkɑmənˏples]

名 平凡的事
形 平凡的
同 general 一般的

英英 a usual or ordinary thing

例 Poets could turn the **commonplace** into gems by vivid imagination.
詩人可以藉由想像力將平凡的事物化為寶石。

☐ 三分熟
☐ 五分熟
☐ 七分熟
☐ 全熟

---

com·mu·nism

[ˋkɑmjʊˏnɪzəm]

名 共產主義

英英 a political and social system whereby all property is owned by the community or government and each person contributes and receives according to their ability and needs

例 Some people believe **communism** exists for a reason.
有些學者相信共產主義有其存在的理由。

☐ 三分熟
☐ 五分熟
☐ 七分熟
☐ 全熟

---

com·mu·nist

[ˋkɑmjʊˏnɪst]

名 共產黨員
形 共產黨的

英英 a system of this kind derived from Marxism, practiced in China and formerly in the Soviet Union

例 The government official is accused of making a deal with the **communist** party member.
這個政府官員被指控與共產黨員做交易。

☐ 三分熟
☐ 五分熟
☐ 七分熟
☐ 全熟

---

com·mute

[kəˋmjut]

動 變換、折合、通勤
同 shuttle 往返

英英 to change something into another; to make the same travel between work and home

例 It takes only 20 minutes to **commute** from my home to the office.
從我家到辦公室通勤只要花二十分鐘。

☐ 三分熟
☐ 五分熟
☐ 七分熟
☐ 全熟

---

com·mut·er

[kəˋmjutɚ]

名 通勤者

英英 someone who travels between home and place of work regularly

例 The MRT was packed with the **commuters**.
捷運裡滿是通勤者。

☐ 三分熟
☐ 五分熟
☐ 七分熟
☐ 全熟

---

com·pact

[ˋkɑmpækt]/[kəmˋpækt]

名 契約
形 緊密的、堅實的

英英 an agreement between two people or companies; consisting of parts that are kept together closely or tightly

例 To take the drugs is like making a **compact** with devil.
吸食毒品就像跟魔鬼訂了契約。

☐ 三分熟
☐ 五分熟
☐ 七分熟
☐ 全熟

C

com·pass
[ˋkʌmpəs]

名 羅盤
動 包圍

英英 a device containing a magnetized pointer which shows the direction of magnetic north; to circle or surround

例 The Golden **Compass** was adapted from a novel written by Sir Philip Pullman.
《黃金羅盤》改編自菲力普‧普曼的小説。

☐ 三分熟
☐ 五分熟
☐ 七分熟
☐ 全熟

com·pas·sion
[kəmˋpæʃən]

名 同情、憐憫
同 sympathy 同情
片 lack of compassion 缺乏同情心

英英 a feeling of sympathetic pity or concern for the sufferings or misfortunes of others

例 **Compassion** is the noblest quality of human beings.
憐憫之心是人類最高貴的特質。

☐ 三分熟
☐ 五分熟
☐ 七分熟
☐ 全熟

com·pas·sion·ate
[kəmˋpæʃənɪt]

形 憐憫的
反 cruel 殘忍的

英英 feeling or showing compassion

例 Mother Teresa has a **compassionate** heart.
德蕾莎修女有顆憐憫之心。

☐ 三分熟
| 五分熟
☐ 七分熟
☐ 全熟

com·pel [kəmˋpɛl]

動 驅使、迫使、逼迫
同 force 迫使

英英 to force or oblige to do something

例 The mayor was **compelled** to make a difficult decision.
市長被迫做出困難的決定。

☐ 三分熟
☐ 五分熟
☐ 七分熟
☐ 全熟

com·pli·ment
[ˋkʌmpləmənt]

名 恭維
反 insult 侮辱

英英 an expression of praise, admiration or respect

例 Don't you think his **compliment** was true?
你真的認為他的恭維是認真的？

☐ 三分熟
☐ 五分熟
☐ 七分熟
☐ 全熟

com·pound
[ˋkʌmpaʊnd]/[kɑmˋpaʊnd]

名 合成物、混合物
動 使混合、達成協定
同 mix 混合

英英 a thing composed of two or more separate substances; to mix things together

例 Paints with organic **compounds** were used to beautify the room.
含有機混合物的油漆被用來美化房間。

☐ 三分熟
☐ 五分熟
☐ 七分熟
☐ 全熟

com·pre·hend
[ˌkɑmprɪˋhɛnd]

動 領悟、理解

英英 to understand or realize something

例 What the old Zen master told was hard to **comprehend**.
老禪師所説的很難理解。

☐ 三分熟
☐ 五分熟
☐ 七分熟
☐ 全熟

🎧 Track 029

com·pre·hen·sion

[ˌkɑmprɪˈhɛnʃən]

名 理解

英英 the action of understanding

例 Reading **comprehension** of the entrance exam is getting harder.
入學考的理解測驗越來越難了。

☐ 三分熟
☐ 五分熟
☐ 七分熟
☐ 全熟

com·pro·mise

[ˈkɑmprəˌmaɪz]

名 和解
動 妥協
同 concession 讓步

英英 an agreement reached by each side making concessions in an argument; to accept the standards that are lower than is desirable

例 To make a **compromise** between ideals and reality is necessary.
在理想和現實間做妥協是必要的。

☐ 三分熟
☐ 五分熟
☐ 七分熟
☐ 全熟

com·pute

[kəmˈpjut]

動 計算
同 calculate 計算

英英 to calculate (a figure or amount)

例 The university's **computing** center is not far away.
這個大學的計算中心不太遠。

☐ 三分熟
☐ 五分熟
☐ 七分熟
☐ 全熟

com·pu·ter·ize

[kəmˈpjutəˌraɪz]

動 用電腦處理

英英 convert to a system or form which is controlled, stored, or processed by computer

例 The library made efforts to **computerize** the illustrations of Russian picture books.
這間圖書館努力用電腦處理俄國繪本的插畫。

☐ 三分熟
☐ 五分熟
☐ 七分熟
☐ 全熟

com·rade

[ˈkɑmræd]

名 同伴、夥伴
同 partner 夥伴

英英 a friend or company, who you have experienced the same difficulties together, such as military or a special activity

例 David's **comrade** lost his way in the Amazon jungle.
大衛的同伴在亞馬遜叢林中迷了路。

☐ 三分熟
☐ 五分熟
☐ 七分熟
☐ 全熟

con·ceal [kənˈsil]

動 隱藏、隱匿
同 hide 隱藏

英英 to prevent something to be seen or known

例 How could you **conceal** such a big secret?
你怎麼可以隱藏這麼大的一個祕密？

☐ 三分熟
☐ 五分熟
☐ 七分熟
☐ 全熟

con·ceive

[kənˈsiv]

動 構想、構思

英英 to imagine something

例 **Conceiving** a good idea for writing a stage play takes time.
構想寫出舞臺劇的好點子主意要花時間。

☐ 三分熟
☐ 五分熟
☐ 七分熟
☐ 全熟

C

con·demn

[kən`dɛm]

動 譴責、非難、判刑
同 denounce 譴責

英英 to criticize something or someone seriously for moral reasons

例 **Condemning** the mob wastes your energy.
譴責暴民浪費的是你的精力。

- [ ] 三分熟
- [ ] 五分熟
- [ ] 七分熟
- [ ] 全熟

con·duct

[`kɑndʌkt]/[kən`dʌkt]

名 行為、舉止
動 指揮、處理

英英 a person's manner or behavior; to manage or direct

例 Do you think we should **conduct** a survey?
你認為我們應該進行個調查嗎？

- [ ] 三分熟
- [ ] 五分熟
- [ ] 七分熟
- [ ] 全熟

con·fes·sion

[kən`fɛʃən]

名 承認、招供

英英 an act of confessing, especially a statement of admitting to a crime

例 Why didn't Vincent make an honest **confession** in front of the policeman?
為什麼文生在警察面前不老實招供？

- [ ] 三分熟
- [ ] 五分熟
- [ ] 七分熟
- [ ] 全熟

con·front

[kən`frʌnt]

動 面對、面臨
同 encounter 遭遇

英英 to deal with a difficult situation or hardship

例 Bravely **confront** the problem.
勇敢面對問題吧。

- [ ] 三分熟
- [ ] 五分熟
- [ ] 七分熟
- [ ] 全熟

con·sent

[kən`sɛnt]

名 贊同
動 同意、應允
同 agree 同意

英英 permission or agreement

例 The manager of Jinsen company hasn't **consented** to the contract yet.
金生公司的經理尚未同意這份契約。

- [ ] 三分熟
- [ ] 五分熟
- [ ] 七分熟
- [ ] 全熟

con·serve

[kən`sɝv]

動 保存、保護
同 preserve 保護

英英 to protect from harm, destruction, or danger

例 It's our duty to **conserve** the historical heritage.
保存歷史遺蹟是我們的責任。

- [ ] 三分熟
- [ ] 五分熟
- [ ] 七分熟
- [ ] 全熟

con·sid·er·ate

[kən`sɪdərɪt]

形 體貼的

英英 very careful; kind and helpful

例 Selena's fiancé is talented and **considerate** to her.
薩琳娜的未婚夫很有才華，對她又體貼。

- [ ] 三分熟
- [ ] 五分熟
- [ ] 七分熟
- [ ] 全熟

🎧 **Track 031**

con·sole
[ˈkɑnsol]/[kənˈsol]

名 操作控制臺
動 安慰、慰問
同 comfort 安慰

英英 a control penal; to give comfort in a time of grief of disappointment

例 Peter **consoled** his wife after the death of their son.
在他們的兒子死去後，彼得安慰他的太太。

☐ 三分熟
☐ 五分熟
☐ 七分熟
☐ 全熟

con·sti·tu·tion·al
[ˌkɑnstəˈtjuʃən!]

名 保健運動
形 有益健康的、憲法的
同 healthful 有益健康的

英英 an exercise which is good for people's health; relating to a person's health; good for a person's health

例 Grandpa is 90 years old and still takes a **constitutional** every day.
爺爺 90 歲了，每天仍然在做保健運動。

☐ 三分熟
☐ 五分熟
☐ 七分熟
☐ 全熟

con·ta·gious
[kənˈtedʒəs]

形 傳染的
同 infectious 傳染的

英英 spread by direct or indirect contact between people or animals

例 Laughter is **contagious**.
笑是有傳染力的。

☐ 三分熟
☐ 五分熟
☐ 七分熟
☐ 全熟

con·tam·i·nate
[kənˈtæməˌnet]

動 污染
同 pollute 污染

英英 to make something impure or make it polluted

例 The factory admitted that they had **contaminated** the river.
這家工廠承認是他們污染了河流。

☐ 三分熟
☐ 五分熟
☐ 七分熟
☐ 全熟

con·tem·plate
[ˈkɑntɛmˌplet]

動 凝視、苦思、盤算

英英 to look at something or think about something thoughtfully

例 Wanda **contemplated** going to Canada to study jewelry design.
汪達盤算著要去加拿大攻讀珠寶設計。

☐ 三分熟
☐ 五分熟
☐ 七分熟
☐ 全熟

con·tem·po·rar·y
[kənˈtɛmpəˌrɛrɪ]

名 同時代的人
形 同時期的、當代的

英英 a person or thing existing at the same time as another

例 Christopher Marlowe is a **contemporary** of Shakespeare.
克里斯托弗‧馬洛是莎士比亞同時代的人。

☐ 三分熟
☐ 五分熟
☐ 七分熟
☐ 全熟

con·tempt
[kənˈtɛmpt]

名 輕蔑、鄙視
同 scorn 輕蔑

英英 the feeling that a person or a thing is worthless or useless

例 His **contempt** on women was showed on his face.
他對女人的鄙視顯露在臉上。

☐ 三分熟
☐ 五分熟
☐ 七分熟
☐ 全熟

C

con·tend
[kən`tɛnd]
動 抗爭、奮鬥

英英 to struggle to deal with a difficulty

例 She **contended** with the unfair administrative system of the company.
她力抗這不公平的公司管理制度。

☐ 三分熟
☐ 五分熟
☐ 七分熟
☐ 全熟

con·ti·nen·tal
[ˌkɑntə`nɛntl̩]
形 大陸的、洲的

英英 (also Continental) usually of or relating to mainland Europe

例 Have you seen the map of the North American **continent**?
你看到北美洲的地圖了嗎？

☐ 三分熟
☐ 五分熟
☐ 七分熟
☐ 全熟

con·ti·nu·i·ty
[ˌkɑntə`njuətɪ]
名 連續的狀態

英英 the unbroken and continuous condition

例 The rain poured in **continuity**, and the children couldn't play outside.
連續下傾盆大雨，小孩不能在外面玩耍。

☐ 三分熟
☐ 五分熟
☐ 七分熟
☐ 全熟

con·vert [kən`vɝt]
動 變換、轉換
同 change 改變

英英 to change in form, character, or religion

例 Don't you think that **converting** the topic of conversation so suddenly is strange?
你難道不認為突然轉換會話的主題是件奇怪的事？

☐ 三分熟
☐ 五分熟
☐ 十分熟
☐ 全熟

con·vict
[`kɑnvɪkt]/[kən`vɪkt]
名 被判罪的人
動 判定有罪

英英 a person who is in prison because they committed a crime; to declare someone is guilty of a crime

例 The **convict** was put to prison.
被判罪的人入獄了。

☐ 三分熟
☐ 五分熟
☐ 七分熟
☐ 全熟

cop·y·right
[`kɑpɪˌraɪt]
名 版權、著作權
動 為……取得版權

英英 the legal right to publish, perform, film, or record literary, artistic, or musical material, and to authorize others to do the same; to get a copyright

例 In the book fair, publishers buy **copyright** of the books from other countries.
在書展中，出版商從其他國家購買書籍的版權。

☐ 三分熟
☐ 五分熟
☐ 七分熟
☐ 全熟

cor·al [`korəl]
名 珊瑚
形 珊瑚製的

英英 a hard stony substance formed in the sea by groups of particular types of small animals; made of coral

例 This pair of earrings was majorly made of the **coral**.
這副耳環主要由珊瑚製成。

☐ 三分熟
☐ 五分熟
☐ 七分熟
☐ 全熟

🎧 **Track 033**

cor·po·ra·tion
[ˈkɔrpəˋreʃən]

名 公司、企業
同 company 公司

英英 a large company or group of companies authorized to act as a single organization
例 The **corporation** announced the date of holding a shareholder meeting.
這間公司宣布舉辦股東大會的日期。

☐ 三分熟
☐ 五分熟
☐ 七分熟
☐ 全熟

cor·re·spon·dence
[ˌkɔrəˋspɑndəns]

名 符合、相似之處
同 accordance 符合

英英 the action or fact of corresponding
例 There is no **correspondence** between the two fingerprints.
這兩枚指紋間並無相似之處。

☐ 三分熟
☐ 五分熟
☐ 七分熟
☐ 全熟

cor·ri·dor
[ˈkɔrədə]

名 走廊、通道

英英 a passage in a building or train, with doors leading into rooms or compartments
例 The butterfly **corridor** was decorated with different butterfly artworks.
這條蝴蝶走廊用不同的蝴蝶藝術作品做裝飾。

☐ 三分熟
☐ 五分熟
☐ 七分熟
☐ 全熟

cor·rupt [kəˋrʌpt]

動 使墮落
形 腐敗的
同 rotten 腐敗的

英英 to make corrupt; using your position or power to your own advantage dishonestly and secretly
例 The thing we should be afraid of is the **corrupt** human heart.
我們應該感到害怕的是腐敗的人心。

☐ 三分熟
☐ 五分熟
☐ 七分熟
☐ 全熟

coun·sel [ˈkaʊnsl̩]

名 忠告、法律顧問
動 勸告、建議
同 advise 勸告

英英 to give an advice formally
例 The lawyer offered useful **counsel** to the couple.
這名律師提供有用的忠告給這對夫婦。

☐ 三分熟
☐ 五分熟
☐ 七分熟
☐ 全熟

coun·sel·or
[ˈkaʊnsl̩ə]

名 顧問、參事

英英 a person who is trained to give guidance on personal or psychological problems
例 The **counselor** will let you know how to maintain mental health.
該名顧問會給你維持心理健康的好建議。

☐ 三分熟
☐ 五分熟
☐ 七分熟
☐ 全熟

coun·ter·clock·wise
[ˌkaʊntəˋklɑkˌwaɪz]

形 反時針方向的
副 反時針方向地

英英 in the opposite direction to the movement of the clock's hand
例 In the midnight, weird things happen; the clock goes **counterclockwise** by itself.
午夜時分，奇怪的事發生了；時鐘自己逆時針轉動。

☐ 三分熟
☐ 五分熟
☐ 七分熟
☐ 全熟

C

cou·pon [ˈkupɑn]
名 優待券

英英 a piece of paper which is used to a discount on a product or a quantity of something rationed

例 The food **coupon** is given to you as you are the birthday girl of this month.
這張食物優待券是送給你的，因為你是本月的壽星。

□三分熟
□五分熟
□七分熟
□全熟

---

court·yard [ˈkortˌjɑrd]
名 庭院、天井

英英 an open area enclosed by walls or buildings

例 It's hard to imagine that there's such a beautiful **courtyard** behind the living room.
很難想像在大廳的後面有如此漂亮的庭院。

□三分熟
□五分熟
□七分熟
□全熟

---

cow·ard·ly [ˈkaʊədlɪ]
形 怯懦的
反 heroic 英勇的

英英 lacking of courage

例 If soldiers fought **cowardly**, they would be punished by the military law.
如果士兵怯戰，他們會被軍法所懲罰。

□三分熟
□五分熟
□七分熟
□全熟

---

co·zy [ˈkozɪ]
形 溫暖而舒適的

英英 very warm and comfortable

例 The room is **cozy**.
這間房間溫暖舒適。

□三分熟
□五分熟
□七分熟
□全熟

---

crack·er [ˈkrækə]
名 薄脆餅乾

英英 a crisp biscuit, which makes slight sound while eating

例 Don't give the puppy the **crackers** you're eating.
不要給小狗你正在吃的薄脆餅乾。

□三分熟
□五分熟
□七分熟
□全熟

---

cra·ter [ˈkretə]
名 火山口
動 噴火、使成坑

英英 a large bowl-shaped hole on the top of a volcano; to form a crater

例 The Bolsena lake was in the **crater** of an ancient volcano.
博賽納湖在古代火山的火山口。

□三分熟
□五分熟
□七分熟
□全熟

---

creak [krik]
名 輾軋聲、嘎吱嘎吱聲
動 發出輾軋聲

英英 make a harsh high-pitched sound when being moved

例 Is it the **creak** of the door or the moaning of a beast?
這是門的嘎吱作響聲，還是某隻野獸的低吼聲？

□三分熟
□五分熟
□七分熟
□全熟

---

creek [krik]
名 小灣、小溪

英英 a narrow area of water that flows into the land from the sea

例 The **creek** is singing a lovely song.
小溪唱著可愛的歌。

□三分熟
□五分熟
□七分熟
□全熟

🎧 Track 035

crib [krɪb]

名 糧倉、木屋
動 放進糧倉、作弊

英英 a baby's bed; to copy someone's work dishonestly; to put something in a crib

例 The woodcutter lived in the **crib** in the mountain.
樵夫住在山裡的木屋裡。

☐ 三分熟
☐ 五分熟
☐ 七分熟
☐ 全熟

croc·o·dile [ˈkrɑkəˌdaɪl]

名 鱷魚

英英 a large reptile with long jaws, long tail, short legs, and hard skin

例 The **crocodiles** were killed and made into purses.
鱷魚被殺死並製成皮包。

☐ 三分熟
☐ 五分熟
☐ 七分熟
☐ 全熟

cross·ing [ˈkrɔsɪŋ]

名 橫越、橫渡

英英 a place where things cross, especially roads or railway lines

例 The ferry aids the **crossing** from Northern Ireland to Scotland or England.
渡輪對從北愛爾蘭到蘇格蘭或英格蘭的橫渡有所幫助。

☐ 三分熟
☐ 五分熟
☐ 七分熟
☐ 全熟

crouch [kraʊtʃ]

名 蹲伏、屈膝姿勢
動 蹲踞
同 squat 蹲

英英 to bend your knees and lower your body down so that you are close to the ground

例 The leopard **crouched** behind the bush.
花豹蹲伏在樹叢後。

☐ 三分熟
☐ 五分熟
☐ 七分熟
☐ 全熟

crunch [krʌntʃ]

名 踩碎、咬碎、嘎吱的聲音、危機、關鍵時刻
動 喀嚓喀嚓地咬嚼、嘎吱嘎吱地碾或踩、壓過

英英 a crunching sound that you make while biting things or stepping on something; to crush something with the teeth, making a grinding sound

例 The **crunch** of autumn leaves delights the little boy.
秋葉被踩碎所發出的嘎吱聲讓這個小男孩感到開心。

☐ 三分熟
☐ 五分熟
☐ 七分熟
☐ 全熟

crys·tal [ˈkrɪstl̩]

名 結晶、水晶
形 清澈的、透明的

英英 a clear glass with very high quality; very clear and pure

例 The **crystal** clear water feels icy.
如水晶般透明清澈的水摸起來很冰冷。

☐ 三分熟
☐ 五分熟
☐ 七分熟
☐ 全熟

cui·sine [kwɪˈzin]

名 烹調、烹飪、菜餚

英英 a style or method of cooking

例 The Thai **cuisine** tastes truly delicious.
泰式料理嚐起來真是美味。

☐ 三分熟
☐ 五分熟
☐ 七分熟
☐ 全熟

curb [kɝb]

名 抑制器
動 遏止、抑制
同 restraint 抑制

英英 to stop or control something

例 Should parents **curb** the spending of children?
父母應該抑制小孩的花費嗎？

☐ 三分熟
☐ 五分熟
☐ 七分熟
☐ 全熟

D

cur·ren·cy
[ˈkɝənsɪ]

名 貨幣、流通的紙幣

英英 a system of money in general use in a particular nation

例 Before traveling, you'd better go to the bank to exchange foreign **currency**.
旅行前,你最好去銀行換外幣。

□ 三分熟
□ 五分熟
□ 七分熟
□ 全熟

cur·ric·u·lum
[kəˈrɪkjələm]

名 課程
片 a core curriculum
主要課程

英英 the subjects studied in a school or college

例 We offer plenty of language **curricula** for the elderly and children.
我們為長者和小孩提供很多的語言課程。

□ 三分熟
□ 五分熟
□ 七分熟
□ 全熟

cur·ry [ˈkɝɪ]

名 咖哩粉
動 用咖哩粉調味

英英 a dish of meat, vegetables, etc., cooked in an Indian-style sauce with strong spicy flavour; to use curry for adding a flavour

例 Cindy loves the **curry** fried rice.
辛蒂喜歡咖哩炒飯。

□ 三分熟
□ 五分熟
□ 七分熟
□ 全熟

cus·toms
[ˈkʌstəmz]

名 海關

英英 the place at an airport or border where traveler's belongings need to be checked to find out if any goods are being carried illegally

例 Keelung **Customs** Office found the illegal jeans on October 16.
基隆海關在 10 月 16 日發現非法的牛仔褲。

□ 三分熟
□ 五分熟
□ 七分熟
□ 全熟

Dd

dart [dɑrt]

名 鏢、鏢槍
動 投擲、發射、猛衝
同 throw 投、丟

英英 a small pointed object with a sharp point which is thrown or fired as a weapon; to throw a dart

例 The guard of the prince was struck by the poisoned **dart**.
王子的守衛被毒鏢射中。

□ 三分熟
□ 五分熟
□ 七分熟
□ 全熟

daz·zle [ˈdæzl]

動 眩目、眼花撩亂
名 耀眼的光

英英 to make someone unable to see clearly for a short time

例 The sad little boy looked at the **dazzling** ocean.
悲傷的小男孩看著眩目的海洋。

□ 三分熟
□ 五分熟
□ 七分熟
□ 全熟

🎧 **Track 037**

---

de·cay [dɪˋke]

名 腐爛的物質
動 腐壞、腐爛
同 rot 腐爛

英英 the state or process of decaying or rotting; rot through the action of bacteria

例 The **decay** of the insect corpse reminds the poet of the meaning of death.
昆蟲腐爛的屍體提醒了詩人死亡的意義。

☐三分熟 ☐五分熟 ☐七分熟 ☐全熟

---

de·ceive [dɪˋsiv]

動 欺詐、詐騙
同 cheat 欺騙

英英 to cheat someone or keep the truth from them

例 You can **deceive** other people, yet you can't **deceive** yourself.
你可以欺騙其他人，但你不可能欺騙你自己。

☐三分熟 ☐五分熟 ☐七分熟 ☐全熟

---

dec·la·ra·tion [ˌdɛkləˋreʃən]

名 正式宣告

英英 a formal statement or announcement

例 The **declaration** of the priest in the wedding brought laughter to the couple.
神父在婚禮中的正式宣告讓這對夫婦笑了。

☐三分熟 ☐五分熟 ☐七分熟 ☐全熟

---

del·e·gate [ˋdɛləˌgɪt]/[ˋdɛləˌget]

名 代表、使節
動 派遣
同 assign 指派

英英 a person sent to represent others, in particular at a conference or meeting; to send a person to represent other

例 The athletes' performance in Australia amazed the **delegates** from other countries.
運動員在澳洲的表現讓來自其他國家的代表很驚豔。

☐三分熟 ☐五分熟 ☐七分熟 ☐全熟

---

del·e·ga·tion [ˌdɛləˋgeʃən]

名 委派、派遣、代表團

英英 the process of delegating or being delegated

例 The **delegation** from Japan congratulated the president on his birthday.
來自日本的代表團在總統生日當天恭喜總統。

☐三分熟 ☐五分熟 ☐七分熟 ☐全熟

---

dem·o·crat [ˋdɛməˌkræt]

名 民主主義者

英英 a supporter of democracy

例 A **democrat** supports same-sex marriage.
民主主義者支持同性婚姻。

☐三分熟 ☐五分熟 ☐七分熟 ☐全熟

---

de·ni·al [dɪˋnaɪəl]

名 否定、否認

英英 the action of denying

例 His **denial** of the cheating pushed his wife even further.
他否認偷吃，甚至把他的太太推得更遠。

☐三分熟 ☐五分熟 ☐七分熟 ☐全熟

---

de·scrip·tive [dɪˋskrɪptɪv]

形 描寫的、說明的

英英 giving a representation or a expression

例 The **descriptive** paragraph includes details of audio and visual aspects and smells.
這個描述性段落包含視聽面向和嗅覺方向的細節。

☐三分熟 ☐五分熟 ☐七分熟 ☐全熟

D

de·spair [dɪˋspɛr]

名 絕望
動 絕望
反 hope 希望

英英 the complete loss of hope

例 The monster could smell the **despair** of human beings.
這頭怪物可以嗅出人類的絕望。

☐ 三分熟
☐ 五分熟
☐ 七分熟
☐ 全熟

de·spise [dɪˋspaɪz]

動 鄙視、輕視
同 scorn 輕視

英英 to feel strong dislike for something or someone; look down on a person

例 Linda **despised** her ex-boyfriend and left him.
琳達鄙視她的前任男友，而離開了他。

☐ 三分熟
☐ 五分熟
☐ 七分熟
☐ 全熟

des·ti·na·tion

[ˌdɛstəˋneʃən]

名 目的地、終點
反 threshold 起點

英英 the place to which someone or something is going or being sent or taken

例 Yangming Mountain, Taipei is the **destination** of this trip.
臺北市的陽明山是這趟旅遊的終點。

☐ 三分熟
☐ 五分熟
☐ 七分熟
☐ 全熟

des·ti·ny [ˋdɛstɪnɪ]

名 命運、宿命
同 fate 命運

英英 the particular thing that will happen to a person, regarded as the fate

例 We have only one Earth and all humans share common **destiny**.
我們只有一個地球，人類共享命運。

☐ 三分熟
☐ 五分熟
☐ 七分熟
☐ 全熟

de·struc·tive

[dɪˋstrʌktɪv]

形 有害的
反 constructive 有建設性的、有益的

英英 causing damage

例 Verbal bullying is **destructive** to relationships.
言語霸凌對人際關係是有害的。

☐ 三分熟
☐ 五分熟
☐ 七分熟
☐ 全熟

de·ter·gent

[dɪˋtɝdʒənt]

名 清潔劑

英英 a chemical substance, usually liquid, for removing dirt from clothes or dishes, etc.

例 Mrs. Smith recommends the brand of **detergent** with the icon of a superman.
史密斯推薦這個有超人圖案的清潔劑。

☐ 三分熟
☐ 五分熟
☐ 七分熟
☐ 全熟

de·vo·tion

[dɪˋvoʃən]

名 摯愛、熱愛、奉獻

英英 great love or loyalty

例 Miss Jiang's **devotion** to the educational career is admirable.
江老師對教育事業的奉獻是令人欽佩的。

☐ 三分熟
☐ 五分熟
☐ 七分熟
☐ 全熟

🎧 **Track 039**

de·vour [dɪˈvaʊr]

動 吞食、吃光
同 swallow 吞嚥

| 英英 | to eat greedily; to eat all of food without anything left |
| 例 | Some natives were amazed when they saw the sun be **devoured**. 有些當地土著看到太陽被吞食時，他們是驚訝的。 |

☐ 三分熟
☐ 五分熟
☐ 七分熟
☐ 全熟

di·a·lect [ˈdaɪəlɛkt]

名 方言

| 英英 | a form of a language which is used by a specific region or social group |
| 例 | The folk song was written in local **dialect**. 這首民謠是由本土方言寫的。 |

☐ 三分熟
☐ 五分熟
☐ 七分熟
☐ 全熟

dis·be·lief

[ˌdɪsbəˈlif]

名 不信、懷疑
反 belief 相信

| 英英 | refusal to accept that something is true or real; lacking of trust |
| 例 | Jimmy was cynical and cherished the **disbelief** of humanity. 吉米憤世嫉俗，對人懷抱著不信任。 |

☐ 三分熟
☐ 五分熟
☐ 七分熟
☐ 全熟

dis·card [dɪsˈkɑrd]

名 被拋棄的人
動 拋棄、丟掉

| 英英 | a person who is gotten rid of; get rid of something or someone as no longer useful or desirable |
| 例 | **Discard** old beliefs and you'll have a new life like a new-born baby. 拋掉舊的信念，你會像個新生兒般的過著新生活。 |

☐ 三分熟
☐ 五分熟
☐ 七分熟
☐ 全熟

dis·ci·ple [dɪˈsaɪp!]

名 信徒、門徒
同 follower 跟隨者

| 英英 | a follower of Christ during his life |
| 例 | The **disciple** follows his master faithfully. 信徒忠實跟隨著他的師父。 |

☐ 三分熟
☐ 五分熟
☐ 七分熟
☐ 全熟

dis·crim·i·nate

[dɪˈskrɪməˌnet]

動 辨別、差別對待
同 distinguish 區別

| 英英 | to recognize a distinction |
| 例 | To **discriminate** the bad and the good is hard for a child. 辨別好與壞，對孩子來講是困難的。 |

☐ 三分熟
☐ 五分熟
☐ 七分熟
☐ 全熟

dis·pense

[dɪˈspɛns]

動 分送、分配、免除
同 distribute 分配

| 英英 | to give out things to a number of people |
| 例 | Kitchen Soups in America **dispensed** food to the homeless people in the 19th century. 在十九世紀時，美國的粥廠為街友分送食物。 |

☐ 三分熟
☐ 五分熟
☐ 七分熟
☐ 全熟

D

dis·pose [dɪˋspoz]

動 佈置、處理
同 arrange 安排、佈置

英英 to arrange in a particular position; to handle or manage

例 The government official monitored how the factory **disposed** the waste.
政府官員監控工廠處理廢料的作業方式。

□三分熟
□五分熟
□七分熟
□全熟

---

dis·tinc·tion

[dɪˋstɪŋkʃən]

名 區別、辨別
同 discrimination 區別

英英 telling the differences between things or people

例 The **distinction** of poisoned fish and non-poisoned fish should be the cook's priority.
區分有毒的魚和無毒的魚，應是廚師的首要之務。

□三分熟
□五分熟
□七分熟
□全熟

---

dis·tinc·tive

[dɪˋstɪŋktɪv]

形 區別的、有特色的

英英 individually characteristic, distinct from others of its kind

例 This dress's color is not quite **distinctive**.
這件洋裝的顏色並沒有很特別。

□三分熟
□五分熟
□十分熟
□全熟

---

dis·tress [dɪˋstrɛs]

名 憂慮、憂傷、苦惱
動 使悲痛
片 a distress signal
求救訊號

英英 extreme anxiety or worry; to make anxious or worried

例 The lad showed obvious signs of **distress**.
少年顯露出明顯憂傷的特徵跡象。

□三分熟
□五分熟
□七分熟
□全熟

---

doc·u·ment

[ˋdɑkjəmənt]

名 文件、公文
動 提供文件

英英 a piece of written or printed paper that provides information or evidence; to record in written

例 Judy has prepared the **document** of the seminar.
茱蒂已經準備好研討會的資料。

□三分熟
□五分熟
□七分熟
□全熟

---

door·step

[ˋdor͵stɛp]

名 門階

英英 a step leading up to the outer door of a house

例 A beggar appeared on the **doorstep** of the mansion.
一名乞丐出現在大廈的門階。

□三分熟
□五分熟
□七分熟
□全熟

---

door·way

[ˋdor͵we]

名 門口、出入口

英英 the space in a wall where a door opens or closes while coming in or out from it

例 The housekeeper was standing in the **doorway** to welcome the guest.
管家站在門口迎接客人。

□三分熟
□五分熟
□七分熟
□全熟

🎧 **Track 041**

dor·mi·to·ry

[`dɔrmə⁄torɪ]

名 學校宿舍

英英 a bedroom for a number of people in an institution or school

例 Not every student is lucky to live in the **dormitory**.
學生並不是都很幸運的可以住在學校宿舍。

☐ 三分熟
☐ 五分熟
☐ 七分熟
☐ 全熟

dough [do]

名 生麵團

英英 a thick mixture of flour and water, for baking into bread or pastry

例 Daphane was kneading the gingerbread **dough**.
黛芬妮正在揉薑餅麵團。

☐ 三分熟
☐ 五分熟
☐ 七分熟
☐ 全熟

down·ward

[`daʊnwəd]

副 下降地、向下地
反 upward 上升地

英英 moving towards a lower point or downside

例 The jeep flew **downward**.
這輛吉普車向下飛奔。

☐ 三分熟
☐ 五分熟
☐ 七分熟
☐ 全熟

down·wards

[`daʊnwədz]

副 下降地、向下地

英英 towards a lower point or level

例 Alice walked to the window and looked **downwards**.
愛麗絲走到窗戶邊，往下看。

☐ 三分熟
☐ 五分熟
☐ 七分熟
☐ 全熟

drape [drep]

名 幔、窗簾
動 覆蓋、裝飾
同 curtain 窗簾

英英 long curtains; to cover up

例 The **drape** with flower patterns is covered with dust.
有花紋的窗簾布滿了灰塵。

☐ 三分熟
☐ 五分熟
☐ 七分熟
☐ 全熟

dread·ful [`drɛdfəl]

形 可怕的、恐怖的
同 fearful 可怕的

英英 extremely bad or terrible

例 My brother's appetite is **dreadful**.
我弟的胃口很可怕。

☐ 三分熟
☐ 五分熟
☐ 七分熟
☐ 全熟

dress·er [`drɛsə]

名 梳妝臺、鏡臺

英英 a cupboard with shelves above for storing and displaying crocker

例 The silver comb on the **dresser** is given by Aunt Debbie.
梳妝臺上的銀色梳子是我的黛比姑姑給的。

☐ 三分熟
☐ 五分熟
☐ 七分熟
☐ 全熟

D

dress·ing [ˋdrɛsɪŋ]

名 服飾、藥膏、裝飾
片 window dressing
　　粉飾的門面

英英 a sauce for salads, usually containing oil and vinegar with herbs or other flavorings

例 The **dressing** of the model attracts girls' eyes.
模特兒的服飾吸引了女孩們的眼光。

☐ 三分熟
☐ 五分熟
☐ 七分熟
☐ 全熟

---

drive·way

[ˋdraɪˏwe]

名 私用車道、車道

英英 a short private path leading to a house

例 Tony's car has appeared on the **driveway**.
湯尼的車出現在車道上。

☐ 三分熟
☐ 五分熟
☐ 七分熟
☐ 全熟

---

du·ra·tion

[djʊˋreʃən]

名 持久、持續

英英 the time during which something continues

例 The **duration** of the course can vary from two years to four years.
這堂課可以持續兩年到四年。

☐ 三分熟
☐ 五分熟
☐ 七分熟
☐ 全熟

---

dusk [dʌsk]

名 黃昏、幽暗
同 twilight 微光、朦朧

英英 the time before night when it is not completely getting dark

例 The **dusk** market (the afternoon market) sells snacks, daily utensils, and clothes.
黃昏市場賣小吃、日常用品和衣服。

☐ 三分熟
☐ 五分熟
☐ 七分熟
☐ 全熟

---

dwarf [dwɔrf]

名 矮子、矮小動物
動 萎縮、使矮小
反 giant 巨人

英英 a creature like little man with magical power, usually in the stories or fairy tales for children; cause to become smaller

例 The little **dwarves** used their wit to defeat the giant.
小矮人用機智打敗了巨人。

☐ 三分熟
☐ 五分熟
☐ 七分熟
☐ 全熟

---

dwell [dwɛl]

動 住、居住、詳述

英英 to live in or at a place; to think, speak, or write about something in details

例 The brown bear **dwelled** in the cave.
棕熊住在山洞裡。

☐ 三分熟
☐ 五分熟
☐ 七分熟
☐ 全熟

---

dwell·ing [ˋdwɛlɪŋ]

名 住宅、住處
同 residence 住宅

英英 a place or a house of residence

例 The architect used seashells and stones to build the **dwelling** near the beach.
建築師用貝殼和石頭建造了靠近海邊的住宅。

☐ 三分熟
☐ 五分熟
☐ 七分熟
☐ 全熟

Ee

🎧 Track 043

e·clipse [ɪ`klɪps]

名 蝕（月蝕等）
動 遮蔽
同 cover 遮蓋

英英 when the sun disappears from view while the moon is moving between it and the Earth, or when the moon becomes darker while the shadow of the Earth moves over it; to obscure the light from something

例 Ancient Chinese people thought the **eclipse** was the moon devoured by a dog.
古代的中國人認為月蝕現象是月亮被狗吞食。

☐三分熟 ☐五分熟 ☐七分熟 ☐全熟

eel [il]

名 鰻魚

英英 a snake-like fish with a slender smooth body

例 The electric **eel** can generate enough electricity to kill human beings.
電鰻可以產出足夠的電力來殺死人類。

☐三分熟 ☐五分熟 ☐七分熟 ☐全熟

e·go [`igo]

名 自我、我
同 self 自我

英英 self-esteem or self-importance of yours

例 Stanley is a man with big **ego**.
史丹利是個很自負的人。

☐三分熟 ☐五分熟 ☐七分熟 ☐全熟

e·lab·o·rate

[ɪ`læbərɪt]/[ɪ`læbəˌret]

形 精心的
動 精心製作、詳述
反 simple 簡樸的

英英 very well-arranged; to develop or present in detail

例 My boss collects **elaborate** purple clay sculptures.
我的上司蒐集精巧的紫砂雕刻作品。

☐三分熟 ☐五分熟 ☐七分熟 ☐全熟

el·e·vate [`ɛləˌvet]

動 舉起
同 lift 舉起

英英 to lift or raise something to a higher position

例 His comments **elevated** men and hurt women.
他的評論舉高男人的地位，傷害了女人。

☐三分熟 ☐五分熟 ☐七分熟 ☐全熟

em·brace

[ɪm`bres]

動 包圍、擁抱
名 擁抱

英英 to hold closely in one's arms, especially to show someone's affection

例 Her **embrace** of love healed her son's frustration.
她愛的擁抱療癒了兒子的挫折感。

☐三分熟 ☐五分熟 ☐七分熟 ☐全熟

en·deav·or

[ɪn`dɛvɚ]

名 努力
動 盡力
同 strive 努力

英英 an effort attempt to achieve something; to try something very hard

例 The **endeavor** of the designer turned the negative outcome to be positive.
設計師的努力使負面結果成為正面。

☐三分熟 ☐五分熟 ☐七分熟 ☐全熟

E

en·roll [ɪnˈrol]

動 登記、註冊
同 register 註冊

英英 officially register to be as a member or student

例 Ryan **enrolled** in the master program in this September.
賴恩今年九月註冊碩士課程。

☐三分熟
☐五分熟
☐七分熟
☐全熟

---

en·roll·ment

[ɪnˈrolmənt]

名 登記、註冊

英英 the action of enrolling or being enrolled

例 The **enrollment** is part of the administrative procedure for the school staff.
註冊是學校職員管理程序的一部分。

☐三分熟
☐五分熟
☐七分熟
☐全熟

---

en·sure/in·sure

[ɪnˈʃʊr]/[ɪnˈʃʊr]

動 確保、保固、保證

英英 to make certain that something will happen or be so; to protect someone or something

例 My uncle adopted any method to **ensure** his future success.
我伯父為了確保未來的成功，而不擇手段。

☐三分熟
☐五分熟
☐七分熟
☐全熟

---

en·ter·prise

[ˈɛntɚˌpraɪz]

名 企業

英英 a business organization

例 The **enterprise** should run the business by the principle of honesty.
企業應秉持誠信原則經營事業。

☐三分熟
☐五分熟
☐七分熟
☐全熟

---

en·thu·si·as·tic

[ɪnˌθjuzɪˈæstɪk]

形 熱心的

英英 having or showing great enthusiasm

例 The insurance salesman is **enthusiastic** in serving his clients.
保險業務員熱心服務客戶。

☐三分熟
☐五分熟
☐七分熟
☐全熟

---

en·ti·tle [ɪnˈtaɪt!]

動 定名、賦予權力
反 deprive 剝奪

英英 give someone a right or power to do something

例 Students are **entitled** to borrow the books.
學生有借書的權力。

☐三分熟
☐五分熟
☐七分熟
☐全熟

---

e·quate [ɪˈkwet]

動 使相等、視為平等
等同

英英 equal to or equivalent to

例 Teachers **equate** cheating with dishonesty.
教師們把作弊視為不誠實。

☐三分熟
☐五分熟
☐七分熟
☐全熟

---

e·rect [ɪˈrɛkt]

動 豎立
形 直立的
同 upright 直立的

英英 to raise something to a straight or vertical position; straight or rigidly upright

例 Jerry **erected** the flag.
傑瑞讓國旗豎立了起來。

☐三分熟
☐五分熟
☐七分熟
☐全熟

🎧 Track 045

e·rupt [ɪˋrʌpt]

動 爆發

英英 to break out suddenly

例 The volcano **erupted** and destroyed the whole village.
火山爆發，毀了整個村莊。

☐三分熟
☐五分熟
☐七分熟
☐全熟

---

es·cort

[ɛsˋkɔrt]/[ˋɛskɔrt]

動 護衛、護送
名 護衛者

英英 to accompany someone as an escort; a person or group accompanying another to make certain that they arrives safely

例 Fanny's boyfriend **escorted** her home.
芬妮的男友護送她回家。

☐三分熟
☐五分熟
☐七分熟
☐全熟

---

es·tate [əˋstet]

名 地產、財產
同 property 財產

英英 a property including a large house and extensive grounds

例 What's the value of the real **estate** in this area?
這個地區的房地產價值是多少？

☐三分熟
☐五分熟
☐七分熟
☐全熟

---

es·teem [əsˋtim]

名 尊重
動 尊敬

英英 respect and admiration

例 Does Willie care about the public **esteem** for him?
威利在乎大眾對他的尊敬嗎？

☐三分熟
☐五分熟
☐七分熟
☐全熟

---

e·ter·nal [ɪˋtɝnl̩]

形 永恆的
同 permanent 永恆的

英英 lasting or existing forever

例 A diamond symbolizes **eternal** love.
鑽石象徵了永恆的愛。

☐三分熟
☐五分熟
☐七分熟
☐全熟

---

eth·ics [ˋɛθɪks]

名 倫理（學）

英英 the study of the moral principles

例 The **ethics** is related to the study of judging what is right and what is wrong.
倫理學與判斷是非對錯的研究有關。

☐三分熟
☐五分熟
☐七分熟
☐全熟

---

ev·er·green

[ˋɛvɚˌgrin]

名 常綠樹
形 常綠的

英英 a tree which has green leaves for all seasons

例 The pine tree is one kind of **evergreen** plants.
松樹是一種常青樹。

☐三分熟
☐五分熟
☐七分熟
☐全熟

---

ex·ag·ger·a·tion

[ɪgˌzædʒəˋreʃən]

名 誇張、誇大

英英 when someone makes something seem bigger, more important or better than it really is

例 Too much **exaggeration** annoyed the interviewer.
過度的誇張惹怒了面試官。

☐三分熟
☐五分熟
☐七分熟
☐全熟

E

ex·ceed [ɪk`sid]

動 超過
同 surpass 勝過

英英 be greater in number or size than

例 The price of the bag **exceeded** my budget.
這個袋子的價錢超過了我的預算。

☐ 三分熟
☐ 五分熟
☐ 七分熟
☐ 全熟

ex·cel [ɪk`sɛl]

動 勝過、突出
同 outdo 勝過

英英 be exceptionally good at something

例 My younger sister **excelled** at chess.
我妹妹擅長下西洋棋。

☐ 三分熟
☐ 五分熟
☐ 七分熟
☐ 全熟

ex·cep·tion·al

[ɪk`sɛpʃənl]

形 優秀的、卓越的

英英 excellent or outstanding

例 Grace is popular because of her **exceptional** piano performance skills.
葛來絲因為卓越的鋼琴演奏技巧而受人歡迎。

☐ 三分熟
☐ 五分熟
☐ 七分熟
☐ 全熟

ex·cess [ɪk`sɛs]

名 超過
形 過量的

英英 an amount that is more than necessary or desirable

例 The **excess** of pressure almost drove Jack crazy.
過多的壓力快把傑克逼瘋了。

☐ 三分熟
☐ 五分熟
☐ 七分熟
☐ 全熟

ex·claim

[ɪk`sklem]

動 驚叫

英英 to cry out suddenly when someone is surprised, angry, or painful

例 The servant **exclaimed** at the sight of the rat.
僕人一看到老鼠就驚叫。

☐ 三分熟
☐ 五分熟
☐ 七分熟
☐ 全熟

ex·clude [ɪk`sklud]

動 拒絕、不包含
反 include 包含

英英 to deny access to, not include

例 The tax is **excluded** from the payment.
這筆付費不包含稅金。

☐ 三分熟
☐ 五分熟
☐ 七分熟
☐ 全熟

ex·e·cute

[`ɛksɪ‚kjut]

動 實行、執行
同 perform 實行

英英 to put your plan into the action

例 Their staff received the command to **execute** the project.
他們的職員收到要執行該專案的命令。

☐ 三分熟
☐ 五分熟
☐ 七分熟
☐ 全熟

ex·ec·u·tive

[ɪg`zɛkjʊtɪv]

名 執行者、管理者
形 執行的

英英 a person with higher responsibility in a business organization; relating to the job of managing a business or organization and making decisions

例 The **executive** of the project is not in the office.
這個專案的執行者不在辦公室。

☐ 三分熟
☐ 五分熟
☐ 七分熟
☐ 全熟

🎧 **Track 047**

ex·ile [ˋɛksaɪl]

名 流亡
動 放逐

英英 the state of being barred from one's country; to bar someone from their country

例 The religious leader is still in **exile**.
宗教領袖流亡中。

☐ 三分熟
☐ 五分熟
☐ 七分熟
☐ 全熟

ex·ten·sion

[ɪkˋstɛnʃən]

名 擴大、延長、電話分機
同 expansion 擴張

英英 action or process of extending

例 The **extension** number of the secretary is 5188.
祕書的分機號碼是 5188。

☐ 三分熟
☐ 五分熟
☐ 七分熟
☐ 全熟

ex·ten·sive

[ɪkˋstɛnsɪv]

形 廣泛的、廣大的
同 spacious 廣闊的

英英 covering a large area; large in amount or scale

例 Cory's researching interest is **extensive**.
克瑞的研究興趣是很廣泛的。

☐ 三分熟
☐ 五分熟
☐ 七分熟
☐ 全熟

ex·te·ri·or

[ɪkˋstɪrɪɚ]

名 外面
形 外部的
反 interior 內部的

英英 the outer surface or from outside

例 The **exterior** of the building is covered by tiles.
這棟建築的外部被磁磚所覆蓋。

☐ 三分熟
☐ 五分熟
☐ 七分熟
☐ 全熟

ex·ter·nal

[ɪkˋstɝnl̩]

名 外表
形 外在的
反 internal 內在的

英英 an external feature or aspect; coming from the outside

例 The **external** appearance of the temple looks like a palace.
這座廟的外表看起來像皇宮。

☐ 三分熟
☐ 五分熟
☐ 七分熟
☐ 全熟

ex·tinct [ɪkˋstɪŋkt]

形 滅絕的
同 dead 死的

英英 of a species are no longer in existence

例 The dodo birds were **extinct** in the seventeenth century.
渡渡鳥十七世紀時絕種。

☐ 三分熟
☐ 五分熟
☐ 七分熟
☐ 全熟

ex·tra·or·di·nar·y

[ɪkˋstrɔrdn̩ˌɛrɪ]

形 特別的
反 normal 正規的

英英 very unusual or special

例 The **extraordinary** quality of being talkative of Anne helps her win a new life.
安這種特別愛說話的特質幫她贏得了新生活。

☐ 三分熟
☐ 五分熟
☐ 七分熟
☐ 全熟

F

eye·lash/lash
[ˈaɪˌlæʃ]/[læʃ]

名 睫毛

英英 each of the short hairs growing on the edges of the eyelids

例 How amazingly long the girl's **eyelashes** are!
這個女孩的眼睫毛長得令人吃驚！

☐ 三分熟
☐ 五分熟
☐ 七分熟
☐ 全熟

eye·lid [ˈaɪˌlɪd]

名 眼皮

英英 each of the two piece of skin which can cover the eye when closed

例 Jill experienced the twitching **eyelids** in the morning.
吉兒今天早上眼皮在跳。

☐ 三分熟
☐ 五分熟
☐ 七分熟
☐ 全熟

Ff

fab·ric [ˈfæbrɪk]

名 紡織品、布料
同 cloth 布料

英英 a cloth produced by knitting, weaving or felting fibers

例 The **fabric** with the phoenix looks gorgeous.
繡有鳳凰的紡織布料看起來好美。

☐ 三分熟
☐ 五分熟
☐ 七分熟
☐ 全熟

fad [fæd]

名 一時的流行
同 fashion 流行

英英 something, such as a style or an activity, which is popular for a short period of time

例 Prize Claw may turn out to be just a **fad**.
抓娃娃有可能變成只是一時的流行。

☐ 三分熟
☐ 五分熟
☐ 七分熟
☐ 全熟

Fahr·en·heit
[ˈfærənˌhaɪt]

名 華氏、華氏溫度計

英英 of a temperature measurement on which water freezes at 32° and boils at 212°

例 It's important to keep warm while climbing the mountain under zero **Fahrenheit** degree.
在華氏零度以下爬山，保暖是件重要的事。

☐ 三分熟
☐ 五分熟
☐ 七分熟
☐ 全熟

fal·ter [ˈfɔltɚ]

動 支吾、結巴地說、猶豫
同 stutter 結巴地說

英英 to lose confidence to do something or speak something and stop

例 Ginnie **faltered** when the policeman questioned her.
當警察質詢她時，金妮支吾其詞。

☐ 三分熟
☐ 五分熟
☐ 七分熟
☐ 全熟

fas·ci·nate
[ˈfæsnˌet]

動 迷惑、使迷惑

英英 to irresistibly interest someone or attract something

例 The piece of pottery vase **fascinated** me.
這隻陶瓷花瓶迷惑了我。

☐ 三分熟
☐ 五分熟
☐ 七分熟
☐ 全熟

Track 049

fa·tigue [fəˋtig]

名 疲勞、破碎
動 衰弱、疲勞

英英 extreme tiredness or weakness; to become weaker

例 The **fatigue** from working pressure can be eased by jogging.
來自工作壓力的疲勞可藉由慢跑得到舒解。

☐ 三分熟
☐ 五分熟
☐ 七分熟
☐ 全熟

fed·er·al [ˋfɛdərəl]

形 同盟的、聯邦（制）的

英英 referring to the central government, in which several states form a unity but still remain independent in internal affairs

例 The **federal** government received taxes from entrepreneurs.
聯邦政府從企業主那邊收到稅金。

☐ 三分熟
☐ 五分熟
☐ 七分熟
☐ 全熟

fee·ble [fibl̩]

形 虛弱的、無力的
同 weak 虛弱的

英英 weak and lacking strength

例 Grandma is **feeble**.
祖母虛弱無力。

☐ 三分熟
☐ 五分熟
☐ 七分熟
☐ 全熟

fem·i·nine [ˋfɛmənɪn]

名 女性
形 婦女的、溫柔的
反 masculine 男性、男子氣概的

英英 female or woman; having qualities that are traditionally associated with women

例 Crying is usually deemed a **feminine** quality.
哭泣通常被視為一種女性的特質。

☐ 三分熟
☐ 五分熟
☐ 七分熟
☐ 全熟

fer·ti·liz·er [ˋfɝtl̩ˌaɪzɚ]

名 肥料、化學肥料

英英 a chemical or natural substance added to soil of land to make plants grow well

例 My uncle uses natural **fertilizer** while growing the vegetable.
我伯父種蔬菜時會使用天然的肥料。

☐ 三分熟
☐ 五分熟
☐ 七分熟
☐ 全熟

fi·an·ce/ fi·an·cee [ˌfiənˋse]

名 未婚夫／未婚妻

英英 a person who is a man or woman has promise to marry

例 Irene's **fiance** works as a bank manager.
艾琳的未婚夫是銀行經理。

☐ 三分熟
☐ 五分熟
☐ 七分熟
☐ 全熟

fi·ber [ˋfaɪbɚ]

名 纖維、纖維質

英英 the substance in a plant or animal tissue, etc., which cannot be digested and helps food pass through your body

例 The **fiber** aids the digestion of intestines.
纖維質對大腸的蠕動有幫助。

☐ 三分熟
☐ 五分熟
☐ 七分熟
☐ 全熟

F

fid·dle [ˈfɪdl̩]

名 小提琴
動 拉提琴、遊蕩
同 violin 小提琴

英英 a violin; an act of dishonesty or cheating; to play the violin

例 The cat is playing the **fiddle** in the famous nursery rhyme.
在有名的童謠中，貓拉小提琴。

☐ 三分熟
☐ 五分熟
☐ 七分熟
☐ 全熟

fil·ter [ˈfɪltɚ]

名 過濾器
動 過濾、滲透
片 a water filter 濾水器

英英 a porous equipment for removing solid particles from a liquid or gas passed through it; to remove unwanted substances from something by passing it through a special substance

例 The **filter** is used to cleanse the drinking water.
過濾器被用來純淨飲用水。

☐ 三分熟
☐ 五分熟
☐ 七分熟
☐ 全熟

fin [fɪn]

名 鰭、手、魚翅

英英 an external organ on the body of a fish, which is used for helping it to swim in the water

例 It's cruel that some people cut the shark's **fin** and throw the shark into the ocean.
有些人殘忍地切掉鯊魚的鰭，再將鯊魚放回海裡。

☐ 三分熟
☐ 五分熟
☐ 七分熟
☐ 全熟

fish·er·y [ˈfɪʃərɪ]

名 漁業、水產業、
養魚場

英英 the business of catching fish

例 The **fishery** has its difficulty of gaining more advanced fish raising technique.
漁業很難獲得更先進的養魚技術。

☐ 三分熟
☐ 五分熟
☐ 七分熟
☐ 全熟

flake [flek]

名 雪花、薄片
動 剝、片片降落、
使成薄片
同 peel 剝

英英 a small, flat, thin piece of something; to come off a surface in small flat pieces

例 The **flake** ice machine is out of order.
製作雪花冰的機器故障了。

☐ 三分熟
☐ 五分熟
☐ 七分熟
☐ 全熟

flap [flæp]

名 興奮狀態、鼓翼
動 拍打、拍動、空談

英英 behave in an excited way; to move something quickly up and down or from side to side, often making a noise

例 The parrot **flaps** its wings and tries to fly away.
鸚鵡拍動翅膀，試圖飛走。

☐ 三分熟
☐ 五分熟
☐ 七分熟
☐ 全熟

flaw [flɔ]

名 瑕疵、缺陷
動 弄破、破裂、糟蹋
同 defect 缺陷

英英 a fault, mistake or weakness causes something or someone not to be perfect; to break or waste something

例 Although the jade bracelet has some **flaws**, it is still quite valuable.
這只手鐲雖然有些瑕疵，但還是有價值的。

☐ 三分熟
☐ 五分熟
☐ 七分熟
☐ 全熟

🎧 Track 051

flick [flɪk]

名 輕打聲、彈開
動 輕打、輕拍
同 pat 輕拍

英英 a sudden movement or hit from up and down or from side to side

例 With a **flick** of the magic wand, the cup changed into a guinea pig.
魔杖一揮，杯子變成了天竺鼠。

☐ 三分熟
☐ 五分熟
☐ 七分熟
☐ 全熟

flip [flɪp]

名 跳動、拍打
動 輕拍、翻轉

英英 a quick or repeated action or movement; to hit something slightly

例 **Flip** the coin and let it decide the way we should go.
翻轉硬幣，讓硬幣決定我們要走的道路吧。

☐ 三分熟
☐ 五分熟
☐ 七分熟
☐ 全熟

flour·ish [ˈflɝɪʃ]

名 繁榮、炫耀、華麗的詞藻
動 誇耀、繁盛
反 decline 衰退

英英 to grow or develop well

例 The commerce of this island country started to **flourish** in the 19th century.
這個島國的經濟十九世紀時開始走向繁榮。

☐ 三分熟
☐ 五分熟
☐ 七分熟
☐ 全熟

flu·en·cy [ˈfluənsɪ]

名 流暢、流利

英英 speaking or writing very well and quickly

例 When you take the oral exam, pay attention to the **fluency**.
當你考口說考試時，留意說話的流暢度。

☐ 三分熟
☐ 五分熟
☐ 七分熟
☐ 全熟

foe [fo]

名 敵人、仇人、敵軍
同 enemy 敵人

英英 an enemy or adversary

例 The **foe** is coming.
敵軍就要來了。

☐ 三分熟
☐ 五分熟
☐ 七分熟
☐ 全熟

foil [fɔɪl]

名 箔片、箔、薄金屬片

英英 a thin sheet of metal, which usually used to wrap food while grilling or in order to keep it fresh

例 Wrap the corn with tin **foil** and put it into the oven.
用錫箔紙把玉米包起來，然後放進烤箱。

☐ 三分熟
☐ 五分熟
☐ 七分熟
☐ 全熟

folk·lore [ˈfokˌlor]

名 沒有隔閡、平民作風、民間傳說、民俗

英英 the traditional beliefs, stories, and customs of a community, passed on by word of mouth

例 The origin of vampire is related to with **folklore**.
吸血鬼的起源與民間傳說有關。

☐ 三分熟
☐ 五分熟
☐ 七分熟
☐ 全熟

F

for·get·ful
[fə˚gɛtfəl]

形 忘掉的、易忘的、
忽略的、健忘的

英英 likely not to remember

例 Grandma is so **forgetful**.
奶奶好健忘。

☐ 三分熟
☐ 五分熟
☐ 七分熟
☐ 全熟

---

for·mat [ˋfɔrmæt]

名 格式、版式
動 格式化

英英 the way in which something is arranged planned; arrange in a particular format for a computer

例 The **format** of the document is illustrated below.
文件的格式如下圖所示。

☐ 三分熟
☐ 五分熟
☐ 七分熟
☐ 全熟

---

foul [faʊl]

動 使污穢、弄髒、使堵塞
形 險惡的、污濁的
反 clean 清潔的

英英 to make something dirty or untidy; very unpleasant or disagreeable

例 Miss Lin was in a **foul** mood this morning.
林小姐今天早上的心情很糟。

☐ 三分熟
☐ 五分熟
☐ 七分熟
☐ 全熟

---

fowl [faʊl]

名 鳥、野禽
同 bird 鳥

英英 a bird derived from a jungle fowl and is used to produce meat or eggs, such as a cock or hen

例 The **fowl** painting was sold last weekend.
野禽的繪畫上個週末賣了出去。

☐ 三分熟
☐ 五分熟
☐ 七分熟
☐ 全熟

---

frac·tion
[ˋfrækʃən]

名 分數、片斷、小部分
同 segment 部分

英英 a numerical quantity that is not a whole number or small part of something

例 A **fraction** of financial loss is nothing to the company.
一部分的財務損失對這家公司來講根本不算什麼。

☐ 三分熟
☐ 五分熟
☐ 七分熟
☐ 全熟

---

frame·work
[ˋfremˌwɝk]

名 架構、骨架、體制
同 structure 結構

英英 a structure of supporting, which is around something can be built

例 The **framework** of the program has been set.
這個課程的架構訂好了。

☐ 三分熟
☐ 五分熟
☐ 七分熟
☐ 全熟

---

fran·tic [ˋfræntɪk]

形 狂暴的、發狂的

英英 out of control or get carried away

例 The scientist went **frantic**.
這名科學家發狂了。

☐ 三分熟
☐ 五分熟
☐ 七分熟
☐ 全熟

---

freight [fret]

名 貨物運輸
動 運輸

英英 transport of goods or products in bulk by truck, train, ship, or aircraft from one place to another

例 The batch of **freight** has been insured.
這批貨物已經有投保。

☐ 三分熟
☐ 五分熟
☐ 七分熟
☐ 全熟

Track 053

fron·tier [frʌnˋtɪr]

名 邊境、國境、新領域
同 border 邊境

英英 a border separating two countries; an area along an international border
例 Mexican immigrants reached the **frontier** of the US.
墨西哥移民抵達美國的邊境。

☐ 三分熟 ☐ 五分熟 ☐ 七分熟 ☐ 全熟

fume [fjum]

名 蒸汽、香氣、煙
動 激怒、冒出（煙、蒸汽等）
同 vapor 蒸汽

英英 a gas that with strong smell and is dangerous to inhale; to get angry and annoyed
例 The giving off of the toxic **fumes** caused the death of the woman.
釋放有毒的煙霧導致這名女子死亡。

☐ 三分熟 ☐ 五分熟 ☐ 七分熟 ☐ 全熟

fu·ry [ˋfjʊrɪ]

名 憤怒、狂怒
同 rage 狂怒
片 provoke fury 激怒

英英 extreme anger or violent anger
例 The daughter's **fury** led her to burn her father's house.
女兒的憤怒使她燒毀了她父親的家。

☐ 三分熟 ☐ 五分熟 ☐ 七分熟 ☐ 全熟

fuse [fjuz]

名 引信、保險絲
動 熔合、裝引信

英英 a safety electrical device of machinery that can interrupt the flow of electrical current when it is overloaded; to fit a fuse to
例 The **fuse** might have been blown.
保險絲很有可能斷了。

☐ 三分熟 ☐ 五分熟 ☐ 七分熟 ☐ 全熟

fuss [fʌs]

名 大驚小怪
動 焦急、使焦急、小題大作、過分講究

英英 needlessly emotions or useless activity, such as a show of anger, worry or lack of satisfaction; to make or become worried
例 Why did you make such a **fuss**?
你為什麼如此大驚小怪？

☐ 三分熟 ☐ 五分熟 ☐ 七分熟 ☐ 全熟

Gg

gal·lop [ˋgæləp]

名 疾馳、飛奔
動 使疾馳、飛奔
同 run 跑

英英 the fast run or speed of a horse; to move at great speed
例 The famous Chinese painting presents **galloping** horses.
這幅有名的國畫呈現出飛奔的馬匹。

☐ 三分熟 ☐ 五分熟 ☐ 七分熟 ☐ 全熟

gar·ment [ˋgɑrmənt]

名 衣服

英英 an item of clothing
例 The women fashion **garments** are mainly exported to Korea.
這些女子流行服飾主要外銷到韓國。

☐ 三分熟 ☐ 五分熟 ☐ 七分熟 ☐ 全熟

gasp [gæsp]

名 喘息、喘
動 喘氣説、喘著氣息

英英 to take a short quick breath with an open mouth, from pain or breathlessness

例 Our class leader **gasped** and said Angela needed our help.
班長喘著氣説安琪拉需要我們的幫忙。

□ 三分熟
□ 五分熟
□ 七分熟
□ 全熟

gath·er·ing

[ˈɡæðərɪŋ]

名 集會、聚集

英英 a get-together; a part when many people get together as a group

例 Would you like to attend the yearly **gathering** of elementary school classmates?
你想要參加小學同學一年一度的聚會嗎？

□ 三分熟
□ 五分熟
□ 七分熟
□ 全熟

gay [ɡe]

名 同性戀
形 快樂的、快活的
反 sad 悲傷的

英英 homosexual or relating to homosexuals; hearted and carefree

例 I heard that Daniel is a **gay**.
我聽説丹尼爾是同性戀。

□ 三分熟
□ 五分熟
□ 七分熟
□ 全熟

gen·der [ˈdʒɛndɚ]

名 性別
同 sex 性別

英英 the physical status of being male or female

例 Do you know the **gender** of Sally's new-born baby?
你知道莎莉所生的新生兒的性別嗎？

□ 三分熟
□ 五分熟
□ 七分熟
□ 全熟

ge·o·graph·i·cal

[ˌdʒiəˈɡræfɪkl̩]

形 地理學的、地理的

英英 relating to geography

例 The National **Geographical** Magazine introduced ocean creatures in this issue.
國家地理雜誌這期介紹海洋生物。

□ 三分熟
□ 五分熟
□ 七分熟
□ 全熟

ge·om·e·try

[dʒɪˈɑmətrɪ]

名 幾何學

英英 the study about mathematics concerned with the properties and relations of points, lines, surfaces, and solids

例 **Geometry** is related to the study of space and lines.
幾何學與空間及線條的研究有關。

□ 三分熟
□ 五分熟
□ 七分熟
□ 全熟

gla·cier [ˈɡleʃɚ]

名 冰河

英英 a huge mass of ice slowly flowing over a land, formed by the accumulation of snow on mountains or near the poles

例 The bottle of mineral water came from the **glacier**.
這罐礦泉水來自冰河。

□ 三分熟
□ 五分熟
□ 七分熟
□ 全熟

G

Track 055

glare [glɛr]

名 怒視、瞪眼
動 怒視瞪眼

英英 a fierce or angry stare

例 The general's **glare** scared his enemy away.
這位將軍的怒視把他的敵人嚇跑了。

☐ 三分熟
☐ 五分熟
☐ 七分熟
☐ 全熟

gleam [glim]

名 一絲光線
動 閃現、閃爍

英英 a faint or brief light; to reflect a small, bright light

例 The sales representative smiled with a **gleam** of confidence.
這名業務代表笑了，笑容中閃現著一絲自信。

☐ 三分熟
☐ 五分熟
☐ 七分熟
☐ 全熟

glee [gli]

名 喜悅、高興
同 joy 高興

英英 great delight or joy

例 He told children a story with **glee**.
他開心地跟孩子們講了個故事。

☐ 三分熟
☐ 五分熟
☐ 七分熟
☐ 全熟

glit·ter [ˈglɪtɚ]

名 光輝、閃光、華麗
動 閃爍、閃亮
同 sparkle 閃爍

英英 bright, shimmering light; to shine with a bright light

例 The diamond apple shines brilliantly with a **glitter**.
這顆鑽石蘋果閃爍著華美的光芒。

☐ 三分熟
☐ 五分熟
☐ 七分熟
☐ 全熟

gloom [glʊm]

名 陰暗、昏暗
動 幽暗、憂鬱
同 shadow 陰暗處

英英 a little or total darkness

例 Some beasts seemed to hide itself in the **gloom**.
黑暗中似乎有隻野獸藏身其中。

☐ 三分熟
☐ 五分熟
☐ 七分熟
☐ 全熟

gnaw [nɔ]

動 咬、噬
同 bite 咬

英英 to bite or nibble something

例 The little black dog is **gnawing** on a bone.
小黑狗在啃咬著骨頭。

☐ 三分熟
☐ 五分熟
☐ 七分熟
☐ 全熟

gob·ble [ˈgɑbl]

動 大口猛吃、狼吞虎嚥
同 devour 狼吞虎嚥

英英 to eat something hurriedly and noisily

例 The bandit was **gobbling** the chicken.
強盜大口猛吃著雞肉。

☐ 三分熟
☐ 五分熟
☐ 七分熟
☐ 全熟

gorge [gɔrdʒ]

名 岩崖、山峽、隘道
動 狼吞虎嚥

英英 a steep, narrow valley or ravine; to swallow something very quickly without chewing it

例 Very few people can climb up the **gorge**.
很少人能爬上這個岩崖。

☐ 三分熟
☐ 五分熟
☐ 七分熟
☐ 全熟

G

gor·geous

[ˈgɔrdʒəs]

形 炫麗的、華麗的、極好的

同 splendid 壯麗的

英英 very beautiful and attractive

例 The traditional Korean wedding dress looks **gorgeous**.
傳統的韓國結婚禮服看起來好華麗。

☐ 三分熟
☐ 五分熟
☐ 七分熟
☐ 全熟

go·ril·la [gəˈrɪlə]

名 大猩猩

英英 a large ape of central Africa, the largest living primate

例 The zoo worker pretends to be a **gorilla**.
動物園的工作人員裝作大猩猩。

☐ 三分熟
☐ 五分熟
☐ 七分熟
☐ 全熟

gos·pel [ˈgɑspl̩]

名 福音、信條

英英 the teachings of Christ

例 To spread the **gospel** is a Christian's duty
傳福音是基督徒的工作。

☐ 三分熟
☐ 五分熟
☐ 七分熟
☐ 全熟

grant [grænt]

名 許可、授與

動 答應、允許、轉讓（財產）

同 permit 允許

英英 to give or allow someone something officially

例 The contract shows that the rental company **grants** you the use of the sports car.
這份合約顯示這家出租公司允許你使用這輛跑車。

☐ 三分熟
☐ 五分熟
☐ 七分熟
☐ 全熟

grav·i·ty [ˈgrævətɪ]

名 重力、嚴重性

英英 seriousness

例 Newton's law of **gravity** is a law of physics.
牛頓的萬有引力定律是物理學的定律。

☐ 三分熟
☐ 五分熟
☐ 七分熟
☐ 全熟

graze [grez]

動 吃草、畜牧

英英 of cattle or sheep to eat grass in a field

例 The sheep in the farm are **grazing**.
農場裡的綿羊吃著草。

☐ 三分熟
☐ 五分熟
☐ 七分熟
☐ 全熟

grease [gris]

名 油脂、獸脂

動 討好、塗脂、用油脂潤滑

英英 animal fat which is soft after melting and used or produced in cooking; to please someone

例 Here are some methods to help you remove the chain **grease**.
這裡有些方法可以幫你去除鏈條油脂。

☐ 三分熟
☐ 五分熟
☐ 七分熟
☐ 全熟

greed [grid]

名 貪心、貪婪

英英 selfish desire for money, food, or power

例 Enormous **greed** turned Peter into a criminal.
過度貪婪讓彼得變成了罪犯。

☐ 三分熟
☐ 五分熟
☐ 七分熟
☐ 全熟

🎧 **Track 057**

---

grim [grɪm]

形 嚴格的、糟糕的
同 stern 嚴格的

英英 very serious or gloomy

例 **Grim** demands should be deemed as reasonable training.
嚴格的要求應該被視為是一種合理的訓練。

□ 三分熟
□ 五分熟
□ 七分熟
□ 全熟

---

grip [grɪp]

名 緊握、抓住
動 緊握、扣住
反 release 鬆開

英英 a firm and tight hold

例 Tight **grip** of the stunt performer on the rope amazed the audience.
特技表演者緊抓著繩子不放讓觀眾頗為吃驚。

□ 三分熟
□ 五分熟
□ 七分熟
□ 全熟

---

groan [gron]

名 哼著說、呻吟
動 呻吟、哼聲
同 moan 呻吟

英英 to make a deep sound of pain or despair

例 The old man **groaned** because of severe stomachache.
這個老人家因為嚴重的胃痛而發出呻吟聲。

□ 三分熟
□ 五分熟
□ 七分熟
□ 全熟

---

gross [gros]

名 總體
動 得到……總收入（或毛利）
形 粗略的、臃腫的
同 total 總數

英英 a particular amount of money you earn before tax is paid; to obtain a particular amount of money

例 The **gross** profit of the shipment is 20% higher than the one of the previous shipment.
這批貨物的毛利潤比前一批貨物的毛利潤高 20%。

□ 三分熟
□ 五分熟
□ 七分熟
□ 全熟

---

growl [graʊl]

名 咆哮聲、吠聲
動 咆哮著說、咆哮
同 snarl 咆哮

英英 to speak in a low sound of hostility in the throat

例 The **growling** lion has scared the monkeys away.
獅子的咆哮聲把猴子嚇跑了。

□ 三分熟
□ 五分熟
□ 七分熟
□ 全熟

---

grum·ble [ˈgrʌmbl̩]

名 牢騷、不高興
動 抱怨、發牢騷
同 complain 抱怨

英英 to complain or protest in an unhappy but muted way

例 **Grumbling** can't solve the problem.
發牢騷仍然無法解決問題。

□ 三分熟
□ 五分熟
□ 七分熟
□ 全熟

---

guide·line [ˈgaɪdˌlaɪn]

名 指導方針、指標
片 breach guidelines 違反指導方針

英英 a general rule, principle, or a piece of advice

例 Clear **guidelines** are necessary.
清楚的指導方針是有必要的。

□ 三分熟
□ 五分熟
□ 七分熟
□ 全熟

H

gulp [gʌlp]

名 滿滿一口
動 牛飲、吞飲

英英 a large mouthful of liquid hastily drunk; an act of gulping

例 The lawyer **gulped** down the iced tea and left.
律師一口吞飲這杯冰茶，之後便離開了。

☐ 三分熟
☐ 五分熟
☐ 七分熟
☐ 全熟

gust [gʌst]

名 一陣狂風
動 吹狂風
同 blast 疾風

英英 a brief, strong rush of wind; to blow in gusts

例 A **gust** sweeps the hut away.
一陣狂風掃飛了一間小屋。

☐ 三分熟
☐ 五分熟
☐ 七分熟
☐ 全熟

gut(s) [gʌt(s)]

名 內臟、腸

英英 the stomach or belly of people or animals

例 Animals' **guts** terrified the monk.
動物的內臟嚇壞該名僧侶。

☐ 三分熟
☐ 五分熟
☐ 七分熟
☐ 全熟

gyp·sy [ˈdʒɪpsɪ]

名 吉普賽人
形 吉普賽人的

英英 a member of a travelling people originally from northern India, who is with dark skin and hair, speaking the Romany language

例 The **gypsy** girl is a fortune teller.
這個吉普賽女孩是算命師。

☐ 三分熟
☐ 五分熟
☐ 七分熟
☐ 全熟

Hh

hail [hel]

名 歡呼、雹
動 歡呼
同 cheer 歡呼

英英 pellets of frozen rain falling from sky; to call someone for drawing their attention

例 When a group of athletes appeared, the audience **hailed** for them.
當一群運動員出現時，觀眾為他們歡呼。

☐ 三分熟
☐ 五分熟
☐ 七分熟
☐ 全熟

hair·style/ hair·do

[ˈhɛrˌstaɪl]/[ˈhɛrˌdu]

名 髮型

英英 a way of someone's hair is cut or arranged

例 The new **hairstyle** gives Professor Jessie a good mood.
新的髮型給傑西教授好心情。

☐ 三分熟
☐ 五分熟
☐ 七分熟
☐ 全熟

hand·i·cap

[ˈhændɪˌkæp]

名 障礙、吃虧
動 妨礙、吃虧、使不利

英英 something makes someone do something more difficult

例 Everyone is moved by the physically **handicapped** athlete's spirit.
每個人都被這個身障運動員的精神所感動。

☐ 三分熟
☐ 五分熟
☐ 七分熟
☐ 全熟

🎧 Track 059

hand·i·craft

[ˈhændɪˌkræft]

名 手工藝品
同 craft 工藝

英英 an object which is made by hand skill

例 The **handicraft** bag is designed by an aboriginal artist.
這手工藝製成的袋子是由原住民藝術家所設計的。

☐ 三分熟
☐ 五分熟
☐ 七分熟
☐ 全熟

har·dy [ˈhɑrdɪ]

形 強健的、能吃苦耐勞的
同 sturdy 強健的

英英 capable of enduring difficult things or hardship

例 The **hardy** mechanic is trusted by many clients.
這個吃苦耐勞型的技師深受許多客戶的信賴。

☐ 三分熟
☐ 五分熟
☐ 七分熟
☐ 全熟

har·ness [ˈhɑrnɪs]

名 馬具
動 裝上馬具、利用、治理

英英 a set of equipment by which a horse or other draught animal is fastened to a cart, plough, etc.; to set a harness

例 The servant has prepared the **harness** for the prince.
僕人已經幫王子把馬具準備好了。

☐ 三分熟
☐ 五分熟
☐ 七分熟
☐ 全熟

haul [hɔl]

名 用力拖拉、一次獲得的量
動 拖、使勁拉
同 drag 拖、拉

英英 to pull something with great effort

例 With a **haul** of the fishing net, the fisherman knew his family has plenty of fish to eat.
用力拖拉漁網，漁夫知道他的家人有很多的魚可以吃。

☐ 三分熟
☐ 五分熟
☐ 七分熟
☐ 全熟

haunt [hɔnt]

名 常到的場所
動 出現、常到（某地）

英英 a place where a person visits frequently; to appear very often in a particular place

例 The piano bar was one of Jackie's son's **haunts**.
這個鋼琴酒吧是傑奇的兒子常去的地方。

☐ 三分熟
☐ 五分熟
☐ 七分熟
☐ 全熟

heart·y [ˈhɑrtɪ]

形 親切的、熱心的
反 cold 冷淡的

英英 enthusiastic and friendly

例 Mrs. Wu is a **hearty** teacher to students.
吳老師對學生來講是位親切的老師。

☐ 三分熟
☐ 五分熟
☐ 七分熟
☐ 全熟

heav·en·ly

[ˈhɛvənlɪ]

形 天空的、天國的

英英 of heaven or sky

例 This rose garden looks like a **heavenly** garden taken care of by angels.
這座玫瑰園看起來就像有天使照顧的天國花園。

☐ 三分熟
☐ 五分熟
☐ 七分熟
☐ 全熟

H

---

hedge [hɛdʒ]

名 樹籬、籬笆
動 制定界線、圍住
片 trim the hedge
修剪樹籬

英英 a fence formed by closely growing bushes or shrubs; to make a boundary

例 The red robin sits on the **hedge** and sings happily.
紅色知更鳥停在樹籬上，開心地唱著歌。

☐ 三分熟
☐ 五分熟
☐ 七分熟
☐ 全熟

---

heed [hid]

名 留心、注意
動 留心、注意
同 notice 注意

英英 to pay careful attention

例 **Heed** the weather warning.
注意天氣預報。

☐ 三分熟
☐ 五分熟
☐ 七分熟
☐ 全熟

---

height·en [ˈhaɪtn̩]

動 增高、加高
反 lower 放低

英英 to make something higher

例 The magic show **heightened** the party atmosphere.
魔術表演增加了派對的氣氛。

☐ 三分熟
☐ 五分熟
☐ 七分熟
☐ 全熟

---

heir [ɛr]

名 繼承人

英英 a person legally received the property from someone after they died

例 The **heir** of this apartment should pay 10% heritage tax.
這間公寓的繼承人應付百分之十的遺產稅。

☐ 三分熟
☐ 五分熟
☐ 七分熟
☐ 全熟

---

hence [hɛns]

副 因此
同 therefore 因此

英英 for this reason; therefore

例 Billy's mother passed away. **Hence**, he needs some time to prepare for the funeral.
比利的母親去世了。因此，他需要一些時間準備葬禮。

☐ 三分熟
☐ 五分熟
☐ 七分熟
☐ 全熟

---

her·ald [ˈhɛrəld]

名 通報者、使者
動 宣示、公告
同 messenger 使者

英英 a person who carried official messages and made announcements; to announce something

例 The Japanese emperor's speech heralded the coming of a new **era**.
日本天皇的演說宣示了新時代的來臨。

☐ 三分熟
☐ 五分熟
☐ 七分熟
☐ 全熟

---

herb [ɝb]

名 草本植物
片 medicinal herbs 藥草

英英 any plant with leaves, seeds, or flowers used for flavoring, medicine, or perfume

例 Take this Chinese **herb** when you feel tired.
當你累的時候，吃這款中藥。

☐ 三分熟
☐ 五分熟
☐ 七分熟
☐ 全熟

---

her·mit [ˈhɝmɪt]

名 隱士、隱居者

英英 a person living along or apart from the society

例 Tao Yuan-ming enjoyed his life of a **hermit**.
陶淵明喜歡隱居的日子。

☐ 三分熟
☐ 五分熟
☐ 七分熟
☐ 全熟

🎧 Track 061

he·ro·ic [hɪˋroʌɪk]

名 史詩
形 英雄的、勇士的
反 cowardly 懦弱的

英英 behavior or talk that is bold or dramatic; very brave

例 The **heroic** epic described the hero's journey to hell.
英雄史詩描寫了英雄的地獄之旅。

☐ 三分熟
☐ 五分熟
☐ 七分熟
☐ 全熟

---

het·er·o·sex·u·al

[ˌhɛtərəˋsɛkʃʊəl]

名 異性戀者
形 異性戀的
反 homosexual 同性戀

英英 sexually attracted to the opposite sex

例 A **heterosexual** should try to understand how a homosexual feels.
異性戀者應該要試著理解同性戀者的感覺。

☐ 三分熟
☐ 五分熟
☐ 七分熟
☐ 全熟

---

hi-fi/
high fi·del·i·ty

[ˋhaɪˋfaɪ]/[ˋhaɪ fɪˋdɛlətɪ]

名 高傳真（靈敏度）音響

英英 a set of equipment which is used to play high fidelity sound

例 The high-quality music is from the **hi-fi** stereo.
高品質的音樂來自這臺音響。

☐ 三分熟
☐ 五分熟
☐ 七分熟
☐ 全熟

---

hi·jack [ˋhaɪdʒæk]

名 搶劫、劫機
動 劫奪

英英 illegally seize control of an aircraft, ship, etc. while it is in transit; to take over something

例 The event of **hijacking** an airplane showed the neglect of the security of flight.
劫機事件透露出飛航安全的疏失。

☐ 三分熟
☐ 五分熟
☐ 七分熟
☐ 全熟

---

hiss [hɪs]

名 噓聲
動 發噓聲

英英 a hissing sound

例 The housekeeper **hissed** and asked me to follow her.
管家發出噓聲，要我跟著她走。

☐ 三分熟
☐ 五分熟
☐ 七分熟
☐ 全熟

---

hoarse [hors]

形 （嗓音）刺耳的、沙啞的

英英 very rough and harsh

例 Mark practiced singing the high-key song so many times and thus had **hoarse** voice.
馬克練習好多次唱這首音準高的歌，因此聲音沙啞。

☐ 三分熟
☐ 五分熟
☐ 七分熟
☐ 全熟

---

hock·ey [ˋhɑkɪ]

名 曲棍球

英英 a game played between two teams of eleven players each on a sport field, using hooked sticks to drive a small hard ball towards a goal

例 The sports of ice **hockey** is an Olympic event.
冰上曲棍球運動是奧運會項目之一。

☐ 三分熟
☐ 五分熟
☐ 七分熟
☐ 全熟

H

ho·mo·sex·u·al
[ˌhoməˋsɛkʃʊəl]

名 同性戀者
形 同性戀的

英英 a homosexual person

例 **Homosexuals** have the right to love and get married.
同性戀者有權利戀愛和結婚。

☐ 三分熟
☐ 五分熟
☐ 七分熟
☐ 全熟

honk [hɔŋk]

名 雁鳴、汽車喇叭聲
動 雁鳴叫、發出汽車喇叭聲

英英 the cry of a goose or the sound of a car horn

例 The car driver behind our back keeps **honking**.
我們後方的汽車駕駛一直在按喇叭。

☐ 三分熟
☐ 五分熟
☐ 七分熟
☐ 全熟

hood [hʊd]

名 罩、蓋
動 掩蔽、覆蓋
反 uncover 揭露

英英 a piece of clothing, which is used to cover the head and neck with an opening for the face; to cover something in order to not being seen

例 The man wearing the black **hood** abducted the rich businessman's daughter.
戴著黑色面罩的男子綁架了富商的女兒。

☐ 三分熟
☐ 五分熟
☐ 七分熟
☐ 全熟

hoof [hʊf]

名 蹄
動 用蹄踢、步行

英英 the hard part of the foot of animals, such as a house or cow, etc.; to kick with a hoof

例 You need special tools to clear the **hooves** of the horse.
你需要特別的工具清理馬蹄。

☐ 三分熟
☐ 五分熟
☐ 七分熟
☐ 全熟

hor·i·zon·tal
[ˌhɑrəˋzɑntl]

名 水平線
形 地平線的、水準線、水平面
反 vertical 垂直的

英英 the apparent parallel line that divides the earth and the sky; relating to the line at which the earth's surface and the sky appear to meet

例 The sun rises from the far-away **horizontal**.
太陽從遠方的地平線昇起。

☐ 三分熟
☐ 五分熟
☐ 七分熟
☐ 全熟

hos·tage [ˋhɑstɪdʒ]

名 人質
同 captive 俘虜

英英 a person who is taken as a prisoner by an enemy in order to force the other do what the enemy wants

例 Currently, the **hostages** are safe.
目前人質安全。

☐ 三分熟
☐ 五分熟
☐ 七分熟
☐ 全熟

hos·tile [ˋhɑstɪl]

形 敵方的、不友善的

英英 not very friendly with something

例 The newcomer has no friends because of his **hostile** attitude.
新來者沒有朋友，因為他那不友善的態度。

☐ 三分熟
☐ 五分熟
☐ 七分熟
☐ 全熟

hound [haʊnd]

名 獵犬、有癮的人
動 追逐、追獵
同 hunt 打獵

英英 a dog of a breed used for hunting; to pursues something eagerly
例 The **hounds** were a part of the royal hunting.
獵犬是皇室狩獵的一部分。

☐ 三分熟
☐ 五分熟
☐ 七分熟
☐ 全熟

---

hous·ing [ˈhaʊzɪŋ]

名 住宅的供給、住宅

英英 houses and flats for people to live in
例 The **housing** in this area is expensive.
這區的住宅很貴。

☐ 三分熟
☐ 五分熟
☐ 七分熟
☐ 全熟

---

hov·er [ˈhʌvɚ]

名 徘徊、翱翔
動 翱翔、盤旋

英英 remain in one place in the air for a while
例 The eagles **hovered** above the temple.
老鷹在寺廟上方盤旋。

☐ 三分熟
☐ 五分熟
☐ 七分熟
☐ 全熟

---

howl [haʊl]

名 吠聲、怒號
動 吼叫、怒號
同 shout 喊叫

英英 a loud crying sound of pain, amusement, etc.
例 The thief heard the **howling** of the dogs and ran away.
小偷聽到狗吠聲，跑走了。

☐ 三分熟
☐ 五分熟
☐ 七分熟
☐ 全熟

---

hurl [hɜl]

名 投
動 投擲
同 fling 丟、擲

英英 to throw something with great energy
例 She **hurled** the comic books across the room in a fit of temper.
在盛怒之下，她把漫畫書丟到房間的另一邊。

☐ 三分熟
☐ 五分熟
☐ 七分熟
☐ 全熟

---

hymn [hɪm]

名 讚美詩
動 唱讚美詩讚美
同 carol 讚美詩

英英 a religious song of praise sung to God by Christians; to sing with hymn
例 The **hymn** is to praise God.
讚美詩是用來讚美神的。

☐ 三分熟
☐ 五分熟
☐ 七分熟
☐ 全熟

Ii

id·i·ot [ˈɪdɪət]

名 傻瓜、笨蛋
同 fool 傻瓜

英英 a stupid person; a fool
例 How can you call your brother an **idiot**?
你怎麼可以叫你的哥哥笨蛋？

☐ 三分熟
☐ 五分熟
☐ 七分熟
☐ 全熟

---

im·mense [ɪˈmɛns]

形 巨大的、極大的
反 tiny 極小的

英英 extremely large or great
例 Can't you see he was under **immense** working pressure?
你難道看不出來他背負著極大的工作壓力？

☐ 三分熟
☐ 五分熟
☐ 七分熟
☐ 全熟

im·pe·ri·al
[ɪmˋpɪrɪəl]

形 帝國的、至高的、
　 皇帝的
同 supreme 至高的

英英 relating to an empire or an emperor

例 This **imperial** palace was reserved quite well.
這座皇宮保存的很好。

☐ 三分熟
☐ 五分熟
☐ 七分熟
☐ 全熟

---

im·pose [ɪmˋpoz]

動 徵收、佔便宜、欺騙

英英 to take unfair advantage of someone or to cheat

例 The first income tax was **imposed** to support the war.
第一筆徵收的所得稅是為了支援戰爭所需。

☐ 三分熟
☐ 五分熟
☐ 七分熟
☐ 全熟

---

im·pulse [ˋɪmpʌls]

名 衝動
片 sudden impulse
　 突然的衝動

英英 a strong wish to do something suddenly and immediately

例 You'll regret for the decision made on **impulse**.
你會為了一時衝動所做的決定而後悔。

☐ 三分熟
☐ 五分熟
☐ 七分熟
☐ 全熟

---

in·cense [ˋɪnsɛns]

名 芳香、香
動 激怒、焚香
同 provoke 激怒

英英 a substance that is burnt to make sweet smell, often used as a part of religious ceremony; a sudden urge to act; to make someone get angry

例 The **incense** of herbs relaxes your body.
草藥的芳香可以放鬆你的身體。

☐ 三分熟
☐ 五分熟
☐ 七分熟
☐ 全熟

---

in·dex [ˋɪndɛks]

名 指數、索引
動 編索引

英英 an alphabetical list of names, subjects, etc., with references to the places in a book where they occur; to record in an index

例 The **index** helps you to find the word analysis of the vocabulary.
這份索引幫你找到字彙的文字分析。

☐ 三分熟
☐ 五分熟
☐ 七分熟
☐ 全熟

---

in·dif·fer·ence
[ɪnˋdɪfərəns]

名 不關心、不在乎
反 concern 關心

英英 having no particular interest on something

例 My son showed **indifference** to his testing performance, which worried me.
我的兒子對考試成績漠不關心，我很擔心。

☐ 三分熟
☐ 五分熟
☐ 七分熟
☐ 全熟

---

in·dif·fer·ent
[ɪnˋdɪfərənt]

形 中立的、不關心的

英英 unconcerned or careless about something

例 As one member of the family, it is not possible to remain **indifferent**.
身為家庭成員之一，要維持中立著實不太可能。

☐ 三分熟
☐ 五分熟
☐ 七分熟
☐ 全熟

🎧 **Track 065**

in·dig·nant
[ɪnˈdɪɡnənt]

形 憤怒的

英英 angry or annoyed because of an unfair treatment

例 Phil's friend was bullied, and he became quite **indignant**.
菲爾的朋友被霸凌，他變得十分憤怒。

☐ 三分熟
☐ 五分熟
☐ 七分熟
☐ 全熟

in·dis·pen·sa·ble
[ˌɪndɪˈspɛnsəbl̩]

形 不可缺少的
同 essential 不可缺少的

英英 absolutely necessary

例 Sense of humor is **indispensable** for being a teacher.
幽默感對身為一個老師來講是不可或缺的。

☐ 三分熟
☐ 五分熟
☐ 七分熟
☐ 全熟

in·duce [ˈɪnˈdjus]

動 引誘、引起

英英 to succeed in persuading or leading someone to do something

例 The coupon **induces** customers to buy expensive products.
這張優惠券引誘消費者購買昂貴的產品。

☐ 三分熟
☐ 五分熟
☐ 七分熟
☐ 全熟

in·dulge [ɪnˈdʌldʒ]

動 沉溺、放縱、遷就

英英 to allow oneself to enjoy the pleasure of something completely

例 **Indulging** in the online games is not a good thing.
沉溺在線上遊戲這件事並不是件好事。

☐ 三分熟
☐ 五分熟
☐ 七分熟
☐ 全熟

in·fi·nite [ˈɪnfənɪt]

形 無限的

英英 limitless in space, extent, size, or degree

例 With **infinite** confidence, he insisted on finishing the rescue task of dogs.
懷抱無限的信心，他堅持完成拯救狗兒的任務。

☐ 三分熟
☐ 五分熟
☐ 七分熟
☐ 全熟

in·her·it [ɪnˈhɛrɪt]

動 繼承、接受
片 be genetically inherited 基因遺傳

英英 to receive money or property as an heir at the death of the previous holder

例 Fanny **inherited** the apartment.
芬妮繼承了這棟公寓。

☐ 三分熟
☐ 五分熟
☐ 七分熟
☐ 全熟

i·ni·ti·ate
[ɪˈnɪʃˌɪt]/[ɪˈnɪʃˌɪet]

名 初學者
動 開始、創始
形 新加入的
同 begin 開始

英英 new comer; to begin or start doing or establishing something

例 The **initiate** needs time to learn how to drive.
初學者需要時間學開車。

☐ 三分熟
☐ 五分熟
☐ 七分熟
☐ 全熟

in·land [ˈɪnlənd]

名 內陸
副 在內陸
形 內陸的

英英 in or into the interior of a nation

例 The **inland** earthquake is shocking.
內陸的地震是令人吃驚的。

---

in·nu·mer·a·ble

[ɪnˈnjumərəbḷ]

形 數不盡的

英英 (something is) too many to be counted

例 **Innumerable** pearls and gold coins are hidden in the cave.
數不盡的珍珠和金幣藏在山洞裡。

---

in·quire [ɪnˈkwaɪr]

動 詢問、調查

英英 to ask for the detail about something or to get the information

例 The detective investigated the murder case by **inquiring** the suspects.
偵探藉由詢問嫌疑犯調查謀殺案。

---

in·sti·tute

[ˈɪnstətjut]

名 協會、機構
動 設立、授職
同 organization 機構

英英 an organization for the promotion of science, education, etc.; to establish or set up

例 This research **institute** will display the new modes of robots this year.
這個研究機構會在今年展示新型的機器人。

---

in·sure [ɪnˈʃʊr]

動 投保、確保

英英 to pay a fixed amount money to a special company for protecting yourself against risk

例 Put the food in these boxes to **insure** its freshness.
把食物放在這些盒子裡，確保食物的新鮮。

---

in·tent [ɪnˈtɛnt]

名 意圖、意思
形 熱心的、急切的、
　專心致志的

英英 the purpose or intention; determined to do something

例 My cousin was **intent** on writing calligraphy.
我的姪子專心致志於寫毛筆字。

---

in·ter·fer·ence

[ˌɪntɚˈfɪrəns]

名 妨礙、干擾

英英 disturbance to radio signals caused by other signals or other sources

例 Humming tunes is a kind of **interference**, don't you think?
哼唱曲子是種干擾，你不這樣認為嗎？

🎧 Track 067

in·te·ri·or [ɪnˈtɪrɪɚ]

名 內部、內務
形 內部的
反 exterior 外部

英英 the internal affairs of a nation; internal

例 Jack is talented in **interior** design.
傑克在室內設計方面有天份。

☐ 三分熟
☐ 五分熟
☐ 七分熟
☐ 全熟

in·ter·pre·ta·tion

[ɪnˌtɝprɪˈteʃən]

名 解釋、說明
同 explanation 解釋

英英 the action of explaining the meaning of something

例 The **interpretation** of the life cycle of the butterfly to kids is meaningful.
對孩子們說明蝴蝶的生命週期有其意義。

☐ 三分熟
☐ 五分熟
☐ 七分熟
☐ 全熟

in·ter·pret·er

[ɪnˈtɝprɪtɚ]

名 解釋者、翻譯員

英英 a person who interprets foreign language orally

例 The **interpreter** of the conference did a good job.
會議的翻譯員做得不錯。

☐ 三分熟
☐ 五分熟
☐ 七分熟
☐ 全熟

in·tu·i·tion

[ˌɪntjuˈɪʃən]

名 直覺
同 hunch 直覺

英英 the ability to understand something immediately, without conscious reasoning

例 Sometime **intuition** helps you create the right style of your own.
直覺有時會幫助你創建自己的正確風格。

☐ 三分熟
☐ 五分熟
☐ 七分熟
☐ 全熟

in·ward [ˈɪnwɚd]

形 裡面的
副 向內、內心裡
反 outward 向外

英英 directed towards the inside

例 **Inward** feelings would reveal themselves through dreams.
內心裡的感覺會透過夢境顯露出來。

☐ 三分熟
☐ 五分熟
☐ 七分熟
☐ 全熟

in·wards [ˈɪnwɚdz]

副 向內

英英 directed or proceeding towards the inside

例 Think **inwards** and then say what is right.
在內心裡想一想，然後說出正確的事。

☐ 三分熟
☐ 五分熟
☐ 七分熟
☐ 全熟

isle [aɪl]

名 島
同 island 島

英英 an island

例 Some people are dreaming of buying a small **isle** and live there.
有些人夢想著要買一座小島，住在島上。

☐ 三分熟
☐ 五分熟
☐ 七分熟
☐ 全熟

is·sue [ˈɪʃjʊ]

名 議題
動 發出、發行

英英 an important subject of a meeting; to produce something official

例 The political **issue** is banned in this company.
在這間公司裡禁止談論政治議題。

☐ 三分熟
☐ 五分熟
☐ 七分熟
☐ 全熟

i·vy [ˋaɪvɪ]

名 常春藤
片 be covered in ivy
布滿常春藤

英英 a woody evergreen plant, typically with shiny five-pointed leaves

例 The **ivy** on the house became quite scary at night.
這間房子上的常春藤在晚上變得相當可怕。

□ 三分熟
□ 五分熟
□ 七分熟
□ 全熟

J

Jj

jack [dʒæk]

名 起重機、千斤頂
動 用起重機舉起

英英 a device which is for lifting heavy objects; to lift up with a jack

例 Use the **jack** to move up the car.
用千斤頂把車舉起來吧。

□ 三分熟
□ 五分熟
□ 七分熟
□ 全熟

jade [dʒed]

名 玉、玉石

英英 a hard stone which is used for ornaments and jewellery

例 The **jade** bracelet shines in the darkness.
這只玉鐲在暗處閃著光芒。

□ 三分熟
□ 五分熟
□ 七分熟
□ 全熟

jan·i·tor [ˋdʒænɪtɚ]

名 管門者、看門者

英英 a caretaker of a building

例 The **janitor** of the university didn't allow the cars to enter the campus.
看門者不允許汽車進校園。

□ 三分熟
□ 五分熟
□ 七分熟
□ 全熟

jas·mine [ˋdʒæsmɪn]

名 茉莉

英英 a shrub or climbing plant with sweet fragrant

例 **Jasmine** perfume is my auntie's favorite.
茉莉香水是我阿姨的最愛。

□ 三分熟
□ 五分熟
□ 七分熟
□ 全熟

jay·walk [ˋdʒeˌwɔk]

動 違規穿越馬路

英英 to across a road without regard for approaching traffic

例 **Jaywalking** is dangerous.
不守交通規則穿越街道，很危險。

□ 三分熟
□ 五分熟
□ 七分熟
□ 全熟

jeer [dʒɪr]

動 戲弄、嘲笑
同 mock 嘲笑

英英 a rude way of making fun of someone or laughing at

例 **Jeering** at poor Justin is wrong.
嘲笑可憐的賈斯汀是錯的。

□ 三分熟
□ 五分熟
□ 七分熟
□ 全熟

🎧 **Track 069**

jin·gle [ˋdʒɪŋḷ]

名 叮鈴聲、節拍十分規則的簡單詩歌

動 使發出鈴聲

英英 a light, loose ringing sound such as that made by metal objects being shaken by a hand

例 Christmas **jingles** delight our ears.
聖誕詩歌很悅耳。

☐ 三分熟
☐ 五分熟
☐ 七分熟
☐ 全熟

---

jol·ly [ˋdʒɑlɪ]

動 開玩笑、戲弄

形 幽默的、快活的、興高采烈的

副 非常地

反 melancholy 憂鬱的

英英 to make fun or tell a joke; being humorous; very, extremely

例 Judy's uncle has **jolly** disposition.
茱蒂的舅舅有著快活的性情。

☐ 三分熟
☐ 五分熟
☐ 七分熟
☐ 全熟

---

jour·nal·ism [ˋdʒɝnḷ͵ɪzəm]

名 新聞學、新聞業

英英 the activity or profession of being a journalist

例 **Journalism** is mainly involved with newspaper media.
新聞業主要與報業媒體相關。

☐ 三分熟
☐ 五分熟
☐ 七分熟
☐ 全熟

---

jour·nal·ist [ˋdʒɝnḷɪst]

名 新聞工作者

英英 a person who writes news for newspapers or magazines to be broadcast on radio or television

例 The **journalist** interviewed the criminals as well as presidents.
新聞工作者探訪罪犯，也採訪總統。

☐ 三分熟
☐ 五分熟
☐ 七分熟
☐ 全熟

---

jug [dʒʌg]

名 帶柄的水壺

英英 a cylindrical container with a handle and a lip, for pouring liquids

例 Pour some coffee from the **jug**.
從這只帶柄的壺中倒出咖啡。

☐ 三分熟
☐ 五分熟
☐ 七分熟
☐ 全熟

---

ju·ry [ˋdʒʊrɪ]

名 陪審團

英英 a group of people sworn to give a verdict in a legal case on the basis of evidence submitted in court

例 The **jury** retired to do further discussions.
陪審團退席去做進一步的討論。

☐ 三分熟
☐ 五分熟
☐ 七分熟
☐ 全熟

---

jus·ti·fy [ˋdʒʌstə͵faɪ]

動 證明……有理

英英 to prove that something is right or reasonable

例 If you didn't kill him, **justify** what you said.
如果你沒有殺他，提出證明表示所說成理。

☐ 三分熟
☐ 五分熟
☐ 七分熟
☐ 全熟

---

ju·ve·nile [ˋdʒuvənḷ]

名 青少年、孩子

形 少年的、孩子氣的

英英 a young child

例 Betty's research interest is **juvenile** literature.
貝蒂的研究興趣是青少年文學。

☐ 三分熟
☐ 五分熟
☐ 七分熟
☐ 全熟

joy·ous [ˈdʒɔɪəs]

形 歡喜的、高興的

英英 full of happiness and joy

例 **Joyous** childhood passed like the spring.
歡樂童年如春天般，一去不返。

Kk

kin [kɪn]

名 親族、親戚
形 有親戚關係的
同 relative 親戚

英英 one's family and relations; of a person related

例 Mr. Scott is her **kin**.
史考特先生是她的親戚。

kin·dle [ˈkɪndl]

動 生火、起火

英英 to set on fire

例 **Kindle** the fire and BBQ some sausages.
起火，烤些香腸。

knowl·cdge·a·ble

[ˈnɑlɪdʒəbl]

形 博學的

英英 very intelligent and well informed

例 Professor Liang is **knowledgeable**.
梁教授博學多聞。

Ll

lad [læd]

名 少年、老友

英英 a boy or young man

例 The **lad** is full of energy.
少年人活力充沛。

lame [lem]

形 跛的、站不住腳的

英英 walking with difficulty because of an injury or illness affecting the leg or foot

例 Tom's excuse of being late is **lame**.
湯姆所給的遲到的理由是站不住腳的。

land·la·dy

[ˈlændˌledɪ]

名 女房東

英英 a woman who leases land or houses

例 The **landlady** is old, yet pretty strong.
女房東雖然年紀大，但滿強壯的。

land·lord [ˈlændˌlɔrd]

名 房東、主人、老闆

英英 a man who leases land or houses

例 I've called the **landlord** to fix the water heater.
我已經打給房東，請他來修熱水器。

🎧 **Track 071**

la·ser [ˈlezɚ]

名 雷射

英英 a device which makes powerful narrow beam of light that can be used to cut metal, or to perform medical operations

例 **Laser** can remove tattoos and scars.
雷射可以去除刺青和疤痕。

☐ 三分熟
☐ 五分熟
☐ 七分熟
☐ 全熟

---

lat·i·tude

[ˈlætəˌtjud]

名 緯度
反 longitude 經度

英英 the position of a place north or south of the equator

例 The flower exhibition was organized by **latitude** and altitude of the flowers.
花卉展會依據花的經緯度做規劃。

☐ 三分熟
☐ 五分熟
☐ 七分熟
☐ 全熟

---

law·mak·er

[ˈlɔˌmekɚ]

名 立法者

英英 a legislator who makes laws or changes laws

例 The **lawmaker** should be wise and just.
立法者應該要有智慧，也要公正。

☐ 三分熟
☐ 五分熟
☐ 七分熟
☐ 全熟

---

lay·er [ˈleɚ]

名 層
動 分層

英英 a sheet or thickness of material; to arrange in a layer

例 The wedding cake has five **layers**.
這個結婚蛋糕有五層。

☐ 三分熟
☐ 五分熟
☐ 七分熟
☐ 全熟

---

league [lig]

名 聯盟
動 同盟
同 union 聯盟

英英 a collection of people, countries, that join together because they have the same goal or interest; to join together and achieve the same goal

例 The National Football **League** consists of 32 teams.
全國足球聯賽由 32 支球隊組成。

☐ 三分熟
☐ 五分熟
☐ 七分熟
☐ 全熟

---

leg·is·la·tion

[ˌlɛdʒɪsˈleʃən]

名 立法

英英 laws suggested by a government

例 **Legislation** of outer space immigration law will be necessary in the future.
未來制定移居外太空法條將會是有必要的。

☐ 三分熟
☐ 五分熟
☐ 七分熟
☐ 全熟

---

less·en [ˈlɛsn̩]

動 減少
同 decrease 減少

英英 to make or become less

例 **Lessening** the number of students of a class increases the teaching efficiency.
減少一個班級的學生人數增加教學效率。

☐ 三分熟
☐ 五分熟
☐ 七分熟
☐ 全熟

---

lest [lɛst]

連 以免

英英 with the intention of preventing or to avoid the risk of

例 We'd better do something about the river pollution, **lest** the pollution gets worse.
我們最好為河川污染做點事，以免污染加劇。

☐ 三分熟
☐ 五分熟
☐ 七分熟
☐ 全熟

lieu·ten·ant

[luˋtɛnənt]

名 海軍上尉、陸軍中尉

英英 a rank of officer in the army, above second lieutenant and below captain

例 **Lieutenant** Liu demanded bribes.
劉姓海軍上尉索賄。

☐ 三分熟
☐ 五分熟
☐ 七分熟
☐ 全熟

---

life·long [ˋlaɪfˋlɔŋ]

形 終身的

英英 lasting or remaining for the whole of a person's life

例 **Lifelong** learning is encouraged.
終身學習是應該鼓勵的。

☐ 三分熟
☐ 五分熟
☐ 七分熟
☐ 全熟

---

like·li·hood

[ˋlaɪklɪˌhʊd]

名 可能性、可能的事物
同 possibility 可能性

英英 the state or fact of being possible

例 The **likelihood** is high.
可能性很高。

☐ 三分熟
☐ 五分熟
☐ 七分熟
☐ 全熟

---

lime [laɪm]

名 萊姆（樹）、石灰
動 灑石灰

英英 a small green fruit, like a lemon, with a lot of sour juice, usually used in cooking and in drinks; a white powdery substance which is used to make grow better; to spray a white powdery substance to soil to control acid

例 The **limes** taste sour.
萊姆嚐起來好酸。

☐ 三分熟
☐ 五分熟
☐ 七分熟
☐ 全熟

---

limp [lɪmp]

動 跛行

英英 to walk with difficulty because of an injured leg or foot

例 Even though Ted had an accident, he **limped** to attend my class.
雖然泰德出了場意外，他仍舊跛著腳來上我的課。

☐ 三分熟
☐ 五分熟
☐ 七分熟
☐ 全熟

---

lin·ger [ˋlɪŋgə]

動 留戀、徘徊
同 stay 停留、逗留

英英 be slow or unwilling to leave

例 Don't **linger** on the hall.
不要在走廊上徘徊。

☐ 三分熟
☐ 五分熟
☐ 七分熟
☐ 全熟

---

live·stock

[ˋlaɪvˌstɑk]

名 家畜

英英 farm animals, such as cows and sheep, regarded as an asset

例 Jason lost all of his **livestock** in the plague.
傑生在這場瘟疫中損失了所有的家畜。

☐ 三分熟
☐ 五分熟
☐ 七分熟
☐ 全熟

---

liz·ard [ˋlɪzəd]

名 蜥蜴

英英 a four-legged reptile with a long body and tail, and a rough, scaly, or spiny skin

例 The snake ate a **lizard**.
這條蛇吃了蜥蜴。

☐ 三分熟
☐ 五分熟
☐ 七分熟
☐ 全熟

L

lo·co·mo·tive
[ˌlokəˈmotɪv]

名 火車頭
形 推動的、運動的

英英 a powered railway vehicle which is used for pulling trains; moving something with pulling

例 The **locomotive** runs out of the track.
火車出軌了。

☐ 三分熟
☐ 五分熟
☐ 七分熟
☐ 全熟

---

lo·cust [ˈlokəst]

名 蝗蟲

英英 a large tropical grasshopper which flies in a large groups and destroys plants and crops

例 The disaster of **locusts** used to harm the harvest of rice.
蝗蟲災害已經危害到稻米的收成了。

☐ 三分熟
☐ 五分熟
☐ 七分熟
☐ 全熟

---

lodge [lɑdʒ]

名 小屋
動 寄宿

英英 a small house at the gates of a large house with grounds; to provide with rented accommodation

例 Some painting tools are left in the **lodge**.
有些作畫的工具留在小屋裡。

☐ 三分熟
☐ 五分熟
☐ 七分熟
☐ 全熟

---

loft·y [ˈlɔftɪ]

形 非常高的、高聳的

英英 of imposing height or noble

例 Chinese painters worshipped **lofty** mountains.
中國畫家們敬仰高山。

☐ 三分熟
☐ 五分熟
☐ 七分熟
☐ 全熟

---

log·o [ˈlɔgo]

名 商標、標誌

英英 a trademark design adopted by an organization to identify its products

例 The **logo** of the movie company looks like a goddess.
電影公司的商標看起來像一位女神。

☐ 三分熟
☐ 五分熟
☐ 七分熟
☐ 全熟

---

lone·some
[ˈlonsəm]

形 孤獨的
同 lonely 孤獨的

英英 very lonely

例 **Lonesome** nights await tired travelers.
孤獨的夜晚等待疲憊的旅客。

☐ 三分熟
☐ 五分熟
☐ 七分熟
☐ 全熟

---

lon·gi·tude
[ˈlɑndʒəˌtjud]

名 經度
反 latitude 緯度

英英 the distance of a place east or west of a standard meridian, especially the Greenwich meridian

例 The map shows clear **longitude** and latitude.
這張地圖秀出清楚的經緯度。

☐ 三分熟
☐ 五分熟
☐ 七分熟
☐ 全熟

lo·tus [ˈlotəs]

名 睡蓮

英英 a large water lily

例 Some carps are swimming under the **lotus**.
有些鯉魚在睡蓮下方游著。

□ 三分熟
□ 五分熟
□ 七分熟
□ 全熟

M

---

lot·ter·y [ˈlɑtərɪ]

名 彩券、樂透

英英 a game of raising money by selling numbered tickets and giving prizes to the holders of numbers drawn at random

例 The shallow news reporting about the **lottery** needs improvement.
這膚淺的樂透新聞報導需要改進。

□ 三分熟
□ 五分熟
□ 七分熟
□ 全熟

---

lum·ber [ˈlʌmbɚ]

名 木材
動 採伐
同 timber 木材

英英 wood which has been prepared for building; to cut down the wood

例 These precious **lumbers** are preserved well.
這些珍貴的木材保管的不錯，

□ 三分熟
□ 五分熟
□ 七分熟
□ 全熟

---

lump [lʌmp]

名 塊
動 結塊、笨重地移動
同 chunk 大塊

英英 a piece of solid substance with no particular shape; to shaped a piece

例 How many sugar **lumps** did you put into this glass of milk?
這杯牛奶裡你放入多少塊糖？

□ 三分熟
□ 五分熟
□ 七分熟
□ 全熟

Mm

mag·ni·fy

[ˈmæɡnəˌfaɪ]

動 擴大
同 enlarge 擴大

英英 to make something appear larger than it used to be

例 When the weak points are **magnified**, it's time to break the relationship.
當弱點被放大時，就是中斷關係的時候了。

□ 三分熟
□ 五分熟
□ 七分熟
□ 全熟

---

maid·en [ˈmedn̩]

名 處女、少女
形 少女的、未婚的、處女的

英英 a girl or young woman or a virgin; being a virgin or single

例 Ophelia is one of the well-known **maidens** in Shakespearean plays.
歐菲莉亞是莎劇裡最有名的少女之一。

□ 三分熟
□ 五分熟
□ 七分熟
□ 全熟

---

main·land

[ˈmenˌlænd]

名 大陸

英英 a large continuous part of a country or continent, not including the islands around it

例 Check the timetable of ferries which travel from **mainland** to Kinmen.
查一下從大陸到金門的渡輪時刻表。

□ 三分熟
□ 五分熟
□ 七分熟
□ 全熟

🎧 **Track 075**

---

main·stream

[ˋmenˌstrim]

名 思潮、主流

英英 the ideas, attitudes, or activities which accepted by most people

例 Hollywood movies have been the **mainstream** in the movie industry.
好萊塢電影一直是電影業中的主流。

☐三分熟
☐五分熟
☐七分熟
☐全熟

---

main·te·nance

[ˋmentənəns]

名 保持

片 regular maintenance 定期保養

英英 the process of maintaining or being maintained

例 **Maintenance** of beauty has long been human being's dream.
保持美麗一直是人類的夢想。

☐三分熟
☐五分熟
☐七分熟
☐全熟

---

ma·jes·tic

[məˋdʒɛstɪk]

形 莊嚴的

同 grand 雄偉的

英英 impressively beautiful or dignified

例 The **majestic** Buddha sculpture arouse believers' inner respect.
莊嚴的佛像引發信徒內心的敬意。

☐三分熟
☐五分熟
☐七分熟
☐全熟

---

maj·es·ty

[ˋmædʒɪstɪ]

名 威嚴

英英 impressive dignity or beauty

例 The **majesty** of the general is said to scare the evil spirits away.
將軍的威嚴據說可以把邪靈嚇走。

☐三分熟
☐五分熟
☐七分熟
☐全熟

---

mam·mal [ˋmæml]

名 哺乳動物

英英 the animals that the female gives birth to babies and feeds them on milk from her own body

例 Whales are a kind of **mammal** living in the ocean.
鯨魚是一種住在海裡的哺乳動物。

☐三分熟
☐五分熟
☐七分熟
☐全熟

---

man·i·fest

[ˋmænəˌfɛst]

動 顯示

形 明顯的

同 apparent 明顯的

英英 to show or demonstrate something; very obvious and clear

例 My sister's emotions are **manifested** clearly on her face.
我姊姊的情緒很清楚的顯露在臉上。

☐三分熟
☐五分熟
☐七分熟
☐全熟

---

man·sion

[ˋmænʃən]

名 宅邸、大廈

英英 a very large, impressive house

例 They plan to hold a rock'n roll party in Tiffany's **mansion**.
他們計劃要在蒂芬妮的大廈裡舉辦搖滾派對。

☐三分熟
☐五分熟
☐七分熟
☐全熟

M

ma·ple [ˈmepḷ]
名 楓樹、槭樹

英英 a tree with lobed leaves, which grows in northern area of the world

例 The autumn **maple** tree leaves while traveling in Canada are impressive.
在加拿大旅遊時看到的秋天楓葉令人印象深刻。

☐ 三分熟
☐ 五分熟
☐ 七分熟
☐ 全熟

---

mar·gin·al [ˈmɑrdʒɪnḷ]
形 邊緣的

英英 constituting a margin, a border

例 The **marginal** people need more opportunities to be accepted by society.
邊緣人需要更多被社會接納的機會。

☐ 三分熟
☐ 五分熟
☐ 七分熟
☐ 全熟

---

ma·rine [məˈrin]
名 海軍
形 海洋的

英英 a member of a body serves on land or sea; relating to shipping or naval matters

例 The design of the **marine** uniform looks youthful.
這款海軍制服的設計看起來充滿青春活力。

☐ 三分熟
☐ 五分熟
☐ 七分熟
☐ 全熟

---

mar·shal [ˈmɑrʃəl]
名 元帥、司儀

英英 an officer of the highest rank in the armed forces of some countries

例 The Young **Marshal** Chang Hsueh-liang rests here.
少帥張學良在此長眠。

☐ 三分熟
☐ 五分熟
☐ 七分熟
☐ 全熟

---

mar·tial [ˈmɑrʃəl]
形 軍事的
同 military 軍事的

英英 relating to or suggestive of war

例 The village headman decided to strengthen the **martial** arts training.
村長決定加強軍事演練。

☐ 三分熟
☐ 五分熟
☐ 七分熟
☐ 全熟

---

mar·vel [ˈmɑrvḷ]
名 令人驚奇的事物、奇蹟
動 驚異
同 miracle 奇蹟

英英 a person or thing that causes a feeling of surprise or admiration; to cause a feeling of surprise or admiration

例 The audience **marveled** at the seal's performance.
觀眾對海豹的表演感到驚奇。

☐ 三分熟
☐ 五分熟
☐ 七分熟
☐ 全熟

---

mas·cu·line [ˈmæskjəlɪn]
名 男性
形 男性的
反 feminine 女性

英英 male; relating to men

例 Is boxing a kind of **masculine** sports or feminine sports?
拳擊是一種男性的運動還是女性的運動？

☐ 三分熟
☐ 五分熟
☐ 七分熟
☐ 全熟

Track 077

mash [mæʃ]

名 麥芽漿
動 搗碎

英英 bran mixed with hot water or liquid; to crush a substance into a pulp

例 **Mashed** potatoes taste good.
馬鈴薯搗泥好吃。

☐三分熟
☐五分熟
☐七分熟
☐全熟

---

mas·sage

[mə`saʒ]

名 按摩
動 按摩

英英 the rubbing and kneading of parts of the body with the hands to make a person relaxed

例 Gently **massaging** the baby can help the baby sleep better.
輕輕地按摩小寶寶可以幫助小寶貝睡得更香。

☐三分熟
☐五分熟
☐七分熟
☐全熟

---

mas·sive [`mæsɪv]

形 笨重的、大量的、巨大的

同 heavy 重的

英英 large and heavy or severe

例 **Massive** homework assignments almost crushed the junior high school student.
大量的課業幾乎壓垮這名國中生。

☐三分熟
☐五分熟
☐七分熟
☐全熟

---

mas·ter·piece

[`mæstɚˌpis]

名 傑作、名著

英英 a work of outstanding skill

例 Auguste Rodin's **masterpiece** is "The Thinker."
奧古斯特・羅丹的傑作是「沉思者」。

☐三分熟
☐五分熟
☐七分熟
☐全熟

---

may·on·naise

[ˌmeə`nez]

名 美乃滋、橄欖油、蛋黃醬

英英 a thick creamy dressing made from egg yolks, oil, and vinegar, which is usually used to make salads

例 My sister-in-law didn't dare to eat the toast paved with **mayonnaise**.
我的弟媳不敢吃塗上美乃滋的吐司。

☐三分熟
☐五分熟
☐七分熟
☐全熟

---

mean·time

[`minˌtaɪm]

名 期間、同時
副 同時

英英 meanwhile; at the same time

例 She studied chemistry. **Meantime**, she researched the way to make poison.
她研讀化學。同時，她研究製作毒藥的方法。

☐三分熟
☐五分熟
☐七分熟
☐全熟

---

me·chan·ics

[mə`kænɪks]

名 機械學、力學

英英 the study concerned with motion and forces producing motion

例 Sam's high score in **mechanics** amazed his parents.
山姆在機械學上考高分，讓他的父母感到驚訝。

☐三分熟
☐五分熟
☐七分熟
☐全熟

M

me·di·ate

[ˈmidɪˌet]

動 調解

英英 to try to settle a dispute between two people or other parties

例 To **mediate** between the two sides takes time.
調解這兩方的紛爭要花點時間。

□ 三分熟
□ 五分熟
□ 七分熟
□ 全熟

men·ace [ˈmɛnɪs]

名 威脅
動 脅迫
同 threat 威脅
片 quiet menace
安靜的威脅

英英 a threatening quality

例 The **menace** from the robber terrified Bill.
來自搶匪的威脅嚇壞了比爾。

□ 二分熟
□ 五分熟
□ 七分熟
□ 全熟

mer·maid

[ˈmɝˌmed]

名 美人魚

英英 a mythical sea creature in the fairy tale, who is with a woman's head and trunk and a fish's tail

例 Starbucks cafe uses the **mermaid** as its logo.
星巴克咖啡店用美人魚當作商標。

□ 三分熟
□ 五分熟
□ 七分熟
□ 全熟

midst [mɪdst]

名 中央、中間
介 在……之中

英英 in the middle point or part

例 Your child was in their **midst**.
你的小孩在那群人中間。

□ 三分熟
□ 五分熟
□ 七分熟
□ 全熟

mi·grant

[ˈmaɪɡrənt]

名 候鳥、移民
形 遷移的

英英 an animal or birds that migrates; to move to another place

例 The **migrant** birds flew down and took a rest beside the river.
遷徙的候鳥飛下來，在河邊休息。

□ 三分熟
□ 五分熟
□ 七分熟
□ 全熟

mile·age [ˈmaɪlɪdʒ]

名 里數

英英 a number of miles travelled or covered

例 The **mileage** of flight is accumulating.
飛行里程數累積中。

□ 三分熟
□ 五分熟
□ 七分熟
□ 全熟

mile·stone

[ˈmaɪlˌston]

名 里程碑

英英 a stone set up at the side of road to mark the distance in miles to a particular place

例 Becoming a mother is the **milestone** of her life.
成為一個母親，是她人生的里程碑。

□ 三分熟
□ 五分熟
□ 七分熟
□ 全熟

Track 079

min·gle [ˋmɪŋɡl̩]

動 混合
同 blend 混合

英英 to mix together
例 Annie likes to drink the **mingling** of the pudding with honey and milk.
安妮喜歡布丁混合著蜂蜜和牛奶一起喝。

□三分熟
□五分熟
□七分熟
□全熟

min·i·mal [ˋmɪnɪml̩]

形 最小的
片 minimal injuries 最小的損傷

英英 of a minimum amount, quantity, or degree
例 The **minimal** charge of this restaurant is NT$200.
這家餐廳最低消費額是臺幣 200 元。

□三分熟
□五分熟
□七分熟
□全熟

mint [mɪnt]

名 薄荷

英英 a herb plant, whose leaves have a strong fresh smell, and usually used for adding flavour to food
例 The soda mixed with **mint** is quite refreshing.
汽水混合薄荷滿提神的。

□三分熟
□五分熟
□七分熟
□全熟

mi·ser [ˋmaɪzɚ]

名 小氣鬼

英英 person who wishes to have great deal of money and hates to spend it
例 The **miser** looked for a way to spend money, yet didn't find any.
小氣鬼尋找花錢的方法，但找不到。

□三分熟
□五分熟
□七分熟
□全熟

mis·tress [ˋmɪstrɪs]

名 女主人

英英 woman in a position of authority or control
例 The **mistress** of the mansion is hospitable.
這棟大宅院的女主人滿好客的。

□三分熟
□五分熟
□七分熟
□全熟

moan [mon]

名 呻吟聲、悲嘆
動 呻吟
同 groan 呻吟

英英 low mournful sound, usually expressive of suffering or pain; to make a low mournful sound
例 The **moaning** of the woman in white sounds miserable.
白衣女子的呻吟聲聽起來滿悲慘的。

□三分熟
□五分熟
□七分熟
□全熟

mock [mɑk]

名 嘲弄、笑柄
動 嘲笑
形 模仿的

英英 to laugh at someone or make fun of someone; not authentic or real
例 The students knew **mocking** is not right, but they did it anyway.
學生們知道嘲笑是不對的，但他們還是這樣做了。

□三分熟
□五分熟
□七分熟
□全熟

M

mode [mod]

名 款式、方法
同 manner 方法

英英 a way in which something happens or is done

例 Heidegger said the most inspiring **mode** of life is the one "being-toward-death."
海德格曾說最有啟發性的人生模式是「走向死亡」。

□ 三分熟
□ 五分熟
□ 七分熟
□ 全熟

---

mod·ern·ize

[`madənˌaɪz]

動 現代化

英英 to make something more modern

例 **Modernized** transportation sometimes is not that convenient at all.
現代化的交通有時並不是那樣的便利。

□ 三分熟
□ 五分熟
□ 七分熟
□ 全熟

---

mod·i·fy

[`madəˌfaɪ]

動 修改

英英 make partial changes to

例 The charge of **modifying** the pants is free.
修改這條褲子不收費。

□ 三分熟
□ 五分熟
□ 七分熟
□ 全熟

---

mold [mold]

名 模型
動 塑造、磨練

英英 a hollow container used to give shape to molten or hot liquid substances when it cools and hardens; to form an object

例 The cake **molds** are sold online.
蛋糕模型網路上有在賣。

□ 三分熟
□ 五分熟
□ 七分熟
□ 全熟

---

mol·e·cule

[`maləˌkjul]

名 分子

英英 the smallest fundamental unit of chemical substance, which is a group of two or more atoms

例 The brand of lotion enables the activation of water **molecules**.
這個牌子的乳液可活化水分子。

□ 三分熟
□ 五分熟
□ 七分熟
□ 全熟

---

mon·arch

[`manək]

名 君主、大王
同 king 君主

英英 a king or lord

例 Heaven, Earth, **Monarch**, Parents, and Teacher belong to traditional Chinese ethics.
天、地、君、親、師屬於傳統中國倫理觀。

□ 三分熟
□ 五分熟
□ 七分熟
□ 全熟

---

mon·strous

[`manstrəs]

形 奇怪的、巨大的
同 bulky 龐大的

英英 very large and ugly or frightening

例 The **monstrous** building was criticized by local residents.
這個奇怪的建築物被當地的居民所批評。

□ 三分熟
□ 五分熟
□ 七分熟
□ 全熟

🎧 **Track 081**

---

mor·tal [`mɔrtl̩]

名 凡人
形 死亡的、致命的
同 deadly 致命的

英英 an ordinary person; causing death

例 Sometimes goddess's love for **mortals** caused tragedies.
有時女神對凡人的愛而造成了悲劇。

☐ 三分熟
☐ 五分熟
☐ 七分熟
☐ 全熟

---

moss [mɔs]

名 苔蘚、用苔覆蓋

英英 a small green plant which grows in wet ground or on rocks, walls and tree trunks; to cover with moss

例 These huge stones are covered with **moss**.
這些巨石被答蘚所覆蓋。

☐ 三分熟
☐ 五分熟
☐ 七分熟
☐ 全熟

---

moth·er·hood

[`mʌðəhʊd]

名 母性

英英 a female parent

例 **Motherhood** is a gift from God to children.
母性是上帝賜給小孩的禮物。

☐ 三分熟
☐ 五分熟
☐ 七分熟
☐ 全熟

---

mo·tive [`motɪv]

名 動機
同 cause 動機

英英 a factor empowering a person to act in a particular way

例 The **motive** of his helping this old beggar without blood relationship is suspicious.
他幫助年老且無血緣關係的乞丐，背後的動機令人起疑。

☐ 三分熟
☐ 五分熟
☐ 七分熟
☐ 全熟

---

mound [maʊnd]

名 丘陵、堆積、築堤

英英 a small hill; to heap up into a mound

例 The fireman found a fire ant **mound** nearby.
消防員在附近發現了一個火蟻丘。

☐ 三分熟
☐ 五分熟
☐ 七分熟
☐ 全熟

---

mount [maʊnt]

名 山
動 攀登
同 climb 攀爬

英英 used as part of the name of a mountain or a hill; to climb onto

例 Tension is **mounting** among the two chess players.
兩名國際象棋棋手之間的緊張感正在加劇。

☐ 三分熟
☐ 五分熟
☐ 七分熟
☐ 全熟

---

mow·er [`moɚ]

名 割草者（機）

英英 a person or machine that cuts down grass or a cereal crop

例 Your uncle borrowed the **mower** yesterday.
你舅舅昨天借走了割草機。

☐ 三分熟
☐ 五分熟
☐ 七分熟
☐ 全熟

---

mum·ble [`mʌmbl̩]

名 含糊不清的話
動 含糊地說
同 mutter 含糊地說

英英 say something unclearly and quietly; unclear words spoken by someone

例 The boy was nervous and **mumbled**.
小男孩很緊張，含糊不清的講了些話。

☐ 三分熟
☐ 五分熟
☐ 七分熟
☐ 全熟

---

mus·cu·lar

[ˈmʌskjələ]

形 肌肉的

英英 of or affecting the muscles

例 **Muscular** strength exercises help weight loss.
肌力練習有助於減重。

☐ 三分熟
☐ 五分熟
☐ 七分熟
☐ 全熟

---

muse [mjuz]

名 深思、靈感來源

英英 an imaginary being inspires someone to write, paint or make music

例 Dora Maar, a French photographer, served as Picasso's **muse**.
法國攝影師朵拉・瑪爾曾經是畢卡索的靈感來源。

☐ 三分熟
☐ 五分熟
☐ 七分熟
☐ 全熟

---

mus·tard

[ˈmʌstəd]

名 芥末

英英 a hot-tasting yellow or brown sauce made from the crushed seeds of a plant, which is eaten cold with meat

例 The self-made honey **mustard** adds flavor to the chicken hamburger.
自製的蜂蜜芥末醬提升了雞肉堡的味道。

☐ 三分熟
☐ 五分熟
☐ 七分熟
☐ 全熟

---

mut·ter [ˈmʌtə]

名 抱怨
動 低語、含糊地説
同 complain 抱怨

英英 to say in a barely audible voice; complain

例 Although Debbie was busy on many tasks, she couldn't stop **muttering**.
雖然黛比手上在忙好幾個任務，她無法停止抱怨。

☐ 三分熟
☐ 五分熟
☐ 七分熟
☐ 全熟

---

mut·ton [ˈmʌtn̩]

名 羊肉

英英 the flesh of adult sheep used as food

例 Chen family's favorite winter food is the **mutton** hot pot.
陳家人冬季最愛的食物是羊肉火鍋。

☐ 三分熟
☐ 五分熟
☐ 七分熟
☐ 全熟

---

myth [mɪθ]

名 神話、傳説
同 tale 傳説
片 Greek myth 希臘神話

英英 an ancient story connecting to the early history of a people or explaining a natural or social phenomenon

例 The **myth** of the dragon has its charm.
龍的神話有其魅力。

☐ 三分熟
☐ 五分熟
☐ 七分熟
☐ 全熟

Nn

🎧 Track 083

nag [næg]

名 嘮叨的人
動 使煩惱、嘮叨
同 annoy 使煩惱

英英 to harass someone constantly to do something

例 Stop **nagging** at me.
不要再對我嘮叨了。

☐ 三分熟
☐ 五分熟
☐ 七分熟
☐ 全熟

---

na·ive [nɑˋiv]

形 天真、幼稚
反 sophisticated 世故的

英英 a person who lacks of experience or wisdom and is willing to believe that someone is telling the truth, that people's intentions in general are good

例 George's sister is so **naive**.
喬治的妹妹好天真。

☐ 三分熟
☐ 五分熟
☐ 七分熟
☐ 全熟

---

nas·ty [ˋnæstɪ]

形 汙穢的、惡意的、使人難受的
片 cheap and nasty 質劣價廉

英英 unpleasant and disgusting

例 He has a **nasty** habit of finding faults with others.
他有個愛找人麻煩的討人厭的習慣。

☐ 三分熟
☐ 五分熟
☐ 七分熟
☐ 全熟

---

nav·i·gate
[ˋnævəˌget]

動 控制航向
同 steer 掌舵

英英 to direct the route or course of a ship, aircraft, or other form of transport

例 Frank has mastered the **navigating** skill of ships.
法蘭克已經掌握了船隻的掌舵技巧。

☐ 三分熟
☐ 五分熟
☐ 七分熟
☐ 全熟

---

news·cast
[ˋnjuzˌkæst]

名 新聞報導

英英 a news report on radio or television

例 We listened to the **newscast** and was worried about Henry who's on business.
我們聽了新聞報導，擔心出公差的亨利。

☐ 三分熟
☐ 五分熟
☐ 七分熟
☐ 全熟

---

nib·ble [ˋnɪbḷ]

名 小撮食物
動 連續地輕咬

英英 a small piece of food bitten off; to bite something lightly and constantly

例 The lovely squirrel was **nibbling** the nut.
可愛的松鼠小口地咬著栗子。

☐ 三分熟
☐ 五分熟
☐ 七分熟
☐ 全熟

---

nick·el [ˋnɪkḷ]

名 鎳
動 覆以鎳……

英英 a silvery-white metallic chemical substance; to cover with nickel

例 **Nickels** can be used to make coins.
鎳可使用來做錢幣。

☐ 三分熟
☐ 五分熟
☐ 七分熟
☐ 全熟

night·in·gale

[ˈnaɪtn̩͵gel]

名 夜鶯、歌聲美妙的歌手

英英 a small brownish bird noted for its rich melodious song, often heard at night

例 The **nightingale** sings beautifully.
夜鶯唱著美妙的歌曲。

□ 三分熟
□ 五分熟
□ 七分熟
□ 全熟

nom·i·nate

[ˈnɑmə͵net]

動 提名、指定
同 propose 提名

英英 to assign or appoint to a job or position

例 Nick was **nominated** as the the director of the association.
尼克被提名為這個協會的理事長。

□ 三分熟
□ 五分熟
□ 七分熟
□ 全熟

none·the·less

[͵nʌnðəˈlɛs]

副 儘管如此、然而

英英 in spite of that, nevertheless

例 Eric behaves badly. **Nonetheless**, he is still our son.
艾瑞克行為舉止不端。然而他還是我們的兒子。

□ 三分熟
□ 五分熟
□ 七分熟
□ 全熟

non·vi·o·lent

[nɑnˈvaɪələnt]

形 非暴力的
反 violent 暴力的

英英 not violent

例 **Nonviolent** behaviors deserve respect.
非暴力的行為值得尊敬。

□ 三分熟
□ 五分熟
□ 七分熟
□ 全熟

nos·tril [ˈnɑstrəl]

名 鼻孔

英英 either of two external openings of the nose which air moves when you breathe

例 The performer imitates a pig's facial expression with flared **nostrils**.
表演者模仿有著大鼻孔的豬隻。

□ 三分熟
□ 五分熟
□ 七分熟
□ 全熟

no·ta·ble [ˈnotəbl̩]

名 名人、出眾的人
形 出色的、著名的
同 famous 著名的
片 particularly notable
　 特別引人注目

英英 a famous or important person; very famous and outstanding

例 My friend devoted herself to zither playing and became a **notable** musician.
我的朋友致力於古箏演奏，並成為著名的音樂家。

□ 三分熟
□ 五分熟
□ 七分熟
□ 全熟

no·tice·a·ble

[ˈnotɪsəbl̩]

形 顯著的、顯眼的

英英 easily seen, clear or apparent

例 The change of the water park is quite **noticeable**.
這座水上樂園的變化還滿明顯的。

□ 三分熟
□ 五分熟
□ 七分熟
□ 全熟

🎧 **Track 085**

no·ti·fy [ˋnotəˌfaɪ]

動 通知、報告
同 inform 通知

英英 to inform in a formal or official manner
例 **Notify** the motorcycle rider's family immediately.
立刻通知這個重機騎士的家人。

☐ 三分熟
☐ 五分熟
☐ 七分熟
☐ 全熟

---

no·tion [ˋnoʃən]

名 觀念、意見
同 opinion 意見

英英 a concept or belief
例 The **notion** of friendly working environment he proposed seemed to be convincing.
他所提出的友善工作環境的概念是很有說服力的。

☐ 三分熟
☐ 五分熟
☐ 七分熟
☐ 全熟

---

nov·ice [ˋnɑvɪs]

名 初學者

英英 a person who is new to a job or situation
例 The **novice** of computer programs learns fast.
這個電腦程式的初學者學得很快。

☐ 三分熟
☐ 五分熟
☐ 七分熟
☐ 全熟

---

no·where

[ˋnoˌhwɛr]

副 無處地
名 不為人知的地方

英英 not anywhere; a place that is not known by people
例 Oliver has **nowhere** to live.
奧利佛沒有地方可住。

☐ 三分熟
☐ 五分熟
☐ 七分熟
☐ 全熟

---

nu·cle·us

[ˋnjuklɪəs]

名 核心、中心、原子核
同 core 核心

英英 the central and most important part of an object or group
例 Dr. Lawrence researched the structure of atomic **nucleus**.
勞倫斯博士研究過原子核的結構。

☐ 三分熟
☐ 五分熟
☐ 七分熟
☐ 全熟

---

nude [njud]

名 裸體、裸體畫
形 裸的
同 naked 裸的

英英 without clothes on
例 The **nude** model was instructed to remain the same posture.
裸體模特兒被要求要保持同一姿勢。

☐ 三分熟
☐ 五分熟
☐ 七分熟
☐ 全熟

Oo

oar [or]

名 槳、櫓

英英 a long pole with a flat blade, used for rowing a boat
例 Use the **oar** to let the boat move forward.
用槳來讓這艘船往前移。

☐ 三分熟
☐ 五分熟
☐ 七分熟
☐ 全熟

O

o·a·sis [o`esɪs]

名 綠洲

英英 a fertile spot in a desert where water rises to ground level or grows plants

例 The **oasis** is real.
這個綠洲是真的。

☐ 三分熟
☐ 五分熟
☐ 七分熟
☐ 全熟

---

oath [oθ]

名 誓約、盟誓
同 vow 誓約

英英 a promise, especially one that you will tell the truth in a law court

例 Take the **oath** by putting your hand on the bible.
把手放在聖經上宣誓。

☐ 三分熟
☐ 五分熟
☐ 七分熟
☐ 全熟

---

oat·meal [`ot͵mil]

名 燕麥片

英英 meal made from ground oats

例 One benefit of eating **oatmeal** is improving digestion.
吃燕麥片的好處之一是改善消化。

☐ 三分熟
☐ 五分熟
☐ 七分熟
☐ 全熟

---

ob·long [`ɑblɔŋ]

名 長方形
形 長方形的

英英 a rectangular shape

例 The **oblong** shoe boxes take too much space.
長方形的鞋盒佔太多空間了。

☐ 三分熟
☐ 五分熟
☐ 七分熟
☐ 全熟

---

ob·serv·er

[əb`zɝvɚ]

名 觀察者、觀察員
反 performer 表演者、執行者

英英 a person who watches what happens but has no active part in it

例 The salary of the forest **observer** is quite low.
森林觀察員的薪水很低。

☐ 三分熟
☐ 五分熟
☐ 七分熟
☐ 全熟

---

ob·sti·nate

[`ɑbstənɪt]

形 執拗的、頑固的

英英 stubbornly refusing to change one's opinion

例 She is very **obstinate** about punctuality.
她對守時很固執。

☐ 三分熟
☐ 五分熟
☐ 七分熟
☐ 全熟

---

oc·cur·rence

[ə`kɝəns]

名 出現、發生
片 frequency of occurrence 出現的頻率

英英 the fact or frequency of something happening

例 Some of the pictures of supernatural **occurrences** are incredible.
有些靈異事件的照片真是不可思議。

☐ 三分熟
☐ 五分熟
☐ 七分熟
☐ 全熟

🎧 Track 087

---

oc·to·pus

[ˋɑktəpəs]

名 章魚

英英 a sea creature with eight sucker-bearing arms, a soft body, beak-like jaws

例 The **octopus** attacked the lady who wants to eat it.
章魚攻擊那位想吃牠的小姐。

☐ 三分熟
☐ 五分熟
☐ 七分熟
☐ 全熟

---

odds [ɑds]

名 勝算、差別

英英 the probability that something will or will not happen

例 The **odds** are Peter will be elected as the leader of the study group.
彼德成為讀書會領導者的勝算很大。

☐ 三分熟
☐ 五分熟
☐ 七分熟
☐ 全熟

---

o·dor [ˋodə]

名 氣味

同 smell 氣味

英英 a distinctive smell

例 The durian has strong **odor**.
榴槤有強烈的氣味。

☐ 三分熟
☐ 五分熟
☐ 七分熟
☐ 全熟

---

ol·ive [ˋɑlɪv]

名 橄欖、橄欖樹

形 橄欖的、橄欖色的

英英 a small green oval fruit with a hard stone and bitter flesh, which is used to produce oil; olive-shaped

例 **Olive** oil can help reduce one's risk for heart disease.
橄欖油可以減少罹患心臟疾病的風險。

☐ 三分熟
☐ 五分熟
☐ 七分熟
☐ 全熟

---

op·po·nent

[əˋponənt]

名 對手、反對者

反 alliance 同盟

英英 a person who competes with or fights another in a contest or game

例 If you're not well prepared, your **opponent** will certainly beat you this time.
如果你不好好做準備，你的對手這次必定會擊敗你。

☐ 三分熟
☐ 五分熟
☐ 七分熟
☐ 全熟

---

op·ti·mism

[ˋɑptəmɪzəm]

名 樂觀主義

反 pessimism 悲觀主義

英英 hopefulness and confidence about things in the future or success of something

例 With a note of **optimism** in her voice, we know she has some good news to announce.
帶著樂觀的聲音，我們知道她有些好消息要宣布。

☐ 三分熟
☐ 五分熟
☐ 七分熟
☐ 全熟

---

or·chard [ˋɔrtʃəd]

名 果園

英英 a piece of land planted with fruit trees

例 Let's go to the **orchard** this weekend to pick some lychees.
讓我們這個週末去果園採一些荔枝。

☐ 三分熟
☐ 五分熟
☐ 七分熟
☐ 全熟

or·gan·i·zer
[ˋɔrgənˌaɪzɚ]

名 組織者

英英 a person who makes arrangements or preparations for

例 The **organizer** of the carnival activity is from Japan.
這次嘉年華活動的組織者來自日本。

□ 三分熟
□ 五分熟
□ 七分熟
□ 全熟

o·ri·ent [ˋorɪənt]

名 東方、東方諸國
動 使適應、定位
同 adapt 使適應

英英 the countries of the East, especially east Asia; to aim something at someone; to make or become adjust

例 The newcomer of the company needs time to **orient** herself.
公司的新人需要時間適應。

□ 三分熟
□ 五分熟
□ 七分熟
□ 全熟

o·ri·en·tal
[ˌorɪˋɛntl̩]

名 東方人
形 東方諸國的

英英 people from the Far East; from or characteristic of the Far East

例 The **oriental** rugs are here for sale.
這裡的東方地毯可供販賣。

□ 三分熟
□ 五分熟
□ 七分熟
□ 全熟

or·na·ment
[ˋɔrnəmənt]

名 裝飾（品）
動 以裝飾品點綴
同 decoration 裝飾品

英英 an object designed to add beauty to something; to decorate with a ornament

例 Aunt Mary used to love the jewel box with the **ornament** of shells.
瑪麗姑姑以前喜歡這個有貝殼裝飾品的珠寶盒。

□ 三分熟
□ 五分熟
□ 七分熟
□ 全熟

or·phan·age
[ˋɔrfənɪdʒ]

名 孤兒院、孤兒

英英 a residential institution for the care and education of orphans; the state or condition of being an orphan

例 Send some Christmas gifts to the **orphanage**.
送一些聖誕節禮物到孤兒院去吧。

□ 三分熟
□ 五分熟
□ 七分熟
□ 全熟

os·trich [ˋɔstrɪtʃ]

名 鴕鳥

英英 a large flightless African bird with a long neck and long legs

例 Samples of **ostrich** eggs and the other eggs were on display in a glass-fronted cabinet.
鴕鳥蛋和其他蛋的樣本陳列在玻璃櫃子中展示。

□ 三分熟
□ 五分熟
□ 七分熟
□ 全熟

ounce [aʊns]

名 盎司

英英 a unit of weight equal to approximately 28 grams

例 Use digital scale to measure the **ounces** of flour you need.
用電子秤去測量你所需要的麵粉盎司份量。

□ 三分熟
□ 五分熟
□ 七分熟
□ 全熟

out·do [aʊtˋdu]

動 勝過、凌駕
同 surpass 勝過

英英 be superior to something

例 Terry **outdid** his classmates in swimming.
泰瑞在游泳方面凌駕他的同學。

☐ 三分熟
☐ 五分熟
☐ 七分熟
☐ 全熟

---

out·go·ing [ˋaʊtˏɡoɪn]

形 擅於社交的、外向的

英英 very friendly and confident

例 **Outgoing** people seem to be more popular.
外向型的人似乎比較受歡迎。

☐ 三分熟
☐ 五分熟
☐ 七分熟
☐ 全熟

---

out·put [ˋaʊtˏpʊt]

名 生產、輸出
動 生產、大量製造、輸出
同 input 輸入

英英 the amount of something produced by a person or factory; to produce goods

例 The factory's main revenue comes from the **output** of soy-cooked chicken wings.
這個工廠的主要收入來自滷翅膀的生產。

☐ 三分熟
☐ 五分熟
☐ 七分熟
☐ 全熟

---

out·sid·er [ˏaʊtˋsaɪdə]

名 門外漢、局外人

英英 a person who does not belong to a particular group or event

例 In the global village, no one is the **outsider**.
在地球村裡，沒有人是局外人。

☐ 三分熟
☐ 五分熟
☐ 七分熟
☐ 全熟

---

out·skirts [ˋaʊtˏskɜts]

名 郊區
同 suburb 郊區

英英 the outer parts of a town or city

例 Mrs. Huang drives to the **outskirts** of the city to meet a friend.
黃太太開車到城市的郊區去跟一個朋友見面。

☐ 三分熟
☐ 五分熟
☐ 七分熟
☐ 全熟

---

out·ward(s) [ˋaʊtwəd(z)]

形 向外的、外面的
副 向外
反 inward 向內

英英 from the outside; going out or away from a place

例 Spreading the notion of management **outwards** takes time.
把這類管理的想法往外散播需要時間。

☐ 三分熟
☐ 五分熟
☐ 七分熟
☐ 全熟

---

o·ver·all [ˋovəˏɔl]

名 罩衫、吊帶褲
形 全部的
副 整體而言
同 whole 全部的

英英 a loose fitting garment worn for protection ; in the whole; taking everything into account

例 The **overall** situation is within our control.
整體的狀況在我們的掌控中。

☐ 三分熟
☐ 五分熟
☐ 七分熟
☐ 全熟

o·ver·do [ˌovɚˋdu]
動 做得過火
同 exaggerate 誇張

英英 to do something excessively or in an exaggerated manner

例 Gill's boyfriend **overdid** it by traveling to Hawaii with his ex-girlfriend.
姬兒的男朋友做得太過份了，竟然跟前女友一同去夏威夷旅行。

☐ 三分熟
☐ 五分熟
☐ 七分熟
☐ 全熟

over·eat [ˌovɚˋit]
動 吃得過多

英英 to eat too much

例 The man vomited because of **overeating** seafood.
那名男子因為吃太多的海鮮而嘔吐。

☐ 三分熟
☐ 五分熟
☐ 七分熟
☐ 全熟

o·ver·flow
[ˌovɚˋflo]
名 滿溢
動 氾濫、溢出、淹沒
同 flood 淹沒

英英 flow over the edges of a container

例 **Overflowing** champagne tower arouse some exclamations from the guests.
溢滿的香檳塔讓賓客驚呼連連。

☐ 三分熟
☐ 五分熟
☐ 七分熟
☐ 全熟

o·ver·hear
[ˌovɚˋhɪr]
動 無意中聽到

英英 to hear something accidentally or secretly

例 I **overheard** the manager said the director of our department would be her son.
我無意中聽到經理說我們部門的主任是她的兒子。

☐ 三分熟
☐ 五分熟
☐ 七分熟
☐ 全熟

over·sleep
[ˌovɚˋslip]
動 睡過頭

英英 to sleep longer or later than one has intended to and so wake up late

例 **Oversleeping** is a bad habit, yet it's hard to change.
睡過頭是壞習慣，但也很難改變。

☐ 三分熟
☐ 五分熟
☐ 七分熟
☐ 全熟

o·ver·whelm
[ˌovɚˋhwɛlm]
動 淹沒、征服、壓倒

英英 to defeat completely, overpower

例 Grandma was **overwhelmed** with grief when she learned her grandson died.
祖母聽到孫子死亡的消息時，悲痛欲絕。

☐ 三分熟
☐ 五分熟
☐ 七分熟
☐ 全熟

o·ver·work
[ˌovɚˋwɝk]
名 過度工作
動 過度工作

英英 to work or cause to work too hard

例 **Overwork** caused the burn-out of the employees of marketing department.
過度工作讓行銷部門的員工精疲力盡。

☐ 三分熟
☐ 五分熟
☐ 七分熟
☐ 全熟

O

🎧 Track 091

oys·ter [ˈɔɪstə]

名 牡蠣、蠔

英英 a flat sea creature with a rough, flattened, irregularly oval shell, several kinds of which are farmed for food or pearls

例 Can **oysters** feel pain?
牡蠣會感受到痛苦嗎？

☐ 三分熟
☐ 五分熟
☐ 七分熟
☐ 全熟

o·zone [ˈozon]

名 臭氧

英英 air that is formed in electrical discharges or by ultraviolet light and is clean and pleasant to breathe

例 The hole in the **ozone** layer is getting bigger.
臭氧層的洞愈來愈大了。

☐ 三分熟
☐ 五分熟
☐ 七分熟
☐ 全熟

Pp

pa·cif·ic [pəˈsɪfɪk]

名 太平洋（首字大寫）
形 平靜的

英英 very quiet and peaceful

例 Japan is an island nation, which is located in the **Pacific** Ocean.
日本是位於太平洋的島國。

☐ 三分熟
☐ 五分熟
☐ 七分熟
☐ 全熟

pack·et [ˈpækɪt]

名 小包
同 package 包裹

英英 a paper or cardboard container

例 Children received the red **packets** happily.
小孩子開心地收下紅包。

☐ 三分熟
☐ 五分熟
☐ 七分熟
☐ 全熟

pad·dle [ˈpædl̩]

名 槳、踏板
動 以槳划動、戲水
同 oar 槳

英英 a short pole with a broad blade at one or both ends, used to move a small boat through the water; to move with a paddle on the water

例 Riding the swan **paddle** boats is a good way to enjoy the lake view.
乘坐天鵝踏板船是個享受湖景的好方法。

☐ 三分熟
☐ 五分熟
☐ 七分熟
☐ 全熟

pane [pen]

名 方框

英英 a single piece of glass in a window or door

例 A yellow bird crashed into the glass **panes** at the school.
一隻黃色的鳥撞上了學校的玻璃窗。

☐ 三分熟
☐ 五分熟
☐ 七分熟
☐ 全熟

par·a·dox [ˈpærəˌdɑks]

名 似是而非的言論、矛盾的事

英英 a self-contradictory statement or situation that seems to be true

例 Colin's argument sounds like a **paradox**.
柯林的辯詞聽起頗為矛盾。

☐ 三分熟
☐ 五分熟
☐ 七分熟
☐ 全熟

par·al·lel

[ˈpærəˌlɛl]

名 平行線
動 平行
形 平行的、類似的

P

英英 two lines having the same distance continuously between them; to move in the same distance continuously between them

例 **Parallel** with the department store is a bank.
跟百貨公司平行而立的是一家銀行。

☐ 三分熟
☐ 五分熟
☐ 七分熟
☐ 全熟

---

par·lor [ˈpɑrlɚ]

名 客廳、起居室

英英 a sitting room or a room of a house used for relaxing

例 A Christmas tree is placed in the **parlor**.
聖誕樹就放在客廳。

☐ 三分熟
☐ 五分熟
☐ 七分熟
☐ 全熟

---

par·tic·i·pant

[pɑrˈtɪsəpənt]

名 參與者

英英 people who takes part of an activity or event

例 Every **participant** of the tug-of-war game gets a coupon of NT$100.
拔河比賽的每位參加者將獲得新臺幣100元的優惠券。

☐ 三分熟
☐ 五分熟
☐ 七分熟
☐ 全熟

---

par·ti·cle [ˈpɑrtɪkl̩]

名 微粒、極少量
片 particle physics
粒子物理學

英英 a small piece of matter

例 The **particles** of dusts are floating in the air.
灰塵的微粒漂浮在空中。

☐ 三分熟
☐ 五分熟
☐ 七分熟
☐ 全熟

---

part·ly [ˈpɑrtlɪ]

副 部分地

英英 to some degree, but not completely

例 The story was **partly** true, **partly** made-up.
這個故事有部分是真的，部分是捏造的。

☐ 三分熟
☐ 五分熟
☐ 七分熟
☐ 全熟

---

pas·sion·ate

[ˈpæʃənɪt]

形 熱情的

英英 showing or caused by passion

例 The tour guide is **passionate** about his job.
導遊對他的工作很有熱情。

☐ 三分熟
☐ 五分熟
☐ 七分熟
☐ 全熟

---

pas·time

[ˈpæsˌtaɪm]

名 消遣
同 recreation 消遣

英英 an activity or thing done for enjoyment; a hobby

例 Carl's **pastime** activities include table tennis playing and doll clothes weaving.
卡爾的消遣活動包含打桌球以及編織娃娃的衣服。

☐ 三分熟
☐ 五分熟
☐ 七分熟
☐ 全熟

---

pas·try [ˈpestrɪ]

名 糕餅

英英 a dough of flour, fat, and water, used as a base of pies for baking

例 Puff **pastry** that Diane made this morning was delicious.
黛安今早做的泡芙糕點好好吃。

☐ 三分熟
☐ 五分熟
☐ 七分熟
☐ 全熟

🎧 **Track 093**

patch [pætʃ]

名 補丁
動 補綴、修補
同 mend 縫補

英英 a piece of material which is used to mend a hole or strengthen a weak point; to mend a hole or strengthen

例 The soldier did a wonderful job of **patching** pants.
這名士兵縫補褲子的工作做得很棒。

☐ 三分熟
☐ 五分熟
☐ 七分熟
☐ 全熟

pat·ent [ˈpetn̩t]

名 專利權
形 公開、專利的
同 copyright 著作權

英英 a government license giving an individual or body the right to make, use, or sell an invention for a particular number of years; relating to the official right to make or sell

例 The lawsuit of the **patent** of the watch has not ended yet.
這場手錶專利權的官司訴訟尚未結束。

☐ 三分熟
☐ 五分熟
☐ 七分熟
☐ 全熟

pa·tri·ot [ˈpetrɪət]

名 愛國者

英英 a person who supports and loves their country very much

例 The **patriot** will fight for his country if necessary.
愛國者會在必要時候為自己的國家作戰。

☐ 三分熟
☐ 五分熟
☐ 七分熟
☐ 全熟

pa·trol [pəˈtrol]

名 巡邏者
動 巡邏

英英 a person or group sent to keep watch in a particular area, especially a detachment of guards or police; to keep watch in a particular area

例 The policemen were **patrolling** around the community at night.
警察夜晚時巡邏整個社區。

☐ 三分熟
☐ 五分熟
☐ 七分熟
☐ 全熟

pa·tron [ˈpetrən]

名 保護者、贊助人

英英 a person who gives financial or other support to a person or organization

例 The **patron** of the music festival is a low-key person.
這個音樂季的贊助人是個低調的人。

☐ 三分熟
☐ 五分熟
☐ 七分熟
☐ 全熟

pea·cock [ˈpiˌkɑk]

名 孔雀

英英 a large bird, which the male has very long tail feathers with eye-like markings that can be fanned out in display

例 The white **peacock** looks elegant.
白色孔雀看起來很優雅。

☐ 三分熟
☐ 五分熟
☐ 七分熟
☐ 全熟

peas·ant [ˈpɛzn̩t]

名 佃農
同 farmer 農夫

英英 a poor person who owns or rents a piece of land and grow crops or keeps animals, who is an agricultural laborer of low social status

例 The **peasant** rented the land and planted rice.
佃農租了塊地，種了些稻米。

三分熟
五分熟
七分熟
全熟

P

---

peck [pɛk]

名 啄、啄痕、輕吻
動 啄食

英英 an act of bird's pecking

例 The sparrows **pecked** the rice on the ground.
麻雀啄食地上的米粒。

三分熟
五分熟
七分熟
全熟

---

ped·dler [ˈpɛdlɚ]

名 小販

英英 a travelling seller who sells small goods

例 The medicine **peddlers** in this park should be chased away.
這個公園裡的賣藥小販應該要被起走。

三分熟
五分熟
七分熟
全熟

---

peek [pik]

名 偷看
動 窺視

英英 to look quickly or secretly

例 **Peeking** satisfied human being's strange desire.
偷窺滿足人類奇怪的慾望。

三分熟
五分熟
七分熟
全熟

---

peg [pɛg]

名 釘子
動 釘牢

英英 a short pin or hook used for hanging things on or securing something in place; to hang things on something tightly

例 The wooden **pegs** of the tent are hammered into the soft ground.
帳篷的木製釘子被敲進了軟軟的土地裡。

三分熟
五分熟
七分熟
全熟

---

pen·e·trate [ˈpɛnəˌtret]

動 刺入、透過、滲透入
同 pierce 刺穿
片 slowly penetrate 緩緩滲入

英英 to force a way to move into or through

例 The cream **penetrated** into the skin.
護膚霜滲入了皮膚。

三分熟
五分熟
七分熟
全熟

---

per·ceive [pɚˈsiv]

動 察覺
同 detect 察覺

英英 to become aware or conscious of something

例 His sadness can be **perceived** through his voice.
他的悲傷可以透過他的聲音察覺出來。

三分熟
五分熟
七分熟
全熟

Track 095

perch [pɝtʃ]

名 鱸魚
動 棲息

英英 a fish that lives in lakes and rivers and is eaten as food; to sit, rest or roost

例 The snowy owl was **perching** on the tree.
雪鴞棲息在樹上。

□三分熟
□五分熟
□七分熟
□全熟

per·form·er

[pɚˋfɔrmɚ]

名 執行者、演出者

英英 a person who completes action, task, or function

例 The ballet **performers** did their best for this performance.
芭蕾舞的演出者為這場演出傾盡全力。

□三分熟
□五分熟
□七分熟
□全熟

per·il [ˋpɛrəl]

名 危險
動 冒險
同 danger 危險

英英 a situation of serious and great danger; to have an adventure

例 The Named **Perils** of this insurance policy include fire or lightning.
這張保單「提及的危險」包含火和雷擊。

□三分熟
□五分熟
□七分熟
□全熟

per·ish [ˋpɛrɪʃ]

動 滅亡
同 die 死亡

英英 to die or suffer complete ruin or destruction

例 The dinosaurs **perished** because of several possible reasons.
由於多種可能的原因，恐龍因此滅絕了。

□三分熟
□五分熟
□七分熟
□全熟

per·mis·si·ble

[pɚˋmɪsəbl̩]

形 可允許的
片 legally permissible
法律上允許的

英英 allowable, permitted

例 Taking a nap at noon is **permissible**.
中午小睡片刻是被允許的。

□三分熟
□五分熟
□七分熟
□全熟

per·sist [pɚˋsɪst]

動 堅持
同 insist 堅持

英英 to continue doing something in no matter how it is difficult or hard

例 Why don't you **persist** in what you love and choose the right job?
你為什麼不堅持自己的愛好並選擇合適的工作？

□三分熟
□五分熟
□七分熟
□全熟

per·son·nel

[ˌpɝsn̩ˋɛl]

名 人員、人事部門
同 staff 工作人員

英英 people employed or hired in an organization or a company

例 The **personnel** department is responsible for planning the year-end party.
人事部負責籌備尾牙。

□三分熟
□五分熟
□七分熟
□全熟

pes·si·mism
[ˈpɛsəmɪzəm]

名 悲觀、悲觀主義

英英 lack of hope or confidence in the future

例 **Pessimism** can't help anything.
悲觀無濟於事。

☐ 三分熟
☐ 五分熟
☐ 七分熟
☐ 全熟

pier [pɪr]

名 碼頭

同 wharf 碼頭

英英 a structure leading out to sea and used as a landing stage for boats

例 Let's travel to Taiwan west coast and enjoy the scenery of **piers**.
讓我們旅行到臺灣的西海岸，欣賞碼頭風光。

☐ 三分熟
☐ 五分熟
☐ 七分熟
☐ 全熟

pil·grim [ˈpɪlgrɪm]

名 朝聖者

英英 a person who journeys to a particular place for religious reasons

例 More than 30,000 **pilgrims** followed the goddess Matsu on a pilgrimage to Peikang.
超過3萬名的香客跟隨媽祖的進香旅程來到了北港。

☐ 三分熟
☐ 五分熟
☐ 七分熟
☐ 全熟

pil·lar [ˈpɪlɚ]

名 樑柱

英英 a strong tall structure used as a support for a building or as an ornament

例 The **pillars** of the palace were decorated with elegant flowers.
宮殿的樑柱是用優雅的花朵做裝飾。

☐ 三分熟
☐ 五分熟
☐ 七分熟
☐ 全熟

pim·ple [ˈpɪmpl̩]

名 面皰；青春痘

英英 a small, hard red spot on the skin

例 **Pimples** often bring trouble to the youngsters.
青春痘經常給年輕人帶來煩惱。

☐ 三分熟
☐ 五分熟
☐ 七分熟
☐ 全熟

pinch [pɪntʃ]

名 掐、少量
動 掐痛、捏
同 squeeze 擠、榨

英英 an act of pinching; a small amount of something

例 **Pinch** me, this isn't a dream, is it?
快捏我，這不是夢吧？是夢嗎？

☐ 三分熟
☐ 五分熟
☐ 七分熟
☐ 全熟

piss [pɪs]

名 小便
動 尿液、激怒

英英 urine or an act of urinating

例 Don't let your pets **piss** here.
不要讓你的寵物在此小便。

☐ 三分熟
☐ 五分熟
☐ 七分熟
☐ 全熟

pis·tol [ˈpɪstl̩]

名 手槍
動 以槍擊傷
同 gun 槍

英英 a small gun designed to be held in one hand; to hurt or harm someone with a small gun

例 The abuse of **pistols** is a serious social problem.
濫用手槍是一個嚴重的社會問題。

☐ 三分熟
☐ 五分熟
☐ 七分熟
☐ 全熟

🎧 Track 097

plague [pleg]

名 瘟疫

英英 a contagious disease spread by bacteria causes illness or death

例 The spread of **plague** during the Black Death killed 20 million people in Europe.
黑死病期間瘟疫的蔓延在歐洲造成兩千萬人死亡。

☐ 三分熟
☐ 五分熟
☐ 七分熟
☐ 全熟

plan·ta·tion

[plenˋteʃən]

名 農場
同 farm 農場

英英 a large farm, in which a particular type of crop is grown

例 The **plantation** in Brazil made Robinson Crusoe rich.
巴西的農場讓魯濱遜・克魯索變得有錢。

☐ 三分熟
☐ 五分熟
☐ 七分熟
☐ 全熟

play·wright

[ˋpleˏraɪt]

名 劇作家

英英 a person who writes plays

例 George Bernard Shaw was an Irish playwright.
蕭伯納是愛爾蘭藉的劇作家。

☐ 三分熟
☐ 五分熟
☐ 七分熟
☐ 全熟

plea [pli]

名 藉口、懇求
同 excuse 藉口

英英 a request made in an urgent manner; an excuse

例 The politician's **plea** sounds false.
這名政客的懇求聽起來滿虛假的。

☐ 三分熟
☐ 五分熟
☐ 七分熟
☐ 全熟

plead [plid]

動 懇求、為……辯護
同 appeal 懇求

英英 to make an emotional request of something

例 His elder sister kneeled on the ground to **plead** for the robber.
他的姊姊跪在地上，向搶匪求情。

☐ 三分熟
☐ 五分熟
☐ 七分熟
☐ 全熟

pledge [plɛdʒ]

名 誓約
動 立誓
同 vow 誓約

英英 a formal promise or undertaking, especially one to give money or to be a friend; to make a formal promise

例 Phoenix's French husband made a **pledge** to love her forever.
菲妮克絲的法國藉老公宣誓要永遠愛她。

☐ 三分熟
☐ 五分熟
☐ 七分熟
☐ 全熟

plow [plaʊ]

名 犁
動 耕作
同 cultivate 耕作

英英 a large farming tool with one or more blades fixed in a frame, drawn over soil to turn it over and cut furrows; to dig land with a plow

例 Grandpa used to **plow** the field of rice when he was young.
爺爺年輕時曾經耕種過稻田。

☐ 三分熟
☐ 五分熟
☐ 七分熟
☐ 全熟

P

pluck [plʌk]

名 勇氣、意志
動 摘、拔、扯

英英 to take hold of something and remove it from its place quickly; a strong wish to be successful

例 The thief **plucked** the flower in our park without asking.
小偷毫不猶豫地就拔走公園裡的花。

☐三分熟
☐五分熟
☐七分熟
☐全熟

---

plunge [plʌndʒ]

名 陷入、急降
動 插入

英英 to move cause something move a long way forward or into something suddenly

例 Steven **plunged** into the lake.
史蒂文縱身跳入湖裡。

☐三分熟
☐五分熟
☐七分熟
☐全熟

---

poc·ket·book
['pɑkɪtˌbʊk]

名 錢包、口袋書

英英 a wallet, purse, or handbag; a notebook

例 **Pocketbooks** are convenient for language learners.
口袋書對語言學習者來講很方便。

☐三分熟
☐五分熟
☐七分熟
☐全熟

---

po·et·ic [po'ɛtɪk]

形 詩意的

英英 relating to poetry

例 To sip a cup of coffee in a café with the ocean view is quite **poetic**.
坐在可享受海景的咖啡店裡喝咖啡是很有詩意的。

☐三分熟
☐五分熟
☐七分熟
☐全熟

---

poke [pʊk]

名 戳
動 戳、刺、刺探

英英 when you push a finger quickly into someone or something; to make a hole by jabbing

例 To **poke** the water balloons is fun.
戳破水球是好玩的。

☐三分熟
☐五分熟
☐七分熟
☐全熟

---

po·lar ['polɚ]

形 極地的、北極的、南極的
同 arctic 北極的

英英 relating to the North or South Poles of the earth

例 **Polar** bears intruded into human houses to look for food.
北極熊闖進民宅覓食。

☐三分熟
☐五分熟
☐七分熟
☐全熟

---

porch [portʃ]

名 玄關

英英 a covered shelter in front of the entrance of a building

例 Take off your shoes and leave them on the **porch**.
脫下鞋子，把鞋放在玄關。

☐三分熟
☐五分熟
☐七分熟
☐全熟

---

po·ten·tial
[pə'tɛnʃəl]

名 潛力
形 潛在的

英英 qualities or abilities that may be developed and lead to future success; having the capacity to achieve something in the future

例 You have great **potential** to be a popular novelist.
你有很大的潛力可以成為受歡迎的小說家。

☐三分熟
☐五分熟
☐七分熟
☐全熟

poul·try [ˈpoltrɪ]

名 家禽
同 fowl 家禽

英英 chickens, turkeys, ducks, and geese; domestic fowl

例 When Thanksgiving is coming, some **poultry** will suffer.
當感恩節即將來臨時，有些家禽就會受苦。

☐三分熟 ☐五分熟 ☐七分熟 ☐全熟

---

prai·rie [ˈprɛrɪ]

名 牧場、大草原

英英 a wide open area of grassland

例 The **prairie** dogs mainly live on the grasslands of North America.
土撥鼠主要住在北美洲的草原上。

☐三分熟 ☐五分熟 ☐七分熟 ☐全熟

---

preach [pritʃ]

動 傳教、說教、鼓吹

英英 to deliver a religious address to a group of people

例 Do some actions rather than **preaching**.
做出一些行動來，而不要只是說教。

☐三分熟 ☐五分熟 ☐七分熟 ☐全熟

---

pre·cau·tion
[prɪˈkɔʃən]

名 警惕、預防

英英 an action taken in advance to prevent something undesirable from happening

例 Take **precautions** to avoid the damage brought by the coming violent storms.
採取預防措施，避免即將來臨的暴風雨造成損害。

☐三分熟 ☐五分熟 ☐七分熟 ☐全熟

---

pref·er·ence
[ˈprɛfərəns]

名 偏好
同 favor 偏愛

英英 a greater liking for a particular thing

例 Choosing vegetarian food was a matter of personal **preference**.
選擇吃素是個人的喜好。

☐三分熟 ☐五分熟 ☐七分熟 ☐全熟

---

pre·hi·stor·ic
[ˌprihɪsˈtɔrɪk]

形 史前的

英英 relating to prehistory

例 **Prehistoric** fossil heritage in Kenya can date back to more than 100 millions years ago.
肯亞的史前化石遺產可以追溯到一億多年前。

☐三分熟 ☐五分熟 ☐七分熟 ☐全熟

---

pre·vail [prɪˈvel]

動 戰勝、普及
同 win 贏

英英 to prove more powerful

例 This kind of clichéd notions **prevailed** in contemporary society.
這種陳腔爛調的想法在當前的社會仍舊十分普及。

☐三分熟 ☐五分熟 ☐七分熟 ☐全熟

---

pre·view [ˈpriˌvju]

名 預演、預習
動 預演、預習、預視

英英 a viewing or display of something before it is acquired

例 Remember to **preview** Lesson 12, kids.
孩子們，記得預習第 12 課。

☐三分熟 ☐五分熟 ☐七分熟 ☐全熟

prey [pre]

名 犧牲品
動 捕食
同 hunt 獵食

英英 an animal which is hunted and killed by another for food; to catch or hunt food

例 The spider slowly approaches its **prey** on the web.
蜘蛛緩緩地接近網上的犧牲品。

□三分熟
□五分熟
□七分熟
□全熟

---

price·less

['praɪslɪs]

形 貴重的、無價的
同 invaluable 無價的

英英 so precious that its value cannot be determined; valuable or priceless

例 Friendship is **priceless**.
友情無價。

□三分熟
□五分熟
□七分熟
□全熟

---

prick [prɪk]

名 刺痛
動 扎、刺、豎起
同 sting 刺

英英 an act of pricking something

例 The queen was **pricked** by a needle.
皇后被針刺到。

□三分熟
□五分熟
□七分熟
□全熟

---

pri·or ['praɪɚ]

形 在前的、優先的
副 居先、先前

英英 existing or coming before in time or in advance

例 **Prior** knowledge of Italian is a must if you'd like to take the course.
如果你要修這堂課,你必須先學過義大利文。

□三分熟
□五分熟
□七分熟
□全熟

---

pri·or·i·ty

[praɪ'ɔrətɪ]

名 優先權

英英 the condition of being regarded as more important than others

例 Stanley seriously considers the **priority** of the new projects.
史丹尼認真考慮新專案的先後順序。

□三分熟
□五分熟
□七分熟
□全熟

---

pro·ces·sion

[prə'sɛʃən]

名 進行、行列

英英 the action of moving in such a way

例 On the day of the funeral **procession**, it was raining.
在葬禮進行的當天,天空下起雨來。

□三分熟
□五分熟
□七分熟
□全熟

---

pro·file ['profaɪl]

名 側面
動 畫側面像、顯出輪廓

英英 an outline of something, especially someone's life, work or character; to draw an outline of something

例 Are you sure this is the **profile** of Oscar Wilde?
你確定這是奧斯卡・王爾德的側面像?

□三分熟
□五分熟
□七分熟
□全熟

P

pro·long [prəˋlɔŋ]

動 延長
反 shorten 縮短

英英 to extend the duration of time or something

例 Jim's training for the marathon was **prolonged**.
吉姆的馬拉松訓練延長了。

☐三分熟
☐五分熟
☐七分熟
☐全熟

---

prop [prɑp]

名 支撐
動 支持

英英 a pole or beam which is used as a temporary support; to support something

例 I need a **prop** to support the mirror.
我需要個支撐物來支撐這面鏡子。

☐三分熟
☐五分熟
☐七分熟
☐全熟

---

proph·et [ˋprɑfɪt]

名 先知

英英 a person who is able to predict the future

例 A **prophet** made a prophecy that the third prince would be next King.
先知做了預言說三王子會是下一任的國王。

☐三分熟
☐五分熟
☐七分熟
☐全熟

---

pro·por·tion

[prəˋporʃən]

名 比例
動 使成比例
同 ratio 比例

英英 a part, share, or number considered in relation to a whole; to have a particular relationship in size or amount

例 Old men made up a large **proportion** of the village.
老人佔這個村落人口很大的比例。

☐三分熟
☐五分熟
☐七分熟
☐全熟

---

pros·pect [ˋprɑspɛkt]

名 期望、前景
動 探勘
同 anticipation 期望

英英 the possibility some future event occurring; to search for mineral deposits

例 The **prospect** of attending the meetings with my boss was stressful.
跟著我老闆參加會議的前景讓我很有壓力。

☐三分熟
☐五分熟
☐七分熟
☐全熟

---

prov·ince

[ˋprɑvɪns]

名 省（行政單位）

英英 a principal administrative division of a nation

例 Qi Baishi, a Chinese painter, was born in Hunan **province**.
中國畫家齊白石生於湖南省。

☐三分熟
☐五分熟
☐七分熟
☐全熟

---

prune [prun]

名 乾梅子
動 修剪

英英 a plum preserved by drying; to remove unwanted parts

例 The **prunes** provide a source of iron.
乾梅子提供了鐵的來源。

☐三分熟
☐五分熟
☐七分熟
☐全熟

---

pub·li·cize

[ˋpʌblɪˏsaɪz]

動 公布、宣傳、廣告

英英 to make widely known in the public

例 The drama competition has been **publicized**.
話劇比賽已經廣為宣傳。

☐三分熟
☐五分熟
☐七分熟
☐全熟

puff [pʌf]

名 噴煙、吹
動 噴出、吹熄

英英 an act of smoking

例 My old uncle **puffed** up the stairs.
我那年邁的叔叔氣喘吁吁地上了樓。

□ 三分熟
□ 五分熟
□ 七分熟
□ 全熟

pulse [pʌls]

名 脈搏
動 脈搏、脈搏跳動

英英 the rhythmical regular beating of the heart, which can be felt at the wrist or side of neck

例 The doctor feels the **pulse** of pregnant woman.
醫生為孕婦診脈。

□ 三分熟
□ 五分熟
□ 七分熟
□ 全熟

pur·chase

[ˈpɝtʃəs]

名 購買
動 購買
同 buy 買

英英 the action of buying; to buy something

例 **Purchase** of the pearl necklace costs Kevin a large sum of money.
買這條珍珠項鍊花了凱文好大一筆錢。

□ 三分熟
□ 五分熟
□ 七分熟
□ 全熟

pyr·a·mid

[ˈpɪrəmɪd]

名 金字塔、角錐
片 population pyramid 人口金字塔

英英 a solid structure with a square or triangular base and sloping sides that meet in a point at the top

例 It was said that the **pyramid** was built by aliens.
據説金字塔是外星人建造的。

□ 三分熟
□ 五分熟
□ 七分熟
□ 全熟

Qq

quack [kwæk]

名 嘎嘎的叫聲
動 嘎嘎叫

英英 the harsh sound made by a duck

例 The ducks are **quacking** loudly.
鴨子大聲地嘎嘎叫。

□ 三分熟
□ 五分熟
□ 七分熟
□ 全熟

qual·i·fy

[ˈkwɑləˌfaɪ]

動 使具有資格、使合格

英英 to successfully finish a training course so that someone is able to do a job

例 Are you **qualified** to take the driver's license test?
你夠資格考駕照嗎？

□ 三分熟
□ 五分熟
□ 七分熟
□ 全熟

quart [kwɔrt]

名 夸脱（容量單位）

英英 unit of liquids, equal to a quarter of 1.14 liters in Britain or 0.95 liters in the US

例 A cup is 8 ounces, which equates one quarter of a **quart**.
一杯的量是八盎司，等於四分之一夸脱。

□ 三分熟
□ 五分熟
□ 七分熟
□ 全熟

🎧 Track 103

quest [kwɛst]

名 尋求、追求、探索、探求

英英 a long search for something or a truth

例 The heroic **quest** of true self is an ongoing process.
英雄式的真我追尋是不斷持續進行的過程。

☐ 三分熟
☐ 五分熟
☐ 七分熟
☐ 全熟

---

quiver [ˋkwɪvɚ]

名 顫抖
動 顫抖

英英 a light shaking

例 After the puppy was saved from the fish pond, it **quivered**.
小狗從魚池裡被解救後，顫抖不已。

☐ 三分熟
☐ 五分熟
☐ 七分熟
☐ 全熟

Rr

rack [ræk]

名 架子、折磨
動 折磨、盡力使用
同 shelf 架子

英英 a framework which is used to hold or store things; to cause physical or mental pain

例 Why don't you use the free bike **racks** in the park?
為什麼你不使用公園裡可免費放腳踏車的架子？

☐ 三分熟
☐ 五分熟
☐ 七分熟
☐ 全熟

---

rad·ish [ˋrædɪʃ]

名 蘿蔔

英英 the small, pungent, red root of a vegetable, which shaped like a finger and is usually eaten raw in salads

例 Claire, feed your pet rabbit with these **radish**.
克萊兒，餵你的寵物兔吃這些蘿蔔吧。

☐ 三分熟
☐ 五分熟
☐ 七分熟
☐ 全熟

---

ra·di·us [ˋredɪəs]

名 半徑

英英 a straight line from the centre to the edge

例 What's the **radius** of the skating rink?
這座溜冰場的半徑是多少？

☐ 三分熟
☐ 五分熟
☐ 七分熟
☐ 全熟

---

rag·ged [ˋrægɪd]

形 破爛的
同 shabby 破爛的

英英 of something old and torn, such as clothes or clothing

例 The **ragged** quilt was the only covering on the old man.
老人身上唯一的覆蓋物是這條破爛的棉被。

☐ 三分熟
☐ 五分熟
☐ 七分熟
☐ 全熟

---

rail [rel]

名 橫杆、鐵軌

英英 a bar or series of bars fixed on upright supports or attached to a wall or ceiling, or used to be a fence or barrier

例 The train to Hualien went out of the **rail**.
往花蓮的列車出軌。

☐ 三分熟
☐ 五分熟
☐ 七分熟
☐ 全熟

R

ral·ly [ˈrælɪ]

名 集合、集會
動 召集
同 gathering 聚集

英英 a mass meeting of a large group of people held as a protest or in support of a cause; to cause to come together

例 The election **rally** will be held next Monday.
選舉大會下星期一舉辦。

☐ 三分熟
☐ 五分熟
☐ 七分熟
☐ 全熟

---

ranch [ræntʃ]

名 大農場
動 經營大農場
同 plantation 大農場

英英 a large farm, especially in the western US and Canada; to run a large farm

例 The hotel was near the sheep **ranch**.
這家旅舍就在綿羊農場附近。

☐ 三分熟
☐ 五分熟
☐ 七分熟
☐ 全熟

---

ras·cal [ˈræskl̩]

名 流氓

英英 a cheeky person who does something that people disapprove or hate of

例 Little **rascal**, don't run away.
小流氓，不要跑。

☐ 三分熟
☐ 五分熟
☐ 七分熟
☐ 全熟

---

ra·tio [ˈreʃo]

名 比率、比例
同 proportion 比率、比例

英英 the quantitative relation between two amounts showing the number of times one value contains or is contained within the other

例 The **ratio** of local and non-local students in this school is 1:10.
這間學校的本地學生和非本地學生的比例是 1 比 10。

☐ 三分熟
☐ 五分熟
☐ 七分熟
☐ 全熟

---

rat·tle [ˈrætl̩]

名 嘎嘎聲
動 發出嘎嘎聲、喋喋不休地講話

英英 to make a rapid noise, such sharp knocking or clinking sounds

例 Anne keeps **rattling**, which annoyed her sister.
安喋喋不休地講話，惹惱了她的姊姊。

☐ 三分熟
☐ 五分熟
☐ 七分熟
☐ 全熟

---

realm [rɛlm]

名 王國、領域

英英 a kingdom

例 The **realm** of the kingdom covers oceans, rivers, and hills.
這個王國的領域包含了海洋、河流和丘陵。

☐ 三分熟
☐ 五分熟
☐ 七分熟
☐ 全熟

---

reap [rip]

動 收割

英英 to cut or gather a crop or harvest

例 Sometimes, we don't **reap** what we sow.
有時候，我們做了耕耘，卻未必會有收獲。

☐ 三分熟
☐ 五分熟
☐ 七分熟
☐ 全熟

---

rear [rɪr]

名 後面
形 後面的
同 front 前面

英英 the back of something

例 Drivers need the **rear** mirrors to predict the changing traffic situation.
駕駛們需要後照鏡，預測變化中的交通狀況。

☐ 三分熟
☐ 五分熟
☐ 七分熟
☐ 全熟

🎧 Track 105

---

reck·less [ˈrɛklɪs]

形 魯莽的、胡亂的
同 rash 魯莽的

英英 without thought or care for something dangerous you're doing

例 Recent **reckless** killing of pigs was horrifying.
近來對豬隻的濫殺令人震驚。

☐ 三分熟
☐ 五分熟
☐ 七分熟
☐ 全熟

---

reck·on [ˈrɛkən]

動 計算、依賴
同 count 計算

英英 to calculate; regard in a specified way

例 Have you **reckoned** the rising percentage of our company's stocks?
你計算出我們公司股票的漲幅了嗎？

☐ 三分熟
☐ 五分熟
☐ 七分熟
☐ 全熟

---

rec·om·mend

[ˌrɛkəˈmɛnd]

動 推薦、託付

英英 to suggestion someone or something would be good or someone should be done

例 What brand of milk powder do you **recommend**?
你推薦哪個牌子的奶粉？

☐ 三分熟
☐ 五分熟
☐ 七分熟
☐ 全熟

---

reef [rif]

名 暗礁

英英 a line of rocks or sand just below the surface of the sea, often dangerous to ships

例 The coral **reef** under the sea has been investigated before.
這塊海底下的珊瑚礁以前曾被探勘過。

☐ 三分熟
☐ 五分熟
☐ 七分熟
☐ 全熟

---

reel [ril]

名 捲軸
動 捲線、搖擺

英英 a cylinder on which film, wire, thread, etc. can be wound or rolled; to roll up

例 The threads on the **reels** are colorful.
捲軸上的線多采多姿。

☐ 三分熟
☐ 五分熟
☐ 七分熟
☐ 全熟

---

ref·e·ree/um·pire

[ˌrɛfəˈri]/[ˈʌmpaɪr]

名 裁判者
動 裁判、調停

英英 a person who is in charge of a sports game or a competition and who makes certain that the rules are followed; to take in charge of a sports game or competition

例 The main purpose of taekwondo **referee** is to make sure fair play.
跆拳道裁判的主要功能是確保比賽的公正性。

☐ 三分熟
☐ 五分熟
☐ 七分熟
☐ 全熟

---

ref·uge/
san·ctu·ar·y

[ˈrɛfjudʒ]/[ˈsæŋktʃuɛrɪ]

名 避難（所）

英英 a place or state of safety from danger or trouble

例 There's a **refuge** nearby.
附近就有避難所。

☐ 三分熟
☐ 五分熟
☐ 七分熟
☐ 全熟

R

re·fute [rɪˋfjut]

動 反駁
同 oppose 反對

英英 to prove a statement or the person advancing it to be wrong

例 Jessica firmly **refuted** what her opponent argued.
傑西卡嚴正反駁她的對手所說的。

☐ 三分熟
☐ 五分熟
☐ 七分熟
☐ 全熟

reign [ren]

名 主權
動 統治
同 rule 統治

英英 the period of time when a king or head rule a country; to rule as monarch

例 The Dragon Queen will **reign** the Seven Kingdoms.
龍后將會統治七國。

☐ 三分熟
☐ 五分熟
☐ 七分熟
☐ 全熟

re·joice [rɪˋdʒɔɪs]

動 歡喜
反 lament 悲痛

英英 to feel or express joy or gladness

例 Beatrix's little readers **rejoiced** when they read her animal tales.
碧雅翠絲的小讀者們欣喜若狂閱讀她的動物故事。

☐ 三分熟
☐ 五分熟
☐ 七分熟
☐ 全熟

rel·ic [ˋrɛlɪk]

名 遺物

英英 an object of interest left from an earlier time

例 More than 100,000 **relics** of the cargo ship from Song Dynasty were discovered.
超過 10 萬件來自中國古代宋朝的遺物被發現了。

☐ 三分熟
☐ 五分熟
☐ 七分熟
☐ 全熟

re·mind·er [rɪˋmaɪndɚ]

名 提醒者、提醒物、提示

英英 a thing that causes someone to remember something

例 The sticky note on your computer serves as a **reminder**.
你電腦上的便利貼有提醒的作用。

☐ 三分熟
☐ 五分熟
☐ 七分熟
☐ 全熟

re·pay [rɪˋpe]

動 償還、報答
同 reward 報答

英英 to pay back a loan or something

例 How many working years can you **repay** the student loan?
你要工作多少年才能還清學貸？

☐ 三分熟
☐ 五分熟
☐ 七分熟
☐ 全熟

re·pro·duce [ˌriprəˋdjus]

動 複製、再生

英英 to produce a copy or representation

例 Tim's artworks were not easy to **reproduce**.
要複製提姆的藝術作品恐怕不太容易。

☐ 三分熟
☐ 五分熟
☐ 七分熟
☐ 全熟

rep·tile [ˋrɛptaɪl]

名 爬蟲類
形 爬行的

英英 an cold-blooded animal which produces eggs and uses the heat of the sun to keep its blood warm; describing an animal which is able to crawl

例 Dinosaurs could be classified as **reptiles** in some ways.
恐龍在某些方面來講，可以被歸為爬蟲類。

☐ 三分熟
☐ 五分熟
☐ 七分熟
☐ 全熟

🎧 Track 107

re·pub·li·can
[rɪˋpʌblɪkən]

名 共和主義者
形 共和主義的
反 democratic 民主主義的

英英 belonging to a republic

例 A member of the **Republican** Party in the US came to visit France.
美國共和黨員前去法國拜訪。

□三分熟
□五分熟
□七分熟
□全熟

re·sent [rɪˋzɛnt]

動 憤恨

英英 to hate or dislike something which you're forced to accept

例 Emily **resents** her best friend because she told a terrible lie.
愛蜜莉憎恨她最好的朋友，因為她撒了一個可怕的謊。

□三分熟
□五分熟
□七分熟
□全熟

re·sent·ment
[rɪˋzɛntmənt]

名 憤慨、怨恨
同 irritation 惱怒

英英 the feeling of hate or dislike

例 Andrew's stepfather became the object of his **resentment** for imperfect life.
安德魯的繼父成為他怨恨不完美人生的對象。

□三分熟
□五分熟
□七分熟
□全熟

re·side [rɪˋzaɪd]

動 居住
同 dwell 居住

英英 to live or stay in a particular place

例 My grandparents **reside** in the mountain.
我的爺爺奶奶居住在山裡。

□三分熟
□五分熟
□七分熟
□全熟

res·i·dence
[ˋrɛzədəns]

名 住家

英英 a place of living; a home

例 The **residence** of the retired doctor is this old apartment.
退休醫生的住家就是這棟老舊公寓。

□三分熟
□五分熟
□七分熟
□全熟

res·i·dent
[ˋrɛzədənt]

名 居民
形 居留的、住校的

英英 a person who lives in a particular place for long term; living in a particular place for long term

例 The **resident** teachers will help handle this accident.
住校的教師會幫忙處理這起意外。

□三分熟
□五分熟
□七分熟
□全熟

re·sort [rɪˋzɔrt]

名 休閒勝地
動 依靠、訴諸

英英 a place frequented for people to spend on the holidays; to use as recourse

例 **Resorting** to fists will never solve the problem.
訴諸於拳頭將永遠不可能解決問題。

□三分熟
□五分熟
□七分熟
□全熟

R

re·strain [rɪˋstren]
動 抑制

英英 to keep under control or within limits

例 Your younger brother is hot tempered and can hardly **restrain** his anger.
你的弟弟脾氣暴躁，很難控制憤怒。

☐ 三分熟
☐ 五分熟
☐ 七分熟
☐ 全熟

re·sume
[ˋrɛzə⁄me]/[rɪˋzjum]
名 摘要、履歷表
動 再開始

英英 brief information about a person's name, age, education background, etc.; to start something again

例 The **resume** is to the point, yet not quite professional.
這份履歷表切中要點，但不太專業。

☐ 三分熟
☐ 五分熟
☐ 七分熟
☐ 全熟

re·tort [rɪˋtɔrt]
名 反駁
動 反駁、回嘴

英英 to reply someone very quickly in an angry way

例 When Andy opened his mouth to **retort**, his father held up his hand to silence him.
當安迪張開嘴要反駁時，他的父親舉起手要他安靜。

☐ 三分熟
☐ 五分熟
☐ 七分熟
☐ 全熟

re·verse [rɪˋvɝs]
名 顛倒
動 反轉
形 相反的

英英 a complete change of direction; to go backwards

例 The twin sister's situations of romantic relationship are **reversed**.
雙胞胎姊妹的戀愛狀況剛好相反。

☐ 三分熟
☐ 五分熟
☐ 七分熟
☐ 全熟

re·vive [rɪˋvaɪv]
動 復甦、復原、恢復生機
同 restore 復原

英英 to restore to what it used to be

例 Kim's fortune is going to **revive**.
金即將時來運轉。

☐ 三分熟
☐ 五分熟
☐ 七分熟
☐ 全熟

re·volt [rɪˋvolt]
名 叛亂、反叛
動 叛變、嫌惡
同 rebel 叛亂

英英 an act of refusing to be controlled or ruled by a group of people

例 The people **revolted** against the nation's military service system.
人們奮起反抗國內的徵兵制。

☐ 三分熟
☐ 五分熟
☐ 七分熟
☐ 全熟

re·volve [rɪˋvɑlv]
動 旋轉、循環

英英 to move in a circle on a central axis

例 Since childhood, Jenny's life has **revolved** around piano contests.
自從兒童時期起，珍妮的日子總圍著鋼琴比賽轉。

☐ 三分熟
☐ 五分熟
☐ 七分熟
☐ 全熟

rhi·noce·r·os/ rhi·no
[raɪˋnɑsərəs]/[ˋraɪno]
名 犀牛

英英 a large, plant-eating gray mammal with one or two horns on the nose and thick folded skin

例 **Rhinoceroses** were shot because hunters wanted their horns.
犀牛遭到射殺因為獵人們要牠們的角。

☐ 三分熟
☐ 五分熟
☐ 七分熟
☐ 全熟

🎧 **Track 109**

rib [rɪb]

名 肋骨
動 支撐、嘲弄

英英 a series of slender bones curves round from your back to your chest for protecting the thoracic cavity and its organs; to support with a rib

例 Jerry fell down from the motorcycle and broke a **rib**.
傑瑞從機車上摔下來，摔斷了一根肋骨。

☐ 三分熟
☐ 五分熟
☐ 七分熟
☐ 全熟

ridge [rɪdʒ]

名 背脊、山脊
動 （使）成脊狀

英英 a long narrow hilltop or mountain range; to make a shape of ridge

例 A mountain climber walked on snow covered **ridge**.
一位登山者走在白雪覆蓋的山脊上。

☐ 三分熟
☐ 五分熟
☐ 七分熟
☐ 全熟

ri·dic·u·lous
[rɪˋdɪkjələs]

形 荒謬的

英英 very unreasonable and stupid

例 What the salesman just said sounded **ridiculous**.
該名業務剛才說的話聽起來簡直就是荒謬的。

☐ 三分熟
☐ 五分熟
☐ 七分熟
☐ 全熟

ri·fle [ˋraɪfl̩]

名 來福槍、步兵
動 掠奪

英英 a gun, especially one fired from shoulder level, and is designed to be accurate at long distances; to steal something quickly

例 A soldier carried a **rifle**.
一名士兵帶著一把來福槍。

☐ 三分熟
☐ 五分熟
☐ 七分熟
☐ 全熟

rig·id [ˋrɪdʒɪd]

形 嚴格的

英英 not able to bend; cannot change its shape

例 Mr. Wilson is a **rigid** judge.
威爾森先生是位嚴格的法官。

☐ 三分熟
☐ 五分熟
☐ 七分熟
☐ 全熟

rim [rɪm]

名 邊緣
動 加邊於

英英 the upper or outer edge of something; to be along the edge of something

例 The **rim** of the cover chipped.
這個蓋子的邊緣裂了。

☐ 三分熟
☐ 五分熟
☐ 七分熟
☐ 全熟

rip [rɪp]

名 裂口
動 扯裂

英英 a tear in a piece of cloth; to tear or pull apart something violently or quickly

例 Wolves **ripped** the throat out of the victims.
野狼扯裂受害者的喉嚨。

☐ 三分熟
☐ 五分熟
☐ 七分熟
☐ 全熟

rip·ple [ˋrɪpl̩]

名 波動
動 起漣漪

英英 a small wave or series of waves on the surface of water; to make small wave

例 The **ripples** of the lake result from the jumping of the carp.
湖水的漣漪由鯉魚的跳躍造成。

☐ 三分熟
☐ 五分熟
☐ 七分熟
☐ 全熟

R

ri·val [ˈraɪvl̩]

名 對手
動 競爭
同 compete 競爭

英英 a person or thing competing with another for the same thing; to compete with someone

例 Molly's **rival** in singing has much clearer tone.
莫莉在歌唱方面的對手有更清亮的音色。

☐ 三分熟
☐ 五分熟
☐ 七分熟
☐ 全熟

roam [rom]

名 漫步
動 徘徊、流浪
同 wander 徘徊

英英 an aimless walk; to walk around when you don't know how to do

例 Jack **roamed** around different European countries while taking pictures.
傑克漫遊在不同歐洲國家時，一路照相。

☐ 三分熟
☐ 五分熟
☐ 七分熟
☐ 全熟

rob·in [ˈrɑbɪn]

名 知更鳥

英英 a small European bird of the thrush family

例 The **robin** flew to the gate of the garden.
知更鳥飛到花園柵欄門口。

☐ 三分熟
☐ 五分熟
☐ 七分熟
☐ 全熟

ro·bust [roˈbʌst]

形 強健的
反 weak 虛弱的

英英 very strong and healthy; good in shape

例 The batman looks **robust**.
蝙蝠俠看起來強健。

☐ 三分熟
☐ 五分熟
☐ 七分熟
☐ 全熟

rod [rɑd]

名 竿、棒、教鞭
同 stick 棒

英英 a fishing rod

例 The fishing **rod** was broken.
釣魚竿斷了。

☐ 三分熟
☐ 五分熟
☐ 七分熟
☐ 全熟

rub·bish [ˈrʌbɪʃ]

名 垃圾
同 garbage 垃圾

英英 waste material or something useless

例 The **rubbish** was drifted to the beach.
垃圾漂流到海邊。

☐ 三分熟
☐ 五分熟
☐ 七分熟
☐ 全熟

rug·ged [ˈrʌgɪd]

形 粗糙的
反 smooth 柔順的

英英 having a rocky surface; not even on the surface

例 The **rugged** landscape didn't stop the runner.
粗糙的地形並沒有阻擋這名跑者。

☐ 三分熟
☐ 五分熟
☐ 七分熟
☐ 全熟

rum·ble [ˈrʌmbl̩]

名 隆隆聲、轆轆聲
動 發出隆隆聲

英英 to make a continuous deep, resonant noise; a continuous deep sound

例 Poor cat, its stomach is **rumbling**.
可憐的貓咪，牠的肚子咕咕叫。

☐ 三分熟
☐ 五分熟
☐ 七分熟
☐ 全熟

rus·tle [ˈrʌsl̩]

名 沙沙響
動 沙沙作響

英英 to make a soft crackling noise by walking on the dry leaves

例 The **rustling** came from the bush.
沙沙聲來自草叢。

☐ 三分熟
☐ 五分熟
☐ 七分熟
☐ 全熟

Ss

🎧 Track 111

sa·cred [ˈsekrɪd]

形 神聖的
同 holy 神聖的
片 be regarded as
　　sacred 視為神聖

英英 relating to be holy and so deserving respect

例 The pilgrims gather the water from the
sacred spring.
朝聖者從神聖的泉水中取水。

☐ 三分熟
☐ 五分熟
☐ 七分熟
☐ 全熟

---

sad·dle [ˈsædl̩]

名 鞍
動 套以馬鞍

英英 a seat, made of leather, fastened on the back of a
horse for riding; to put a saddle on a horse

例 The **saddle** of the horse is made of silver.
這匹馬的馬鞍是銀製的。

☐ 三分熟
☐ 五分熟
☐ 七分熟
☐ 全熟

---

saint [sent]

名 聖、聖人
動 列為聖徒

英英 a person who has received an official honor and
regarded in Christian faith as being in heaven after
death; to be a saint

例 Only **saints** forgive.
只有聖人才會原諒。

☐ 三分熟
☐ 五分熟
☐ 七分熟
☐ 全熟

---

salm·on [ˈsæmən]

名 鮭
形 鮭肉色的、淺橙色的

英英 a large slivery fish, that lives in the sea and
migrates to rivers to produce its eggs; orange-pink

例 Brown bears catch **salmons** for food.
棕熊抓鮭魚當作食物。

☐ 三分熟
☐ 五分熟
☐ 七分熟
☐ 全熟

---

sa·lute [səˈlut]

名 招呼、敬禮
動 致意、致敬
同 greeting 招呼

英英 an act of showing respect, especially of people in
the armed forces

例 **Salute** the general.
向將軍敬禮。

☐ 三分熟
☐ 五分熟
☐ 七分熟
☐ 全熟

---

san·dal [ˈsændl̩]

名 涼鞋、便鞋

英英 a shoe with straps attaching the sole to the foot,
which is wore in warm weather

例 Hermes, a messenger god, usually wears a
pair of **sandals** with wings.
信使神荷密斯通常穿著一雙有翅膀的涼鞋。

☐ 三分熟
☐ 五分熟
☐ 七分熟
☐ 全熟

---

sav·age [ˈsævɪdʒ]

名 野蠻人
形 荒野的、野性的
同 fierce 兇猛的
片 increasingly savage
　　更加野蠻

英英 a person who is living in the way of very early
stage of development; wild land

例 The **savage** beast is wounded.
這隻具野性的野獸受傷了。

☐ 三分熟
☐ 五分熟
☐ 七分熟
☐ 全熟

S

scan [skæn]

名 掃描
動 掃描、審視

英英 to look at something quickly with eyes or a machine in order to identify relevant features or information

例 **Scan** your ID card and send a copy to me.
掃描你的身份證,寄一份複本給我。

☐三分熟
☐五分熟
☐七分熟
☐全熟

scan·dal [ˈskændl̩]

名 醜聞、恥辱
同 disgrace 恥辱

英英 an action or event regarded as legally wrong and causing general public outrage

例 The political **scandal** followed him all his life.
這件政治醜聞一輩子都跟著他。

☐三分熟
☐五分熟
☐七分熟
☐全熟

scar [skɑr]

名 傷痕、疤痕
動 使留下疤痕

英英 a mark left on the part of body after the healing of a wound or burn; to make a scar on the skin

例 The red **scar** on the pirate's face scared us.
海盜臉上的疤痕嚇壞我們了。

☐三分熟
☐五分熟
☐七分熟
☐全熟

scent [sɛnt]

名 氣味、痕跡
動 聞、嗅
同 smell 氣味

英英 a distinctive and pleasant smell, to smell something

例 The ant is able to leave certain **scent**.
螞蟻會留下某些氣味。

☐三分熟
☐五分熟
☐七分熟
☐全熟

scheme [skim]

名 計畫、陰謀
動 計畫、密謀、擬訂

英英 a systematic plan or arrangement for achieving a particular goal

例 Her **scheme** won't work out.
她的陰謀不會成功的。

☐三分熟
☐五分熟
☐七分熟
☐全熟

scorn [skɔrn]

名 輕蔑、蔑視
動 不屑做、鄙視
同 contempt 輕蔑

英英 a strong feeling of something that you think is stupid or has no value; not willing to do something you think is stupid

例 Vincent's **scorn** on the new manager is clearly shown on his face.
文生對新任經理的鄙視,清楚地表現在他的臉上。

☐三分熟
☐五分熟
☐七分熟
☐全熟

scram·ble [ˈskræmbl̩]

名 攀爬、爭奪
動 爭奪、湊合

英英 to move or make one's way quickly; to take off very quickly

例 The passengers **scrambled** to the door.
旅客們爭先恐後地跑到門邊。

☐三分熟
☐五分熟
☐七分熟
☐全熟

🎧 **Track 113**

scrap [skræp]

名 小片、少許、碎片
動 去棄、爭吵
同 quarrel 爭吵

英英 a small piece or amount of something; to get rid of something or throw something away

例 These shiny **scraps** of paper were used to decorate the windows.
這些閃亮的紙片用來裝飾窗戶。

☐ 三分熟
☐ 五分熟
☐ 七分熟
☐ 全熟

---

scrape [skrep]

名 磨擦聲、擦掉
動 磨擦、擦刮
同 rub 磨擦

英英 a sound made from dragging a hard implement across to remove dirt; to drag or pull a hard implement across to remove dirt or waste matter

例 The biker's elbow **scraped** the ground and bled.
騎自行車者的手肘與地板磨擦到，因而流血。

☐ 三分熟
☐ 五分熟
☐ 七分熟
☐ 全熟

---

scroll [skrol]

名 卷軸
動 把……寫在捲軸上、（電腦術語）捲頁

英英 a roll of paper or similar material for writing or painting on; to write something on a scroll

例 The **scroll** of Chinese painting has been delivered to your residence.
這幅國畫卷軸已經送到你的住處。

☐ 三分熟
☐ 五分熟
☐ 七分熟
☐ 全熟

---

sculp·tor

[`skʌlptə]

名 雕刻家、雕刻師

英英 an artist who makes sculptures

例 Jay McDougall is a contemporary wood **sculptor**.
傑・麥克杜格爾是位當代的木雕師。

☐ 三分熟
☐ 五分熟
☐ 七分熟
☐ 全熟

---

se·cure [sɪ`kjʊr]

動 保護
形 安心的、安全的
同 safe 安全的

英英 certain to keep safe and unthreatened from being harmed; protection or keeping safe

例 To **secure** the government official's safety should be the priority.
保護政府官員的安全為首要之務。

☐ 三分熟
☐ 五分熟
☐ 七分熟
☐ 全熟

---

seg·ment

[`sɛgmənt]

名 部分、段
動 分割、劃分
同 section 部分

英英 each of the parts into which something is divided; to divide something

例 The **segment** of the population in this area increased rapidly.
這個地區人口部分快速增加。

☐ 三分熟
☐ 五分熟
☐ 七分熟
☐ 全熟

---

sen·sa·tion

[sɛn`seʃən]

名 感覺、知覺
同 feeling 感覺

英英 a physical feeling from something that comes into contact with the body

例 Cooks should learn to open up the possibility of countless taste **sensations**.
廚師應學著打開味覺千變萬化的可能性。

☐ 三分熟
☐ 五分熟
☐ 七分熟
☐ 全熟

sen·si·tiv·i·ty
[ˌsɛnsəˈtɪvətɪ]

名 敏感度、靈敏度

英英 the condition of being sensitive

例 Before you give criticism, remember to have **sensitivity**.
當你給出評論前，記得要有敏感度。

☐ 三分熟
☐ 五分熟
☐ 七分熟
☐ 全熟

sen·ti·ment
[ˈsɛntəmənt]

名 情緒

英英 an emotion or feeling, such as sympathy, love, etc.

例 When you have this kind of **sentiment**, don't hurry to deny it.
當你有這樣的情緒時，不要急於否定。

☐ 三分熟
☐ 五分熟
☐ 七分熟
☐ 全熟

ser·geant
[ˈsɑrdʒənt]

名 士官

英英 a soldier of middle rank in the army or air force, above corporal and below staff sergeant

例 A **sergeant** should fulfill his duties.
士官理應履行自己的職責。

☐ 三分熟
☐ 五分熟
☐ 七分熟
☐ 全熟

se·ries [ˈsɪrɪz]

名 連續
同 succession 連續

英英 a number of related things coming one after another

例 A **series** of murders of prostitutes shocked the Londoners.
一連串的妓女謀殺事件，震驚了倫敦人。

☐ 三分熟
☐ 五分熟
☐ 七分熟
☐ 全熟

ser·mon [ˈsɝmən]

名 佈道、講道
同 detect 察覺

英英 a religious talk, especially one given during a church service

例 The **sermon** of the priest moved the audience to tears.
牧師的講道讓聽眾感動落淚。

☐ 三分熟
☐ 五分熟
☐ 七分熟
☐ 全熟

serv·er [ˈsɝvə]

名 侍者、服役者
同 waiter 侍者

英英 a person or thing that serves food

例 Lin's boyfriend used to be a **server** in an Australian restaurant.
林的男友過去曾在澳洲的餐廳當侍者。

☐ 三分熟
☐ 五分熟
☐ 七分熟
☐ 全熟

set·ting [ˈsɛtɪŋ]

名 安置的地點、背景

英英 the position or place in which something is set

例 The **setting** of the TV series is in Northern Ireland.
這部電視影集的場景在北愛爾蘭。

☐ 三分熟
☐ 五分熟
☐ 七分熟
☐ 全熟

shab·by [ˈʃæbɪ]

形 衣衫襤褸的
反 decent 體面的

英英 dressed in old or worn clothes

例 **Shabby** clothes didn't dim the girl's inner nobility.
破舊的服飾並沒有讓這個女孩內心的高貴失色。

☐ 三分熟
☐ 五分熟
☐ 七分熟
☐ 全熟

S

🎧 **Track 115**

---

sharp·en [ˈʃɑrpn̩]

動 使銳利、使尖銳

英英 make something stronger or become sharp

例 I need to **sharpen** these pencils.
我必需要要削這些鉛筆。

☐三分熟
☐五分熟
☐七分熟
☐全熟

---

shat·ter [ˈʃætɚ]

動 粉碎、砸破

同 break 砸破

英英 to break something violently into pieces; to damage or destroy something

例 The glass fell to the ground and thoroughly **shattered** to pieces.
玻璃杯掉到地上，徹底粉碎。

☐三分熟
☐五分熟
☐七分熟
☐全熟

---

sher·iff [ˈʃɛrɪf]

名 警長

英英 the chief executive officer who is in charge of performing the orders of the law courts

例 The **sheriff** just caught the gang.
警長剛捉到幫派份子。

☐三分熟
☐五分熟
☐七分熟
☐全熟

---

shield [ʃild]

名 盾

動 遮蔽

英英 a broad piece of object, usually made of metal, held for protection against blows or missiles; to cover or protect

例 Captain America uses his **shield** as a defensive equipment.
美國隊長用他的盾牌當作防衛性的裝備。

☐三分熟
☐五分熟
☐七分熟
☐全熟

---

shiv·er [ˈʃɪvɚ]

名 顫抖

動 冷得發抖

同 quake 顫抖

英英 shaking lightly because of feeling cold; to shake lightly because of feeling cold or frightened

例 The black and white cat was **shivering** under the car.
黑白貓在車下冷得發抖。

☐三分熟
☐五分熟
☐七分熟
☐全熟

---

short·age [ˈʃɔrtɪdʒ]

名 不足、短缺

同 deficiency 不足

英英 a situation in which something is not in sufficient amounts

例 It's hard to bear water **shortage**.
缺水是難以忍受的。

☐三分熟
☐五分熟
☐七分熟
☐全熟

---

short·com·ing [ˈʃɔrtkʌmɪŋ]

名 短處、缺點

同 deficiency 不足

英英 a failure to meet a certain standard

例 Everyone has his **shortcoming**.
每個人都有自身的缺點。

☐三分熟
☐五分熟
☐七分熟
☐全熟

---

shove [ʃʌv]

名 推

動 推、推動

英英 to push something roughly

例 The fans **shoved** to see their idol.
粉絲們推來擠去，想見偶像。

☐三分熟
☐五分熟
☐七分熟
☐全熟

S

shred [ʃrɛd]

名 細長的片段
動 撕成碎布

英英 a strip of material that has been torn or cut; to tear something into pieces

例 The **shreds** of dresses and shirts are placed in the basement.
洋裝和襯衫的碎布放在地下室。

☐ 三分熟
☐ 五分熟
☐ 七分熟
☐ 全熟

shriek [ʃrik]

名 尖叫
動 尖叫、叫喊
同 scream 尖叫

英英 a high-pitched cry or sound

例 A boy **shrieked** and threw the toys around.
小男孩放聲尖叫，亂丟玩具。

☐ 三分熟
☐ 五分熟
☐ 七分熟
☐ 全熟

shrine [ʃraɪn]

名 廟、祠

英英 a place regarded as holy because of a connection with a holy person or object

例 The **shrine** has exquisite stone sculpture.
這座廟有精巧的石雕。

☐ 三分熟
☐ 五分熟
☐ 七分熟
☐ 全熟

shrub [ʃrʌb]

名 灌木
同 bush 灌木

英英 a woody plant which is smaller than a tree and has many small branches from several main stems arising at or near the ground

例 In the mountain behind our house are some flowering **shrubs**.
屋後的山裡有些開花的灌木。

☐ 三分熟
☐ 五分熟
☐ 七分熟
☐ 全熟

shud·der [ˈʃʌdɚ]

名 發抖、顫抖
動 顫抖、戰慄
同 tremble 顫抖

英英 to shake suddenly, especially as a result of fear or other unpleasant thought

例 The kitty was **shuddering**.
小貓咪在發抖。

☐ 三分熟
☐ 五分熟
☐ 七分熟
☐ 全熟

shut·ter [ˈʃʌtɚ]

名 百葉窗
動 關上窗
片 behind shutters
　 在百葉窗後方

英英 a wooden cover on the outside of window, that can be closed for security or privacy or to keep out the light; to close window

例 The **shutter** was down.
百葉窗是關上的。

☐ 三分熟
☐ 五分熟
☐ 七分熟
☐ 全熟

silk·worm

[ˈsɪlkwɝm]

名 蠶

英英 a caterpillar of a domesticated silk moth, which produces thread of silk from which it makes a cocoon

例 The **silkworm** is eating the mulberry leaf.
蠶在吃桑葉。

☐ 三分熟
☐ 五分熟
☐ 七分熟
☐ 全熟

🎧 Track 117

sim·mer [ˈsɪmɚ]

名 沸騰的狀態
動 煲、怒氣爆發
同 stew 燉、燜

英英 a status or temperature just below boiling point; to cook something liquid at a temperature slightly below boiling

例 Leave the chicken soup to **simmer** for a few minutes.
讓雞湯再沸騰個幾分鐘。

☐ 三分熟
☐ 五分熟
☐ 七分熟
☐ 全熟

---

skel·e·ton

[ˈskɛlətn̩]

名 骨骼、骨架
同 bone 骨骼

英英 an internal framework for supporting or containing the body of an animal or plant

例 Dinosaur's **skeleton** is huge.
恐龍的骨骼好大。

☐ 三分熟
☐ 五分熟
☐ 七分熟
☐ 全熟

---

skull [skʌl]

名 頭蓋骨

英英 a bone framework enclosing a person or animal's brain

例 A bullet passed through the man's **skull**.
一顆子彈穿過男子的頭蓋骨。

☐ 三分熟
☐ 五分熟
☐ 七分熟
☐ 全熟

---

slam [slæm]

名 砰然聲
動 砰地關上

英英 a loud sound made by shutting a door; to shut loudly with great force

例 His daughter **slammed** the door.
他的女兒砰然一聲地關上門。

☐ 三分熟
☐ 五分熟
☐ 七分熟
☐ 全熟

---

slap [slæp]

名 掌擊
動 用掌拍擊

英英 to hit or strike with the palm of one's hand

例 Mr. Wu **slapped** hard on his wife's face.
吳先生用力甩了他太太一巴掌。

☐ 三分熟
☐ 五分熟
☐ 七分熟
☐ 全熟

---

slaugh·ter [ˈslɔtɚ]

名 屠宰
動 屠宰
片 cruelly slaughtered 殘酷的屠殺

英英 to kill farm animals for food

例 There must be some ways to reduce the **slaughter** of animals.
一定有方法可以減少屠宰動物。

☐ 三分熟
☐ 五分熟
☐ 七分熟
☐ 全熟

---

slay [sle]

動 殺害、殺
同 kill 殺

英英 to kill something in a violent way

例 The Japanese soldier **slew** the woman.
日本兵殺了該名女子。

☐ 三分熟
☐ 五分熟
☐ 七分熟
☐ 全熟

---

slop·py [ˈslɑpɪ]

形 不整潔的、邋遢的
同 neat 整潔的

英英 untidy, unclean or unsystematic

例 The puppy looked **sloppy**.
這隻幼犬看起來邋遢。

☐ 三分熟
☐ 五分熟
☐ 七分熟
☐ 全熟

slump [slʌmp]

名 下跌
動 暴跌

英英 an instance of sinking; to sink or go down quickly

例 The value of the restaurant has **slumped**.
這間餐廳的價值突然下跌。

□ 三分熟
□ 五分熟
□ 七分熟
□ 全熟

sly [slaɪ]

形 狡猾的、陰險的
反 frank 坦白的

英英 having a cunning and deceitful nature

例 What does that **sly** smile mean?
那抹詭笑是何用意？

□ 三分熟
□ 五分熟
□ 七分熟
□ 全熟

smash [smæʃ]

名 激烈的碰撞
動 粉碎、碰撞
同 shatter 粉碎

英英 an act or sound of smashing; to break something noisily

例 **Smashed** windows scared the guests inside the hotel.
粉碎的窗戶嚇壞了飯店內的客人。

□ 三分熟
□ 五分熟
□ 七分熟
□ 全熟

snarl [snɑrl]

名 謾罵、爭吵
動 吼叫著說、糾結

英英 an act or sound of snarling, usually made in anger; to yell or say something loudly

例 Two drunkards **snarled** at each other.
兩名酒客互相謾罵。

□ 三分熟
□ 五分熟
□ 七分熟
□ 全熟

snatch [snætʃ]

名 片段
動 奪取、抓住
同 grab 抓取

英英 a small or short part of something; an act of snatching; to take or grasp something quickly and roughly

例 Mike's physical check-up report was **snatched** by his girlfriend.
麥克的身體檢查報告被他的女友一把搶走。

□ 三分熟
□ 五分熟
□ 七分熟
□ 全熟

sneak [snik]

動 潛行、偷偷地做

英英 to move or go somewhere secretly

例 The two ninjas **sneaked** into the palace.
兩名忍者潛進宮殿。

□ 三分熟
□ 五分熟
□ 七分熟
□ 全熟

sneak·er(s)

[ˈsnikɚ(s)]

名 慢跑鞋

英英 a soft shoe which is usually worn for sports or casual occasions

例 Why don't you put on these **sneakers**?
為什麼你不穿這雙慢跑鞋？

□ 三分熟
□ 五分熟
□ 七分熟
□ 全熟

sniff [snɪf]

名 吸氣
動 用鼻吸、嗅、聞
同 scent 嗅、聞

英英 an act or sound of sniffing

例 Helen **sniffed** Jeff's socks and almost fainted.
海倫聞了聞傑夫的襪子，差點昏了過去。

□ 三分熟
□ 五分熟
□ 七分熟
□ 全熟

snore [snor]

名 鼾聲
動 打鼾

英英 a sound of snorting or grunting in a person's breathing while they are asleep; to make snorting sound while sleeping

例 My roommate **snored** like a piglet.
我室友的打鼾聲像隻小豬。

☐ 三分熟 ☐ 五分熟 ☐ 七分熟 ☐ 全熟

---

snort [snɔrt]

名 鼻息、哼氣
動 哼著鼻子説

英英 a loud sound made by the sudden forcing of breath through the nose; to say something with a snorting sound

例 Jason **snorted** "Is this what you called the top jade?"
傑森哼著鼻子説：「這就是你所説的頂級玉？」

☐ 三分熟 ☐ 五分熟 ☐ 七分熟 ☐ 全熟

---

soak [sok]

名 浸泡
動 浸、滲入

英英 an act or spell of soaking; to make something very wet in the liquid

例 Tomato juice **soaked** into the carpet.
番茄汁滲進地毯裡。

☐ 三分熟 ☐ 五分熟 ☐ 七分熟 ☐ 全熟

---

so·ber [ˋsobɚ]

動 使清醒
形 節制的、清醒的

英英 to make awake; not affected by alcohol, not drunk

例 Are you **sober** now?
你清醒了嗎？

☐ 三分熟 ☐ 五分熟 ☐ 七分熟 ☐ 全熟

---

soft·en [ˋsɔfən]

動 使柔軟
反 harden 使變硬

英英 to make something soft or softer or become soft or softer

例 **Softened** mochi tastes good.
柔軟的麻糬好吃。

☐ 三分熟 ☐ 五分熟 ☐ 七分熟 ☐ 全熟

---

sole [sol]

形 唯一的、單一的

英英 being only one; unique

例 The **sole** objective is to finish the two final reports by the end of June.
我唯一的目標是在六月底前完成兩份期末報告。

☐ 三分熟 ☐ 五分熟 ☐ 七分熟 ☐ 全熟

---

sol·emn [ˋsɑləm]

形 鄭重的、莊嚴的
同 serious 莊嚴的

英英 very formal and serious

例 Ted's **solemn** face shows he is willing to consider the contract we offered.
泰德嚴肅的臉顯示他願意考慮我們所提供的合約。

☐ 三分熟 ☐ 五分熟 ☐ 七分熟 ☐ 全熟

---

sol·i·tar·y [ˋsɑləˏtɛrɪ]

名 隱士、獨居者
形 單獨的
同 single 單獨的

英英 a person who lives alone; being alone

例 The **solitary** lives alone beside the lake.
隱士獨自一人生活在湖邊。

☐ 三分熟 ☐ 五分熟 ☐ 七分熟 ☐ 全熟

so·lo [ˈsolo]

名 獨唱、獨奏、單獨表演
形 單獨的

英英 a piece of music, song, or dance for only one performer; being alone

例 While Susan was performing the **solo**, the judges were stunned.
當蘇珊在表演獨唱時，評審感到十分震驚。

☐ 三分熟
☐ 五分熟
☐ 七分熟
☐ 全熟

---

sov·er·eign

[ˈsɑvrɪn]

名 最高統治、獨立國家
形 自決的、獨立的

英英 a king or queen who is the supreme ruler of a country; able to deal with problems alone

例 It takes time to a country with the **sovereign** status.
要成為有獨立地位的國家需要時間。

☐ 三分熟
☐ 五分熟
☐ 七分熟
☐ 全熟

---

sow [so]

動 播、播種

英英 to plant seed by scattering it in the soil

例 Plow the field and **sow** the seeds.
犁這塊地，播下這些種子。

☐ 三分熟
☐ 五分熟
☐ 七分熟
☐ 全熟

---

space·craft/ space·ship

[ˈspes͵kræft]/[ˈspesͺʃɪp]

名 太空船

英英 a vehicle used for travelling in space

例 The **spacecraft** cruises to Mars.
太空船航行到火星去。

☐ 三分熟
☐ 五分熟
☐ 七分熟
☐ 全熟

---

spe·cial·ist

[ˈspɛʃəlɪst]

名 專家
同 expert 專家

英英 a person who is with high skill or knowledge in a particular field

例 Jane is a **specialist** in Children's Literature.
珍是兒童文學的專家。

☐ 三分熟
☐ 五分熟
☐ 七分熟
☐ 全熟

---

spec·i·men

[ˈspɛsəmən]

名 樣本、樣品
同 sample 樣本

英英 an individual animal, plant, object, etc. shown as an example for scientific study or display

例 Miller sent many butterfly **specimen** to the artist's studio.
米勒送很多的蝴蝶樣本到藝術家的工作室去。

☐ 三分熟
☐ 五分熟
☐ 七分熟
☐ 全熟

---

spec·ta·cle

[ˈspɛktəkl̩]

名 奇觀

英英 an unusual event or situation which attracts interesting or disapproval

例 The waterfall was a wonderful **spectacle**.
這條瀑布可說是奇觀。

☐ 三分熟
☐ 五分熟
☐ 七分熟
☐ 全熟

S

129

🎧 **Track 121**

spec·ta·tor

[ˋspɛktetɚ]

名 觀眾、旁觀者

英英 a person who watches a game, an activity or other event, without taking part

例 The clown was surrounded by **spectators**.
小丑被觀眾圍者。

☐ 三分熟
☐ 五分熟
☐ 七分熟
☐ 全熟

---

spine [spaɪn]

名 脊柱、背骨

英英 the backbone, the line of bones down centre of the back, which provides support for the body

例 Judy fell down from the stairs and hurt he **spine**.
茱蒂從樓梯摔了下來，傷了脊柱。

☐ 三分熟
☐ 五分熟
☐ 七分熟
☐ 全熟

---

splen·dor

[ˋsplɛndɚ]

名 燦爛、光輝

英英 magnificent and attractive appearance

例 The **splendor** of the morning sun is unforgettable.
晨曦的光輝難以忘懷。

☐ 三分熟
☐ 五分熟
☐ 七分熟
☐ 全熟

---

sponge [spʌndʒ]

名 海綿
動 依賴、（用海綿）
　　擦拭

英英 a soft substance with small holes and is able to absorb a lot of liquid; to depend or rely on someone or something

例 Use the **sponge** to clean the basin.
用海綿清理臉盆。

☐ 三分熟
☐ 五分熟
☐ 七分熟
☐ 全熟

---

spot·light

[ˋspɑtˌlaɪt]

名 聚光燈
動 用聚光燈照明

英英 a lamp projecting a narrow, and its beam can be directly on to a place or person; to light up something with spotlight

例 One of the **spotlights** was broken.
其中一個聚光燈壞了。

☐ 三分熟
☐ 五分熟
☐ 七分熟
☐ 全熟

---

sprint [sprɪnt]

名 短距離賽跑
動 衝刺、全力奔跑
同 speed 迅速前進

英英 a short, fast race; to run fast

例 100-meter **sprint** is going to begin.
100 公尺短跑即將開始。

☐ 三分熟
☐ 五分熟
☐ 七分熟
☐ 全熟

---

spur [spɝ]

名 馬刺
動 策馬、飛奔

英英 a sharp, metal device, which is worn on a rider's heel for urging a horse forward; to urge a horse forward

例 The **spur** was used to encourage the horse to run faster.
馬刺用以鼓勵馬匹跑快一點。

☐ 三分熟
☐ 五分熟
☐ 七分熟
☐ 全熟

squash [skwɑʃ]

名 擠壓的聲音
動 壓扁、壓爛

英英 a state of being squashed; to crash something into a flat shape

例 My garlic bread was **squashed**.
我的大蒜麵包被壓爛了。

□ 三分熟
□ 五分熟
□ 七分熟
□ 全熟

---

squat [skwɑt]

名 蹲下的姿勢
動 蹲下、蹲
形 蹲著的

英英 a position or movement of squatting position

例 The boy **squatted** down and observed the marching ants.
小男孩蹲下，觀察著行進中的螞蟻。

□ 三分熟
□ 五分熟
□ 七分熟
□ 全熟

---

stack [stæk]

名 堆、堆疊
動 堆疊
同 heap 堆

英英 a neat pile of things

例 Sam signed on a **stack** of books.
山姆在這堆書上簽名。

□ 三分熟
□ 五分熟
□ 七分熟
□ 全熟

---

stag·ger [ˈstæɡɚ]

名 搖晃、蹣跚
動 蹣跚
同 sway 搖動

英英 to move or walk with difficulty just like someone's going to fall down

例 The baby **staggered** after the other children.
寶寶在其他小朋友後面搖搖晃晃的走著。

□ 三分熟
□ 五分熟
□ 七分熟
□ 全熟

---

stain [sten]

動 弄髒、汙染
名 汙點
同 spot 汙點

英英 to make unclean; a dirty mark on something

例 The blood **stain** is still on his shirt.
血的汙點還在他的襯衫上。

□ 三分熟
□ 五分熟
□ 七分熟
□ 全熟

---

stake [stek]

名 椿
動 把……綁在椿上、以……作為賭注
片 the stake 火刑柱

英英 a strong stick or metal bar with a point at one end, driven into the ground to support a tree, or form part of a fence; to tie something on a stake

例 On the gambling table, Mina **staked** $20,000 on number 13.
在賭桌上，米娜押了二萬美元賭 13 號。

□ 三分熟
□ 五分熟
□ 七分熟
□ 全熟

---

stalk [stɔk]

名 莖
同 stem 莖

英英 the main stem of a plant

例 The bean **stalk** continues to grow up.
豆莖持續成長。

□ 三分熟
□ 五分熟
□ 七分熟
□ 全熟

---

stall [stɔl]

名 商品陳列臺、攤位

英英 a stand or booth for the sale of goods in a market

例 The fruits on the **stalls** attract traveler's eyes.
攤位上的水果吸引旅客的目光。

□ 三分熟
□ 五分熟
□ 七分熟
□ 全熟

S

🎧 Track 123

stan·za [ˈstænzə]

名 節、段

英英 a group of lines forming the unit in a poem, a verse

例 Let's begin with the first **stanza** of the poem.
讓我們從這首詩的第一節開始。

☐ 三分熟
☐ 五分熟
☐ 七分熟
☐ 全熟

---

star·tle [ˈstɑrtl̩]

動 使驚跳
同 surprise 使吃驚

英英 cause to feel sudden shock or alarm

例 The lizard was **startled** by the sudden light.
蜥蜴被突然出現的光給嚇了一跳。

☐ 三分熟
☐ 五分熟
☐ 七分熟
☐ 全熟

---

states·man

[ˈstetsmən]

名 政治家

英英 a skilled, experienced, and respected political leader

例 **Statesmen** deserve respect.
政治家值得尊敬。

☐ 三分熟
☐ 五分熟
☐ 七分熟
☐ 全熟

---

sta·tis·tic(s)

[stəˈtɪstɪk(s)]

名 統計值、統計量

英英 the collection and analysis of numerical data or numerical fats in large quantities

例 The **statistics** are accurate.
這些統計數字是正確的。

☐ 三分熟
☐ 五分熟
☐ 七分熟
☐ 全熟

---

sta·tis·ti·cal

[stəˈtɪstɪkl̩]

形 統計的、統計學的

英英 relating to statistics

例 To prove our presumption is right, we need some **statistical** evidence.
要證明我們的假設是正確的，我們需要一些統計上的證據。

☐ 三分熟
☐ 五分熟
☐ 七分熟
☐ 全熟

---

steam·er [ˈstimɚ]

名 汽船、輪船

英英 a ship or boat which is powered by steam

例 You may consider taking a paddle **steamer** to explore the key sights of London.
你可以考慮搭乘外輪船去探索倫敦的重要景點。

☐ 三分熟
☐ 五分熟
☐ 七分熟
☐ 全熟

---

steer [stɪr]

名 忠告、建議
動 駕駛、掌舵

英英 a piece of advice or information; to drive or take a wheel

例 **Steering** the car in the mountain seems to be easy for Bonnie.
在山區內駕駛車輛對邦妮來說似乎是很簡單的。

☐ 三分熟
☐ 五分熟
☐ 七分熟
☐ 全熟

---

ster·e·o·type

[ˈstɛrɪəˌtaɪp]

名 鉛版、刻板印象
動 把……澆成鉛版、定型

英英 a fixed and over-simplified idea that people have about a person or thing; to fix something in a particular shape

例 The **stereotype** of females as family angels should be corrected.
女性當成家庭天使的這種刻板印象應該要糾正。

☐ 三分熟
☐ 五分熟
☐ 七分熟
☐ 全熟

S

stern [stɝn]

形 嚴格的
同 severe 嚴格的

英英 very serious or strict, especially in the exercise of discipline

例 Iris's father is the **sternest** critic for her.
艾莉絲的父親對她而言是最為嚴格的評論家。

☐ 三分熟
☐ 五分熟
☐ 七分熟
☐ 全熟

---

stew [stju]

名 燉菜
動 燉煮、燉

英英 a dish of mixing meat and vegetables cooked slowly in liquid

例 The chef specializes in **stewing** pig's trotters.
這位主廚特別擅長於燉豬腳。

☐ 三分熟
☐ 五分熟
☐ 七分熟
☐ 全熟

---

stew·ard/ stew·ard·ess/ at·tend·ant

[`stjuwəd]/[`stjuwədɪs]/ [ə`tendənt]

名 服務生、空服員

英英 a male or female person who looks after the passengers on a ship or aircraft

例 Can you call the **steward** to give us a cup of hot water?
可否叫服務生給我們　杯熱水？

☐ 三分熟
☐ 五分熟
☐ 七分熟
☐ 全熟

---

stink [stɪŋk]

名 惡臭、臭
動 弄臭
反 perfume 弄香

英英 a strong, unpleasant smell; to make something smell unpleasant

例 The kitchen **stinks**.
廚房發出惡臭。

☐ 三分熟
☐ 五分熟
☐ 七分熟
☐ 全熟

---

stock [stɑk]

名 庫存、紫羅蘭、股票

英英 a supply of goods available for sale or use; the amount of money which a company sells shares to people

例 The dress of your size is currently out of **stock**.
符合您尺寸的洋裝目前缺貨中。

☐ 三分熟
☐ 五分熟
☐ 七分熟
☐ 全熟

---

stoop [stup]

名 駝背
動 自貶、使屈服

英英 a person stands or walks with their head and shoulders bend slightly; to bend one's head or body forwards and downwards; to look down on oneself

例 Anyone can **stoop** to failure, not you.
每個人都可以向挫折屈服，但不包含你。

☐ 三分熟
☐ 五分熟
☐ 七分熟
☐ 全熟

---

stor·age [`storɪdʒ]

名 儲存、倉庫
同 warehouse 倉庫

英英 the action of storing

例 We don't have enough **storage** space.
我們沒有足夠的儲存空間。

☐ 三分熟
☐ 五分熟
☐ 七分熟
☐ 全熟

🎧 Track 125

---

stout [staʊt]

形 強壯的、堅固的
反 feeble 虛弱的

英英 describes something that is strongly made from strong materials

例 The pigeon has **stout** body.
這隻鴿子有強健的身體。

☐ 三分熟
☐ 五分熟
☐ 七分熟
☐ 全熟

---

straight·en [ˋstretn̩]

動 弄直、整頓

英英 to make or become straight; to make something tidy or in order

例 **Straighten** the tablecloth quickly.
趕快把桌布弄直。

☐ 三分熟
☐ 五分熟
☐ 七分熟
☐ 全熟

---

straight·for·ward [ˋstretˏfɔrwəd]

形 直接的、正直的
同 straight 正直的

英英 very easy to do or understand; very honest

例 John is a **straightforward** man who helps anyone in need.
正直的 John，會幫助任何需要被幫助的人。

☐ 三分熟
☐ 五分熟
☐ 七分熟
☐ 全熟

---

strain [stren]

名 緊張
動 拉緊、強逼、盡全力
反 relax 放鬆
片 strain every nerve 竭盡全力

英英 a force or influence tending to strain something to an extreme degree; to pull tightly

例 Jamie tried her best to cope with the **strain** of the job.
婕咪盡全力去處理工作壓力。

☐ 三分熟
☐ 五分熟
☐ 七分熟
☐ 全熟

---

strait [stret]

名 海峽

英英 a narrow passage of water which connects two seas or other large areas of water

例 The relation between the two sides of the Taiwan **Straits** is complex.
兩岸的關係是複雜的。

☐ 三分熟
☐ 五分熟
☐ 七分熟
☐ 全熟

---

strand [strænd]

名 濱
動 擱淺、處於困境

英英 the shore of a sea, lake, or wide river; to abandon

例 Another whale **stranded** on shore.
另一條鯨魚擱淺在岸邊。

☐ 三分熟
☐ 五分熟
☐ 七分熟
☐ 全熟

---

strap [stræp]

名 皮帶
動 約束、用帶子捆
同 bind 捆、綁

英英 a narrow piece of leather or other strong material used for fastening something or giving support

例 **Strap** this box of books.
用帶子把這個書箱捆起來。

☐ 三分熟
☐ 五分熟
☐ 七分熟
☐ 全熟

S

stray [stre]

名 漂泊者
動 迷路、漂泊
形 迷途的

英英 a person or pet that on longer has a home; to travel along

例 The group of explorers **strayed** into an unknown jungle.
一群探險者誤入了一個未知的叢林。

□三分熟
□五分熟
□七分熟
□全熟

---

streak [strik]

動 加條紋
名 條紋
同 stripe 條紋

英英 to make a long thin mark on something; a long, thin mark of a different substance which is easily noticed because it has different color from its surroundings

例 The designer added a few **streaks** for the character in the film.
設計師為電影中的人物加些條紋。

□三分熟
□五分熟
□七分熟
□全熟

---

stride [straɪd]

名 跨步、大步
動 邁過、跨過
同 step 步伐

英英 a long, big step; to make a big step

例 The length of **stride** made her a winner of the race.
大跨步讓她成為賽跑中的贏家。

□三分熟
□五分熟
□七分熟
□全熟

---

stripe [straɪp]

名 斑紋、條紋

英英 a long narrow band or strip of a different color

例 The black and white **stripes** on the model's face turned him into a zebra.
這個模特兒臉上的黑白條紋讓他變成了一隻斑馬。

□三分熟
□五分熟
□七分熟
□全熟

---

stroll [strol]

名 漫步、閒逛
動 漫步
片 after-lunch stroll
午後散步

英英 a short leisurely walk

例 Take a **stroll** in the park is relaxing.
在公園裡漫步是很悠哉的。

□三分熟
□五分熟
□七分熟
□全熟

---

struc·tur·al

[ˈstrʌktʃərəl]

形 構造的、結構上的

英英 relating to or forming part of a structure

例 The **structural** design of the lake café is astounding.
湖邊咖啡廳結構上的設計令人吃驚。

□三分熟
□五分熟
□七分熟
□全熟

---

stum·ble [ˈstʌmbl̩]

名 絆倒
動 跌倒、偶然發現

英英 to trip or lose someone's balance; to walk unsteadily

例 The robber **stumbled** on a stick.
搶匪因為一支木棍而跌了一跤。

□三分熟
□五分熟
□七分熟
□全熟

🎧 **Track 127**

stump [stʌmp]

名　（樹的）殘株、殘餘部分

動　遊說、難倒

同　remainder 殘餘物

英英　the part of a tree trunk left from the ground after the rest has fallen or been felled; to persuade someone

例　The **stump** of the tree serves as the man's stool.
樹的殘株成為這名男子的矮凳。

☐三分熟
☐五分熟
☐七分熟
☐全熟

---

stun [stʌn]

動　嚇呆

英英　to shock or surprise somebody very much

例　The monkey was **stunned** at the sight the leopard.
一看到花豹，猴子嚇呆了。

☐三分熟
☐五分熟
☐七分熟
☐全熟

---

stur·dy [ˈstɝdɪ]

形　強健的、穩固的

同　strong 強壯的

英英　in the state of strongly and solidly built or made

例　I need a **sturdy** table.
我需要一張穩固的桌子。

☐三分熟
☐五分熟
☐七分熟
☐全熟

---

stut·ter [ˈstʌtɚ]

名　結巴

動　結結巴巴地說

同　stammer 結結巴巴地說

英英　to speak something with difficulty, usually pausing it or repeating it several times

例　Laura made a mistake and **stuttered** to explain.
蘿拉犯了錯，結結巴巴地解釋。

☐三分熟
☐五分熟
☐七分熟
☐全熟

---

styl·ish [ˈstaɪlɪʃ]

形　時髦的、漂亮的

同　fashionable 時髦的

英英　having a good sense of style; very fashion

例　That **stylish** carpet is hung outside.
那條漂亮的地毯掛在外面。

☐三分熟
☐五分熟
☐七分熟
☐全熟

---

sub·mit [səbˈmɪt]

動　屈服、提交

英英　to accept or yield to a superior force or stronger person

例　**Submit** your report to me before 4 p.m.
下午 4 點前把報告交給我。

☐三分熟
☐五分熟
☐七分熟
☐全熟

---

sub·stan·tial
[səbˈstænʃəl]

形　實際的、重大的

同　actual 實際的

英英　of considerable importance, size, or worth

例　A **substantial** difference between the two clerks is working attitude.
這兩個店員間最大的不同在工作態度。

☐三分熟
☐五分熟
☐七分熟
☐全熟

sub·sti·tute

[ˈsʌbstəˌtjut]

名 代替者
動 代替
同 replace 代替

英英 a person or thing acting or serving in place of another; to use something or someone instead

例 The **substitute** teacher hasn't arrived yet.
代理教師還沒到。

☐ 三分熟
☐ 五分熟
☐ 七分熟
☐ 全熟

suit·case

[ˈsutˌkes]

名 手提箱

英英 a case with a handle and a hinged lid, used for carrying documents and other personal possessions

例 The **suitcase** is made of real leather.
這只手提箱是用真皮製成的。

☐ 三分熟
☐ 五分熟
☐ 七分熟
☐ 全熟

sul·fur [ˈsʌlfɚ]

名 硫磺

英英 a non-metallic chemical element which typically occurs as yellow crystals

例 Beitou is famous for its hot spring with **sulfur**.
北投以含有硫磺的溫泉聞名。

☐ 三分熟
☐ 五分熟
☐ 七分熟
☐ 全熟

sum·mon [ˈsʌmən]

動 召集

英英 to order someone to be present or appear in a particular event

例 Several students were **summoned** to the teacher's office.
幾個學生被召集到教師辦公室去。

☐ 三分熟
☐ 五分熟
☐ 七分熟
☐ 全熟

su·per·fi·cial

[ˈsupɚˈfɪʃəl]

形 表面的、外表的、粗略的
反 essential 本質的

英英 existing or occurring at or on the surface

例 Toby has **superficial** knowledge of Korean.
托比略懂一點韓文。

☐ 三分熟
☐ 五分熟
☐ 七分熟
☐ 全熟

su·per·sti·tion

[ˌsupɚˈstɪʃən]

名 迷信

英英 belief in the supernatural, which is connected with old ideas about magic, etc.

例 Dislike of the number of 4 results from certain **superstition**.
不喜歡數字 4 是由某些迷信所造成的。

☐ 三分熟
☐ 五分熟
☐ 七分熟
☐ 全熟

su·per·vise

[ˈsupɚvaɪz]

動 監督、管理
同 administer 管理

英英 to observe and direct a task or the work of someone

例 The students were taking the tests while the teacher **supervised**.
在教師監督之下，學生們在考試。

☐ 三分熟
☐ 五分熟
☐ 七分熟
☐ 全熟

🎧 Track 129

su·per·vi·sor

[ˌsupɚˋvaɪzɚ]

名 監督者、管理人
同 administrator 管理人

英英 a person who observes and directs a task or the work of a person

例 My **supervisor** is on a business trip.
我的主管出公差。

☐ 三分熟
☐ 五分熟
☐ 七分熟
☐ 全熟

---

sup·press

[səˋprɛs]

動 壓抑、制止
同 restrain 抑制

英英 to forcibly put an end to something or stop something

例 He **suppressed** his anger and left without a word.
他把怒氣壓抑下來，不發一語離開。

☐ 三分熟
☐ 五分熟
☐ 七分熟
☐ 全熟

---

su·preme

[səˋprim]

形 至高無上的

英英 highest or most important in authority or rank

例 The **Supreme** Court will decide if you can win the lawsuit.
最高法院會決定你是否能贏得這個訟案。

☐ 三分熟
☐ 五分熟
☐ 七分熟
☐ 全熟

---

surge [sɝdʒ]

名 大浪
動 洶湧

英英 a sudden powerful increase; to move quickly and powerfully

例 There's a **surge** of shoppers into the department store.
潮湧般的購買者湧入百貨公司。

☐ 三分熟
☐ 五分熟
☐ 七分熟
☐ 全熟

---

sus·pend

[səˋspɛnd]

動 懸掛、暫停
同 hang 懸掛
片 be forced to suspend
被迫要暫停

英英 to stop something either temporarily or permanently

例 **Suspend** what you imagine for a minute.
暫停你現在所想像的。

☐ 三分熟
☐ 五分熟
☐ 七分熟
☐ 全熟

---

sus·tain [səˋsten]

動 支持、支撐
同 support 支持

英英 to bear the weight of something

例 Your younger sister needs your faith on her to **sustain** her decision.
你妹妹需要你對她的信心，以支持她的決定。

☐ 三分熟
☐ 五分熟
☐ 七分熟
☐ 全熟

swamp [swɑmp]

名 沼澤
動 陷入泥沼
同 bog 沼澤

英英 wet soft land; to overwhelm or flood with water

例 The alligators await their preys in the **swamp**.
鱷魚在沼澤等待獵物。

☐ 三分熟
☐ 五分熟
☐ 七分熟
☐ 全熟

swarm [swɔrm]

名 群、群集
動 聚集、一塊
同 cluster 群、組

英英 a large group of flying insects; to come together

例 A **swarm** of bees are attacking the man.
群蜂攻擊該名男子。

☐ 三分熟
☐ 五分熟
☐ 七分熟
☐ 全熟

sym·pa·thize

[ˈsɪmpəˌθaɪz]

動 同情、有同感
同 pity 同情

英英 to feel or express sympathy

例 I **sympathize** with Cathy, who doesn't sleep well at night.
我同情凱蒂，她夜裡常常睡不好。

☐ 三分熟
☐ 五分熟
☐ 七分熟
☐ 全熟

S

Tt

🔊 Track 130

---

tack·le [ˈtækl̩]

動 著手處理、捉住
同 undertake 著手處理
片 attempt to tackle
試著去處理

英英 to try to handle or deal with something or someone

例 **Tackle** the problem immediately.
趕快著手處理這個問題。

☐ 三分熟
☐ 五分熟
☐ 七分熟
☐ 全熟

---

tan [tæn]

名 日曬後的顏色、
曬成棕褐色
形 棕褐色的

英英 a yellowish-brown color getting after exposure to the sun

例 Jeff looks strong with deep **tan**.
傑夫看起來強壯，有深褐色的肌色。

☐ 三分熟
☐ 五分熟
☐ 七分熟
☐ 全熟

---

tan·gle [ˈtæŋgl̩]

名 混亂、糾結
動 使混亂、使糾結、纏結

英英 a confused or complicated state

例 My cat likes to play with a **tangled** ball of yarn.
我的貓喜歡玩纏結在一起毛線團。

☐ 三分熟
☐ 五分熟
☐ 七分熟
☐ 全熟

---

tar [tɑr]

名 焦油、柏油
動 塗焦油於

英英 a dark substance becomes sticky when hot, which is used in road-making and for coating and preserving timber; to spread tar on something

例 The road was just paved with **tar**.
這條路才鋪了柏油。

☐ 三分熟
☐ 五分熟
☐ 七分熟
☐ 全熟

---

tart [ˈtɑrt]

形 酸的、尖酸的
同 sour 酸的

英英 having a sour taste

例 Add sugar on the fruit; it's a little **tart**.
加糖到水果上，水果有點酸。

☐ 三分熟
☐ 五分熟
☐ 七分熟
☐ 全熟

---

taunt [tɔnt]

名 辱罵
動 嘲弄

英英 to annoy or upset someone by laughing at them

例 Bard was **taunted** by other students this morning.
巴德今天早上被其他學生嘲弄。

☐ 三分熟
☐ 五分熟
☐ 七分熟
☐ 全熟

---

tav·ern [ˈtævən]

名 酒店、酒館

英英 a places where sells alcohol

例 Let's go to the **tavern** and have a drink.
我們到酒館裡喝一杯吧。

☐ 三分熟
☐ 五分熟
☐ 七分熟
☐ 全熟

---

tell·er [ˈtɛlə]

名 講話者、敘述者、
出納員

英英 a person who speaks or gives a speech

例 The bank **teller** is quite friendly.
這名銀行出納員還滿友善的。

☐ 三分熟
☐ 五分熟
☐ 七分熟
☐ 全熟

T

tem·po [ˈtɛmpo]

名 速度、拍子
同 rhythm 節拍

英英 the speed at which a passage of music is played

例 They had to up the **tempo** in order to finish this project.
他們必須加快節奏，才能完成這個項目。

☐ 三分熟
☐ 五分熟
☐ 七分熟
☐ 全熟

tempt [tɛmpt]

動 誘惑、慫恿

英英 to make someone to do something against their better judgement

例 Some youngsters are easily **tempted** by drugs.
有些年輕人很容易被毒品誘惑。

☐ 三分熟
☐ 五分熟
☐ 七分熟
☐ 全熟

temp·ta·tion

[tɛmpˈteʃən]

名 誘惑

英英 a person who rents land or a house from a landlord; to rent something

例 The job offering high salary is a great **temptation**.
這份提供高薪的工作是很大的誘惑。

☐ 三分熟
☐ 五分熟
☐ 七分熟
☐ 全熟

ten·ant [ˈtɛnənt]

名 承租人、房客
動 租賃
同 landlord 房東

英英 a person who pays rent for the use of land or a building

例 The **tenant** needs to pay the rent on the 15th of each month.
房客每月 15 號都要付房租。

☐ 三分熟
☐ 五分熟
☐ 七分熟
☐ 全熟

ten·ta·tive

[ˈtɛntətɪv]

形 暫時的

英英 not final or fully worked out

例 To find a part-time job is a **tentative** plan.
找兼差的工作是暫時的計畫。

☐ 二分熟
☐ 五分熟
☐ 十分熟
☐ 全熟

ter·mi·nal

[ˈtɝmən!]

名 終點、終站、碼頭
形 終點的

英英 the final stop; situated at the end

例 There's a busy fair near the ferry **terminal**.
在碼頭的附近有忙碌的市集。

☐ 三分熟
☐ 五分熟
☐ 七分熟
☐ 全熟

ter·race [ˈtɛrəs]

名 房屋的平頂、陽臺
動 使成梯形的

英英 a platform extending outdoors from a floor of a building; to make narrow strips of land

例 The **terrace** of the house is painted in blue.
這棟房子的陽臺油漆成藍色。

☐ 三分熟
☐ 五分熟
☐ 七分熟
☐ 全熟

🎧 Track 132

thigh [θaɪ]

名 大腿

英英 a platform extending outdoors from a floor of a building; to make narrow strips of land

例 Take some exercise to relax the strained **thigh**.
做些運動來放鬆緊繃的大腿。

☐ 三分熟
☐ 五分熟
☐ 七分熟
☐ 全熟

---

thorn [θɔrn]

名 刺、荊棘

英英 a small sharp pointed grow on the stem or other part of a plant

例 The **thorns** of the rose bring out its uniqueness.
玫瑰的刺彰顯其獨特之處。

☐ 三分熟
☐ 五分熟
☐ 七分熟
☐ 全熟

---

thrill [θrɪl]

名 戰慄
動 使激動
同 excite 使激動

英英 a feeling of excitement and pleasure; to make something excited

例 Vincent van Gogh's painting gave me a real **thrill**.
梵谷的畫作讓我激動不已。

☐ 三分熟
☐ 五分熟
☐ 七分熟
☐ 全熟

---

thrill·er [ˈθrɪlɚ]

名 恐怖小說、令人震顫的人事物

英英 a novel, play, or film with an exciting story, typically involving a crime

例 Stephen King is the master of horror and **thriller** novels.
史蒂芬・金是恐怖小說的大師。

☐ 三分熟
☐ 五分熟
☐ 七分熟
☐ 全熟

---

throne [θron]

名 王位、寶座

英英 a ceremonial chair for a ruler, especially a king or queen

例 Princes compete with each other to gain the **throne**.
王子們彼此競爭以取得王位。

☐ 三分熟
☐ 五分熟
☐ 七分熟
☐ 全熟

---

throng [θrɔn]

名 群眾
動 擠入

英英 a large and packed crowd; to go somewhere in very large numbers

例 A huge **throng** yelled loudly and pushed to move forward.
一大群人大聲喊叫，往前擠。

☐ 三分熟
☐ 五分熟
☐ 七分熟
☐ 全熟

---

thrust [θrʌst]

名 用力推
動 猛推
同 shove 推

英英 a sudden or violent push or attack

例 Clark **thrust** past the crowd to save a woman.
克拉克推開群眾去救一名女子。

☐ 三分熟
☐ 五分熟
☐ 七分熟
☐ 全熟

T

tick [tɪk]

名 滴答聲
動 發出滴答聲、標上記號

英英 the sound of clocks or watches make every second; of a clock or a watch, to make short, regular repeated sounds to mark time passing

例 The clock stops **ticking** at midnight.
這座鐘在半夜即停止發出滴答聲。

☐ 三分熟
☐ 五分熟
☐ 七分熟
☐ 全熟

---

tile [taɪl]

名 瓷磚
動 用瓦蓋
同 slope 傾斜

英英 a thin square or rectangular piece of baked clay, used for covering roofs, floors, or walls, etc.; to cover with a tiles

例 The floor **tiles** of the villa were imported from Italy.
這棟別墅的地板瓷磚是從義大利進口的。

☐ 三分熟
☐ 五分熟
☐ 七分熟
☐ 全熟

---

tilt [tɪlt]

動 傾斜、刺擊
同 pierce 刺穿

英英 a leaning position; to attack with a weapon

例 Jay's head **tilted** to one side, looking at Nicole curiously.
傑的腦袋傾向一邊，好奇地看著妮可。

☐ 三分熟
☐ 五分熟
☐ 七分熟
☐ 全熟

---

tin [tɪn]

名 錫
動 鍍錫

英英 a silvery-white chemical element, used for covering and protecting other metals; to cover with a layer of tin

例 Ancient Chinese people used **tin** and copper to make bronze ware.
古代中國人用錫和銅造銅器。

☐ 三分熟
☐ 五分熟
☐ 七分熟
☐ 全熟

---

tip·toe [ˈtɪpˌto]

名 腳尖
動 用腳尖走路
副 以腳尖著地

英英 to walk quietly and carefully with one's heels lifted off the ground

例 The thief **tiptoed** to enter the bedroom.
小偷用腳尖走路，進入臥房。

☐ 三分熟
☐ 五分熟
☐ 七分熟
☐ 全熟

---

toad [tod]

名 癩蛤蟆

英英 a brownish green animal, typically having dry warty skin that can exude poison

例 **Toads** are often associated with witches.
癩蛤蟆常跟巫婆聯想在一起。

☐ 三分熟
☐ 五分熟
☐ 七分熟
☐ 全熟

---

toil [tɔɪl]

名 辛勞
動 辛勞
反 leisure 悠閒

英英 to work extremely hard or incessantly

例 Farmers **toiled** on the land.
農夫們在土地上辛勞工作。

☐ 三分熟
☐ 五分熟
☐ 七分熟
☐ 全熟

🎧 **Track 134**

to·ken [ˈtokən]

名 表徵、代幣
同 sign 象徵

英英 a thing serving to represent a fact or feeling

例 The gift is nothing, just a **token** of our friendship.
這份禮物沒有什麼，只代表我們的友誼。

□ 三分熟
□ 五分熟
□ 七分熟
□ 全熟

torch [tɔrtʃ]

名 火炬、引火燃燒、手電筒

英英 a small light which is held in the hand and usually gets its power from a portable battery; to set fire to

例 The statue of liberty in New York held the **torch** high in the sky.
紐約的自由女神像高舉著火炬。

□ 三分熟
□ 五分熟
□ 七分熟
□ 全熟

tor·ment

[ˈtɔrˌmɛnt][tɔrˈmɛnt]

名 苦惱
動 使受苦、煩擾
同 comfort 安慰

英英 great physical or mental suffering; to make physical or mental suffer

例 The frustration of single-love has **tormented** her for almost a year.
單戀的挫折感已經困擾她將近一年。

□ 三分熟
□ 五分熟
□ 七分熟
□ 全熟

tor·rent [ˈtɔrɛnt]

名 洪流、急流
片 torrents of rain 傾盆大雨

英英 a strong and fast-moving stream of water

例 A lad was drowned in this **torrent**.
一名少年在急流中溺斃。

□ 三分熟
□ 五分熟
□ 七分熟
□ 全熟

tor·ture [ˈtɔrtʃɚ]

名 折磨、拷打
動 使……受折磨

英英 the acting of causing severe pain as a punishment or a forcible means of persuasion

例 The prisoner suffered terrible **torture** and died in the prison.
囚犯受到可怕的折磨，死在獄中。

□ 三分熟
□ 五分熟
□ 七分熟
□ 全熟

tour·na·ment

[ˈtɝnəmənt]

名 競賽、比賽
同 contest 競賽

英英 a series of contests between a number of competitors or groups

例 He has won the table tennis **tournament**.
他已經贏得桌球比賽。

□ 三分熟
□ 五分熟
□ 七分熟
□ 全熟

tox·ic [ˈtɑksɪk]

形 有毒的
同 poisonous 有毒的

英英 poisonous

例 The bottle of paint includes **toxic** substances.
這罐油漆含有毒物質。

□ 三分熟
□ 五分熟
□ 七分熟
□ 全熟

trade·mark

[ˈtredˌmɑrk]

名 標記、商標
同 brand 商標

英英 a symbol or words, legally registered, which is put on a product to show that is made by a particular company or producer

例 Triumph is a **trademark** of underwear.
黛安芬是內衣商標。

☐ 三分熟
☐ 五分熟
☐ 七分熟
☐ 全熟

trai·tor [ˈtretɚ]

名 叛徒

英英 a person who betrays their country or an organization

例 He feels guilty of being called a **traitor**.
他因為被叫做叛徒而感到內疚。

☐ 三分熟
☐ 五分熟
☐ 七分熟
☐ 全熟

tramp [træmp]

名 不定期貨船、長途跋涉、徒步旅行
動 踐踏、長途跋涉

英英 a long walk or journey by walking

例 My brothers went for a **tramp** to small villages in the mountain.
我的兄弟們長途跋涉到山裡的小村落。

☐ 三分熟
☐ 五分熟
☐ 七分熟
☐ 全熟

tram·ple [ˈtræmpl̩]

動 踐踏
名 踐踏、踐踏聲

英英 to tread on and crush something

例 Don't **trample** on the grassland.
不要踐踏草地。

☐ 三分熟
☐ 五分熟
☐ 七分熟
☐ 全熟

trans·par·ent

[trænsˈpɛrənt]

形 透明的

英英 allowing light to pass through so that objects behind can be clearly seen

例 Those shrimps look **transparent**.
那些蝦看起來呈現是透明的。

☐ 三分熟
☐ 五分熟
☐ 七分熟
☐ 全熟

trea·sur·y

[ˈtrɛʒərɪ]

名 寶庫、金庫、財政部

英英 a place in which treasure or money is kept

例 Tax revenue was the main source for the national **treasury**.
稅收是國庫的主要來源。

☐ 三分熟
☐ 五分熟
☐ 七分熟
☐ 全熟

trea·ty [ˈtritɪ]

名 協議、條約
同 contract 合約

英英 a formally concluded agreement between states and signed by their leaders

例 The two countries had signed a cultural exchange **treaty**.
兩國已簽署文化交流條約。

☐ 三分熟
☐ 五分熟
☐ 七分熟
☐ 全熟

trench [trɛntʃ]

名 溝、渠
動 挖溝渠
同 ditch 渠

英英 a long, narrow ditch; to dig a ditch

例 During war time, many soldiers died in the **trench**.
戰爭期間，許多士兵死在溝渠裡。

☐ 三分熟
☐ 五分熟
☐ 七分熟
☐ 全熟

🎧 **Track 136**

trib·ute [ˈtrɪbjut]

名 致敬、進貢

英英 an act, statement that is intended to show respect or admiration

例 Some people visited here to pay **tribute** to Princess Diana.
有些人造訪這裡，向黛安娜王妃致敬。

☐ 三分熟
☐ 五分熟
☐ 七分熟
☐ 全熟

---

tri·fle [ˈtraɪfl̩]

名 瑣事
動 疏忽、輕忽、戲弄

英英 a thing without value or importance; to do something carelessly

例 Ruby often argued with her sister for **trifles**.
露比常和姐姐因為瑣事爭吵。

☐ 三分熟
☐ 五分熟
☐ 七分熟
☐ 全熟

---

trim [trɪm]

名 修剪、整潔、整齊
動 整理、修剪、削減
形 整齊的、整潔的、苗條的
同 shave 修剪

英英 tidy and organized; to make something neat by cutting unwanted parts; cutting something to make it tider

例 I need to **trim** my hair this afternoon.
今天下午，我需要去整理我的頭髮。

☐ 三分熟
☐ 五分熟
☐ 七分熟
☐ 全熟

---

tri·ple [ˈtrɪpl̩]

名 三倍的數量
動 變成三倍
形 三倍的

英英 a thing that is three times as large as usual; to become three times as much; having three times the usual size or quality

例 If you offer **triple** payment, the detective will agree to work for you.
如果你付三倍的錢，那個偵探會答應為你工作。

☐ 三分熟
☐ 五分熟
☐ 七分熟
☐ 全熟

---

trot [trɑt]

動 使小跑步
名 小跑步
片 break into a trot
開始小跑了起來

英英 to run in small pace; a slow run

例 John came **trotting** down the street after his girlfriend.
約翰跟在他女友身後，沿著街道小跑著。

☐ 三分熟
☐ 五分熟
☐ 七分熟
☐ 全熟

---

trout [traʊt]

名 鱒魚

英英 an edible fish of the salmon family, which lives in rivers and lakes

例 The **trout** jumped energetically.
這隻鱒魚活蹦亂跳。

☐ 三分熟
☐ 五分熟
☐ 七分熟
☐ 全熟

---

tuck [tʌk]

名 縫褶
動 打褶、把……塞進

英英 a narrow fold sewn into something, especially a piece of material; to fold something

例 Greg **tucked** the shirt into his pants nervously.
葛列格緊張地把襯衫下擺塞進褲子裡。

☐ 三分熟
☐ 五分熟
☐ 七分熟
☐ 全熟

tu·i·tion [tjuˋɪʃən]

名 教學、講授、學費
同 instruction 教學

英英 teaching or instruction, especially given to individuals or small groups

例 Many college students take part-time jobs in order to pay the **tuition**.
很多的大學生打工是為了付學費。

□三分熟
□五分熟
□七分熟
□全熟

---

tu·na [ˋtunə]

名 鮪魚

英英 a large fish of warm seas

例 Put some **tuna** fish cans into your backpack.
把一些鮪魚罐頭放進你的背包裡。

□三分熟
□五分熟
□七分熟
□全熟

---

ty·rant [ˋtaɪrənt]

名 暴君、獨裁者

英英 a cruel and harsh ruler

例 People rebelled against the **tyrant**.
人民反抗暴君。

□三分熟
□五分熟
□七分熟
□全熟

Uu

🎧 Track 137

um·pire [ˋʌmpaɪr]

名 仲裁者、裁判員
動 擔任裁判
同 judge 裁判員

英英 an official who makes certain rules a particular game and settles disputes arising from the play; to play a role as an umpire

例 The **umpire** is not fair.
這名裁判員並不公平。

□ 三分熟
□ 五分熟
□ 七分熟
□ 全熟

un·der·grad·u·ate

[ˌʌndɚˋgrædʒʊɪt]

名 大學生

英英 a student at a university who has not have his first degree

例 The **undergraduate** cut two classes this morning.
該名大學生今天蹺了兩堂課。

□ 三分熟
□ 五分熟
□ 七分熟
□ 全熟

un·der·line

[ˌʌndɚˋlaɪn]

名 底線
動 畫底線

英英 (to draw) or a line drawn under a word

例 **Underline** the complete sentences.
在完整句子下畫底線。

□ 三分熟
□ 五分熟
□ 七分熟
□ 全熟

un·der·neath

[ˌʌndɚˋniθ]

介 在下面
同 below 在下面

英英 under or below

例 A ruler is **underneath** the table.
一把尺就在桌下。

□ 三分熟
□ 五分熟
□ 七分熟
□ 全熟

un·der·stand·a·ble

[ˌʌndɚˋstændəbl]

形 可理解的

英英 be able to be understood

例 Her situation of being bullied is **understandable**.
她被霸凌的情況是可以理解的。

□ 三分熟
□ 五分熟
□ 七分熟
□ 全熟

un·doubt·ed·ly

[ʌnˋdaʊtɪdlɪ]

副 無庸置疑地

英英 ot questioned or doubted by anyone

例 **Undoubtedly**, Emily is the most popular girl in our school.
無庸置疑地，愛蜜莉是我們學校最受歡迎的女孩。

□ 三分熟
□ 五分熟
□ 七分熟
□ 全熟

up·date [ʌpˋdet]

名 最新資訊
動 更新
片 fully updated 完全更新

英英 the newest information; to make more modern; to give the latest information to

例 Login in the website and **update** your personal information.
登入此網址，更新你的個人資訊。

□ 三分熟
□ 五分熟
□ 七分熟
□ 全熟

up·right [ˈʌpˌraɪt]

名 直立的姿勢
形 直立的
副 直立地
同 erect 直立的

英英 a straight up or vertical post; very straight

例 It seemed weird to see a dog stand **upright** like a man.
看到狗像人一樣直立起來，似乎很奇怪。

☐ 三分熟
☐ 五分熟
☐ 七分熟
☐ 全熟

up·ward(s)

[ˈʌpwəd(z)]

形 向上的
副 向上地
同 downward 向下

英英 moving or leading towards a higher position

例 Walk **upwards** and you'll be there soon.
往上走，你很快地會到那裡。

☐ 三分熟
☐ 五分熟
☐ 七分熟
☐ 全熟

ut·ter [ˈʌtɚ]

形 完全的
動 發言、發出
同 complete 完全的

英英 complete, absolute; to say something

例 What she **uttered** was a lie.
她所說的話全是謊言。

☐ 三分熟
☐ 五分熟
☐ 七分熟
☐ 全熟

U

Vv

🔊 **Track 139**

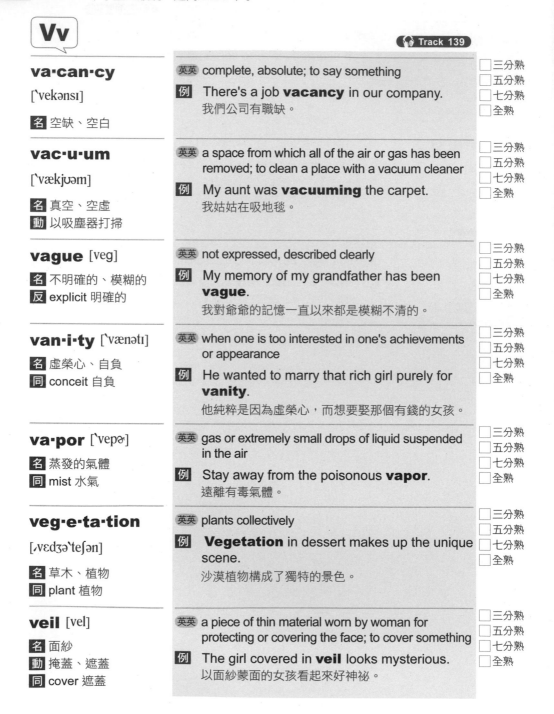

va·can·cy

[`vekənsɪ]

名 空缺、空白

英英 complete, absolute; to say something

例 There's a job **vacancy** in our company.
我們公司有職缺。

☐ 三分熟
☐ 五分熟
☐ 七分熟
☐ 全熟

vac·u·um

[`vækjʊəm]

名 真空、空虛
動 以吸塵器打掃

英英 a space from which all of the air or gas has been removed; to clean a place with a vacuum cleaner

例 My aunt was **vacuuming** the carpet.
我姑姑在吸地毯。

☐ 三分熟
☐ 五分熟
☐ 七分熟
☐ 全熟

vague [veg]

名 不明確的、模糊的
反 explicit 明確的

英英 not expressed, described clearly

例 My memory of my grandfather has been **vague**.
我對爺爺的記憶一直以來都是模糊不清的。

☐ 三分熟
☐ 五分熟
☐ 七分熟
☐ 全熟

van·i·ty [`vænətɪ]

名 虛榮心、自負
同 conceit 自負

英英 when one is too interested in one's achievements or appearance

例 He wanted to marry that rich girl purely for **vanity**.
他純粹是因為虛榮心，而想要娶那個有錢的女孩。

☐ 三分熟
☐ 五分熟
☐ 七分熟
☐ 全熟

va·por [`vepɚ]

名 蒸發的氣體
同 mist 水氣

英英 gas or extremely small drops of liquid suspended in the air

例 Stay away from the poisonous **vapor**.
遠離有毒氣體。

☐ 三分熟
☐ 五分熟
☐ 七分熟
☐ 全熟

veg·e·ta·tion

[ˌvɛdʒəˋteʃən]

名 草木、植物
同 plant 植物

英英 plants collectively

例 **Vegetation** in dessert makes up the unique scene.
沙漠植物構成了獨特的景色。

☐ 三分熟
☐ 五分熟
☐ 七分熟
☐ 全熟

veil [vel]

名 面紗
動 掩蓋、遮蓋
同 cover 遮蓋

英英 a piece of thin material worn by woman for protecting or covering the face; to cover something

例 The girl covered in **veil** looks mysterious.
以面紗蒙面的女孩看起來好神祕。

☐ 三分熟
☐ 五分熟
☐ 七分熟
☐ 全熟

vein [ven]

名 靜脈
反 artery 動脈

英英 tubes by which blood is conveyed from all parts of the body towards the heart

例 The nurse has found the **vein** and made an injection for David.
護士找到了大衛的靜脈，也為其打針了。

☐ 三分熟
☐ 五分熟
☐ 七分熟
☐ 全熟

---

vel·vet [ˈvɛlvɪt]

名 天鵝絨
形 柔軟的、平滑的、天鵝絨製的
同 soft 柔軟的

英英 a closely woven tabric of silk or cotton with a thin soft furry; very soft and smooth

例 The green **velvet** dress suits Betty.
這條綠色天鵝絨洋裝很適合貝蒂。

☐ 三分熟
☐ 五分熟
☐ 七分熟
☐ 全熟

---

ven·ture [ˈvɛntʃɚ]

名 冒險
動 以……為賭注、冒險

英英 a risky or daring journey or uncertainty; to dare to do something risky

例 They are well-prepared and dare to **venture** into the jungle.
他們準備充份，膽敢進入叢林冒險。

☐ 三分熟
☐ 五分熟
☐ 七分熟
☐ 全熟

---

ver·bal [ˈvɝbḷ]

形 言詞上的、口頭的
同 oral 口頭的

英英 relating to words

例 The **verbal** abuse forced the girl to do foolish things.
言語暴力讓女孩做了傻事。

☐ 三分熟
☐ 五分熟
☐ 七分熟
☐ 全熟

---

ver·sus [ˈvɝsəs]

介 ……對……
（縮寫為 vs.）

英英 against; in contrast to

例 Italy's football team **versus** Brazil's football team, which team will win?
義大利的橄欖球隊對巴西的橄欖球隊，哪一隊會贏？

☐ 三分熟
☐ 五分熟
☐ 七分熟
☐ 全熟

---

ver·ti·cal [ˈvɝtɪkḷ]

名 垂直線、垂直面
形 垂直的、豎的

英英 a vertical line or surface; having the top; having the top directly above the bottom

例 The coat with the **vertical** stripes matches the white pants well.
有垂直線條的大衣與白色褲子十分搭配。

☐ 三分熟
☐ 五分熟
☐ 七分熟
☐ 全熟

---

ve·to [ˈvito]

名 否決
動 否決
同 deny 否定

英英 refusal to something or refusal to allow something to be done

例 The president has promised to **veto** the bill.
總統已承諾否決該議案。

☐ 三分熟
☐ 五分熟
☐ 七分熟
☐ 全熟

🎧 **Track 141**

---

vi·a [ˈvaɪə]

介 經由
同 through 經由

英英 through; by; using

例 The couple contacts each other **via** the communication software.
這對情侶經由通訊軟體相互聯絡彼此。

☐ 三分熟
☐ 五分熟
☐ 七分熟
☐ 全熟

---

vi·brate [ˈvaɪbret]

動 震動

英英 to move with small movements quickly

例 Your cellphone is **vibrating**.
你的手機在震動。

☐ 三分熟
☐ 五分熟
☐ 七分熟
☐ 全熟

---

video·tape

[ˈvɪdɪoˌtep]

名 錄影帶
動 錄影

英英 a video cassette; to record something with a video cassette

例 **Videotape** the baby's swimming with his father.
錄影帶裡嬰兒和他的父親一起游泳。

☐ 三分熟
☐ 五分熟
☐ 七分熟
☐ 全熟

---

view·er [ˈvjuə]

名 觀看者、電視觀眾
同 spectator 旁觀者
片 attract viewers
吸引觀看者

英英 a person who views something, especially TV programs

例 Analyze the data of **viewers**.
分析觀看者的資料。

☐ 三分熟
☐ 五分熟
☐ 七分熟
☐ 全熟

---

vig·or [ˈvɪgə]

名 精力、活力
同 energy 精力

英英 physical strength, energy, and enthusiasm

例 Billy completed the job with **vigor**.
比利活力十足地完成這份工作。

☐ 三分熟
☐ 五分熟
☐ 七分熟
☐ 全熟

---

vig·or·ous

[ˈvɪgərəs]

形 有活力的
同 energetic 有活力的

英英 strong and full of energy

例 Grandma is 85, and is still **vigorous**.
奶奶 85 歲了，還是很有活力。

☐ 三分熟
☐ 五分熟
☐ 七分熟
☐ 全熟

---

vil·lain [ˈvɪlən]

名 惡棍
同 rascal 惡棍

英英 a person who is guilty or harms other people

例 The **villain** pretends to be good.
惡棍假裝是好人。

☐ 三分熟
☐ 五分熟
☐ 七分熟
☐ 全熟

---

vine [vaɪn]

名 葡萄樹、藤蔓

英英 a climbing or trailing plant which produces grapes as its fruit

例 The fox looks at the grapes on the **vine**.
狐狸看著葡萄樹上的葡萄。

☐ 三分熟
☐ 五分熟
☐ 七分熟
☐ 全熟

---

vi·o·lin·ist

[ˌvaɪəˈlɪnɪst]

名 小提琴手

英英 a person who plays violin

例 The **violinist** with the pianist will give us a great show tonight.
小提琴手搭鋼琴家，將在今晚呈現精采的表演。

□三分熟
□五分熟
□七分熟
□全熟

vi·sa [ˈvizə]

名 簽證

英英 an official mark on a passport which is allowed a person to enter, leave, or stay for a specified period of time in a country

例 You don't need a **visa** if you'd like to go to Japan.
如果你想去日本，你並不需要簽證。

□三分熟
□五分熟
□七分熟
□全熟

vow [vaʊ]

名 誓約、誓言
動 立誓、發誓
同 swear 發誓

英英 (to make) a solemn promise or decision

例 Carol made a **vow** not to go nightclubs.
卡蘿發誓不再上夜店。

□三分熟
□五分熟
□七分熟
□全熟

Ww

wade [wed]

名 涉水、跋涉
動 艱辛地進行、跋涉

英英 to walk through water or mud

例 The travel guide **waded** across the river.
導遊涉水過河。

□三分熟
□五分熟
□七分熟
□全熟

wail [wel]

名 哀泣
動 哭泣

英英 a long high-pitched cry of pain or anger

例 Her **wailing** gives us goose bumps.
她的哀泣讓我們起雞皮疙瘩。

□三分熟
□五分熟
□七分熟
□全熟

ward [wɔrd]

名 行政區、守護、病房
動 守護、避開
同 avoid 避開

英英 an area of a city or a country, which has its own organizations for managing services; to prevent from harming

例 He was in the cancer **ward**.
他在癌症安寧病房。

□三分熟
□五分熟
□十分熟
□全熟

ware [wɛr]

名 製品、貨品

英英 manufactured products or goods

例 The shop sells a great variety of blue-and-white ware.
這家商店出售種類繁多的青花瓷器。

□三分熟
□五分熟
□七分熟
□全熟

🎧 **Track 143**

ware·house

[ˈwɛrˌhaʊs]

名 倉庫、貨棧
動 將貨物存放於倉庫中

英英 a large building where manufactured products are stored; to put the goods or products in a large building

例 We need to help our **warehouse** co-workers this afternoon.
我們今天下午需要幫忙倉庫的同事。

☐ 三分熟
☐ 五分熟
☐ 七分熟
☐ 全熟

---

war·rior [ˈwɔrɪɚ]

名 武士、戰士
同 fighter 戰士

英英 a soldier or fighter who is brave and experienced in fighting

例 Avita is a cyborg **warrior**.
艾薇塔是個半機器半人類的戰士。

☐ 三分熟
☐ 五分熟
☐ 七分熟
☐ 全熟

---

war·y [ˈwɛrɪ]

形 注意的、小心的
同 cautious 小心的

英英 cautious about possible dangers; be very careful about something

例 Be **wary** of the mudslide in the mountain.
小心山裡的土石流。

☐ 三分熟
☐ 五分熟
☐ 七分熟
☐ 全熟

---

wea·ry [ˈwɪrɪ]

形 疲倦的
動 使疲倦

英英 tired or exhausted; to become or make tired or exhausted

例 **Weary** mothers need to know how to take care of themselves.
疲倦的母親必需知道如何照顧自己。

☐ 三分熟
☐ 五分熟
☐ 七分熟
☐ 全熟

---

weird [wɪrd]

形 怪異的、不可思議的
同 strange 奇怪的

英英 very strange, bizarre and impossible to believe

例 It is **weird** that the tiger takes the pig as its friend.
這隻老虎竟把豬當成朋友，真是不可思議。

☐ 三分熟
☐ 五分熟
☐ 七分熟
☐ 全熟

---

wharf [hwɔrf]

名 碼頭
同 pier 碼頭

英英 an area where a ship may be moored to load and unload

例 There will be one more deep-water **wharf** here.
這邊會再多一個深水碼頭。

☐ 三分熟
☐ 五分熟
☐ 七分熟
☐ 全熟

---

where·a·bouts

[ˈhwɛrəbaʊts]

名 所在的地方
副 在何處
同 location 位置、所在地

英英 the place where someone or something is; where

例 The little girl's family is anxious to know the **whereabouts** of her.
小女孩的家人急著知道她的下落。

☐ 三分熟
☐ 五分熟
☐ 七分熟
☐ 全熟

where·as

[hwɛrˋæz]

連 雖然、卻、然而

英英 but; although

例 I finished cleaning three rooms, **whereas** May finished one.
我打掃了三間房，然而梅卻只完成了一間。

---

whine [hwaɪn]

名 哀泣聲、嗚嗚聲
動 發牢騷、怨聲載道

英英 a long, high-pitched cry; to complain in a feeble way

例 Can't you stop **whining** about your life?
你難道不能停止抱怨你的人生？

---

whirl [hwɝl]

名 迴轉
動 旋轉
同 turn 旋轉

英英 a rapid movement round and round; to move rapidly round and round

例 Her stepdaughter walked into the **whirling** snow.
她的繼女走進飛旋的雪花中。

---

whisk [hwɪsk]

名 小掃帚
動 掃、揮
同 sweep 掃

英英 a bunch of grass for flicking away dust or flies; to sweep with a cleaning tool

例 Use the **whisk** to get rid of the dirt.
用小掃帚清除灰塵。

---

whis·key/

whis·ky [ˋhwɪskɪ]

名 威士忌

英英 a strong alcoholic drink, originally from Scotland and Ireland, made from grain

例 He likes his **whiskey** neat.
他喜歡純威士忌。

---

whole·sale

[ˋholˌsel]

名 批發
動 批發賣出
形 批發的、大批的、成批的

英英 the selling of goods in large amounts to be retailed by others; to sell goods in large amounts

例 The batch of children's clothing was sold out in **wholesale** price.
這批童裝以批發價賣出。

---

whole·some

[ˋholsəm]

形 有益健康的
反 harmful 有害的

英英 good for health and physical or moral well-being

例 Yogurt is a kind of **wholesome** food.
優格是有益健康的食品。

🎧 **Track 145**

---

wide·spread

[ˋwaɪdˌsprɛd]

形 流傳很廣的、廣泛的
同 extensive 廣泛的

英英 spread around a group of people or over a large area

例 The legend is **widespread**.
這則傳說流傳很廣。

□ 三分熟
□ 五分熟
□ 七分熟
□ 全熟

**wid·ow/
wid·ow·er**

[ˋwɪdo]/[ˋwɪdəwɚ]

名 寡婦／鰥夫

英英 a woman / a man who has lost her husband / his wife by death and still keeps single

例 Mary used to be a happy **widow**.
瑪麗以前是個快樂的寡婦。

□ 三分熟
□ 五分熟
□ 七分熟
□ 全熟

---

wig [wɪg]

名 假髮

英英 artificial hair

例 The judge wears a **wig**.
法官戴一頂假髮。

□ 三分熟
□ 五分熟
□ 七分熟
□ 全熟

---

wil·der·ness

[ˋwɪldənɪs]

名 荒野

英英 an uncultivated and uninhabited area

例 To survive in the **wilderness** is challenging.
在荒野求生是件有挑戰的事。

□ 三分熟
□ 五分熟
□ 七分熟
□ 全熟

---

wild·life

[ˋwaɪldˌlaɪf]

名 野生生物

英英 the native living creatures of a region

例 To protect the **wildlife** in this area is our duty.
保護這個區域的野生生物是我們的責任。

□ 三分熟
□ 五分熟
□ 七分熟
□ 全熟

---

with·er [ˋwɪðɚ]

動 枯萎、凋謝
同 fade 枯萎、凋謝

英英 to become shrunken or weak from age or disease

例 Flowers grow and then **wither**.
花兒生長，然後凋謝。

□ 三分熟
□ 五分熟
□ 七分熟
□ 全熟

---

woe [wo]

名 悲哀、悲痛
同 sorrow 悲痛

英英 great sorrow or distress

例 The letter is surely full of a mother's **woe**.
這封信的確滿溢母親的悲痛。

□ 三分熟
□ 五分熟
□ 七分熟
□ 全熟

---

wood·peck·er

[ˋwʊdˌpɛkɚ]

名 啄木鳥

英英 a bird with a strong bill and a stiff tail, typically making holes to find insects on a tree

例 The **woodpecker's** beak is strong.
啄木鳥的鳥喙強而有力。

□ 三分熟
□ 五分熟
□ 七分熟
□ 全熟

---

work·shop

[ˈwɝkˌʃɑp]

名 小工廠、研討會

英英 a meeting for people to discuss a subject or perform practical work

例 Tim taught us how to make paper cutting in a **workshop**.
提姆在研討會中教我們如何做紙雕。

---

wor·ship [ˈwɝʃɪp]

名 禮拜
動 做禮拜

英英 religious ceremonies (in a church); to show a strong respect and admiration for God

例 Angie **worships** weekly.
安琪每週都做禮拜。

---

worth·while

[ˈwɝθˈhwaɪl]

形 值得的
同 worthy 值得的

英英 worth the time, money, or effort spent

例 It is **worthwhile** to let my son go to the cram school.
讓我的兒子上補習班是值得的。

---

wor·thy [ˈwɝðɪ]

形 有價值的、值得的

英英 something or someone important in a particular sphere; valuable

例 This is a **worthy** novel.
這是一本值得讀的小說。

---

wreath [riθ]

名 花環、花圈

英英 an arrangement of flowers, leaves, or stems fastened in a ring and used for decoration

例 The bridal **wreath** is a piece of art.
這個新娘花圈是藝術傑作。

---

wring [rɪŋ]

名 絞、絞扭、擰掉（水）
動 握緊、絞
同 twist 絞、扭

英英 to squeeze and twist to force liquid from

例 He **wrung** out some T-shirts.
他擰乾了一些 T 恤。

W

Yy

🎧 Track 147

yacht [jɑt]

名 遊艇
動 駕駛遊艇、乘遊艇

英英 a medium-sized sailing boat used for racing or travelling; to cruise in a medium-sized sailing boat

例 Bill's dream is to buy a luxury **yacht** and travel around the world.
比爾的夢想是買艘遊艇，環遊世界。

☐ 三分熟
☐ 五分熟
☐ 七分熟
☐ 全熟

---

yarn [jɑrn]

名 冒險故事、紗
動 講故事

英英 a long or rambling story; spun thread used for making clothes or sewing; to tell a long or rambling story

例 The **yarn** excites children's imagination.
這則冒險故事激起孩子們的想像力。

☐ 三分熟
☐ 五分熟
☐ 七分熟
☐ 全熟

---

yeast [jist]

名 酵母、發酵粉

英英 a microscopic fungus capable of converting sugar into alcohol and carbon dioxide

例 The bread includes high-vitamin **yeast**.
這塊麵包含有高維他命的酵母。

☐ 三分熟
☐ 五分熟
☐ 七分熟
☐ 全熟

---

yield [jild]

名 產出
動 生產、讓出
同 produce 生產

英英 to produce or provide something, such as a natural, agricultural, or industrial product

例 We should work hard to help the company **yield** profits.
我們要努力工作，幫忙公司產出利潤。

☐ 三分熟
☐ 五分熟
☐ 七分熟
☐ 全熟

---

yo·ga [ˈjogə]

名 瑜珈

英英 a Hindu spiritual and ascetic discipline, a part of which, including breath control, simple meditation, and the adoption of specific bodily postures, is widely practiced for health and relaxation

例 They attended the **yoga** class together.
他們一起去上瑜珈課。

☐ 三分熟
☐ 五分熟
☐ 七分熟
☐ 全熟

Zz

zinc [zɪŋk]

名 鋅
動 鍍鋅

英英 a silvery-white metallic chemical element which is a constituent of brass and is used for making iron and steel; to make something coated with zinc

例 **Zinc** makes your immune system strong.
鋅讓你的免疫系統強壯。

☐ 三分熟
☐ 五分熟
☐ 七分熟
☐ 全熟

---

zip [zɪp]

名 尖嘯聲、拉鍊
動 呼嘯而過、拉開或扣上拉鍊
片 the zip is stuck
拉鍊卡住

英英 a fastener consisting of two row of metal or plastic with interlocking projections closed or opened by pulling a slide along them; to move at high speed

例 **Zip** your jacket.
把夾克的拉鍊拉上。

☐ 三分熟
☐ 五分熟
☐ 七分熟
☐ 全熟

ZIP [zɪp]

名 郵遞區號

英英 series of numbers that forms part of an address, usually used to help organize post so that it can be delivered faster

例 You can find the **zip** code you want through the website.
你可以透過這個網站找到你要的郵遞區號。

☐ 三分熟
☐ 五分熟
☐ 七分熟
☐ 全熟

---

zoom [zum]

動 調整焦距使物體放大或縮小

英英 to move or travel very quickly

例 The camera **zoomed** in to focus on the leaving train.
鏡頭拉近，聚焦在離去的火車。

☐ 三分熟
☐ 五分熟
☐ 七分熟
☐ 全熟

Y
Z

Level 6 音檔雲端連結

因各家手機系統不同，若無法直接掃描，
仍可以至以下電腦雲端連結下載收聽。
（https://tinyurl.com/428s4rnk）

Level 6

英文力
全面提升

挑戰
7000單字

Aa

Track 149

---

ab·bre·vi·ate
[əˈbrivɪˌet]

動 將……縮寫成
同 shorten 縮短

英英 to shorten words or phrases

例 The United Nations Education, Scientific and Cultural Organization is **abbreviated** as UNESCO.
聯合國教育科學與文化組織被縮寫成 UNESCO。

□ 三分熟
□ 五分熟
□ 七分熟
□ 全熟

---

ab·bre·vi·a·tion
[əˌbrivɪˈeʃən]

名 縮寫

英英 a form of shortening a word or a phrase, used especially in writing

例 CFO is the **abbreviation** of "Chief Financial Officer."
CFO 是「首席財務官」的縮寫。

□ 三分熟
□ 五分熟
□ 七分熟
□ 全熟

---

ab·nor·mal
[æbˈnɔrml̩]

形 反常的

英英 different from what is considered normal

例 The **abnormal** rise in temperature causes concern of the environmental protectionists.
反常的氣溫上升，引起環境保護份子的擔心。

□ 三分熟
□ 五分熟
□ 七分熟
□ 全熟

---

ab·o·rig·i·nal
[ˌæbəˈrɪdʒənl̩]

名 土著、原住民
形 土著的、原始的
片 aboriginal language 原住民語言

英英 describes a person or living thing that has inhabited or existed on a land from the earliest times or from before the arrival of colonists; indigenous

例 Professor Chou devotes herself in revitalizing the **aboriginal** languages.
周教授致力於恢復原住民語言。

□ 三分熟
□ 五分熟
□ 七分熟
□ 全熟

---

ab·o·rig·i·ne
[ˌæbəˈrɪdʒəni]

名 原住民

英英 an aboriginal person, animal, or plant

例 The local government offers education subsidies to the **aborigines**.
當地政府提供教育補助給原住民。

□ 三分熟
□ 五分熟
□ 七分熟
□ 全熟

---

a·bound [əˈbaʊnd]

動 充滿
同 overflow 充滿

英英 to be full of, or exist in large numbers or amounts

例 Her lyrics **abounds** in metaphors and similes.
她的歌詞中充滿暗喻與明喻。

□ 三分熟
□ 五分熟
□ 七分熟
□ 全熟

---

ab·sent·mind·ed

[ˈæbsn̩tˈmaɪndɪd]

形 茫然的

英英 someone who is inattentive, forgetful, or isn't clear about what is happening around them

例 The drunk driver appeared **absentminded** when he was stopped by the police officer.
酒醉駕駛被警察攔下時顯得很茫然。

□ 三分熟
□ 五分熟
□ 七分熟
□ 全熟

ab·strac·tion

[æbˈstrækʃən]

名 抽象、出神

英英 a very general topic that isn't based on real situations

例 The **abstraction** in her talk made the whole lecture rather obscure.
她演講中的抽象特色使得整個演講相當難懂。

□ 三分熟
□ 五分熟
□ 七分熟
□ 全熟

a·bun·dance

[əˈbʌndəns]

名 充裕、富足

英英 a very large amount of something

例 The **abundance** of rain in this region makes it a suitable place to grow tea plant.
此區域充足的雨量，適合種植茶葉植物。

□ 三分熟
□ 五分熟
□ 七分熟
□ 全熟

a·buse [əˈbjuz]

名 濫用、虐待
動 濫用、虐待、傷害
同 injure 傷害

英英 to use something excessively, or improperly

例 The man was accused of **abusing** endangered animals.
這名男子遭指控虐待瀕危動物。

□ 三分熟
□ 五分熟
□ 七分熟
□ 全熟

ac·cel·er·ate

[ækˈsɛləˌret]

動 促進、加速進行

英英 to increase in speed, begin or cause to move more quickly

例 It takes the car 10 seconds to **accelerate** from 0 m/ph to 60 m/ph.
這輛車可以用 10 秒從零加速到每小時 60 英里。

□ 三分熟
□ 五分熟
□ 七分熟
□ 全熟

ac·cel·er·a·tion

[ækˌsɛləˈreʃən]

名 加速、促進

英英 the ability to increase in speed

例 I have difficulty distinguishing the concepts of velocity and **acceleration**.
我分不清楚速度和加速度的概念。

□ 三分熟
□ 五分熟
□ 七分熟
□ 全熟

ac·ces·si·ble

[ækˈsɛsəbl̩]

形 可親的、容易接近的、可使用的

英英 easily obtained, or reached

例 There are a lot of online learning resources **accessible** for the public.
有很多線上學習資源供大眾利用。

□ 三分熟
□ 五分熟
□ 七分熟
□ 全熟

ac·ces·so·ry

[ækˈsɛsərɪ]

名 附件、零件、幫兇、配件
形 附屬的

英英 a thing which can be added to something else to make it more useful, versatile, or attractive; supplementary

例 The **accessories** in this outfit shop are in sale.
這家服飾店的飾品特價中。

□ 三分熟
□ 五分熟
□ 七分熟
□ 全熟

A

🎧 **Track 151**

ac·com·mo·date

[əˋkɑmə͵det]

動 能容納、使⋯⋯適
應、提供

同 conform 適應

英英 to provide sufficient space for lodging or storage

例 The theater can **accommodate** over two thousand viewers.
這間劇院可容納兩千名觀眾。

- [ ] 三分熟
- [ ] 五分熟
- [ ] 七分熟
- [ ] 全熟

ac·com·mo·da·tion

[ə͵kɑməˋdeʃən]

名 便利、適應、住宿

英英 making suitable or becoming suitable

例 They are looking for suitable **accommodation** in Sydney.
他們正在尋找雪梨適合住宿的地點。

- [ ] 三分熟
- [ ] 五分熟
- [ ] 七分熟
- [ ] 全熟

ac·cord [əˋkɔrd]

名 一致、和諧
動 和⋯⋯一致
片 accord with
與⋯⋯符合

英英 give or grant someone with (power or recognition)

例 His self-introduction did not **accord** with what he stated in his resume.
她自我介紹的內容和履歷表上寫的不一致。

- [ ] 三分熟
- [ ] 五分熟
- [ ] 七分熟
- [ ] 全熟

ac·cor·dance

[əˋkɔrdn̩s]

名 給予、根據、依照
片 in accordance with
依照

英英 in a manner agreeing or conforming with a law, rule, wish, etc.

例 The guidelines of the association are established in **accordance** with the relevant laws.
本協會的章程是依照相關法令制定的。

- [ ] 三分熟
- [ ] 五分熟
- [ ] 七分熟
- [ ] 全熟

ac·cord·ing·ly

[əˋkɔrdɪŋlɪ]

副 因此、於是、相應地

英英 in a way that is appropriate to the particular circumstances; consequently; therefore

例 Both parties agree with the terms in the contract and will act **accordingly**.
兩方都同意合約的條款，並將採取相應地行動。

- [ ] 三分熟
- [ ] 五分熟
- [ ] 七分熟
- [ ] 全熟

ac·count·a·ble

[əˋkaʊntəbl̩]

形 應負責的、有責
任的、可說明的
同 responsible 有責任的

英英 required, held responsible for, or expected to justify actions or decisions

例 The director is **accountable** for the execution of the project.
主任負責這個計畫的執行。

- [ ] 三分熟
- [ ] 五分熟
- [ ] 七分熟
- [ ] 全熟

ac·count·ing

[əˋkaʊntɪŋ]

名 會計、會計學

英英 to increase, or gather together a number or quantity of the keeping of financial records

例 The **accounting** majors are required to obtain the professional certificate before they graduate.
主修會計的學生被要求要在畢業前取得專業證照。

- [ ] 三分熟
- [ ] 五分熟
- [ ] 七分熟
- [ ] 全熟

A

ac·cu·mu·late
[əˈkjumjəˌlet]

動 累積、積蓄
同 gather 聚集

英英 an amount of something that has been gathered

例 Mr. Guo **accumulated** a large sum of fortune over the years.
郭先生多年來累積了大筆的財富。

☐ 三分熟
☐ 五分熟
☐ 七分熟
☐ 全熟

ac·cu·mu·la·tion
[əˌkjumjəˈleʃən]

名 累積

英英 to charge or claim that someone has done something illegal or wrong

例 Education is not about the **accumulation** of knowledge but cultivation of good attitude in learning.
教育不是在累積知識，而是在發展好的學習態度。

☐ 三分熟
☐ 五分熟
☐ 七分熟
☐ 全熟

ac·cu·sa·tion
[ˌækjəˈzeʃən]

名 控告、罪名

英英 a statement saying that someone has done something morally wrong, illegal, or unkind, or the fact of accusing someone

例 The politician denied the **accusation** of bribery.
政治人物否認了賄選的指控。

☐ 三分熟
☐ 五分熟
☐ 七分熟
☐ 全熟

ac·qui·si·tion
[ˌækwəˈzɪʃən]

名 獲得、取得

英英 the act of acquiring

例 The **acquisition** of property should be conducted in accordance with the following guidelines.
資產的取得，應遵照下列的規定。

☐ 三分熟
☐ 五分熟
☐ 七分熟
☐ 全熟

ac·tiv·ist
[ˈæktɪvɪst]

名 行動者

英英 someone who tries to cause political or social change with the use of vigorous campaigning

例 Several political **activists** are arrested in the illegal demonstration.
有幾位政治行動者在非法抗議行動中遭到逮補。

☐ 三分熟
☐ 五分熟
☐ 七分熟
☐ 全熟

a·cute [əˈkjut]

形 敏銳的、激烈的
同 keen 敏銳的

英英 something that is extremely bad, critical, or serious

例 The runner felt **acute** pain in his ankle when approaching the goal.
跑者在接近終點的時候感覺腳踝激烈疼痛。

☐ 三分熟
☐ 五分熟
☐ 七分熟
☐ 全熟

ad·ap·ta·tion
[ˌædəpˈteʃən]

名 適應、順應、改編

英英 the action or process of adapting or being adapted

例 The new movie **adaptation** of Aladdin was very popular.
阿拉丁的新版電影改編相當受歡迎。

☐ 三分熟
☐ 五分熟
☐ 七分熟
☐ 全熟

🎧 Track 153

ad·dict

[ˋædɪkt]/[əˋdɪkt]

名 有毒癮的人
動 對……有癮、使入迷

英英 a person who cannot stop taking a drug or doing something; to cause someone to be dependent on something

例 He is a social media **addict** who could never spend a day without his smartphone.
他是社群媒體上癮者，不能一天沒有手機在身邊。

☐ 三分熟
☐ 五分熟
☐ 七分熟
☐ 全熟

ad·dic·tion

[əˋdɪkʃən]

名 熱衷、上癮

英英 when you cannot stop doing or taking something because you are addicted to it; the fact or condition of being addicted

例 His **addiction** to online games has hindered his academic achievement.
他對線上遊戲成癮，影響了學業成績。

☐ 三分熟
☐ 五分熟
☐ 七分熟
☐ 全熟

ad·min·is·ter/ ad·min·is·trate

[ədˋmɪnəstɚ]/
[ədˋmɪnəˏstret]

動 管理、照料

英英 to arrange, to organize, or the use of something

例 The CFO **administers** the budget and financing for the company.
財務長管理公司的預算和財經事務。

☐ 三分熟
☐ 五分熟
☐ 七分熟
☐ 全熟

ad·min·is·tra·tion

[ədˏmɪnəˋstreʃən]

名 經營、管理、政府
同 government 管理

英英 the work of organizing or arranging of a business or system

例 The **administration** has not made any response to the students' request.
當局還未針對學生的要求予以回應。

☐ 三分熟
☐ 五分熟
☐ 七分熟
☐ 全熟

ad·min·is·tra·tive

[ədˋmɪnəˏstretɪv]

形 行政上的、管理上的

英英 relating to the administration and organization of something; carry out administration

例 The civil servants are just fulfilling their **administrative** duties.
這些公務人員只是在行使管理職務。

☐ 三分熟
☐ 五分熟
☐ 七分熟
☐ 全熟

ad·min·is·tra·tor

[ədˋmɪnəˏstretɚ]

名 管理者

英英 someone whose job is to control the operation of a business, organization or plan

例 The **administrator** of the bulletin board will delete posts of offensive remarks.
留言板的管理者會刪除有冒犯言論的貼文。

☐ 三分熟
☐ 五分熟
☐ 七分熟
☐ 全熟

A

ad·vo·cate

[ˈædvəkɪt]/[ˈædvəˌket]

名 提倡者
動 提倡、主張
同 support 擁護

英英 a person who publicly supports or recommends a particular cause, policy, or way of doing things; to recommend or support

例 Martin Luther King is an **advocate** of peaceful protests.
馬丁路德是和平抗爭的倡導者。

☐ 三分熟
☐ 五分熟
☐ 七分熟
☐ 全熟

af·fec·tion·ate

[əˈfɛkʃənɪt]

形 摯愛的

英英 readily showing love or like for someone or something

例 Mr. and Mrs. Smith are an **affectionate** couple.
史密斯夫婦是一對恩愛的夫妻。

☐ 三分熟
☐ 五分熟
☐ 七分熟
☐ 全熟

af·firm [əˈfɝm]

動 斷言、證實
同 declare 斷言

英英 to state that something is true; emphatically or publicly

例 They **affirm** that receiving education is a human right.
他們斷言受教育是人權的一種。

☐ 三分熟
☐ 五分熟
☐ 七分熟
☐ 全熟

ag·gres·sion

[əˈgrɛʃən]

名 進攻、侵略

英英 hostile or violent behavior or attitudes toward someone

例 His verbal **aggression** on the conference was condemned by the other attendees.
他在會議上的言語攻擊受到其他與會者的譴責。

☐ 三分熟
☐ 五分熟
☐ 七分熟
☐ 全熟

al·co·hol·ic

[ˌælkəˈhɔlɪk]

名 酗酒者
形 含酒精的

英英 relating or containing to alcohol; a person who is affected by alcoholism

例 The **alcoholic** died of liver cancer in his early forties.
這名酗酒者在四十歲出頭因肝癌而過世。

☐ 三分熟
☐ 五分熟
☐ 七分熟
☐ 全熟

a·li·en·ate

[ˈeljənˌet]

動 使感情疏遠
同 separate 使疏遠

英英 to make yourself isolated from others

例 Alice tends to **alienate** her half-sister.
愛麗絲刻意疏遠她同母異父的姐姐。

☐ 三分熟
☐ 五分熟
☐ 七分熟
☐ 全熟

al·li·ance

[əˈlaɪəns]

名 聯盟、同盟

英英 the state of working together or being associated

例 The **alliance** between the two neighboring countries lasted over 20 years.
這兩個鄰國結盟維持二十多年。

☐ 三分熟
☐ 五分熟
☐ 七分熟
☐ 全熟

al·lo·cate
[`æləˌket]

動 分配
同 distribute 分配

英英 to give time, money, space to be assigned or distributed for a particular purpose

例 The NGO is responsible for **allocating** the donated necessities to the needy people.
非政府組織負責將捐贈的物資分配給需要的人。

☐ 三分熟
☐ 五分熟
☐ 七分熟
☐ 全熟

a·long·side
[ə`lɔŋsaɪd]

副 沿著、並排地
介 在……旁邊

英英 close to the side of; next to someone or something

例 The tourists appreciated the beautiful lighting **alongside** the street.
觀光客欣賞沿街的美麗燈飾。

☐ 三分熟
☐ 五分熟
☐ 七分熟
☐ 全熟

al·ter·na·tive
[ɔl`tɝnətɪv]

名 二選一、供選擇的東西
形 二選一的
同 substitute 代替

英英 available as another possibility or choice between two or more things; one or more available possibilities

例 He has no **alternative** but to withdraw from the political campaign.
他別無選擇，只能退出這次競選。

☐ 三分熟
☐ 五分熟
☐ 七分熟
☐ 全熟

am·bi·gu·i·ty
[ˌæmbɪ`gjuətɪ]

名 曖昧、模稜兩可

英英 uncertain or not clear in meaning

例 **Ambiguity** in a bilateral contract can cause trouble to both parties.
雙邊協定曖昧不明可能會造成雙方的困擾。

☐ 三分熟
☐ 五分熟
☐ 七分熟
☐ 全熟

am·big·u·ous
[æm`bɪgjʊəs]

形 曖昧的
同 doubtful 含糊的

英英 having more than one possible meaning

例 **Ambiguous** expressions may cause misunderstanding.
曖昧的用語可能會造成誤會。

☐ 三分熟
☐ 五分熟
☐ 七分熟
☐ 全熟

am·bu·lance
[`æmbjələns]

名 救護車

英英 a vehicle equipped for taking sick or injured people to and from hospital

例 Three paramedics arrived with the **ambulance**.
三位醫護人員隨救護車抵達。

☐ 三分熟
☐ 五分熟
☐ 七分熟
☐ 全熟

am·bush [`æmbʊʃ]

名 埋伏、伏兵
動 埋伏並突擊
同 trap 陷阱

英英 a surprise attack by people lying in wait or in a hidden position; to attack in ambush

例 They fell into an **ambush** when they passed through the village.
他們經過小鎮時遭遇埋伏。

☐ 三分熟
☐ 五分熟
☐ 七分熟
☐ 全熟

A

a·mi·a·ble
[ˈemɪəbļ]
形 友善的、可親的

英英 friendly and pleasant in behavior
例 Her **amiable** manner made the visitors feel more relaxed.
她友善的態度令來訪者感覺更放鬆。

☐ 三分熟 ☐ 五分熟 ☐ 七分熟 ☐ 全熟

am·pli·fy
[ˈæmpləˌfaɪ]
動 擴大、放大

英英 to increase the volume or strength by using electronic equipment
例 The actor's voice was **amplified** with an electronic device.
演員的聲音用電子設備放大了。

☐ 三分熟 ☐ 五分熟 ☐ 七分熟 ☐ 全熟

an·a·lects
[ˈænəˌlɛkts]
名 語錄、選集
同 collection 收集品

英英 selected works; literary selections
例 The **Analects** of Confucius are considered a classic of ancient Chinese literature.
孔子的語錄被認為是中國古代文學的經典。

☐ 三分熟 ☐ 五分熟 ☐ 七分熟 ☐ 全熟

a·nal·o·gy
[əˈnælədʒɪ]
名 類似

英英 a comparison between two things made to explain or clarify
例 The project manager pointed out the **analogy** between the two cases.
專案經理指出這兩個案子之間的相似之處。

☐ 三分熟 ☐ 五分熟 ☐ 七分熟 ☐ 全熟

an·a·lyst [ˈænəlɪst]
名 分解者、分析者

英英 a person who conducts a study or examination of something in detail
例 The statistical **analyst** is responsible to interpret the data.
數據分析師負責解釋資料。

☐ 三分熟 ☐ 五分熟 ☐ 七分熟 ☐ 全熟

an·a·lyt·i·cal
[ˌænəˈlɪtɪkḷ]
形 分析的

英英 examining something in detail; relating to or using analysis or logical reasoning
例 Does she adopt a holistic approach or an **analytical** method in this study?
她這個研究是採用整體的方式或分析的方式呢？

☐ 三分熟 ☐ 五分熟 ☐ 七分熟 ☐ 全熟

an·ec·dote
[ˈænɪkˌdot]
名 趣聞

英英 a short entertaining, and often funny story about a real incident or person
例 The students enjoy listening to the **anecdotes** of the poet.
學生喜歡聽詩人的趣聞。

☐ 三分熟 ☐ 五分熟 ☐ 七分熟 ☐ 全熟

🎧 Track 157

---

an·i·mate

[ˈænəˌmet]

動 賦予……生命、激勵
形 活的
同 encourage 激發、助長

英英 to bring to life or make something active; being alive or active

例 We were **animated** by the news that we would all get a pay raise next month.
聽説下個月我們都可以加薪，這使我們感到振奮。

☐ 三分熟
☐ 五分熟
☐ 七分熟
☐ 全熟

---

an·noy·ance

[əˈnɔɪəns]

名 煩惱、困擾

英英 to make slightly angry

例 The complicated procedure to apply for the document could be an **annoyance**.
申請文件的複雜程序，可能是一件很令人煩惱的事。

☐ 三分熟
☐ 五分熟
☐ 七分熟
☐ 全熟

---

a·non·y·mous

[əˈnɑnəməs]

形 匿名的

英英 unknown by name or identity

例 The person who offered us this scoop news wished to remain **anonymous**.
提供這個獨家消息的人希望保持匿名。

☐ 三分熟
☐ 五分熟
☐ 七分熟
☐ 全熟

Ant·arc·tic/ ant·arc·tic

[ænˈtɑrktɪk]

名 南極洲
形 南極的

英英 relating to the very cold region surrounding the South Pole; the Antarctic

例 Several countries have claimed territorial sovereignty in the **Antarctic**.
好幾個國家宣稱擁有南極土地的主權。

☐ 三分熟
☐ 五分熟
☐ 七分熟
☐ 全熟

---

an·ten·na

[ænˈtɛnə]

名 觸角、觸鬚、天線

英英 each of a pair of long, thin sensory organs on the heads of insects, crustaceans, etc.

例 The **antenna** receives signals from the TV station.
天線接收來自電視臺的訊息。

☐ 三分熟
☐ 五分熟
☐ 七分熟
☐ 全熟

---

an·ti·bi·ot·ic

[ˌæntɪbaɪˈɑtɪk]

名 抗生素、盤尼西林
形 抗生的、抗菌的
同 medicine 藥物

英英 a medicine or chemical that inhibits the growth of or destroys harmful bacteria; be able to destroy harmful bacteria

例 Some bacteria have evolved to be immune to **antibiotics**.
有些細菌演變成能對抗生素免疫。

☐ 三分熟
☐ 五分熟
☐ 七分熟
☐ 全熟

---

an·ti·bod·y

[ˈæntɪˌbɑdɪ]

名 抗體

英英 a protein produced in the blood to counteract diseases and harmful bacteria

例 People can have **antibodies** against influenza virus by vaccination.
人們可以在接種疫苗之後具有流感的抗體。

☐ 三分熟
☐ 五分熟
☐ 七分熟
☐ 全熟

A

an·tic·i·pate
[æn'tɪsə‚pet]

動 預期、預料、提前支用
同 expect 預期

英英 to be aware of a future event and prepare for it

例 It is **anticipated** that the typhoon may cause great damage to the island.
可以預期到這個颱風會對本島帶來很大的損害。

☐ 三分熟
☐ 五分熟
☐ 七分熟
☐ 全熟

an·tic·i·pa·tion
[æn‚tɪsə'peʃən]

名 預想、預期、預料

英英 a feeling of excitement, anticipating; expectation or prediction or something that is going to happen in the future

例 The outcome of the contest was beyond our **anticipation**.
比賽的結果超出我們的預期。

☐ 三分熟
☐ 五分熟
☐ 七分熟
☐ 全熟

an·to·nym
['æntə‚nɪm]

名 反義字

英英 a word opposite in meaning to another

例 "Agony" is an **antonym** of "joy."
「痛苦」是「喜悅」的反義字。

☐ 三分熟
☐ 五分熟
☐ 七分熟
☐ 全熟

ap·pli·ca·ble
['æplɪkəbl]

形 適用的、適當的
同 appropriate 適當的

英英 relating to or appropriate

例 The rule is **applicable** to all students enrolled this year.
這項規定適用於所有今年入學的新生。

☐ 三分熟
☐ 五分熟
☐ 七分熟
☐ 全熟

ap·pren·tice
[ə'prɛntɪs]

名 學徒
動 使……做學徒
同 beginner 新手

英英 a person learning a skilled practical trade from one who is skilled in that trade; to make someone become a apprentice

例 He has been a baking **apprentice** for three months.
他已經當了三個月的烘焙學徒。

☐ 三分熟
☐ 五分熟
☐ 七分熟
☐ 全熟

ap·prox·i·mate
[ə'prɑksəmɪt]

動 相近
形 近似的、大致準確的

英英 to fairly accurate but not completely precise

例 Can you tell me the **approximate** number of participants in the party?
可以告訴我這個派對大約有多少人參加嗎？

☐ 三分熟
☐ 五分熟
☐ 七分熟
☐ 全熟

ap·ti·tude
['æptə‚tjud]

名 才能、資質、天資
同 ability 才能

英英 a natural skill, ability or inclination

例 The result of the **aptitude** test showed that he was suitable to pursue a career in art.
性向測驗結果顯示，他適合從事藝術工作。

☐ 三分熟
☐ 五分熟
☐ 七分熟
☐ 全熟

🎧 Track 159

Arc·tic/arc·tic
[ˋɑrktɪk]

名 北極地區
形 北極的

英英 relating to the very cold regions around the North Pole

例 The decline of **Arctic** sea ice has raised concerns about climate change.
北極海面冰層減少，引起人們對氣候變遷的擔憂。

☐ 三分熟
☐ 五分熟
☐ 七分熟
☐ 全熟

ar·ro·gant
[ˋærəgənt]

形 自大的、傲慢的
反 humble 謙虛的

英英 believing that one's own importance or abilities are better than others

例 The **arrogant** movie star refused to work with the less famous actor.
傲慢的電影明星拒絕和比較不有名的演員合作。

☐ 三分熟
☐ 五分熟
☐ 七分熟
☐ 全熟

ar·ter·y [ˋɑrtərɪ]

名 動脈、主要道路

英英 any of the muscular-walled tubes through which blood flows from the heart around the body

例 Clogged **arteries** may cause heart attack and stroke.
主動脈阻塞可能導致心臟病發或者中風。

☐ 三分熟
☐ 五分熟
☐ 七分熟
☐ 全熟

ar·tic·u·late
[ɑrˋtɪkjəˏlet]/[ɑrˋtɪkjəlɪt]

動 清晰地發音
形 清晰的

英英 to express feelings and ideas fluently and clear in speech; able to express feelings and ideas fluently and clear in speech

例 The anchor **articulated** to make her report as clear as possible.
主播清晰地發音，盡可能讓自己的報導變清楚。

☐ 三分熟
☐ 五分熟
☐ 七分熟
☐ 全熟

ar·ti·fact
[ˋɑrtɪˏfækt]

名 加工品

英英 an object, a functional or decorative man-made object especially of historical interest

例 These **artifacts** were found to contain substances harmful to human beings.
這些加工品被發現含有對人類有害的物質。

☐ 三分熟
☐ 五分熟
☐ 七分熟
☐ 全熟

as·sas·si·nate
[əˋsæsnˏet]

動 行刺
同 kill 殺死

英英 to murder (a political or religious leader)

例 The antigovernment activist was **assassinated** at the venue of the demonstration.
反政府行動份子在抗議現場被暗殺。

☐ 三分熟
☐ 五分熟
☐ 七分熟
☐ 全熟

as·sert [əˋsɝt]

動 斷言、主張

英英 to speak or state a fact confidently and forcefully

例 The governor **asserted** that crime fighting would be the most important issue in his term of office.
州長主張在他任期內，打擊犯罪是最重要的議題。

☐ 三分熟
☐ 五分熟
☐ 七分熟
☐ 全熟

A

as·sess [əˈsɛs]

動 估計價值、課稅

英英 to make judgments, evaluate or estimate

例 The value of the property was **assessed** by the real estate appraiser.
由不動產估價師來估計這個房產的價值。

☐ 三分熟
☐ 五分熟
☐ 七分熟
☐ 全熟

---

as·sess·ment

[əˈsɛsmənt]

名 評估、稅額

英英 the act of making a judgment, evaluate, or estimate

例 More teachers adopt the process-based **assessment** in their class.
越來越多老師在課堂中採用重視歷程的評量方式。

☐ 三分熟
☐ 五分熟
☐ 七分熟
☐ 全熟

---

as·sump·tion

[əˈsʌmpʃən]

名 前提、假設、假定
反 conclusion 結論

英英 a thing that is thought of as true without any proof

例 Don't make **assumptions** about others based on the stereotypes.
不要以刻板印象對別人妄加臆斷。

☐ 三分熟
☐ 五分熟
☐ 七分熟
☐ 全熟

---

asth·ma [ˈæzmə]

名 【醫】氣喘

英英 a medical condition which makes it difficult to breathe

例 The girl who suffers from **asthma** carries an inhaler with her all the time.
有氣喘疾病的女孩，總是將吸入器帶在身邊。

☐ 三分熟
☐ 五分熟
☐ 七分熟
☐ 全熟

---

a·sy·lum [əˈsaɪləm]

名 收容所、避難、庇護

英英 shelter or protection; protection granted by a state to a political refugee

例 The Russian activist sought political **asylum** in the U.S.
俄國激進份子在美國尋求政治庇護。

☐ 三分熟
☐ 五分熟
☐ 七分熟
☐ 全熟

---

at·tain [əˈten]

動 達成
反 fail 失敗

英英 to succeed in accomplishing or achieving something after hard work

例 He **attained** his goal and became a billionaire.
他達成目標，成為一位億萬富翁。

☐ 三分熟
☐ 五分熟
☐ 七分熟
☐ 全熟

---

at·tain·ment

[əˈtenmənt]

名 到達、實現

英英 the action of achieving; an achievement

例 The alliance was established for **attainment** of the shared goal.
聯盟的成立是為了達成共同目標。

☐ 三分熟
☐ 五分熟
☐ 七分熟
☐ 全熟

---

at·ten·dant

[əˈtɛndənt]

名 侍者、隨從、隨員
形 陪從的

英英 a person whose job is to provide a service to the public; providing a service to the public

例 The flight **attendant** will serve the meal in about thirty minutes.
空服員大約三十分鐘之後會送餐。

☐ 三分熟
☐ 五分熟
☐ 七分熟
☐ 全熟

🎧 Track 161

at·tic [ˈætɪk]

名 閣樓、頂樓

英英 a space or room under the roof of a building or house

例 Mr. Benson had his stepchild live in the **attic**.
班森先生讓他的繼子住在閣樓裡面。

☐三分熟
☐五分熟
☐七分熟
☐全熟

---

auc·tion [ˈɔkʃən]

名 拍賣
動 拍賣
同 sale 拍賣

英英 a public sale in which goods or property are sold to the highest bidder; to sell something at an auction

例 The painting was sold at a record-high price at the **auction**.
這幅畫在拍賣會上以高價賣出。

☐三分熟
☐五分熟
☐七分熟
☐全熟

---

au·then·tic

[ɔˈθɛntɪk]

形 真實的、可靠的

英英 of undisputed origin; genuine, real

例 **Authentic** materials for language learning can benefit the students the most.
真實的語言學習材料對學生的幫助是最大的。

☐三分熟
☐五分熟
☐七分熟
☐全熟

---

au·thor·ize

[ˈɔθəˌraɪz]

動 委託、授權、委任

英英 to give official permission for or approval to

例 The committee was **authorized** to appoint the manager of the company.
委員會獲得授權任命公司的經理。

☐三分熟
☐五分熟
☐七分熟
☐全熟

---

au·to·graph/ sig·na·ture

[ˈɔtəˌgræf]/[ˈsɪgnətʃə]

名 親筆簽名
動 親筆寫於……
同 sign 簽名

英英 a celebrity's signature written for an admirer; a celebrity's name written by that person; to write someone's signature on

例 The photo with the Michael Jackson's **autograph** was considered to be very precious.
麥可‧傑克森的親筆簽名照被視為是相當珍貴的。

☐三分熟
☐五分熟
☐七分熟
☐全熟

---

au·ton·o·my

[ɔˈtɑnəmɪ]

名 自治、自治權

英英 the self-government of a country or group; freedom of action

例 Many teachers joined the campaign for school **autonomy**.
許多教師參與爭取學校自主權的運動。

☐三分熟
☐五分熟
☐七分熟
☐全熟

---

a·vi·a·tion

[ˌevɪˈeʃən]

名 航空、飛行
同 flight 飛行

英英 the activity of operating and flying an aircraft

例 Jason is looking for an **aviation** security job.
傑森在找機場保全人員的工作。

☐三分熟
☐五分熟
☐七分熟
☐全熟

awe·some

[`ɔsəm]

形 有威嚴的、令人驚嘆的

英英 inspiring awe, very great or large making you feel respect and sometimes fear

例 The tourists were impressed by the **awesome** view at the top of the mountain.
山頂極佳的視野令遊客印象深刻。

□三分熟
□五分熟
□七分熟
□全熟

B

Bb

ba·rom·e·ter

[bə`rɑmətə]

名 氣壓計、晴雨錶

英英 an instrument measuring air pressure, used especially in forecasting the weather

例 The online poll is considered a **barometer** of the public opinion.
線上調查被視為是人眾意見的晴雨錶。

□三分熟
□五分熟
□七分熟
□全熟

beck·on [`bɛkn̩]

動 點頭示意、招手、吸引

英英 to make a gesture to encourage or instruct someone to approach or follow

例 He **beckoned** for a cab, but the driver didn't see him.
他招手攔計程車,但是司機沒有看到他。

□三分熟
□五分熟
□七分熟
□全熟

be·siege [bɪ`sidʒ]

動 包圍、圍攻
反 release 釋放

英英 to surround a place with armed forces in order attack, capture, or force it to surrender

例 The minister was **besieged** by the journalists who kept asking whether he would step down for the scandal.
部長被記者包圍,他們一直追問是否他會因為醜聞而下臺。

□三分熟
□五分熟
□七分熟
□全熟

be·tray [bɪ`tre]

動 出賣、背叛
同 deceive 欺騙

英英 to act treacherously or in a dishonest way towards a person, country, etc. by revealing information to or otherwise aiding an enemy

例 He went bankrupt after his business partner **betrayed** him.
被生意夥伴背叛後,他破產了。

□三分熟
□五分熟
□七分熟
□全熟

bev·er·age

[`bɛvrədʒ]

名 飲料

英英 a drink

例 Sugar-loaded **beverages** can increase the risk of diabetes.
含糖飲料會增加罹患糖尿病的風險。

□三分熟
□五分熟
□七分熟
□全熟

🎧 Track 163

bi·as [ˈbaɪəs]

名 偏心、偏袒
動 使存偏見

英英 inclination or prejudice in favor of a particular person, thing, or viewpoint influenced by your personal opinions; prejudice

例 The government tried to eliminate the public's **bias** against the minorities.
政府試圖消弭大眾對少數族群的偏見。

☐ 三分熟
☐ 五分熟
☐ 七分熟
☐ 全熟

bin·oc·u·lars

[baɪˈnɑkjələz]

名 雙筒望遠鏡

英英 an optical instrument with a separate lens for each eye, used for making distant objects clearer to view

例 He observed the rare birds with his **binoculars**.
他用雙筒望遠鏡觀察稀有的鳥類。

☐ 三分熟
☐ 五分熟
☐ 七分熟
☐ 全熟

bi·o·chem·i·stry

[ˌbaɪoˈkɛmɪstrɪ]

名 生物化學

英英 the study of the chemical processes which occur within living organisms

例 A **biochemistry** major can pursue a career in scientific research.
主修生物化學的學生可以往科學研究的生涯發展。

☐ 三分熟
☐ 五分熟
☐ 七分熟
☐ 全熟

bi·o·log·i·cal

[ˌbaɪoˈlɑdʒɪk!]

形 生物學的、有關生物學的

英英 related to biology or living organisms

例 He spent three years looking for his **biological** brother after the war separated them.
他花了三年時間尋找因戰爭失散的親生弟弟。

☐ 三分熟
☐ 五分熟
☐ 七分熟
☐ 全熟

bi·zarre [bɪˈzɑr]

形 古怪的、奇異的

英英 something really strange, abnormal

例 The newcomer's **bizarre** behaviors raised concerns of the local residents.
新來的人言行古怪，引起當地居民的擔憂。

☐ 三分熟
☐ 五分熟
☐ 七分熟
☐ 全熟

bleak [blik]

形 淒涼的、暗淡的

英英 bare and exposed, unattractive

例 The open, **bleak** desert ahead of the traveler made her rather distressed.
旅行者眼前廣大蒼涼的沙漠，令她心情低落。

☐ 三分熟
☐ 五分熟
☐ 七分熟
☐ 全熟

blun·der [ˈblʌndɚ]

名 大錯
動 犯錯

英英 a stupid or careless mistake; make a mistake

例 He never served any official position after the political **blunder**.
這次政治失誤之後，他就沒再擔任過任何公職。

☐ 三分熟
☐ 五分熟
☐ 七分熟
☐ 全熟

B

blunt [blʌnt]

動 使遲鈍、減弱
形 遲鈍的
反 sharp 敏銳的

英英 not having a sharp edge or point; to make someone become blunt

例 The frustrating experience during the trip has **blunted** his enthusiasm for travel.
旅行中令人挫敗的經驗，削弱了他對旅行的熱情。

□ 三分熟
□ 五分熟
□ 七分熟
□ 全熟

bom·bard [bɑm`bɑrd]

動 砲轟、轟擊

英英 to attack a place continuously with bombs, guns, or other missiles

例 The journalists **bombarded** the movie star with questions about his love affair.
記者用關於緋聞的問題砲轟這位電影明星。

□ 三分熟
□ 五分熟
□ 七分熟
□ 全熟

bond·age [`bɑndɪdʒ]

名 奴役、囚禁

英英 the state of being completely controlled by someone or something as a slave or feudal serf

例 He became a **bondage** of money as he was addicted to luxuries.
他因為對奢侈品上癮而成為金錢的奴隸。

□ 三分熟
□ 五分熟
□ 七分熟
□ 全熟

boost [bust]

名 幫助、促進
動 推動、增強、提高
同 increase 增加

英英 help or encourage to increase or improve something

例 The establishment of infrastructure can help **boost** the economy.
基礎設施的建立可以幫助促進經濟。

□ 三分熟
□ 五分熟
□ 七分熟
□ 全熟

bout [baʊt]

名 比賽、競賽的一回合

英英 a short period of illness or activity

例 The boxing **bout** ended abruptly as one of the players passed out after getting a critical hit.
這名拳擊選手因重擊而昏過去，導致比賽突然中止。

□ 三分熟
□ 五分熟
□ 七分熟
□ 全熟

boy·cott [`bɔɪˌkɑt]

名 杯葛、排斥
動 杯葛、聯合抵制

英英 to refuse to buy, use, or do something with a person, organization, or country as a punishment or in protest

例 They **boycotted** the company for that its manufacturing procedure may harm the environment.
他們抵制該公司的產品，因為製造過程會傷害環境。

□ 三分熟
□ 五分熟
□ 七分熟
□ 全熟

break·down [`brekˌdaʊn]

名 故障、崩潰

英英 a failure or collapse of communication, or health

例 He almost had an emotional **breakdown** when he lost the tournament.
他輸掉錦標賽之後，幾乎情緒崩潰。

□ 三分熟
□ 五分熟
□ 七分熟
□ 全熟

🎧 **Track 165**

break·through

[`brekˌθru]

名 突破

英英 a sudden important development, discovery, or success that helps solve a problem

例 Face recognition was one of the major **breakthroughs** in artificial intelligence.
臉部辨識是人工智慧的一項主要突破。

☐ 三分熟
☐ 五分熟
☐ 七分熟
☐ 全熟

break·up

[`brekˌʌp]

名 分散、瓦解

英英 a gradual division of something large into smaller pieces

例 Sammy tried to help her friend get over a **breakup**.
珊米試圖幫助她的朋友克服分手的難過心情。

☐ 三分熟
☐ 五分熟
☐ 七分熟
☐ 全熟

brew [bru]

名 釀製物
動 釀製

英英 something brewed; to make (beer) by soaking, boiling, and fermentation

例 My uncle used to **brew** beers in his house.
我叔叔以前會在自己家裡釀造啤酒。

☐ 三分熟
☐ 五分熟
☐ 七分熟
☐ 全熟

brink [brɪŋk]

名 陡峭邊緣

英英 the extreme edge of land before a steep slope or a body of water; when something bad is about to happen

例 The reckless youngster risks his life to take a picture at the **brink** of the cliff.
冒失的年輕人，冒生命危險在懸崖旁邊拍照。

☐ 三分熟
☐ 五分熟
☐ 七分熟
☐ 全熟

brisk [brɪsk]

形 活潑的、輕快的

英英 active, quick, and energetic

例 The **brisk** tempo of the music lightened up the atmosphere.
音樂的輕快節奏使氣氛變愉快。

☐ 三分熟
☐ 五分熟
☐ 七分熟
☐ 全熟

bro·chure

[broˋʃʊr]

名 小冊子
同 pamphlet 小冊子

英英 a thick book containing pictures and information about a product or service

例 The museum offers **brochures** in five languages for the visitors.
博物館提供五種語言的導覽手冊給參觀者。

☐ 三分熟
☐ 五分熟
☐ 七分熟
☐ 全熟

brute [brut]

名 殘暴的人
形 粗暴的

英英 a person who behaves in a violent or savage way; behaving in a violent way

例 The **brute** attacked the passersby for unspecified reasons.
殘暴的人因為不明原因而攻擊了路過的人。

☐ 三分熟
☐ 五分熟
☐ 七分熟
☐ 全熟

C

buck·le [ˈbʌkl]

名 皮帶扣環
動 用扣環扣住
同 fasten 扣緊

英英 a metal object with a hinged pin, used for fastening a belt or strap; to fasten with a buckle

例 The passengers were asked to **buckle** up the seatbelt as soon as they got onboard.
乘客一上飛機就被要求要繫好安全帶。

☐ 三分熟
☐ 五分熟
☐ 七分熟
☐ 全熟

---

bulk·y [ˈbʌlkɪ]

形 龐大的、笨重的

英英 in large amounts

例 Few people carry a **bulky** paper dictionary around; most people use electronic dictionaries or their smart phones.
很少人會把笨重的紙本字典帶在身邊；大多數人用電子字典或者手機。

☐ 三分熟
☐ 五分熟
☐ 七分熟
☐ 全熟

---

bu·reau·cra·cy
[bjʊˈrɑkrəsɪ]

名 官僚政治

英英 a system of government in which most decisions are taken by state officials rather than by elected representatives

例 The corrupt system in the **bureaucracy** was condemned by the public.
大眾譴責官僚政治的腐敗體系。

☐ 三分熟
☐ 五分熟
☐ 七分熟
☐ 全熟

---

bur·i·al [ˈbɛrɪəl]

名 埋葬、下葬
同 funeral 葬儀、出殯

英英 the act of burying a dead body

例 The atmosphere at the **burial** was solemn yet peaceful.
喪禮上的氣氛是嚴肅但平和的。

☐ 三分熟
☐ 五分熟
☐ 七分熟
☐ 全熟

---

byte [baɪt]

名 【電算】位元組

英英 a unit for measuring the amount of information a computer can store in a group of binary digits (usually eight) operated on as a unit

例 One **byte** equals 8 bits of data.
一個位元組等於八個位元。

☐ 三分熟
☐ 五分熟
☐ 七分熟
☐ 全熟

Cc

caf·feine [ˈkæfiin]

名 咖啡因

英英 n.a crystalline compound that is found especially in tea and coffee plants and is a stimulant of the central nervous system

例 **Caffeine** dependence or addiction may have some negative effects on your body.
過度依賴咖啡因或者咖啡因上癮，可能會對你的身體有一些負面的影響。

☐ 三分熟
☐ 五分熟
☐ 七分熟
☐ 全熟

🎧 Track 167

cal·ci·um
[ˈkælsɪəm]

名 鈣

英英 a soft grey reactive metallic chemical element in teeth, bones, and chalk

例 **Calcium** deficiency may cause hypocalcemia.
缺鈣會導致低血鈣症。

☐三分熟 ☐五分熟 ☐七分熟 ☐全熟

can·vass
[ˈkænvəs]

名 審視、討論
動 詳細調查

英英 an act of canvassing; to persuade people to vote in certain ways

例 The association is **canvassing** students' opinions about the school's new policy.
該協會正在調查學生對於學校新政策的意見。

☐三分熟 ☐五分熟 ☐七分熟 ☐全熟

ca·pa·bil·i·ty
[ˌkepəˈbɪlətɪ]

名 能力

英英 the power or ability to do something

例 As a project manager, he has the **capability** to be a bridge of communication between the clients and the product developers.
作為專案經理，他有能力在客戶和產品開發者之間擔任溝通的橋樑。

☐三分熟 ☐五分熟 ☐七分熟 ☐全熟

cap·sule [ˈkæpsl̩]

名 膠囊
片 time capsule 時空膠囊

英英 a small container of gelatin containing a dose of medicine, swallowed whole

例 They opened the time **capsule** from 1914 and found several precious antiques.
他們打開 1914 年留下的時空膠囊，發現幾樣珍貴的古董。

☐三分熟 ☐五分熟 ☐七分熟 ☐全熟

cap·tion [ˈkæpʃən]

名 標題、簡短說明、字幕
動 加標題

英英 a title or brief explanation added to an illustration or cartoon; to add a title or brief explanation

例 American viewers prefer watching a movie without the **captions**.
美國觀眾比較喜歡看電視時沒有字幕。

☐三分熟 ☐五分熟 ☐七分熟 ☐全熟

cap·tive [ˈkæptɪv]

名 俘虜
形 被俘的
同 hostage 人質

英英 a person who has been taken prisoner or held in confinement; losing freedom or being imprisoned

例 The soldier fell **captive** to the enemy.
這名軍人被敵軍俘虜。

☐三分熟 ☐五分熟 ☐七分熟 ☐全熟

cap·tiv·i·ty
[kæpˈtɪvətɪ]

名 監禁、囚禁

英英 the state of being kept in imprisonment or enclosed

例 Years of **captivity** has made him lose the ability to communicate with others.
被監禁多年後，他失去了和他人溝通的能力。

☐三分熟 ☐五分熟 ☐七分熟 ☐全熟

C

car·b·o·hy·drate

[ˌkɑrboˈhaɪdret]

名 碳水化合物、醣

英英 substances, found in certain kinds of food, such as potatoes, sugar, etc. that provide you with energy

例 Excessive consumption of **carbohydrates** may lead to obesity and other diseases.
吃過多的碳水化合物，可能會導致肥胖以及其他疾病。

□三分熟
□五分熟
□七分熟
□全熟

---

ca·ress [kəˈrɛs]

名 愛撫
動 撫觸
同 touch 碰觸

英英 to touch or stroke in a gentle and loving or endearing manner

例 She gently **caressed** the baby.
她溫柔地輕撫著小嬰兒。

□三分熟
□五分熟
□七分熟
□全熟

---

car·ol [ˈkærəl]

名 頌歌、讚美詞

英英 joyful religious song celebrating the birth of Christ and sung at Christmas time

例 "Joy to the World" is a well-known Christmas **carol**.
「普世歡騰」是一首有名的聖誕頌歌。

□三分熟
□五分熟
□七分熟
□全熟

---

cash·ier [kæˈʃɪr]

名 出納員、收銀員

英英 a person responsible for receiving payments for goods and services in a shop, bank, etc.

例 She takes a part-time job as a **cashier** at the mall.
她在購物中心當兼職的收銀員。

□三分熟
□五分熟
□七分熟
□全熟

---

cas·u·al·ty

[ˈkæʒʊəltɪ]

名 意外事故、橫禍、受害者、傷亡人員、急診室

英英 fatal accident; an accident in which people or someone die

例 The authority has not announced the number of **casualties** in the earthquake.
當局還沒公佈地震的傷亡人數。

□三分熟
□五分熟
□七分熟
□全熟

---

ca·tas·tro·phe

[kəˈtæstrəfɪ]

名 大災難

英英 an unexpected event that causes great damage, destruction or suffering

例 It is believed that climate change may lead to **catastrophe** for human beings.
氣候變遷可能會為人類帶來大災難。

□三分熟
□五分熟
□七分熟
□全熟

---

ca·ter [ˈketɚ]

動 提供食物、提供娛樂

英英 to provide what is desired or needed, especially support, and food

例 The restaurant offers various dishes that can **cater** to diners with different preferences.
這間餐廳提供不同餐點來迎合不同喜好的用餐者。

□三分熟
□五分熟
□七分熟
□全熟

Track 169

cav·al·ry [ˈkævl̩rɪ]

名 騎兵隊、騎兵

英英 the part of an army that uses armored vehicles or horses for fighting

例 The crowd watched in awe as the **cavalry** passed through the street.
騎兵隊經過街道的時候，群眾尊敬地看著。

□ 三分熟
□ 五分熟
□ 七分熟
□ 全熟

cav·i·ty [ˈkævətɪ]

名 洞、穴

英英 a space or hole in a solid object or a person's body

例 The dentist didn't say what caused the tooth **cavities**.
牙醫師沒有說明是什麼導致蛀牙的。

□ 三分熟
□ 五分熟
□ 七分熟
□ 全熟

cem·e·ter·y

[ˈsɛməˌtɛrɪ]

名 公墓

英英 a place in which the bodies or ashes of dead people are buried

例 The spooky atmosphere in the **cemetery** kept the children away.
公墓的陰森氣氛把小朋友嚇得遠遠的。

□ 三分熟
□ 五分熟
□ 七分熟
□ 全熟

cer·tain·ty

[ˈsɝtn̩tɪ]

名 事實、確定的情況

英英 the state of being definite or sure and doubtless about something

例 The testimony of the witnesses laid **certainty** of the case.
目擊者的證詞，使這次案件實情能夠釐清。

□ 三分熟
□ 五分熟
□ 七分熟
□ 全熟

cer·ti·fy [ˈsɝtəˌfaɪ]

動 證明

英英 to provide evidence for; stand as proof of; show by one's behavior, attitude

例 Frank was **certified** as a qualified teacher by the university.
法蘭克得到大學證明為一位合格教師。

□ 三分熟
□ 五分熟
□ 七分熟
□ 全熟

cham·pagne

[ʃæmˈpen]

名 香檳

英英 an expensive French white wine with bubbles in it, often drunk for celebratory reasons

例 They had some **champagne** at the gala.
他們在慶功宴上喝了一些香檳。

□ 三分熟
□ 五分熟
□ 七分熟
□ 全熟

cha·os [ˈkeɑs]

名 無秩序、大混亂
同 confusion 混亂

英英 a state of complete disorder and confusion

例 The **chaos** in the town after the typhoon astonished the international volunteers.
颱風過後，小鎮的混亂狀況令國際志工感到震驚。

□ 三分熟
□ 五分熟
□ 七分熟
□ 全熟

char·ac·ter·ize

[ˈkærɪktəˌraɪz]

動 描述……的性質、
具有……特徵

英英 to describe or portray the character or the qualities or peculiarities of

例 The tree frogs are **characterized** with the adhesive pads on their fingers and toes.
樹蛙的特徵在於指尖有黏性的吸盤。

□ 三分熟
□ 五分熟
□ 七分熟
□ 全熟

char·coal

[ˈtʃɑrˌkol]

名 炭、木炭

英英 hard blackened substance obtained by burning wood without much air, usually be burned as a fuel

例 They prepared some **charcoals** for the barbecue.
他們準備一些木炭要用來烤肉。

---

char·i·ot [ˈtʃærɪət]

名 戰車、駕駛戰車

英英 vehicles with two wheels that were pulled by horses; to drive a vehicle which is with two wheels that were pulled by horses

例 They built a prop of **chariot** for the stage play.
他們為這次舞臺劇建立一個戰車的道具。

---

char·i·ta·ble

[ˈtʃærətəbl]

形 溫和的、仁慈的

英英 organization or activity helps and supports people who are ill, physically disabled, or very poor

例 The **charitable** organization is raising funds for homeless children.
慈善機構在為無家可歸的孩子募款。

---

cho·les·ter·ol

[kəˈlɛstəˌrol]

名 膽固醇

英英 substance that exists in the fat, tissues, and blood of all animals

例 High levels of **cholesterol** in your diet may put your health at risk.
飲食中的高膽固醇，會使你的健康產生風險。

---

chron·ic [ˈkrɑnɪk]

形 長期的、持續的
同 constant 持續的

英英 an illness or something being long-lasting and recurrent or characterized by long suffering

例 Some office workers suffer from **chronic** fatigue due to lack of exercise and unbalanced diets.
有些辦公室員工因為缺乏運動和不均衡的飲食，而有持續疲勞的現象。

---

chuck·le [ˈtʃʌkl]

名 滿足的輕笑
動 輕輕地笑

英英 a small quiet laugh

例 The toddler **chuckled** as the clown handed him a balloon.
小丑拿氣球給小朋友時，他滿足地笑了。

---

chunk [tʃʌŋk]

名 厚塊、厚片、相當大的部分

英英 a thick solid pieces of something

例 A large **chunk** of our profit comes from the sales of dietary supplement.
我們有很大一部分利益是來自營養食品的銷售。

C

🎧 Track 171

civ·i·lize [ˈsɪvəˌlaɪz]

動 啟發、使開化
同 educate 教育

英英 to teach or refine a society to be more organized and advanced

例 The child was **civilized** by his parents' disciplinary measures.
小孩因為父母親的紀律措施而被教化。

☐ 三分熟
☐ 五分熟
☐ 七分熟
☐ 全熟

---

clamp [klæmp]

名 夾子、鉗子
動 以鉗子轉緊、強行實施
片 clamp down on 強行實施

英英 an instrument that holds two things firmly together; to hold things firmly together with a clamp

例 They **clamped** a curfew on the town to prevent crime.
他們對該城鎮強行實施宵禁以防止犯罪。

☐ 三分熟
☐ 五分熟
☐ 七分熟
☐ 全熟

---

cla·ri·ty [ˈklærətɪ]

名 清澈透明、清楚

英英 the quality of being clear in voice or sound

例 Please **clarity** the message in your email.
請在 email 中把訊息表達清楚。

☐ 三分熟
☐ 五分熟
☐ 七分熟
☐ 全熟

---

cleanse [klɛnz]

動 淨化、弄清潔

英英 to clean one's body or parts by washing

例 She uses soap to **cleanse** her skin.
她使用肥皂清潔臉部肌膚。

☐ 三分熟
☐ 五分熟
☐ 七分熟
☐ 全熟

---

clear·ance [ˈklɪrəns]

名 清潔、清掃、間隙、出空

英英 the removal of unwanted old buildings, trees, or other things from an area

例 The shop will go on **clearance** of Christmas decorations in January.
商店將在一月份舉行聖誕飾品清倉拍賣。

☐ 三分熟
☐ 五分熟
☐ 七分熟
☐ 全熟

---

clench [klɛntʃ]

名 緊握
動 握緊、咬緊

英英 to hold in a tight grasp

例 He **clenched** his fist as he heard the offensive remarks, but he repressed his anger.
他聽到冒犯的言論就握緊了拳頭，但他壓抑了怒氣。

☐ 三分熟
☐ 五分熟
☐ 七分熟
☐ 全熟

---

clin·i·cal [ˈklɪnɪkl̩]

形 門診的、臨床的
片 clinical trial 臨床試驗

英英 involving or relating to the direct medical treatment or testing of patients

例 The medical research center conducts hundreds of **clinical** trials every year.
這間醫學研究中心每年進行數百項臨床試驗。

☐ 三分熟
☐ 五分熟
☐ 七分熟
☐ 全熟

---

clone [klon]

名 無性繁殖、複製
動 複製
同 copy 複製

英英 someone or something that is so similar to the person or thing that they seem to be exactly the same as them

例 Some people would **clone** a deceased pet for they miss their furry friend too much.
有些人因為太過想念毛小孩而複製他們已過世的寵物。

☐ 三分熟
☐ 五分熟
☐ 七分熟
☐ 全熟

clo·sure [ˈkloʒɚ]

名 封閉、結尾
同 conclusion 結尾

英英 approaching a particular destination; a coming closer; the narrowing of a gap

例 The **closure** in an essay usually contains a summary of the content.
文章的結尾通常包含內容的摘要。

☐ 三分熟
☐ 五分熟
☐ 七分熟
☐ 全熟

---

coffin [ˈkɔfɪn]

名 棺材

英英 a long box in which a dead body is buried or cremated

例 The wooden **coffin** would decay in a few years.
木頭棺材可能會在幾年之後腐壞。

☐ 三分熟
☐ 五分熟
☐ 七分熟
☐ 全熟

---

co·her·ent

[koˈhɪrənt]

形 連貫的、有條理的

英英 well-planned, so that it is clear and understandable and all its parts go well with each other

例 They had a **coherent** plan for innovating the company.
他們有一個具條理的計畫要來改革公司。

☐ 三分熟
☐ 五分熟
☐ 七分熟
☐ 全熟

---

co·in·cide

[koɪnˈsaɪd]

動 一致、同意
同 accord 一致

英英 to be at the same time as

例 The research outcome **coincided** with his prediction.
研究的結果和他的預期一致。

☐ 三分熟
☐ 五分熟
☐ 七分熟
☐ 全熟

---

co·in·ci·dence

[koˈɪnsdəns]

名 巧合

英英 when two or more similar or related events occur at the same time by chance and without any previous planning

例 It was a **coincidence** that he graduated from the same university where his mother studied.
他碰巧是從他母親唸過的同一所大學畢業。

☐ 三分熟
☐ 五分熟
☐ 七分熟
☐ 全熟

---

col·lec·tive

[kəˈlɛktɪv]

名 集體
形 共同的、集體的

英英 actions, situations, or feelings involved or are shared by every member of a group of people; taken as a whole

例 The **collective** intelligence can increase the efficiency and accuracy in decision making.
集體智慧可以增進決策的效率和準確度。

☐ 三分熟
☐ 五分熟
☐ 七分熟
☐ 全熟

---

col·lec·tor

[kəˈlɛktɚ]

名 收集的器具、收藏家、收款人

英英 a person who's hobby is collecting things of a particular type

例 He is a **collector** of cartoon character figurines.
他是卡通角色公仔的收藏家。

☐ 三分熟
☐ 五分熟
☐ 七分熟
☐ 全熟

🎧 **Track 173**

---

col·lide [kə`laɪd]

動 碰撞

同 bump 碰撞

英英 to be incompatible with; be or come into conflict with

例 The truck **collided** with a tour bus, causing severe casualties.
卡車與遊覽車相撞，造成嚴重死傷。

☐ 三分熟
☐ 五分熟
☐ 七分熟
☐ 全熟

---

col·li·sion

[kə`lɪʒən]

名 相撞、碰撞、猛撞

英英 occurs when a moving object crashes into another object

例 If the asteroid headed for **collision** with Earth, there will be a catastrophe.
如果這個小行星與地球相撞，將會有大災難發生。

☐ 三分熟
☐ 五分熟
☐ 七分熟
☐ 全熟

---

col·lo·qui·al

[kə`lokwɪəl]

形 白話的、通俗的、口語的

英英 informal spoken language or conversation characteristics

例 Urban Dictionary offers various **colloquial** usages of words and phrases.
都會字典提供各種口語用法。

☐ 三分熟
☐ 五分熟
☐ 七分熟
☐ 全熟

---

col·um·nist

[`kɑləmɪst]

名 專欄作家

英英 a journalist who regularly writes articles of a particular subject in a newspaper or magazine

例 The local newspaper **columnist** writes about stories of successful people who started their business in the town.
本地報紙的專欄作家會寫在這個小鎮發跡的成功商人故事。

☐ 三分熟
☐ 五分熟
☐ 七分熟
☐ 全熟

---

com·mem·o·rate

[kə`mɛməˌret]

動 祝賀、慶祝

同 celebrate 慶祝

英英 to mark by some ceremony or observation

例 They gathered to **commemorate** the 100th anniversary of the organization.
他們聚在一起慶祝組織成立一百週年。

☐ 三分熟
☐ 五分熟
☐ 七分熟
☐ 全熟

---

com·mence

[kə`mɛns]

動 開始、著手

英英 to start to take the first step or steps in carrying out an action

例 They **commenced** the project to develop the autopilot system three years ago.
他們三年前開始開發這個自動駕駛系統。

☐ 三分熟
☐ 五分熟
☐ 七分熟
☐ 全熟

---

com·men·tar·y

[`kɑmənˌtɛrɪ]

名 注釋、說明

英英 a description given by a person of an event that is broadcast on radio or television while the event is taking place

例 The journalist revealed his political orientation in the **commentary** of the article.
記者在文章評註的地方顯露出他的政治傾向。

☐ 三分熟
☐ 五分熟
☐ 七分熟
☐ 全熟

com·mit·ment

[kə`mɪtmənt]

名 承諾、拘禁、託付

英英 a strong belief in an idea or system and staying with it

例 Raising a pet is a long-term **commitment**.
養寵物是長期的承諾。

☐三分熟 ☐五分熟 ☐七分熟 ☐全熟

---

com·mu·ni·ca·tive

[kə`mjunə`ketɪv]

形 愛說話的、口無遮攔的

英英 willing to talk and give information to

例 He was a **communicative** person who would quickly tell whatever he knew.
他是個多話的人，很快便全盤托出他所知道的事。

☐三分熟 ☐五分熟 ☐七分熟 ☐全熟

---

com·pan·ion·ship

[kəm`pænjənʃɪp]

名 友誼、交往

英英 having someone you know and like with you, rather than being on your own

例 May our **companionship** last forever.
願我們的友誼長存。

☐三分熟 ☐五分熟 ☐七分熟 ☐全熟

---

com·pa·ra·ble

[`kɑmpərəbḷ]

形 可對照的、可比較的

英英 able to be compared or worthy of comparison

例 The quality of the handbag is **comparable** to the brand-named ones.
這個手提包的品質比得上名牌包包。

☐三分熟 ☐五分熟 ☐七分熟 ☐全熟

---

com·pa·ra·tive

[kɑm`pərətɪv]

形 比較上的、相對的

英英 relating to or based on or involving comparison

例 **Comparative** Literature is an optional course for students in Department of English.
比較文學是英語系學生的選修課。

☐三分熟 ☐五分熟 ☐七分熟 ☐全熟

---

com·pat·i·ble

[kəm`pætəbḷ]

形 一致的、和諧的、【電腦】相容的

英英 able to exist and perform in a harmonious or agreeable combination

例 The software is **compatible** with the operating system.
這個軟體和作業系統相容。

☐三分熟 ☐五分熟 ☐七分熟 ☐全熟

---

com·pen·sate

[`kɑmpən`set]

動 抵銷、彌補

英英 to make amends for; pay money as compensation for

例 The organizer will **compensate** for those who suffer from injury in the event.
主辦單位會補償這個活動中受傷的人。

☐三分熟 ☐五分熟 ☐七分熟 ☐全熟

---

com·pen·sa·tion

[`kɑmpən`seʃən]

名 報酬、賠償

英英 money that someone who has experienced loss, injury, or suffering claims from the person or organization responsible, or from the state

例 Some passengers claimed for **compensation** because of the flight delay.
有些乘客要求班機延誤的賠償費。

☐三分熟 ☐五分熟 ☐七分熟 ☐全熟

🎧 **Track 175**

com·pe·tence

[ˈkɑmpətəns]

名 能力、才能

英英 the ability to do something well or effectively

例 To manage a company is beyond his **competence**.
他的能力還不夠去經營一家公司。

☐ 三分熟
☐ 五分熟
☐ 七分熟
☐ 全熟

com·pe·tent

[ˈkɑmpətənt]

形 能幹的、有能力的

英英 able to do something properly, sufficiently, or efficiently

例 He is **competent** enough to take this position.
他有足夠能力接下這個職務。

☐ 三分熟
☐ 五分熟
☐ 七分熟
☐ 全熟

com·pile

[kəmˈpaɪl]

動 收集、資料彙編
同 collect 收集

英英 to compose; to put something together out of existing material

例 Martin Clifton **compiled** an anthology of Shakespeare.
馬丁克理夫頓編撰了莎士比亞的選集。

☐ 三分熟
☐ 五分熟
☐ 七分熟
☐ 全熟

com·ple·ment

[ˈkɑmpləmənt]

名 補充物
動 補充、補足

英英 a word or phrase used to complete a grammatical construction; to make things complete

例 The two tennis players could **complement** each other perfectly.
這兩位網球選手可以完美地互補。

☐ 三分熟
☐ 五分熟
☐ 七分熟
☐ 全熟

com·plex·ion

[kəmˈplɛkʃən]

名 氣色、血色

英英 the color of a person's face

例 He used some skin care products to brighten his **complexion**.
他用一些護膚產品想讓自己的膚色變亮。

☐ 三分熟
☐ 五分熟
☐ 七分熟
☐ 全熟

com·plex·i·ty

[kəmˈplɛksətɪ]

名 複雜

英英 the quality of involving different yet connected parts that is difficult to understand

例 The **complexity** of the ethnic issue makes it a thorny problem for the government.
種族議題的複雜性，使它成為政府的燙手山芋。

☐ 三分熟
☐ 五分熟
☐ 七分熟
☐ 全熟

com·pli·ca·tion

[ˌkɑmpləˈkeʃən]

名 複製、混亂、複雜、併發症

英英 a circumstance that complicates something or a situation; a difficulty

例 It takes the viewers some time to understand the plot due to the **complication** of the story.
因為故事的複雜性，使得觀眾花了一些時間才看懂情節。

☐ 三分熟
☐ 五分熟
☐ 七分熟
☐ 全熟

C

com·po·nent
[kəmˋponənt]

名 成分、部件
形 合成的、構成的
同 part 部分

英英 a part or component of a larger whole; being part of a whole

例 Most **components** of the machine were manufactured in Vietnam.
這臺機器大部分零件是在越南製造的。

☐ 三分熟
☐ 五分熟
☐ 七分熟
☐ 全熟

com·pre·hen·sive
[ˌkɑmprɪˋhɛnsɪv]

形 廣泛的、包羅萬象的、全面的

英英 including or dealing with all or nearly all aspects or studies of something

例 The curator gave a **comprehensive** introduction to the relics in the museum.
館長針對館內文物作了全面的介紹。

☐ 三分熟
☐ 五分熟
☐ 七分熟
☐ 全熟

com·prise
[kəmˋpraɪz]

動 由……構成、包含

英英 to be made up of; consist of

例 Students from aboriginal community **comprises** over half of the class.
原住民學生佔這班級人數的一半以上。

☐ 三分熟
☐ 五分熟
☐ 七分熟
☐ 全熟

con·cede [kənˋsid]

動 承認、讓步
同 confess 承認

英英 to finally begrudgingly admit or agree that something is true

例 He wouldn't **concede** to your unreasonable request.
他不會對你無禮的要求讓步的。

☐ 三分熟
☐ 五分熟
☐ 七分熟
☐ 全熟

con·ceit [kənˋsit]

名 自負、自大

英英 excessive pride in oneself and one's own actions

例 None of his colleague could tolerate his **conceit**.
沒有同事能夠忍受他的自負。

☐ 三分熟
☐ 五分熟
☐ 七分熟
☐ 全熟

con·cep·tion
[kənˋsɛpʃən]

名 概念、計畫、想法
同 idea 計畫、概念

英英 the action of conceiving a child or of one being conceived; an idea or a plan

例 According to the author, the **conception** of the protagonist was inspired by his sister.
作者說，主角的角色構想是受到他妹妹的啟發。

☐ 三分熟
☐ 五分熟
☐ 七分熟
☐ 全熟

con·ces·sion
[kənˋsɛʃən]

名 讓步、妥協

英英 a thing that is agreed to be done; a reduction in price for a certain category of person

例 Mutual **concession** may be the only way to reach an agreement.
互相妥協可能是達成協議的唯一方法。

☐ 三分熟
☐ 五分熟
☐ 七分熟
☐ 全熟

🎧 Track 177

---

con·cise [kənˋsaɪs]

形 簡潔的、簡明的

英英 giving a lot of information in a clear manner with few words

例 The final essay for the course's assignment should be **concise** and informative.
這堂課的期末文章需要簡短而資訊豐富。

☐ 三分熟
☐ 五分熟
☐ 七分熟
☐ 全熟

---

con·dense

[kənˋdɛns]

動 縮小、濃縮
片 condensed milk 煉乳

英英 to make denser or more concentrated

例 He **condensed** his report from 1,500 words to 1,000.
他將報告從 2000 字濃縮到 1000 字。。

☐ 三分熟
☐ 五分熟
☐ 七分熟
☐ 全熟

---

con·fer [kənˋfɝ]

動 商議、商討

英英 to discuss with other people before making a decision

例 They **conferred** on the marketing strategies for the next quarter.
他們商討下一季的行銷策略。

☐ 三分熟
☐ 五分熟
☐ 七分熟
☐ 全熟

---

con·fi·den·tial

[ˌkɑnfəˋdɛnʃəl]

形 可信任的、機密的
同 secret 機密的

英英 intended to be kept private

例 If your computer is infected with malware, the **confidential** information could be stolen.
如果你的電腦受到惡意軟體感染，機密的資料可能會被竊取。

☐ 三分熟
☐ 五分熟
☐ 七分熟
☐ 全熟

---

con·form

[kənˋfɔrm]

動 使符合、遵照
片 conform to 遵守

英英 comply with rules, standards, or conventions

例 If you don't **conform** to the aviation protocols, you will be fined.
如果你不遵守航空規定，你就會遭到罰款。

☐ 三分熟
☐ 五分熟
☐ 七分熟
☐ 全熟

---

con·fron·ta·tion

[ˌkɑnfrʌnˋteʃən]

名 對抗、對峙

英英 a dispute, fight, or argument between two groups of people

例 There was a heated **confrontation** between the conservatives and liberalists.
保守份子和自由主義者之間產生激烈的對抗。

☐ 三分熟
☐ 五分熟
☐ 七分熟
☐ 全熟

---

con·gress·man/ con·gress·wom·an

[ˋkɑŋgrəsˌmæn]/
[ˋkɑŋgrəsˌwʊmən]

名 眾議員／女眾議員

英英 a member of the US Congress

例 The actor participated in the campaign and got elected to be a **congressman**.
演員參加競選並獲選為眾議員。

☐ 三分熟
☐ 五分熟
☐ 七分熟
☐ 全熟

con·quest

[ˈkɑŋkwɛst]

名 征服、獲勝
同 submit 使屈服

英英 the action of taking control of an country, situation, or area

例 The **conquest** of Egypt established the empire's dominant status in north Africa.
征服埃及使這個帝國在北非奠定主宰的基礎。

☐ 三分熟
☐ 五分熟
☐ 七分熟
☐ 全熟

con·sci·en·tious

[ˌkɑnʃɪˈɛnʃəs]

形 本著良心的、有原則的
同 faithful 忠誠的

英英 diligent, responsible, and thorough in carrying out one's work or duties

例 The assistant is **conscientious** about planning for the details of the event.
助理用心規劃這個活動的細節。

☐ 三分熟
☐ 五分熟
☐ 七分熟
☐ 全熟

con·sen·sus

[kənˈsɛnsəs]

名 一致、全體意見

英英 general agreement

例 After a thorough discussion, the **consensus** is established.
詳細討論之後，有了全體的共識。

☐ 三分熟
☐ 五分熟
☐ 七分熟
☐ 全熟

con·ser·va·tion

[ˌkɑnsəˈveʃən]

名 保存、維護

英英 preservation or restoration of the natural environment, resources, and wildlife

例 The organization aims to raise public's awareness for **conservation** of the endangered species.
這個組織宗旨在提升大眾對保護瀕危物種的重視。

☐ 三分熟
☐ 五分熟
☐ 七分熟
☐ 全熟

con·so·la·tion

[ˌkɑnsəˈleʃən]

名 撫恤、安慰、慰藉
反 pain 使痛苦

英英 comfort or prize received after a loss or disappointment

例 The cats and dogs have brought some **consolation** to the patients with depression.
這些貓和狗為憂鬱的病患帶來一些安慰。

☐ 三分熟
☐ 五分熟
☐ 七分熟
☐ 全熟

con·spir·a·cy

[kənˈspɪrəsɪ]

名 陰謀

英英 a secret plan by a group to do something unlawful or harmful

例 The **conspiracy** of embezzlement was revealed by the clerk.
櫃檯員工揭露了盜用公款的陰謀。

☐ 三分熟
☐ 五分熟
☐ 七分熟
☐ 全熟

con·stit·u·ent

[kənˈstɪtʃʊənt]

名 成分、組成要素
形 組成的、成分的
同 component 成分

英英 being a part of a whole; parts or elements which form something

例 The **constituents** of the mixture are specified on the label.
標籤上有寫這種混合物的成分。

☐ 三分熟
☐ 五分熟
☐ 七分熟
☐ 全熟

C

🎧 **Track 179**

con·sul·ta·tion
[ˌkɑnsl̩ˈteʃən]

名 討教、諮詢

英英 to seek advice and information from

例 The director conducts individual **consultation** meetings with his subordinates once in a while.
這位主任偶爾會和屬下進行個別的諮詢會議。

☐ 三分熟
☐ 五分熟
☐ 七分熟
☐ 全熟

con·sump·tion
[kənˈsʌmpʃən]

名 消費、消費量
同 waste 消耗

英英 the action or process of consuming

例 New policies have been implemented to reduce **consumption** of plastic products.
減少塑膠產品使用量的新政策已開始施行。

☐ 三分熟
☐ 五分熟
☐ 七分熟
☐ 全熟

con·tem·pla·tion
[ˌkɑntɛmˈpleʃən]

名 注視、凝視、冥想

英英 the action of thinking over something

例 She spends some time in quiet **contemplation** and meditation before sleep every day.
她每天睡前都會花一些時間安靜冥想和沉思。

☐ 三分熟
☐ 五分熟
☐ 七分熟
☐ 全熟

con·test·ant
[kənˈtɛstənt]

名 競爭者、參賽者

英英 a person who takes part in a contest

例 The **contestants** had to provide a urine sample for drug test.
參賽者需要提供尿液樣本以進行禁藥檢測。

☐ 三分熟
☐ 五分熟
☐ 七分熟
☐ 全熟

con·trac·tor
[ˈkɑntræktɚ]

名 立契約者、承包商

英英 a person who undertakes a project to provide materials or labor for a job

例 A compensation should be paid if one of the **contractors** wants to withdraw from the deal.
如果立契約者其中一方想要退出協定，需支付補償金。

☐ 三分熟
☐ 五分熟
☐ 七分熟
☐ 全熟

con·tra·dict
[ˌkɑntrəˈdɪkt]

動 反駁、矛盾、否認

英英 (of people) to say the opposite of what someone else has said, or (of one fact or statement) to be so different from another fact or statement that one of them must be wrong

例 We would not trust him for his deeds often **contradict** with his words.
我們不願意再相信他，因為他的行為和他說的話互相矛盾。

☐ 三分熟
☐ 五分熟
☐ 七分熟
☐ 全熟

con·tra·dic·tion
[ˌkɑntrəˈdɪkʃən]

名 否定、矛盾
同 denial 否認

英英 a combination of statements, ideas, or features in opposition to one another

例 The cartoon is a sarcasm for **contradiction** in the politician's statements before and after the election.
這個卡通諷刺了政治人物選前和選後言論的矛盾之處。

☐ 三分熟
☐ 五分熟
☐ 七分熟
☐ 全熟

con·tro·ver·sial
[ˌkɑntrəˈvɝʃəl]

形 爭論的、議論的

英英 causing or likely to cause disagreement or argument

例 Racism is one of the **controversial** issues that could tear society apart.
種族主義是其中一項可能撕裂社會的爭論議題。

☐ 三分熟
☐ 五分熟
☐ 七分熟
☐ 全熟

con·tro·ver·sy
[ˈkɑntrəˌvɝsɪ]

名 辯論、爭論

英英 debate or disagreement about a matter which arouse strong contradicting reactions

例 There was a huge **controversy** over the new pension policy.
新的退休金政策有很大的爭議。

☐ 三分熟
☐ 五分熟
☐ 七分熟
☐ 全熟

con·vic·tion
[kənˈvɪkʃən]

名 定罪、說服力

英英 an instance of being convicted of a criminal offence

例 The penalty for an aggravated assault **conviction** could be a fine of over $200,000.
重傷害罪的懲罰可能是二十萬元以上的罰金。

☐ 三分熟
☐ 五分熟
☐ 七分熟
☐ 全熟

co·or·di·nate
[koˈɔrdṇet]/[koˈɔrdṇɪt]

動 調和、使同等
形 同等的
同 equal 同等的

英英 to bring the different elements of a complex activity or organization into an efficient and harmonious relationship

例 The sectors of the company should **coordinate** with each other in the event.
公司的各部門必須要為了這次活動而互相協調。

☐ 三分熟
☐ 五分熟
☐ 七分熟
☐ 全熟

cor·dial [ˈkɔrdʒəl]

形 熱忱的、和善的

英英 warm and friendly

例 The foreign visitors were impressed with the **cordial** reception of the student representatives.
外賓對於學生代表的熱情接待印象深刻。

☐ 三分熟
☐ 五分熟
☐ 七分熟
☐ 全熟

core [kor]

名 果核、核心

英英 he tough heart of various fruits, containing the seeds

例 Filial piety is one of the **core** values in traditional Chinese culture.
孝順是傳統中國文化的核心價值之一。

☐ 三分熟
☐ 五分熟
☐ 七分熟
☐ 全熟

cor·po·rate
[ˈkɔrpərɪt]

形 社團的、公司的

英英 relating to a business corporation

例 Working overtime is not a positive **corporate** culture.
加班不是一個正向的公司文化。

☐ 三分熟
☐ 五分熟
☐ 七分熟
☐ 全熟

corps [korps]

名 軍團、兵團

英英 a main subdivision of an army in the field, consisting of two or more divisions

例 The volunteer **corps** from Britain have created changes in several underdeveloped areas.
來自英國的志願軍已經為好幾個落後地區帶來改變。

☐ 三分熟
☐ 五分熟
☐ 七分熟
☐ 全熟

---

corpse [korps]

名 屍體、屍首

英英 a dead body of a human or animal

例 The shocking photo of **corpse** on the battlefield reminded people the value of peace.
令人震驚的戰場屍體相片提醒人們和平的價值。

☐ 三分熟
☐ 五分熟
☐ 七分熟
☐ 全熟

---

cor·re·spon·dent

[ˌkɔrə`spɑndənt]

名 通信者、通訊記者
同 journalist 新聞工作者

英英 a person who writes letters in response to another, usually on a regular basis

例 He worked as a foreign **correspondent** for AFP.
他曾是法新社的駐外記者。

☐ 三分熟
☐ 五分熟
☐ 七分熟
☐ 全熟

---

cor·rup·tion

[kə`rʌpʃən]

名 敗壞、墮落

英英 the act of acting dishonestly in return for money or personal gain

例 **Corruption** in public administration has a negative influence on the nation.
公共行政的腐敗對國家有負面的影響。

☐ 三分熟
☐ 五分熟
☐ 七分熟
☐ 全熟

---

cos·met·ic

[kɑz`mɛtɪk]

形 化妝用的

英英 relating to treatment with the intention to improve a person's appearance

例 She spent a quarter of her monthly wage on luxury **cosmetic** products.
她花掉四分之一的月薪買昂貴的化妝品。

☐ 三分熟
☐ 五分熟
☐ 七分熟
☐ 全熟

---

cos·met·ics

[kɑz`mɛtɪks]

名 化妝品

英英 substances such as lipstick or powder, which people apply on their face to make themselves look more attractive

例 Using **cosmetics** containing harmful chemicals may ruin your skin.
使用含有有害化學物質的化妝品可能會損壞皮膚。

☐ 三分熟
☐ 五分熟
☐ 七分熟
☐ 全熟

cos·mo·pol·i·tan

[ˌkɑzmə`pɑlətn̩]

名 世界主義者、
四海為家的人
形 世界主義的、世界性
的、國際性的
同 international 國際的

英英 a person with experience of many different countries and cultures; consisting of people from many different nations and cultures

例 A **cosmopolitan** crowd resides in this area peacefully.
來自各國的居民在此區和平共處。

□三分熟
□五分熟
□七分熟
□全熟

coun·ter·part

[`kaʊntɚpart]

名 副本、極相像的人、
配對物、對應的人

英英 a duplicate copy

例 The high school students in Taiwan are under greater pressure than their **counterparts** in the U.S.
臺灣的高中生比美國的高中生承受更多的學業壓力。

□三分熟
□五分熟
□七分熟
□全熟

cov·er·age

[`kʌvərɪdʒ]

名 覆蓋範圍、保險範圍

英英 the extent to which something is covered

例 The car insurance **coverage** is specified in the contract.
汽車保險範圍在合約書中有詳細說明。

□三分熟
□五分熟
□七分熟
□全熟

cov·et [`kʌvɪt]

動 垂涎、貪圖

英英 to want or yearn to possess something belonging to someone else

例 The ambitious young man **coveted** greater political power.
有野心的年輕人垂涎更大的政治權利。

□三分熟
□五分熟
□七分熟
□全熟

cramp [kræmp]

名 抽筋、鉗子
動 用鉗子夾緊、使抽筋

英英 an instrument used for clamping two objects together; to clamp two things together with a cramp

例 Most swimmers would warm up themselves before getting into the pool to prevent leg **cramp**.
大部分游泳者進到泳池之前會暖身以預防腳抽筋。

□三分熟
□五分熟
□七分熟
□全熟

cred·i·bil·i·ty

[ˌkrɛdə`bɪlətɪ]

名 可信度、確實性

英英 the quality of being believed and trusted

例 The entrepreneur emphasizes honesty and **credibility** in business.
企業家強調做生意要講求誠實信用。

□三分熟
□五分熟
□七分熟
□全熟

cred·i·ble

[`krɛdəbl̩]

形 可信的、可靠的

英英 able to be believed; convincing, trusted

例 Is the source of the news **credible**?
這個新聞的來源可靠嗎？

□三分熟
□五分熟
□七分熟
□全熟

🎧 Track 183

cri·te·ri·on

[kraɪˋtɪrɪən]

名 標準、基準
同 standard 標準

英英 a set of principles or standards by which something may be judged or decided

例 He fulfills the **criteria** for undertaking the position.
他符合接下這個職位的標準。

☐三分熟
☐五分熟
☐七分熟
☐全熟

crook [krʊk]

名 彎曲、彎處
動 使彎曲

英英 the inside part of the arm that bends; to make something bend

例 Turn left at the **crook** on the road, and you will see your destination.
在彎路左轉，你就會看到你的目的地。

☐三分熟
☐五分熟
☐七分熟
☐全熟

crooked [ˋkrʊkɪd]

形 彎曲的、歪曲的

英英 bent or twisted out of shape or position

例 We passed through the **crooked** trail in the woods.
我們經過樹林裡彎曲的小路。

☐三分熟
☐五分熟
☐七分熟
☐全熟

cru·cial [ˋkruʃəl]

形 關係重大的
同 important 重大的

英英 important, decisive or critical

例 Budging is the **crucial** factor to consider for the interior renovation.
預算是室內裝修的重要考量因素。

☐三分熟
☐五分熟
☐七分熟
☐全熟

crude [krʊd]

形 天然的、未加工的
片 crude oil 原油

英英 in a natural or raw state; not yet processed or refined

例 The price of **crude** oil has been fluctuating over the past few years.
過去幾年，原油價格一直在波動。

☐三分熟
☐五分熟
☐七分熟
☐全熟

cruise [kruz]

動 航行、巡航

英英 to move slowly around at a constant speed without a precise destination, especially for pleasure

例 The U.S. military naval vessel **cruised** through Taiwan Strait.
美國軍艦航行經過臺灣海峽。

☐三分熟
☐五分熟
☐七分熟
☐全熟

cruis·er [ˋkruzɚ]

名 遊艇、巡洋艦、巡邏車

英英 a fast warship larger than a destroyer and less heavily armed than a battleship

例 The cabins of the **cruiser** are equipped with entertainment systems.
這艘遊艇的船艙有配備娛樂系統。

☐三分熟
☐五分熟
☐七分熟
☐全熟

crumb [krʌm]

名 小塊、碎屑、少許

英英 a small fragment of bread, cake, or biscuit

例 The sparrows are enjoying the bread **crumbs** left by the child.
麻雀在享用小朋友留下的麵包屑。

□ 三分熟
□ 五分熟
□ 七分熟
□ 全熟

---

crum·ble [ˈkrʌmbl̩]

名 碎屑、碎片
動 弄成碎屑、崩潰
同 mash 壓碎
片 that's the way the cookie crumbles 事已定局

英英 a whole breaking or falling apart into small fragments, to break something apart into small fragments

例 She **crumbled** a bread in her fingers.
她用手指捏碎了一塊麵包。

□ 三分熟
□ 五分熟
□ 七分熟
□ 全熟

---

crust [krʌst]

名 麵包皮、派皮
動 覆以外皮

英英 the tough outer part of a loaf or slice of bread; to cover with an outer part

例 Shiny **crust** and tender interior are crucial for delicious baguettes.
長棍麵包好吃的祕訣，就是在閃亮的外皮和柔軟的內裡。

□ 三分熟
□ 五分熟
□ 七分熟
□ 全熟

---

cul·ti·vate

[ˈkʌltəˌvet]

動 耕種

英英 to prepare (land) for crops or gardening

例 The soil in this area is suitable to **cultivate** tea plants.
這個地區的土壤適合種植茶葉植物。

□ 三分熟
□ 五分熟
□ 七分熟
□ 全熟

---

cu·mu·la·tive

[ˈkjumjəˌletɪv]

形 累增的、累加的

英英 increasing or increased by gradual additions

例 The **cumulative** effect of inhaling chemical fumes can be harmful to human body.
吸入含有化學物質的煙霧，長期累積，會對身體有不好的影響。

□ 三分熟
□ 五分熟
□ 七分熟
□ 全熟

---

cus·tom·ar·y

[ˈkʌstəmˌɛrɪ]

形 慣例的、平常的

英英 according to customs; usual

例 It is **customary** for Muslim women to wear hijabs.
穆斯林女性習慣穿頭巾。

□ 三分熟
□ 五分熟
□ 七分熟
□ 全熟

C

Dd

🎧 Track 185

daf·fo·dil [ˋdæfədɪl]

名 黃水仙、水仙花

英英 a bright yellow flower with a long trumpet-shaped center that usually grows in spring

例 **Daffodils** are often used to decorate the house during Chinese New Year.
水仙花在中國新年的時候常常被用來裝飾家中。

☐ 三分熟
☐ 五分熟
☐ 七分熟
☐ 全熟

---

dan·druff

[ˋdændrəf]

名 頭皮屑

英英 pieces of dead skin on a person's scalp and in the hair

例 **Dandruff** is a flaky skin condition that affects up to 50% of people.
頭皮屑是一種皮膚片狀脫落的狀況，影響多達 50% 的人。

☐ 三分熟
☐ 五分熟
☐ 七分熟
☐ 全熟

---

day·break

[ˋdeˌbrek]

名 破曉、黎明

英英 dawn; when the first light of the day appears in the sky

例 The travelers set off at the **daybreak**.
旅人在破曉時出發。

☐ 三分熟
☐ 五分熟
☐ 七分熟
☐ 全熟

---

dead·ly [ˋdɛdlɪ]

形 致命的
副 極度地

英英 causing or potential to cause death; of a voice, glance, etc. filled with hate; extremely

例 Ebola is one of the **deadliest** kinds of virus in the 21st century.
伊波拉是 21 世紀最致命的病毒種類之一。

☐ 三分熟
☐ 五分熟
☐ 七分熟
☐ 全熟

---

de·cent [ˋdisn̩t]

形 端正的、正當的、
體面的、還不錯的
同 correct 端正的

英英 of a satisfactory level; conforming with generally accepted standards of morality or respectability

例 She attended several interviews, hoping to find a **decent** job.
她去過幾次面試，希望可以找到體面的工作。

☐ 三分熟
☐ 五分熟
☐ 七分熟
☐ 全熟

---

de·ci·sive

[dɪˋsaɪsɪv]

形 有決斷力的

英英 settling an issue quickly; having the ability to make decisions quickly

例 A leader needs to be **decisive** and motivating.
領導者應該要有決斷力，以及懂得激勵人心。

☐ 三分熟
☐ 五分熟
☐ 七分熟
☐ 全熟

---

de·cline [dɪˋklaɪn]

名 衰敗
動 下降、衰敗、婉拒

英英 to become smaller, weaker, lessening quality or quantity

例 Many elderly people have **declining** health conditions after they are sent to the nursing home.
許多老年人被送到養護中心之後，健康情況就衰退。

☐ 三分熟
☐ 五分熟
☐ 七分熟
☐ 全熟

D

ded·i·cate

[ˈdɛdəˌket]

動 供奉、奉獻、致力於
同 devote 奉獻

英英 to devote or give most of one's energy to a particular subject, task, or purpose

例 He **dedicated** himself to protecting endangered species.
他致力於保護瀕危的動物。

☐ 三分熟
☐ 五分熟
☐ 七分熟
☐ 全熟

ded·i·ca·tion

[ˌdɛdəˈkeʃən]

名 奉獻、供奉

英英 the quality of being devoted to a purpose or task

例 Mr. Jackson was presented an award for his **dedication** to music industry.
傑克森先生獲頒獎項表揚他對音樂產業的奉獻。

☐ 三分熟
☐ 五分熟
☐ 七分熟
☐ 全熟

deem [dim]

動 認為、視為
同 consider 認為

英英 to regard, judge, or consider in a specified way

例 Jamie Oliver is **deemed** one of the most successful chefs in the modern time.
傑米奧利佛被認為是現代最成功的廚師之一。

☐ 三分熟
☐ 五分熟
☐ 七分熟
☐ 全熟

de·fect [dɪˈfɛkt]

名 缺陷、缺點
動 脫逃、脫離

英英 something or someone that is faulty or has a problem; to escape from a place

例 She suffers from congenital heart **defect**, so she could not do intense exercise.
她有先天性心臟病，所以她不能做激烈的運動。

☐ 三分熟
☐ 五分熟
☐ 七分熟
☐ 全熟

de·fi·cien·cy

[dɪˈfɪʃənsɪ]

名 匱乏、不足
同 shortage 短缺

英英 a lack or shortage; a failure or shortcoming of something

例 Severe vitamin D **deficiency** may cause kidney and liver diseases.
嚴重缺乏維生素 D 可能會導致腎臟和肝臟的疾病。

☐ 三分熟
☐ 五分熟
☐ 七分熟
☐ 全熟

de·grade [dɪˈgred]

動 降級、降等

英英 to cause someone to feel a loss of dignity or self-respect

例 He was **degraded** for being involved in the scandal.
他因為涉及醜聞而遭到降級。

☐ 三分熟
☐ 五分熟
☐ 七分熟
☐ 全熟

de·lib·er·ate

[dɪˈlɪbəˌret]/[dɪˈlɪbərɪt]

動 仔細考慮
形 慎重的

英英 done consciously, with intentions; careful and unhurried

例 A scam is a **deliberate** plan to deceive people into handing over their property or personal information.
詐騙是一個仔細考慮過的計畫，要欺騙人交出自己的財產或者個人資訊。

☐ 三分熟
☐ 五分熟
☐ 七分熟
☐ 全熟

de·lin·quent

[dɪˈlɪŋkwənt]

名 違法者
形 拖欠的、違法的

英英 (especially of young people) potential to commit crime; a person who commits a crime

例 He was fined for being **delinquent** in paying his income tax.
他因為拖欠所得稅而遭到罰款。

☐三分熟
☐五分熟
☐七分熟
☐全熟

de·nounce

[dɪˈnaʊns]

動 公然抨擊、譴責

英英 to publicly declare or accuse to be wrong or evil

例 The actor was **denounced** for saying something obscene in public.
演員因為在公開場合開黃腔受到譴責。

☐三分熟
☐五分熟
☐七分熟
☐全熟

den·si·ty [ˈdɛnsətɪ]

名 稠密、濃密
片 population density
人口密度

英英 the degree of compactness of a substance; mass per unit volume

例 Macau is the country of the highest population **density** in 2019.
澳門是 2019 年人口密度最高的國家。

☐三分熟
☐五分熟
☐七分熟
☐全熟

den·tal [ˈdɛntl̩]

形 牙齒的

英英 elating to the teeth or to dentistry

例 Brushing and flossing are important for **dental** care.
要照顧好牙齒，刷牙和使用牙線很重要。

☐三分熟
☐五分熟
☐七分熟
☐全熟

de·pict [dɪˈpɪkt]

動 描述、敘述

英英 to represent by a drawing, picture, or other art form

例 The poet **depicts** the scenery with metaphors and similes in his works.
詩人在作品中用明喻和暗喻描述景色。

☐三分熟
☐五分熟
☐七分熟
☐全熟

de·prive [dɪˈpraɪv]

動 剝奪、使……喪失

英英 to prevent from having, using, or enjoying something

例 People under the rule of a dictatorial system are **deprived** the right of speech.
在專制制度統治下的人被剝奪言論自由。

☐三分熟
☐五分熟
☐七分熟
☐全熟

de·rive [dəˈraɪv]

動 引出、源自

英英 to obtain something from a source; base something on a modification of

例 The writer's inspiration for the novel **derives** from her daily experience.
作家寫小說的靈感源自於她的生活經驗。

☐三分熟
☐五分熟
☐七分熟
☐全熟

dep·u·ty [ˈdɛpjətɪ]
名 代表、代理人、副職
同 agent 代理人

英英 a person appointed to undertake the duties of a superior in the superior's absence; the one with the second most important job in the organization

例 He was promoted as a **deputy** manager last month.
他上個月被晉升為副經理。

---

de·scend [dɪˈsɛnd]
動 下降、突襲
同 drop 下降

英英 to move in a downward motion; slope or lead downwards

例 The pilot made accurate decision about when to **descend**.
駕駛員很精準地決定何時要下降。

---

de·scen·dant
[dɪˈsɛndənt]
名 子孫、後裔

英英 a person, animal, etc. that is related to a particular ancestor

例 She left a huge sum of heritage for her **descendants**.
她留下一大筆遺產給子孫。

---

de·scent [dɪˈsɛnt]
名 下降、下坡

英英 an act or the action of going in a downward motion

例 There is a sign by the road warning drivers about a steep **descent** ahead.
路旁有個標語在警告駕駛前方有陡峭的下坡。

---

des·ig·nate
[ˈdɛzɪɡˌnet]
動 指出
形 選派的

英英 to choose someone for a specified status; officially choosing someone for a specified status or name to

例 He was **designated** to represent the company on the industry conference.
他被指派代表公司參加產業研討會。

---

des·tined
[ˈdɛstɪnd]
形 命運註定的

英英 intended (for a particular purpose)

例 The tyrant claimed that he was **destined** to be a sovereign.
暴君宣稱他命中註定要成為君主。

---

de·tach [dɪˈtætʃ]
動 派遣、分開
同 separate 分開

英英 to unattach something and remove it

例 The booster **detached** from the space shuttle.
推進器由太空梭分離了。

de·tain [dɪˋten]

動 阻止、妨礙、拘留、扣留

英英 to keep someone somewhere without allowing to leave

例 The journalist was **detained** for three months before the international human right organization intervened.
在國際人權組織介入前，這名記者已被拘禁三個月。

☐ 三分熟
☐ 五分熟
☐ 七分熟
☐ 全熟

---

de·ter [dɪˋtɜ]

動 使停止做、威攝住、使斷念

英英 to discourage someone from doing something through fear of the consequences

例 Severe penalty is deemed as an effective method to **deter** crime.
嚴刑被視為遏止犯罪的有效方式。

☐ 三分熟
☐ 五分熟
☐ 七分熟
☐ 全熟

---

de·te·ri·o·rate

[dɪˋtɪrɪəˌret]

動 使惡化、降低

英英 to become progressively worse

例 The air quality in the urban area **deteriorates** with the increasing number of vehicles.
隨著車輛增加，都市地區的空氣品質愈加惡化。

☐ 三分熟
☐ 五分熟
☐ 七分熟
☐ 全熟

---

de·val·ue

[diˋvælju]

動 降低價值

英英 to reduce the worth of; reduce the official value of (a currency) relating to other currencies

例 A second-hand car may **devalue** because of high mileage.
二手車可能會因為里程數高而價值降低。

☐ 三分熟
☐ 五分熟
☐ 七分熟
☐ 全熟

---

di·a·be·tes

[ˌdaɪəˋbitiz]

名 糖尿病

英英 a medical condition in which the body cannot control the blood sugar level

例 Type 1 **diabetes** is often treated with insulin injection.
第一型糖尿病常是以注射胰島素來治療。

☐ 三分熟
☐ 五分熟
☐ 七分熟
☐ 全熟

---

di·ag·nose

[ˋdaɪəgnoz]

動 診斷

英英 to say what is wrong with a person who is ill

例 The doctor was able to **diagnose** her condition based on her symptoms.
醫生可以根據她的症狀診斷出她的狀況。

☐ 三分熟
☐ 五分熟
☐ 七分熟
☐ 全熟

---

di·ag·no·sis

[ˌdaɪəgˋnosɪs]

名 診斷（複數）

英英 the identification of the nature of an illness or other problem by examining the symptoms

例 The clinic could not issue a certificate of **diagnosis**.
診所無法開立診斷證明書。

☐ 三分熟
☐ 五分熟
☐ 七分熟
☐ 全熟

D

di·a·gram
[ˈdaɪəˌgræm]

名 圖表、圖樣
動 圖解
同 design 圖樣

英英 a drawing schematically representing of the appearance or structure of something; to make a drawing schematically representing of the appearance or structure of something

例 The **diagram** shows the unemployment rate over the past years.
圖表顯示出過去幾年的失業率。

☐ 三分熟
☐ 五分熟
☐ 七分熟
☐ 全熟

di·am·e·ter
[daɪˈæmətɚ]

名 直徑

英英 a straight line going from one side to another side of a circle

例 The arena is 100 meters in **diameter**, and it can accommodate 3000 viewers.
這個圓形競技場直徑有一百公尺，而且可以容納三千位觀眾。

☐ 三分熟
☐ 五分熟
☐ 七分熟
☐ 全熟

dic·tate [ˈdɪktet]

動 口授、聽寫、下令

英英 to state or order authoritatively

例 The doctor **dictated** the proper ways of attending the patient.
醫生口述照顧病人的適當方式。

☐ 三分熟
☐ 五分熟
☐ 七分熟
☐ 全熟

dic·ta·tion
[dɪkˈteʃən]

名 口述、口授、命令

英英 the activity of dictating something for someone else to write down

例 We **defied** that dictation from the brutal leader.
我們違抗了殘暴領導者的命令。

☐ 三分熟
☐ 五分熟
☐ 七分熟
☐ 全熟

dic·ta·tor
[ˈdɪkˌtetɚ]

名 獨裁者、發號施令者

英英 a ruler with complete and total power over a country

例 The **dictator** was overthrown for his despotism.
獨裁者因為過於專制而被推翻。

☐ 三分熟
☐ 五分熟
☐ 七分熟
☐ 全熟

dif·fer·en·ti·ate
[dɪfəˈrɛnʃɪˌet]

動 辨別、區分

英英 to recognize or identify as different; distinguish

例 The morals of the fables teach people to **differentiate** between good and evil.
寓言的啟示，教導人們要區辨善惡。

☐ 三分熟
☐ 五分熟
☐ 七分熟
☐ 全熟

di·lem·ma
[dəˈlɛmə]

名 左右為難、窘境

英英 a situation in which a difficult choice has to be made between two alternatives, especially when a decision will bring undesirable results either way

例 We faced the **dilemma** of telling a white lie or speaking of the truth.
我們陷入兩難，不知道要說善意謊言還是說出實情。

☐ 三分熟
☐ 五分熟
☐ 七分熟
☐ 全熟

di·men·sion

[dəˈmɛnʃən]

名 尺寸、方面
同 size 尺寸

英英 an extent that is measurable, such as length, breadth, or height

例 The model of the house was presented in three **dimensions**.
這個房子的尺寸是用三個面向立體呈現。

☐ 三分熟
☐ 五分熟
☐ 七分熟
☐ 全熟

di·min·ish

[dəˈmɪnɪʃ]

動 縮小、減少

英英 to make or become less

例 The company's revenue **diminished** due to the economic depression.
公司的收入因為經濟蕭條而減少。

☐ 三分熟
☐ 五分熟
☐ 七分熟
☐ 全熟

di·plo·ma·cy

[dɪˈploməsɪ]

名 外交、外交手腕
同 politics 手腕

英英 the profession, activity, or skill of managing international relations with governments

例 Her experience in international **diplomacy** makes her a suitable candidate for the Minister of Foreign Affairs.
她豐富的國際外交經驗，使她成為外交部長的合適人選。

☐ 三分熟
☐ 五分熟
☐ 七分熟
☐ 全熟

dip·lo·ma·tic

[ˌdɪpləˈmætɪk]

形 外交的、外交官的
片 diplomatic allies 邦交國

英英 concerning diplomacy

例 His brother had been in the **diplomatic** service.
他的哥哥曾在外交部門工作。。

☐ 三分熟
☐ 五分熟
☐ 七分熟
☐ 全熟

di·rec·to·ry

[dəˈrɛktərɪ]

名 姓名地址錄、電話簿

英英 a book listing details such as addresses and telephone numbers of individuals or organizations

例 I checked the telephone **directory** for contact number of the plumber in the community.
我在電話簿查詢社區裡水電師傅的聯絡方式。

☐ 三分熟
☐ 五分熟
☐ 七分熟
☐ 全熟

dis·a·bil·i·ty

[ˌdɪsəˈbɪlətɪ]

名 無能、無力、殘疾

英英 a physical or mental condition that inhibits a person's movements, senses, or activities

例 Dr. Hawking continued with his researches despite his physical **disabilities**.
霍金博士儘管身體殘障，還是繼續從事研究。

☐ 三分熟
☐ 五分熟
☐ 七分熟
☐ 全熟

dis·a·ble [dɪsˈebl̩]

動 使無能力、使無作用

英英 to limit someone in their movements, sense or activities because of a disease or an accident

例 The alarm system in the house was **disabled** by the burglar.
家中的防盜系統被小偷破壞了。

☐ 三分熟
☐ 五分熟
☐ 七分熟
☐ 全熟

D

dis·ap·prove

[ˌdɪsəˈpruv]

動 反對、不贊成
同 oppose 反對

英英 to have or express disdain

例 Our proposal was **disapproved** by the Board of Directors.
我們的提案被董事會否決了。

☐ 三分熟
☐ 五分熟
☐ 七分熟
☐ 全熟

dis·as·trous

[dɪzˈæstrəs]

形 災害的、悲慘的
同 tragic 悲慘的

英英 causing great damage resulting in disaster

例 The **disastrous** typhoon left hundreds of people homeless in this area.
這次慘烈的颱風，造成此區域數百人無家可歸。

☐ 三分熟
☐ 五分熟
☐ 七分熟
☐ 全熟

dis·charge

[dɪsˈtʃɑrdʒ]

名 排出、卸下
動 卸下

英英 to let go, dismiss or allow to leave

例 The water pollution was caused by the waste water **discharged** from the factory.
水污染是工廠排放的污水導致的。

☐ 三分熟
☐ 五分熟
☐ 七分熟
☐ 全熟

dis·ci·pli·nar·y

[ˈdɪsəplɪnˌɛrɪ]

形 訓練上的、訓育的、懲戒的

英英 the practice of punishing people when rules or a code of behavior is broken

例 Physical punishment was considered an inappropriate **disciplinary** measure.
體罰被視為是不妥當的紀律措施。

☐ 三分熟
☐ 五分熟
☐ 七分熟
☐ 全熟

dis·close

[dɪsˈkloz]

動 暴露、露出

英英 to make secret or new information known

例 The bribery scandal was **disclosed** by a veteran journalist.
賄賂醜聞是由一位資深記者揭露的。

☐ 三分熟
☐ 五分熟
☐ 七分熟
☐ 全熟

dis·clo·sure

[dɪsˈkloʒɚ]

名 暴露、揭發

英英 the action of disclosing information; a fact, especially a secret, that is disclosed

例 The company has limited **disclosure** about the components in its products.
公司對於其產品的成分只揭露一部分。

☐ 三分熟
☐ 五分熟
☐ 七分熟
☐ 全熟

dis·com·fort

[dɪsˈkʌmfət]

名 不安、不自在、不適
動 使不安、使不自在

英英 slight pain; slight anxiety or embarrassment; to make someone anxious or embarrassed

例 The **discomfort** caused by the new pair of shoes made her unable to focus on the job.
因為新鞋子帶來的不適感，使她無法專注於工作上。

☐ 三分熟
☐ 五分熟
☐ 七分熟
☐ 全熟

🎧 **Track 193**

---

dis·creet [dɪˋskrit]

形 謹慎的、慎重的

英英 careful not to attract attention, cause embarrassment, or give offence

例 **Discreet** analysis is needed before we could make any inference from the survey.
從這問卷調查推論出結論，我們需要做謹慎的分析。

□ 三分熟
□ 五分熟
□ 七分熟
□ 全熟

---

dis·crim·i·na·tion

[dɪˌskrɪməˋneʃən]

名 辨別
片 gender discrimination 性別歧視

英英 the act of discriminating against people of different sex, race, religion, etc.

例 The "glass ceiling" for female workers is considered a sign of gender **discrimination** in workplace.
女性員工的「玻璃天花板」被認為是職場上性別歧視的徵象。

□ 三分熟
□ 五分熟
□ 七分熟
□ 全熟

---

dis·grace

[dɪsˋgres]

名 不名譽
動 羞辱
同 shame 羞恥

英英 loss of reputation as the result of a doing something dishonorable

例 If you cheat in the contest, you will bring **disgrace** to your school.
如果你在比賽中作弊，將會給學校帶來羞辱。

□ 三分熟
□ 五分熟
□ 七分熟
□ 全熟

---

dis·grace·ful

[dɪsˋgresfəl]

形 可恥的、不名譽的

英英 shockingly unacceptable, something that is very bad

例 It is **disgraceful** to speak ill of people behind them.
在別人背後說他們壞話是不名譽的行為。

□ 三分熟
□ 五分熟
□ 七分熟
□ 全熟

---

dis·man·tle

[dɪsˋmæntḷ]

動 拆開、分解、扯下

英英 to take something down into pieces

例 The robot can be programmed to perform a task of **dismantling** a bomb.
這個機器人可以被設定去執行拆除炸彈的任務。

□ 三分熟
□ 五分熟
□ 七分熟
□ 全熟

---

dis·may [dɪsˋme]

名 恐慌、沮喪
動 狼狽、恐慌

英英 feeling disappointment, discouragement, and distress

例 To our **dismay**, the field trip was cancelled because of the typhoon.
令我們沮喪的是，校外教學因颱風而取消了。

□ 三分熟
□ 五分熟
□ 七分熟
□ 全熟

---

dis·patch [dɪˋspætʃ]

名 急速、快速處理
動 派遣、發送
同 send 發送

英英 send off to a destination or for a purpose; the action of being quick

例 The troops were **dispatched** to Middle East to suppress the local civil war.
軍隊被派至中東壓制當地的內戰。

□ 三分熟
□ 五分熟
□ 七分熟
□ 全熟

---

dis·pens·a·ble

[dɪˋspɛnsəbḷ]

形 非必要的、可有可無的

英英 easily or able to be replaced or done without

例 Those decorative props were regarded **dispensable**.
那些裝飾的道具被視為是可有可無的。

☐ 三分熟
☐ 五分熟
☐ 七分熟
☐ 全熟

dis·perse [dɪˋspɝs]

動 使散開、驅散

英英 to go or spread in different directions or over a wide area

例 The crowd of demonstrators were **dispersed** by the police.
抗議群眾被警察驅散。

☐ 三分熟
☐ 五分熟
☐ 七分熟
☐ 全熟

dis·place [dɪsˋples]

動 移置、移走、使離鄉背井

英英 to change or shift from the proper or usual position

例 The **displaced** person sought asylum in the European country.
離鄉背井的人在歐洲國家尋求庇護。

☐ 三分熟
☐ 五分熟
☐ 七分熟
☐ 全熟

dis·please

[dɪsˋpliz]

動 得罪、使不快

英英 to annoy or upset

例 The man was degraded for he **displeased** his supervisor.
這人因為得罪了主管而被降級。

☐ 三分熟
☐ 五分熟
☐ 七分熟
☐ 全熟

dis·pos·a·ble

[dɪˋspozəbḷ]

形 可任意使用的、免洗的

英英 meant to be used once and then thrown away

例 The woman advocates for replacing **disposable** diapers with reusable ones.
這位女士提倡用可再次使用尿布取代免洗尿布。

☐ 三分熟
☐ 五分熟
☐ 七分熟
☐ 全熟

dis·pos·al

[dɪˋspozḷ]

名 分佈、配置
片 at your disposal
任你使用

英英 the action or process of disposing or getting rid of something

例 Once you get connected to the Internet, lots of online learning resources are at your **disposal**.
只要連上網路，大量的線上學習資源任你使用。

☐ 三分熟
☐ 五分熟
☐ 七分熟
☐ 全熟

dis·re·gard

[ˌdɪsrɪˋgard]

名 蔑視、忽視
動 不理、蔑視

英英 disregarding something or the state of being disregarded; to pay no attention to

例 My roommate **disregarded** my complaint and remained his lousy lifestyle.
我的室友不理會我的抱怨，繼續髒亂的生活方式。

☐ 三分熟
☐ 五分熟
☐ 七分熟
☐ 全熟

🎧 **Track 195**

dis·si·dent
['dɪsədənt]

名 異議者
形 有異議的

英英 a person who opposes official policy in a public way; being in opposition to official policy

例 The tyrant used extreme measures to quiet the **dissidents**.
暴君用極端手段使異議者無法表達意見。

☐ 三分熟
☐ 五分熟
☐ 七分熟
☐ 全熟

dis·solve [dɪ'zɑlv]

動 使溶解

英英 to become a part of a liquid so as to form a solution

例 The laundry detergent can easily **dissolve** in water.
這種洗衣粉易溶解於水中。

☐ 三分熟
☐ 五分熟
☐ 七分熟
☐ 全熟

dis·suade
[dɪ'swed]

動 勸阻、勸止
同 discourage 勸阻

英英 to persuade or advise not to do, to discourage from doing

例 He **dissuaded** me from taking a leave of absence from school.
他勸我不要休學。

☐ 三分熟
☐ 五分熟
☐ 七分熟
☐ 全熟

dis·tort [dɪs'tɔrt]

動 曲解、扭曲

英英 to pull or twist out of shape. 2 give a misleading account of

例 He tends to **distort** my message for negative meanings.
他常會把我的話曲解成負面的意思。

☐ 三分熟
☐ 五分熟
☐ 七分熟
☐ 全熟

dis·tract
[dɪ'strækt]

動 分散

英英 to prevent someone from giving their complete attention to something

例 The music on the radio **distracted** me from my studies.
收音機音樂分散我讀書的注意力。

☐ 三分熟
☐ 五分熟
☐ 七分熟
☐ 全熟

dis·trac·tion
[dɪ'strækʃən]

名 分心、精神渙散、
心煩不安

英英 a thing that diverts attention

例 The **distraction** caused by the smartphone may hinder your academic performance.
智慧型手機造成分心，可能會使你的學業表現變差。

☐ 三分熟
☐ 五分熟
☐ 七分熟
☐ 全熟

dis·trust [dɪs'trʌst]

名 不信任、不信
動 不信

英英 lacking in trust; have little trust in; to regard with suspicion

例 Mutual **distrust** is what causes the negotiation to break down.
互不信任是使談判破裂的主因。

☐ 三分熟
☐ 五分熟
☐ 七分熟
☐ 全熟

dis·tur·bance

[dɪˋstɝbəns]

名 擾亂、騷亂

英英 the action of disturbing or the process of being disturbed

例 The noise from the traditional market was the **disturbance** that kept us from concentrating on our work.
傳統市場噪音的干擾令我們無法專心工作。

☐ 三分熟
☐ 五分熟
☐ 七分熟
☐ 全熟

di·verse [dəˋvɝs]

形 互異的、不同的
同 different 不同的

英英 including many different types, widely varied

例 The **diverse** backgrounds of students in this class make it a miniature society.
班上學生不同的背景使它成為一個社會的縮影。

☐ 三分熟
☐ 五分熟
☐ 七分熟
☐ 全熟

di·ver·si·fy

[daɪˋvɝsəˌfaɪ]

動 使……多樣化

英英 to make or become more diverse; to enlarge or vary its range of products or field of operation

例 The teacher tried to **diversify** in-class activities to motivate students to learn.
老師試圖讓教學活動多樣化來激勵學生學習。

☐ 三分熟
☐ 五分熟
☐ 七分熟
☐ 全熟

di·ver·sion

[dəˋvɝʒən]

名 脫離、轉向、轉換

英英 an instance of diverting attention

例 Some drivers complained about the traffic **diversion** during the festival.
節慶期間交通改道引起一些駕駛的抱怨。

☐ 三分熟
☐ 五分熟
☐ 七分熟
☐ 全熟

di·ver·si·ty

[dəˋvɝsətɪ]

名 差異處、不同點、多樣性

英英 the state of being diverse

例 Biological **diversity** is a criterion for an unspoiled ecosystem.
生物多樣性是完整生態系統的條件。

☐ 三分熟
☐ 五分熟
☐ 七分熟
☐ 全熟

di·vert [dəˋvɝt]

動 使轉向

英英 to send someone somewhere; to cause to change course or take a different route

例 The plane was **diverted** to another runway.
飛機被引導轉向到另一個跑道。

☐ 三分熟
☐ 五分熟
☐ 七分熟
☐ 全熟

doc·trine

[ˋdɑktrɪn]

名 教義

英英 a set of beliefs or principles held and taught by a Church, political party, or other group

例 Philanthropy is considered a principle in Christian **doctrine**.
博愛被視為是基督教義的一個原則。

☐ 三分熟
☐ 五分熟
☐ 七分熟
☐ 全熟

D

🎧 **Track 197**

doc·u·men·ta·ry

[ˌdɑkjə`mɛntərɪ]

名 紀錄
形 文件的

英英 consisting of documents and other material providing an factual account

例 The international **documentary** film festival was held in Berlin.
國際紀錄片影展在柏林舉行。

☐三分熟 ☐五分熟 ☐七分熟 ☐全熟

---

dome [dom]

名 拱形圓屋頂、穹窿
動 覆以圓頂、使成圓頂、拱形屋頂上的

英英 a rounded vault forming the roof of a building, typically with a circular base; to make a dome as a top or head

例 The tourists were amazed by the magnificent paintings on the **dome** of the cathedral.
遊客為教堂圓頂的壯觀畫作感到驚訝。

☐三分熟 ☐五分熟 ☐七分熟 ☐全熟

---

do·nate [`donet]

動 贈與、捐贈
同 contribute 捐獻

英英 to give something for a good cause

例 Gary makes a routine to **donate** blood to those who need it.
蓋瑞有固定捐血的習慣。

☐三分熟 ☐五分熟 ☐七分熟 ☐全熟

---

do·na·tion

[`donefən]

名 捐贈物、捐款

英英 something that is given to a charity or foundation

例 We decided to make a **donation** after we saw the report about earthquake victims in Chili.
我們看到智利地震受難者的報導之後，決定要捐款。

☐三分熟 ☐五分熟 ☐七分熟 ☐全熟

---

do·nor [`donɚ]

名 寄贈者、捐贈人

英英 a person who donates money, blood, etc.

例 The anonymous kidney **donor** saved my mother's life.
匿名腎臟捐贈者救了我母親一命。

☐三分熟 ☐五分熟 ☐七分熟 ☐全熟

---

doom [dum]

名 命運
動 注定

英英 death, destruction, or another terrible fate; condemn to certain destruction or failure

例 He was **doomed** to failure for he never thought twice before making a decision.
他從來不會想清楚再做決定，註定要失敗的。

☐三分熟 ☐五分熟 ☐七分熟 ☐全熟

---

dos·age [`dosɪdʒ]

名 藥量、劑量

英英 the size of a dose of medicine or radiation

例 Don't exceed the prescribed **dosage** when you take the medicine.
服藥時不要超過處方的劑量。

☐三分熟 ☐五分熟 ☐七分熟 ☐全熟

---

dras·tic [ˈdræstɪk]

形 激烈的、猛烈的
同 rough 劇烈的

英英 having a strong or extreme effect
例 The local government may take **drastic** measures to curb emission of harmful fumes.
當地政府會採取激烈手段來減少有害氣體的排放。

☐三分熟
☐五分熟
☐七分熟
☐全熟

draw·back

[ˈdrɔˌbæk]

名 缺點、弊端

英英 a disadvantage or problem
例 The **drawback** of the plan is that it may take a long time to complete.
這個計畫的缺點就是可能要花很多時間才能完成。

☐三分熟
☐五分熟
☐七分熟
☐全熟

drear·y [ˈdrɪərɪ]

形 陰鬱的、淒涼的

英英 dull, bleak, and depressing
例 The **dreary** scene in winter makes me feel gloomy.
冬天陰沉的景色令我感到憂鬱。

☐三分熟
☐五分熟
☐七分熟
☐全熟

driz·zle [ˈdrɪzl̩]

名 細雨、毛毛雨
動 下毛毛雨
同 rain 雨

英英 light rain falling in a very fine mist; pour a thin stream of a liquid ingredient over a dish
例 According to the weather forecast, it may **drizzle** in the afternoon.
氣象報導指出下午可能會下毛毛雨。

☐三分熟
☐五分熟
☐七分熟
☐全熟

drought [draʊt]

名 乾旱、久旱

英英 a prolonged period of low rainfall; a shortage of water
例 Long-term **drought** may cause poor harvest or even famine.
長期乾旱可能會造成農作物欠收或甚至乾旱。

☐一分熟
☐五分熟
☐七分熟
☐全熟

du·al [ˈdjuəl]

形 成雙的、雙重的
同 double 成雙的

英英 to consist of two parts, elements, or aspects
例 The tennis **dual** match will be held in Europe this year.
網球雙打比賽今年會在歐洲舉行。

☐三分熟
☐五分熟
☐七分熟
☐全熟

du·bi·ous

[ˈdjubɪəs]

形 曖昧的、含糊的

英英 hesitating or doubting; not to be relied upon
例 The wording in the official press release script was rather **dubious**.
官方新聞稿中的說法相當模糊。

☐三分熟
☐五分熟
☐七分熟
☐全熟

dy·na·mite

[ˈdaɪnəˌmaɪt]

名 炸藥
動 爆破、炸破
同 explosive 炸藥

英英 a high explosive consisting of nitroglycerine mixed with an absorbent material; to blow up with dynamite
例 The terrorist smuggled highly-explosive **dynamite** into the country.
恐怖份子將炸藥走私進這個國家裡。

☐三分熟
☐五分熟
☐七分熟
☐全熟

Ee

🎧 Track 199

ebb [ɛb]

名 退潮
動 衰落
片 ebb and flow
　潮起潮落、起伏

英英 the movement of sea away from the land; to recede or reduce

例 Some people enjoy the **ebb** and flow of love in a romantic relationship.
有些人很享受戀愛過程中的起起伏伏。

☐ 三分熟
☐ 五分熟
☐ 七分熟
☐ 全熟

ec·cen·tric

[ɪk`sɛntrɪk]

名 古怪的人
形 異常的

英英 unconventional and slightly strange behavior; a person who is strange

例 The **eccentric** man has a habit of hoarding cartons in his house.
這個古怪的人習慣在房子裡囤積紙箱。

☐ 三分熟
☐ 五分熟
☐ 七分熟
☐ 全熟

e·col·o·gy

[ɪ`kɑlədʒɪ]

名 生態學

英英 the branch of biology involved with the relations of organisms to one another and to their physical surroundings.

例 **Ecology** is a subject that may involve biology studies and environmental protection.
生態學是牽涉到生物學研究和環境保護的學科。

☐ 三分熟
☐ 五分熟
☐ 七分熟
☐ 全熟

ec·sta·sy

[`ɛkstəsɪ]

名 狂喜、入迷
同 joy 歡樂

英英 feeling extreme happiness

例 The students hailed in **ecstasy** when they realized that they won the champion in the contest.
一聽說在比賽中得到冠軍，學生們就高興地歡呼。

☐ 三分熟
☐ 五分熟
☐ 七分熟
☐ 全熟

ed·i·ble [`ɛdəbḷ]

形 可食用的

英英 able to be eaten

例 A Japanese farmer has cultivated a kind of banana with **edible** peels.
一名日本農夫種植出皮可以食用的香蕉。

☐ 三分熟
☐ 五分熟
☐ 七分熟
☐ 全熟

ed·i·to·ri·al

[ˌɛdə`torɪəl]

名 社論
形 編輯的

英英 relating to the commissioning or preparation of material for publication; an article which gives an opinion on an issue or event

例 The **editorial** staff of the magazine conducted a survey on its subscribers.
雜誌編輯群針對訂戶進行一項問卷調查。

☐ 三分熟
☐ 五分熟
☐ 七分熟
☐ 全熟

E

e·lec·tron
[ɪˋlɛktrɑn]

名 電子

英英 a stable negatively charged subatomic particle with a mass 1,836 times less than that of the proton, found in all atoms and acting as the primary carrier of electricity in solids

例 They observed the bacteria with the **electron** microscope.
他們用電子顯微鏡觀察細菌。

☐ 三分熟
☐ 五分熟
☐ 七分熟
☐ 全熟

el·i·gi·ble
[ˋɛlɪdʒəbl̩]

形 適當的、合適的

英英 satisfying the conditions to be able to do or receive something

例 He is **eligible** to apply for the subsidy.
他符合申請這個補助金的資格。

☐ 三分熟
☐ 五分熟
☐ 七分熟
☐ 全熟

e·lite [eˋlit]

名 精英
形 傑出的
片 elite high school
　　重點高中

英英 a group of people regarded as the best or most privileged in a particular society or organization; very outstanding or excellent

例 He worked hard to be admitted to the **elite** high school.
他為了能錄取就讀明星高中而努力用功。

☐ 三分熟
☐ 五分熟
☐ 七分熟
☐ 全熟

el·o·quence
[ˋɛləkwəns]

名 雄辯、口才

英英 fluent, charming, or persuasive speaking or writing

例 We were impressed by his **eloquence** in the debate.
我們對他在辯論中的口才感到印象深刻。

☐ 三分熟
☐ 五分熟
☐ 七分熟
☐ 全熟

el·o·quent
[ˋɛləkwənt]

形 辯才無礙的

英英 showing eloquence

例 The politician is an **eloquent** public speaker.
這位政客是辯才無礙的演講者。

☐ 三分熟
☐ 五分熟
☐ 七分熟
☐ 全熟

em·bark [ɪmˋbɑrk]

動 從事、搭乘
片 embark on
　　著手進行、從事

英英 to go on board a ship or aircraft

例 They **embarked** on a new project following the direction of their boss.
他們在老闆指示下著手進行新的計畫。

☐ 三分熟
☐ 五分熟
☐ 七分熟
☐ 全熟

em·i·grant
[ˋɛməgrənt]

名 移民者、移出者
形 移民的、移居他國的
同 immigrant 外來移民

英英 a person who leaves their country to live in another one; move to another country from one's country

例 The **emigrants** have to apply for identification for long-term residence in the area.
移民者需要申請身分證件才能在此區域長久居住。

☐ 三分熟
☐ 五分熟
☐ 七分熟
☐ 全熟

🎧 **Track 201**

em·i·grate
[ˋɛməˌgret]

動 移居

英英 to leave a country permanently and go to live in another one

例 Since she was employed by a Canadian company, she decided to **emigrate** to the foreign country.

因為受到加拿大公司的雇用，她決定要移居至該國。

☐三分熟
☐五分熟
☐七分熟
☐全熟

em·i·gra·tion
[ˌɛməˋgreʃən]

名 移民

英英 leave one's own country in order to settle or live permanently in another

例 **Emigration** may bring both opportunities and challenges.

移民會同時帶來機會和挑戰。

☐三分熟
☐五分熟
☐七分熟
☐全熟

em·phat·ic
[ɪmˋfætɪk]

形 強調的

英英 expressing something forcibly and clearly; (of an action or its result) definite and clear

例 He repeated the rules in an **emphatic** tone.

他用強調的語氣重述了這些規定。

☐三分熟
☐五分熟
☐七分熟
☐全熟

en·act [ɪnˋækt]

動 制定

英英 to make law; act out a role or play

例 The legal package was **enacted** to boycott the goods from certain countries.

抵制某些國家商品的法案已被制定。

☐三分熟
☐五分熟
☐七分熟
☐全熟

en·act·ment
[ɪnˋæktmənt]

名 法規

英英 the process of enacting

例 The racist **enactment** was condemned by human right organizations.

這個種族歧視的法規受到人權組織的譴責。

☐三分熟
☐五分熟
☐七分熟
☐全熟

en·clo·sure
[ɪnˋkloʒɚ]

名 圍住

英英 an area that is closed off by a fence, wall, or other barrier

例 The **enclosure** of the park means entrance is not allowed.

公園被圍住，代表禁止進入。

☐三分熟
☐五分熟
☐七分熟
☐全熟

en·cy·clo·pe·di·a/ en·cy·clo·pae·di·a
[ɪnˌsaɪkləˋpidɪə]

名 百科全書

英英 a book or set of books giving information on many subjects or on many aspects of one subject, typically arranged in an alphabetical fashion

例 He is so knowledgeable that we nickname him as a walking **encyclopedia**.

他是如此博學多聞，以至於我們暱稱他為行走的百科全書。

☐三分熟
☐五分熟
☐七分熟
☐全熟

en·dur·ance
[ɪnˈdjʊrəns]

名 耐力、忍耐

英英 the fact or power to endure something for a prolonged period of time

例 The severe pain was beyond **endurance**.
劇痛令人難以忍受。

☐ 三分熟
☐ 五分熟
☐ 七分熟
☐ 全熟

en·hance
[ɪnˈhæns]

動 提高、增強
同 improve 提高、增進

英英 to improve the quality, amount, or strength of something

例 Several strategies are applied to **enhance** students' learning efficiency.
已實施幾項策略來增進學生的學習效率。

☐ 三分熟
☐ 五分熟
☐ 七分熟
☐ 全熟

en·hance·ment
[ɪnˈhænsmənt]

名 增進

英英 increase the quality, value, or extent of

例 The managerial team put emphasis on **enhancement** of employees' work efficiency.
管理團隊強調增進員工的工作效率。

☐ 三分熟
☐ 五分熟
☐ 七分熟
☐ 全熟

en·light·en
[ɪnˈlaɪtn̩]

動 啟發、教導

英英 to give greater knowledge and understanding to

例 Can you **enlighten** me on the theme of the lecture?
您可以指點我一下這個演講的主題嗎？

☐ 三分熟
☐ 五分熟
☐ 七分熟
☐ 全熟

en·light·en·ment
[ɪnˈlaɪtn̩mənt]

名 文明、啟發

英英 the action of enlightening or the state of being enlightened

例 The **enlightenment** of Buddha about the truth of life is the foundation of Buddhism.
佛祖受到有關人生真諦的啟發，是佛教信仰的基礎。

☐ 三分熟
☐ 五分熟
☐ 七分熟
☐ 全熟

en·rich [ɪnˈrɪtʃ]

動 使富有、使豐富

英英 to improve the quality or value of; make wealthy or wealthier

例 The culture of the community has been **enriched** because more immigrants moved in.
社區的文化因為外來移入者的加入變得更加豐富。

☐ 三分熟
☐ 五分熟
☐ 七分熟
☐ 全熟

en·rich·ment
[ɪnˈrɪtʃmənt]

名 豐富

英英 to improve the quality of something by adding something else

例 The school offers various **enrichment** courses.
學校提供各種豐富的課程。

☐ 三分熟
☐ 五分熟
☐ 七分熟
☐ 全熟

E

🎧 **Track 203**

ep·i·dem·ic
[ˌɛpɪˋdɛmɪk]

名 傳染病
形 流行的

英英 an infectious disease that is a widespread occurrence in a community at a particular time; affecting many people in an area

例 The authorities concerned are fighting against the **epidemics** like Dengue Fever.
當局正在對抗登革熱等等的傳染病。

☐ 三分熟
☐ 五分熟
☐ 七分熟
☐ 全熟

ep·i·sode
[ˋɛpəˌsod]

名 插曲、連續劇的一齣
（或一集）

英英 a single event or a group of events occurring as part of a series of events

例 I watched all the ten **episodes** of the Japanese drama in one day.
我在一天之內看完這部十集的日劇。

☐ 三分熟
☐ 五分熟
☐ 七分熟
☐ 全熟

EQ/e·motion·al quo·tient e·mo·tion·al in·tel·li·gence
[i kju]/[ɪˋmoʃənḷ ˋkwoʃənt]/
[ɪˋmoʃənḷ ɪnˋtɛlədʒəns]

名 情緒智商

英英 the awareness of and ability to manage one's emotions in a healthy an productive manner

例 Being adaptable to the surroundings is one of the hallmarks of the high **EQ**.
高情緒智商的其中一項特徵是能適應環境。

☐ 三分熟
☐ 五分熟
☐ 七分熟
☐ 全熟

e·qua·tion
[ɪˋkweʃən]

名 相等

英英 the process of showing that two amounts equate with another using mathematics

例 I had difficulty understanding the mathematical **equation**.
我看不懂這個數學等式。

☐ 三分熟
☐ 五分熟
☐ 七分熟
☐ 全熟

e·quiv·a·lent
[ɪˋkwɪvələnt]

名 相等物、方程式、相
　 等
形 相當的

英英 equal in value, amount, function, meaning, etc; having the same meaning or effect

例 His silence is **equivalent** with his reluctant acceptance of the suggestion.
他的沉默相當於他勉強接受了這個建議。

☐ 三分熟
☐ 五分熟
☐ 七分熟
☐ 全熟

e·rode [ɪˋrod]

動 蝕

英英 to gradually wear down or be worn away; to gradually destroy over time

例 The challenges have not **eroded** my determination.
挑戰沒有侵蝕掉我的決心。

☐ 三分熟
☐ 五分熟
☐ 七分熟
☐ 全熟

E

e·rup·tion
[ɪˋrʌpʃən]

名 爆發

英英 a sudden act, or act violently

例 The volcanic **eruption** caused dozens of deaths.
火山爆發造成數十人死亡。

☐ 三分熟
☐ 五分熟
☐ 七分熟
☐ 全熟

es·ca·late
[ˋɛskəˌlet]

動 擴大、延長、（戰爭）逐步升級

英英 increase or rise rapidly; become more intense or serious

例 The conflict between ethnic groups in this area is **escalating**.
這個區域的種族衝突越發激烈。

☐ 三分熟
☐ 五分熟
☐ 七分熟
☐ 全熟

es·sence [ˋɛsṇs]

名 本質、精華

英英 the basic or most important idea of something; the quality which determines character of something

例 They have to capture the **essence** of the problem before they can figure out the solution.
他們必須要掌握問題的本質，才能想出解決的方式。

☐ 三分熟
☐ 五分熟
☐ 七分熟
☐ 全熟

e·ter·ni·ty
[ɪˋtɝnətɪ]

名 永遠、永恆

英英 infinite or unending time, without limits; endless life after death

例 Diamond is often considered as a symbol of love lasting for **eternity**.
鑽石常被視為是永恆之愛的象徵。

☐ 三分熟
☐ 五分熟
☐ 七分熟
☐ 全熟

e·thi·cal [ˋɛθɪk!]

形 道德的

英英 relating to moral responsibilities or the branch of knowledge concerned with these

例 The use of non-human animals in experiment has raised **ethical** concerns.
實驗中涉及動物會引起道德問題。

☐ 三分熟
☐ 五分熟
☐ 七分熟
☐ 全熟

eth·nic [ˋɛθnɪk]

名 少數民族的成員
形 人種的、民族的

英英 relating to a group of people having a common culture or nationality; a small group of people having a common culture or nationality

例 There are more than ten major **ethnic** groups on the island.
這個島上有超過十個主要的民族族群。

☐ 三分熟
☐ 五分熟
☐ 七分熟
☐ 全熟

e·vac·u·ate
[ɪˋvækjʊˌet]

動 撤離
同 leave 離開

英英 to move people or things from a place of danger to a safer place

例 Residents of the village were **evacuated** before the typhoon hit.
颱風來襲之前，這個小鎮的居民被撤離。

☐ 三分熟
☐ 五分熟
☐ 七分熟
☐ 全熟

ev·o·lu·tion

[ˌɛvəˈluʃən]

名 發展、演化

英英 the process by which different kinds of living organism are believed to have developed, especially by natural selection

例 This article is about the **evolution** of Android system.

這篇文章是關於安卓系統的演變。

☐ 三分熟
☐ 五分熟
☐ 七分熟
☐ 全熟

---

e·volve [ɪˈvɑlv]

動 演化
同 develop 發展

英英 to gradually develop from other forms of life

例 The convenience store has **evolved** a lot over the past decade, and now it offers a great variety of services.

便利商店在過去十年演化很多，現在提供相當多種的服務。

☐ 三分熟
☐ 五分熟
☐ 七分熟
☐ 全熟

---

ex·cerpt

[ˈɛksɝpt]/[ɪkˈsɝpt]

名 摘錄
動 引用

英英 a short extract from a film, book, or piece of music or writing; a passage taken from a book, article or play

例 The writer used an **excerpt** of Analects to illustrate his ideas.

作者摘錄論語的一段話來說明他的想法。

☐ 三分熟
☐ 五分熟
☐ 七分熟
☐ 全熟

---

ex·ces·sive

[ɪkˈsɛsɪv]

形 過度的

英英 more than is necessary, normal, or wanted

例 **Excessive** UV exposure may cause skin disease.

過度接觸紫外線可能會引發皮膚病變。

☐ 三分熟
☐ 五分熟
☐ 七分熟
☐ 全熟

---

ex·clu·sive

[ɪkˈsklusɪv]

形 唯一的、排外的、獨家的

英英 excluding or not admitting other things

例 The journalist had an **exclusive** interview with the former prime minister.

記者進行了與前首相的獨家專訪。

☐ 三分熟
☐ 五分熟
☐ 七分熟
☐ 全熟

---

ex·e·cu·tion

[ˌɛksɪˈkjuʃən]

名 實行、處決

英英 to follow a plan or order or put into effect

例 The **execution** of the project will take about a month.

這個計畫的實行需要花一個月左右的時間。

☐ 三分熟
☐ 五分熟
☐ 七分熟
☐ 全熟

---

ex·ert [ɪgˈzɝt]

動 運用、盡力
同 employ 利用

英英 to apply strength or bring to bear

例 We will **exert** all out efforts to create good reputation for the corporation.

我們盡力為公司創造良好的名聲。

☐ 三分熟
☐ 五分熟
☐ 七分熟
☐ 全熟

ex·ot·ic [ɛgˋzɑtɪk]

形 外來的、舶來品

英英 things which are from other natives; originating in or characteristic of a distant foreign country

例 They enjoyed sampling **exotic** foods when traveling abroad.
他們出國旅行時很享受異國風情的食物。

☐ 三分熟
☐ 五分熟
☐ 七分熟
☐ 全熟

ex·pe·di·tion
[ˌɛkspɪˋdɪʃən]

名 探險、遠征

英英 an organized journey undertaken by a group of people with a particular purpose

例 The adventurers going for the **expedition** in Antarctica returned with glory.
至南極遠征的探險家們光榮返回。

☐ 三分熟
☐ 五分熟
☐ 七分熟
☐ 全熟

ex·pel [ɪkˋspɛl]

動 逐出、趕走

英英 to force out or to drive out; force a student to leave a school

例 The soldier convicted of treason was **expelled** by the government.
背上叛國罪的軍人被政府驅逐。

☐ 三分熟
☐ 五分熟
☐ 七分熟
☐ 全熟

ex·per·tise
[ˌɛkspɚˋtiz]

名 專門知識

英英 highly skilled or have great knowledge in a particular field

例 The question is beyond my area of **expertise**.
這個問題超過我專業知識範圍。

☐ 三分熟
☐ 五分熟
☐ 七分熟
☐ 全熟

ex·pi·ra·tion
[ˌɛkspəˋreʃən]

名 終結、期滿

英英 the end of the period of validity

例 The **expiration** date is specified in the label on the packaging.
產品有效期限有在包裝的標籤上寫明。

☐ 三分熟
☐ 五分熟
☐ 七分熟
☐ 全熟

ex·pire [ɪkˋspaɪr]

動 終止

英英 to come to an end

例 The contract has **expired** at the end of the last month.
這個合約到上個月底就終止了。

☐ 三分熟
☐ 五分熟
☐ 七分熟
☐ 全熟

ex·plic·it
[ɪkˋsplɪsɪt]

形 明確的、清楚的

英英 clear, exact, and detailed, with no room for confusion or doubt

例 **Explicit** communication and avoidance of ambiguity may make the negotiation go smoothly.
清楚溝通和避免模糊可以使協商更順利。

☐ 三分熟
☐ 五分熟
☐ 七分熟
☐ 全熟

E

🎧 Track 207

ex·ploit [ɪkˋsplɔɪt]

名 剝削、功績
動 利用

英英 a remarkable effect or result; to make good use of something

例 In some underdeveloped countries, immoral employers may **exploit** child labors.
在一些落後國家，不道德的雇主會剝削童工。

☐ 三分熟
☐ 五分熟
☐ 七分熟
☐ 全熟

---

ex·plo·ra·tion

[ˏɛkspləˋreʃən]

名 探測

英英 travel through an unfamiliar area in search of something and learning about it

例 China has conducted **exploration** on the back of the moon.
中國已經進行過月球背面的探測。

☐ 三分熟
☐ 五分熟
☐ 七分熟
☐ 全熟

---

ex·qui·site

[ˋɛkskwɪzɪt]

形 精巧的

英英 of great beauty and delicacy; perfect

例 The **exquisite** desserts in the bakery are really eye-catching.
這家烘焙坊裡面精巧的點心真是引人注目。

☐ 三分熟
☐ 五分熟
☐ 七分熟
☐ 全熟

---

ex·tract

[ˋɛkstrækt]/[ɪkˋstrækt]

名 摘錄
動 引出、源出

英英 to remove with care or effort; a short passage taken from an article, text or book

例 She put an **extract** of her favorite novel in her blog post.
她從喜愛的小說中摘錄出一句話放在她部落格裡。

☐ 三分熟
☐ 五分熟
☐ 七分熟
☐ 全熟

---

extra·cur·ric·u·lar

[ˏɛkstrəkəˋrɪkjələ]

形 課外的

英英 describing an activity or subject that is extra, not part of the usual school or college course

例 The **extracurricular** activities took up most of his time after school.
他放學以後大部分的時間都花在課外活動上。

☐ 三分熟
☐ 五分熟
☐ 七分熟
☐ 全熟

---

eye·sight [ˋaɪˏsaɪt]

名 視力

英英 a person's ability to see

例 It is vital that a pilot should have good **eyesight**.
飛行員有好的視力是很重要的。

☐ 三分熟
☐ 五分熟
☐ 七分熟
☐ 全熟

fa·bu·lous

[ˈfæbjələs]

形 傳說、神話中的、極好的
同 marvelous 不可思議的

英英 extremely good; great; extraordinary

例 The musician has composed several **fabulous** hit songs since his debut five years ago.
這位音樂家從五年前出道開始，已經作了好幾首極佳的暢銷歌曲。

☐ 三分熟
☐ 五分熟
☐ 七分熟
☐ 全熟

fa·cil·i·tate

[fəˈsɪləˌtet]

動 利於、使容易、促進
同 assist 促進

英英 to make possible or easier

例 Sometimes visual aids can **facilitate** the process of communication.
有時候視覺輔助可以促進溝通。

☐ 三分熟
☐ 五分熟
☐ 七分熟
☐ 全熟

fac·tion [ˈfækʃən]

名 黨派、當中之派系

英英 a small group which is part of a larger one

例 The legislator quit a political party because of conflicts between petty **factions**.
這位立法委員因為派系之間的衝突而退黨。

☐ 三分熟
☐ 五分熟
☐ 七分熟
☐ 全熟

fac·ul·ty [ˈfækḷtɪ]

名 全體教員、系所

英英 a natural ability, mental, or physical power

例 The **faculty** of this graduate institution are all Christians.
這所研究所的教職員都是基督徒。

☐ 三分熟
☐ 五分熟
☐ 七分熟
☐ 全熟

fa·mil·i·ar·i·ty

[fəˌmɪlɪˈærətɪ]

名 熟悉、親密、精通

英英 to know something or someone well through long or close association

例 **Familiarity** breeds contempt.
熟悉會滋生蔑視。

☐ 三分熟
☐ 五分熟
☐ 七分熟
☐ 全熟

fam·ine [ˈfæmɪn]

名 饑荒、饑饉、缺乏
同 starvation 饑餓

英英 extreme scarcity of food

例 The **famine** was caused by persistent drought.
連續乾旱造成饑荒。

☐ 三分熟
☐ 五分熟
☐ 七分熟
☐ 全熟

fas·ci·na·tion

[ˌfæsəˈneʃən]

名 迷惑、魅力、魅惑、迷戀

英英 irresistibly attractive or interesting

例 My five-year-old daughter has a **fascination** for barbie dolls.
我五歲的女兒對芭比娃娃十分著迷。

☐ 三分熟
☐ 五分熟
☐ 七分熟
☐ 全熟

🎧 **Track 209**

fea·si·ble [ˈfizəbḷ]

形 可實行的、可能的

英英 possible and practical to achieve easily or conveniently

例 The plan they proposed sounds **feasible**.
他們提出的計畫聽起來是可行的。

☐ 三分熟
☐ 五分熟
☐ 七分熟
☐ 全熟

fed·er·a·tion
[ˌfɛdəˈreʃən]

名 聯合、同盟、聯邦政府

英英 groups of states, countries, regions, organizations, etc. that have come together to form a larger organization or government

例 The conference is hosted by the National **Federation** of Women's Institutes.
這次研討會是由全國婦女協會聯盟所舉辦的。

☐ 三分熟
☐ 五分熟
☐ 七分熟
☐ 全熟

feed·back
[ˈfidˌbæk]

名 回饋
同 response 反應

英英 information given in response to a product, performance etc., used as a basis for improvement

例 The speaker is expecting some **feedback** from the audience.
講者正期待得到一些觀眾的回應。

☐ 三分熟
☐ 五分熟
☐ 七分熟
☐ 全熟

fer·til·i·ty [fɝˈtɪlətɪ]

名 肥沃、多產、繁殖力
片 fertility rate 生育率

英英 producing, suitable, or capable of producing abundant vegetation or crops

例 The declining **fertility** rate reflects the youngsters' lack of confidence in economic development.
下降的生育率，反映出年輕人對經濟發展缺乏信心。

☐ 三分熟
☐ 五分熟
☐ 七分熟
☐ 全熟

fi·del·i·ty [fɪˈdɛlətɪ]

名 忠實、精準度、誠實
同 faith 誠實

英英 continuing loyalty to a person, cause, or belief

例 **Fidelity** and credibility can be considered basic criteria for a good leader.
誠實可信是一位好的領導者基本的條件。

☐ 三分熟
☐ 五分熟
☐ 七分熟
☐ 全熟

fire·proof
[ˈfairˌpruf]

形 耐火的、防火的

英英 able to withstand fire or great heat

例 The apartment is furnished with **fireproof** materials.
這間公寓是用防火材質裝潢的。

☐ 三分熟
☐ 五分熟
☐ 七分熟
☐ 全熟

flare [flɛr]

名 閃光、燃燒
動 搖曳、閃亮、發怒

英英 to burn in a sudden brief burst of flame or light

例 His eyes **flared** with excitement.
他的眼神因為興奮而閃閃發光。

☐ 三分熟
☐ 五分熟
☐ 七分熟
☐ 全熟

fleet [flit]

名 船隊、艦隊、車隊

英英 a group of ships sailing together

例 The **fleet** consists thirty vessels.
這個船隊包含三十艘船。

☐ 三分熟
☐ 五分熟
☐ 七分熟
☐ 全熟

F

flick·er [ˈflɪkɚ]

名 閃耀
動 飄揚、震動

英英 a quick movement or light; to make a quick movement

例 The candle fire **flickered** in the wind.
燭火在風中閃爍。

□三分熟
□五分熟
□七分熟
□全熟

---

fling [flɪŋ]

名 投、丟、猛衝
動 投擲、踢、跳躍

英英 throw forcefully and suddenly; hurl

例 He **flung** the crumbled script into the trash can.
他把揉成一團的手稿丟進垃圾桶。

□三分熟
□五分熟
□七分熟
□全熟

---

flu·id [ˈfluɪd]

名 流體
形 流質的
反 solid 固體

英英 a substance, such as a liquid or gas, without a fixed shape and yields easily to external pressure; able to flow easily

例 Taking in enough **fluid** on a hot day can prevent heat stroke.
補充足夠的流質可以預防中暑。

□三分熟
□五分熟
□七分熟
□全熟

---

flut·ter [ˈflʌtɚ]

名 心亂、不安
動 拍翅、飄動

英英 a state of being tremulous excitement; to fly quickly and gently by flapping the wings quickly and lightly

例 The pigeon **fluttered** its wings and flew away.
鴿子拍動翅膀飛走了。

□三分熟
□五分熟
□七分熟
□全熟

---

fore·see [forˈsi]

動 預知、看穿

英英 to be aware or conscious of beforehand; predict

例 The witch claimed that she could **foresee** the disaster.
巫婆宣稱他可以預知災難。

□三分熟
□五分熟
□七分熟
□全熟

---

for·mi·da·ble [ˈfɔrmɪdəbl̩]

形 可怕的、難應付的

英英 inspiring fear or respect through being impressively large, powerful, or capable

例 He was quite nervous before the tennis match against the **formidable** opponent.
和這位難應付的對手進行網球比賽之前，他很緊張。

□三分熟
□五分熟
□七分熟
□全熟

---

for·mu·late [ˈfɔrmjəlet]

動 明確地陳述、
　用公式表示
同 define 使明確

英英 to develop the ideas of a plan, create or prepare methodically

例 He **formulated** a hypothesis for the scientific research.
他清楚陳述這個科學研究的假設。

□三分熟
□五分熟
□七分熟
□全熟

🎧 Track 211

for·sake [fɚˋsek]

動 拋棄、放棄、捨棄
同 abandon 拋棄

英英 to abandon; renounce or give up
例 The **forsaken** baby was rescued by the volunteers.
志工救回了棄嬰。

☐ 三分熟
☐ 五分熟
☐ 七分熟
☐ 全熟

---

forth·com·ing
[ˌforθˋkʌmɪŋ]

形 不久就要來的、下一次的

英英 ready to happen or appear
例 Thousands of athletes from around the world will participate the **forthcoming** Summer Olympics.
數千名來自世界各地的運動員將會參加下一次的夏季奧運。

☐ 三分熟
☐ 五分熟
☐ 七分熟
☐ 全熟

---

for·ti·fy [ˋfɔrtəˌfaɪ]

動 加固、強化工事

英英 to provide more strength with defensive works as protection against attack
例 They adopted a firewall system to **fortify** against cyber attacks.
他們採用一個防火牆系統來強化對抗網路攻擊。

☐ 三分熟
☐ 五分熟
☐ 七分熟
☐ 全熟

---

fos·ter [ˋfɔstɚ]

動 養育、收養
形 收養的

英英 to encourage, promote the development of; bringing up a child that is not your own by birth
例 The actress **fostered** four homeless children.
這位女演員收養了四位無家可歸的孩子。

☐ 三分熟
☐ 五分熟
☐ 七分熟
☐ 全熟

---

frac·ture
[ˋfræktʃɚ]

名 破碎、骨折
動 挫傷、破碎
同 crack 破裂

英英 the cracking or a slight break of a hard object or material
例 It took the patient three months to heal the bone **fracture**.
病人花了三個月時間，骨折才痊癒。

☐ 三分熟
☐ 五分熟
☐ 七分熟
☐ 全熟

---

frag·ile [ˋfrædʒəl]

形 脆的、易碎的

英英 easily broken or damaged
例 When you send **fragile** items, remember to place a warning sticker on the package.
寄送易碎物品時，記得在包裝上面貼警告標籤。

☐ 三分熟
☐ 五分熟
☐ 七分熟
☐ 全熟

---

frag·ment
[ˋfrægmənt]

名 破片、碎片、未完成部分
動 裂成碎片

英英 a small part broken off or detached from a larger whole; to break into small pieces
例 The sentence **fragments** were ungrammatical, but the message has been conveyed.
這些不完整的句子是不合文法的，但訊息已送達。

☐ 三分熟
☐ 五分熟
☐ 七分熟
☐ 全熟

frail [frel]

形 脆弱的、虛弱的
同 weak 虛弱的

英英 easily damaged or broken

例 The patient is too **frail** to walk without assistance of the nurse.
病人很脆弱，沒有護士的攙扶無法自己走路。

☐ 三分熟 ☐ 五分熟 ☐ 七分熟 ☐ 全熟

G

fraud [frɔd]

名 欺騙、詐欺

英英 to deceit in a wrongful or criminal way intended to result in financial or personal gain

例 The teenager fell victim of the Internet **fraud**.
這名青少年成為網路詐欺的受害者。

☐ 三分熟 ☐ 五分熟 ☐ 七分熟 ☐ 全熟

freak [frik]

名 怪胎、異想天開
形 怪異的

英英 a person, animal, or plant which is abnormal or deformed; very weird, not normal

例 The gifted child was regarded as a **freak** for he seldom interacts with his peers.
這個大賦異稟的孩子，因為很少跟同儕互動而被認為是個怪胎。

☐ 三分熟 ☐ 五分熟 ☐ 七分熟 ☐ 全熟

fret [frɛt]

動 煩躁、焦慮

英英 to be constantly or visibly nervous, or anxious

例 He was constantly **fretting** about his lack of social connection.
他總是在煩惱自己缺少社會聯繫。

☐ 三分熟 ☐ 五分熟 ☐ 七分熟 ☐ 全熟

fric·tion [ˈfrɪkʃən]

名 摩擦、衝突
同 conflict 衝突

英英 the resistance that one surface or object encounters when rubbing against another

例 Leaders of the two countries are trying to reduce **friction** between the two sides.
兩國的元首正試圖減少雙邊的衝突。

☐ 三分熟 ☐ 五分熟 ☐ 七分熟 ☐ 全熟

Gg

gal·ax·y [ˈgæləksɪ]

名 星雲、星系

英英 a system of millions or billions of stars, held together with gas and dust

例 The **galaxy** is a constantly evolving system.
這個星系是一個不斷演化的系統。

☐ 三分熟 ☐ 五分熟 ☐ 七分熟 ☐ 全熟

gen·er·a·lize
[ˈdʒɛnərəˌlaɪz]

動 一般化、推斷

英英 to say something simple and basic about a group of people or things that are often true, but sometimes untrue

例 She **generalized** from the incident that all truck drivers are rude.
她由這次事件推論，所有的貨車司機都很魯莽。

☐ 三分熟 ☐ 五分熟 ☐ 七分熟 ☐ 全熟

🎧 Track 213

gen·er·ate
[ˈdʒɛnəˌret]

動 產生、引起、發生
（熱、電、光等等）

英英 to cause something to exist, to create something

例 The local people **generated** electricity with water power.
當地人用水力發電。

三分熟／五分熟／七分熟／全熟

gen·er·a·tor
[ˈdʒɛnəˌretɚ]

名 發電機、創始者、產生者

英英 someone who makes a general or broad statement by inferring from specific cases

例 The company offers electricity **generator** for rent.
這間公司出租發電機。

三分熟／五分熟／七分熟／全熟

ge·net·ic
[dʒəˈnɛtɪk]

形 遺傳學的、基因的

英英 relating to genes or heredity; relating to genetics

例 Some people think **genetic** engineering is an ethically flawed science.
有些人認為基因工程是一門有道德缺陷的科學。

三分熟／五分熟／七分熟／全熟

ge·net·ics
[dʒəˈnɛtɪks]

名 遺傳學

英英 the study of heredity and the variation of inherited characteristics

例 The progress in **genetics** makes it possible to control some inherited diseases.
遺傳學的進步，使得有些遺傳的疾病得以被控制。

三分熟／五分熟／七分熟／全熟

glam·our [ˈɡlæmɚ]

名 魅力

英英 the quality of being attractive, special, and exciting

例 I was impressed with the **glamour** of the movie star.
我對電影明星的魅力感到印象深刻。

三分熟／五分熟／七分熟／全熟

glass·ware
[ˈɡlæsˌwɛr]

名 玻璃製品、玻璃器皿

英英 drinking glasses or other objects made of glass

例 She cleaned the **glassware** with hot soapy water.
她使用熱的肥皂水來清潔玻璃器皿。

三分熟／五分熟／七分熟／全熟

glis·ten [ˈɡlɪsn̩]

動 閃耀、閃爍

英英 shine or sparkle; a sparkling light reflected in the sun from something wet

例 The silverware **glistened** in the moonlight.
銀器在月光下閃耀。

三分熟／五分熟／七分熟／全熟

gloom·y [ˈɡlumɪ]

形 幽暗的、暗淡的

英英 gray skies, dark or poorly lit, especially so as to cause fear or depression

例 I don't like the **gloomy** and dark atmosphere in this film.
我不喜歡這部電影當中憂鬱晦暗的氣氛。

三分熟／五分熟／七分熟／全熟

G

GMO/ge·net·i·cal·ly mod·i·fied or·gan·ism

[dʒəˋnɛtɪklɪ ˋmɑdəˌfaɪd ˋɔrgəˌnɪzm̩]

名 基因改造生物

英英 a plant or animal whose genes have been scientifically changed

例 The **GMO** may cause allergic reaction to some people.
基因改造食品會令某些人產生過敏反應。

□ 三分熟
□ 五分熟
□ 七分熟
□ 全熟

---

graph [græf]

名 曲線圖、圖表
動 圖解

英英 a picture with lines and curves drawn or written in a specified way to compare things or show development; to explain with a picture with lines and curves drawn or written in a specified way to compare things or show development

例 The **graph** shows the population structure of the country.
此圖片顯示這個國家的人口結構。

□ 三分熟
□ 五分熟
□ 七分熟
□ 全熟

---

graph·ic [ˋgræfɪk]

形 圖解的、生動的
片 graphic design
　　平面造型設計

英英 in relation to visual art, especially involving drawing, engraving, or lettering

例 She has a portfolio for her works of **graphic** design.
她有一個平面設計作品集。

□ 三分熟
□ 五分熟
□ 七分熟
□ 全熟

---

grill [grɪl]

名 烤架
動 烤
同 broil 烤

英英 a device that cooks food from direct heat from above; to cook with a grill

例 The beef is sizzling on the **grill**.
牛肉在烤肉架上面滋滋作響。

□ 三分熟
□ 五分熟
□ 七分熟
□ 全熟

---

gro·cer [ˋgrosɚ]

名 雜貨商

英英 a person who sells food and household goods

例 The local **grocer** provides daily necessities for residents in the community.
本地雜貨商提供社區居民日常用品。

□ 三分熟
□ 五分熟
□ 七分熟
□ 全熟

---

grope [grop]

名 摸索
動 摸索找尋

英英 to blindly feel about or search uncertainly with the hands

例 They **groped** their way out of the cave.
他們一邊摸索一邊找尋走出洞穴的路。

□ 三分熟
□ 五分熟
□ 七分熟
□ 全熟

---

guer·ril·la [gəˋrɪlə]

名 非正規的軍隊、游擊隊
同 soldier 軍人

英英 member of a small independent group of unofficial soldiers fighting against the government or regular forces

例 The soldiers were ambushed by **guerrillas**.
軍人遭到游擊隊埋伏。

□ 三分熟
□ 五分熟
□ 七分熟
□ 全熟

Hh

Track 215

---

hab·it·at

[ˈhæbəˌtæt]

名 棲息地

英英 the natural home or environment of an organism

例 The environmental conservationists appeal that the **habitat** of tree frogs should be preserved.
環保人士呼籲樹蛙的棲息地應該被保留。

☐ 三分熟
☐ 五分熟
☐ 七分熟
☐ 全熟

---

hack [hæk]

動 割、劈、砍

英英 to cut with rough or heavy hits

例 He **hacked** away the twigs in the yard for the whole afternoon.
他花了一下午砍掉庭院裡的樹枝。

☐ 三分熟
☐ 五分熟
☐ 七分熟
☐ 全熟

---

hack·er [ˈhækɚ]

名 駭客

英英 a person who illegally works their way into the computers of others

例 The **hacker** who paralyzed the internal network of the company was a teenager.
癱瘓公司內部網路的駭客原來是一名青少年。

☐ 三分熟
☐ 五分熟
☐ 七分熟
☐ 全熟

---

hail [hel]

名 歡呼、冰雹
動 歡呼
同 cheer 歡呼

英英 pellets of frozen rain falling in heavy showers; to acclaim enthusiastically

例 They **hailed** for the candidate's victory in the campaign.
他們為候選人勝選而歡呼。

☐ 三分熟
☐ 五分熟
☐ 七分熟
☐ 全熟

---

ha·rass [ˈhærəs]

動 使困擾、不斷騷擾
同 bother 打擾

英英 to torment someone by subjecting them to constant threat or intimidation

例 They complained about the salesperson who **harassed** them through phone calls and emails.
他們投訴那個用電話和電子郵件騷擾他們的業務員。

☐ 三分熟
☐ 五分熟
☐ 七分熟
☐ 全熟

---

ha·rass·ment

[ˈhærəsmənt]

名 煩惱、侵擾

英英 behavior that annoys, causing fear, or upsets someone

例 The sexual **harassment** case was made public by the journalist.
這椿性騷擾案件被記者揭露。

☐ 三分熟
☐ 五分熟
☐ 七分熟
☐ 全熟

---

haz·ard [ˈhæzɚd]

名 偶然、危險
動 冒險、受傷害

英英 a danger or risk; to take a risk

例 The tornado may cause severe **hazard** to the village.
龍捲風可能會對這個村莊造成很大的危害。

☐ 三分熟
☐ 五分熟
☐ 七分熟
☐ 全熟

hem·i·sphere

[ˈhɛməsˌfɪr]

名 半球體、半球

英英 a half of a sphere

例 The seasonal cycle of the northern **hemisphere** is opposite to that of the other.
北半球的季節循環是南半球的相反。

☐ 三分熟
☐ 五分熟
☐ 七分熟
☐ 全熟

here·af·ter

[ˌhɪrˈæftɚ]

名 來世、將來、未來
副 隨後、從此以後

英英 after death; at sometime in the future

例 She is determined to be self-employed **hereafter**.
她下定決心以後要從事自由職業。

☐ 三分熟
☐ 五分熟
☐ 七分熟
☐ 全熟

her·i·tage

[ˈhɛrətɪdʒ]

名 遺產

英英 property that is or may be inherited; an inheritance

例 The historical site is listed as a world cultural **heritage** by the UNESCO.
這個歷史景點被聯合國教科文組織列為世界文化遺產。

☐ 三分熟
☐ 五分熟
☐ 七分熟
☐ 全熟

he·ro·in [ˈhɛroɪn]

名 海洛因

英英 a highly addictive painkilling drug derived from morphine, often used as a narcotic for pleasure

例 The man was accused of smuggling **heroin** to Japan.
這名男子遭控走私海洛因到日本。

☐ 三分熟
☐ 五分熟
☐ 七分熟
☐ 全熟

high·light

[ˈhaɪˌlaɪt]

名 精彩場面
動 使顯著、強調
同 emphasize 強調

英英 to emphasize something, or make noticeable part of an event or period of time; to make an outstanding part of an event

例 In the speech, she **highlighted** the importance of spontaneity in education.
在演講中,她強調教育中自主的重要性。

☐ 三分熟
☐ 五分熟
☐ 七分熟
☐ 全熟

hon·or·ar·y

[ˈɑnəˌrɛrɪ]

形 榮譽的
片 honorary degree 榮譽學位

英英 given as an reward to show respect and honor

例 The entrepreneur received an **honorary** degree from the prestigious university.
企業家獲得著名大學的榮譽學位。

☐ 三分熟
☐ 五分熟
☐ 七分熟
☐ 全熟

hor·mone

[ˈhɔrmon]

名 荷爾蒙

英英 a substance produced by a living thing and transported in tissue fluids to specific cells or tissues to stimulate them into growth and development

例 Endorphin is a **hormone** in human body that can suppress pain.
腦內啡是一種可以壓抑疼痛的荷爾蒙。

☐ 三分熟
☐ 五分熟
☐ 七分熟
☐ 全熟

🎧 **Track 217**

hos·pi·ta·ble

[`hɑspɪtəbḷ]

形 善於待客的、好客的
同 generous 慷慨的

英英 someone who is friendly, pleasant, and welcomes guests

例 The host family were **hospitable** to the exchange student.
接待家庭對這位交換生很熱情好客。

☐三分熟 ☐五分熟 ☐七分熟 ☐全熟

hos·pi·tal·i·ty

[ˌhɑspɪˋtælətɪ]

名 款待、好客

英英 the friendly and generous treatment towards guests or strangers

例 The host showed her **hospitality** to the foreign visitors.
主人款待外國訪客。

☐三分熟 ☐五分熟 ☐七分熟 ☐全熟

hos·pi·tal·ize

[`hɑspɪtəˌlaɪz]

動 使入院治療

英英 to admit or cause someone to be admitted to hospital for treatment

例 She was **hospitalized** for severe chronic heart failure.
她因為嚴重的慢性心臟衰竭而住院。

☐三分熟 ☐五分熟 ☐七分熟 ☐全熟

hos·til·i·ty

[hɑsˋtɪlətɪ]

名 敵意

英英 unfriendly, angry behavior towards someone to show contempt

例 Don't show **hostility** toward the immigrants.
不要對移民者表現敵意。

☐三分熟 ☐五分熟 ☐七分熟 ☐全熟

hu·man·i·tar·i·an

[hjuˌmænəˋtɛrɪən]

名 人道主義者、博愛
形 人道主義的

英英 concerned with or seeking to promote the welfare of human beings; a humanitarian person

例 The aim of the philanthropic organization is to promote **humanitarian** thoughts.
這個慈善組織的目標就是宣傳人道主義的想法。

☐三分熟 ☐五分熟 ☐七分熟 ☐全熟

hu·mil·i·ate

[hjuˋmɪlɪˌet]

動 侮辱、羞辱

英英 to make someone lose dignity and self-respect

例 She felt **humiliated** when the client refused to read her proposal.
顧客拒絕看她的提案，讓她感覺受辱。

☐三分熟 ☐五分熟 ☐七分熟 ☐全熟

hunch [hʌntʃ]

名 瘤
動 突出、弓起背部、隆起
同 bump 凸塊

英英 a lump or tumor; to raise and bend the top of one's body forward

例 She tends to **hunch** her shoulders when she feels nervous.
她感覺緊張的時候會聳起肩膀。

☐三分熟 ☐五分熟 ☐七分熟 ☐全熟

hur·dle [ˋhɝdḷ]

名 障礙物、跨欄
動 跳過障礙

英英 one of a series of upright frames which athletes run and jump over in a race; to run in a hurdle race

例 She overcame the **hurdles** and became a famous actress.
她克服許多障礙並成為一位名演員。

☐ 三分熟
☐ 五分熟
☐ 七分熟
☐ 全熟

hy·giene [ˋhaɪdʒin]

名 衛生學、衛生
片 personal hygiene
個人衛生

英英 conditions or practices that help to maintain cleanliness, health, and prevent disease

例 Keeping good personal **hygiene** is important for preventing epidemic diseases.
保持好的個人衛生對防止傳染病很重要。

☐ 三分熟
☐ 五分熟
☐ 七分熟
☐ 全熟

hy·poc·ri·sy

[hɪˋpɑkrəsɪ]

名 偽善、虛偽

英英 the practice of claiming believe a set of standards or beliefs when that is not the case

例 **Hypocrisy** is rather common in the bureaucratic system.
偽善在官僚體系中相當普遍。

☐ 三分熟
☐ 五分熟
☐ 七分熟
☐ 全熟

hyp·o·crite

[ˋhɪpəˌkrɪt]

名 偽君子

英英 a person who is given to hypocrisy

例 The **hypocrite** always wears a fake smile on his face.
偽君子的臉上總是掛著假笑。

☐ 三分熟
☐ 五分熟
☐ 七分熟
☐ 全熟

hys·ter·i·cal

[hɪsˋtɛrɪkḷ]

形 歇斯底里的
同 upset 心煩的

英英 associated with or suffering from hysteria

例 He became **hysterical** whenever we mention his ex-wife.
我們一提到他的前妻，他就會變得歇斯底里。

☐ 三分熟
☐ 五分熟
☐ 七分熟
☐ 全熟

Ii

il·lu·mi·nate

[ɪˋluməˌnet]

動 照明、點亮、啟發

英英 to light up; help to clarify or explain

例 The streetlamps **illuminated** our way home.
街燈照亮了我們回家的路。

☐ 三分熟
☐ 五分熟
☐ 七分熟
☐ 全熟

il·lu·sion [ɪˋljuʒən]

名 錯覺、幻覺

英英 a false or artificial perception or belief

例 She is under the **illusion** that the guy has a crush on her.
她幻想那名男子對她有意思。

☐ 三分熟
☐ 五分熟
☐ 七分熟
☐ 全熟

🎧 Track 219

im·mune [ɪˋmjun]

形 免除的

英英 resistant to a certain infection owing to the presence of specific antibodies or sensitized white blood cells

例 I was **immune** to the sarcasm of the online haters.
我對網路酸民的諷刺言論已經免疫了。

☐ 三分熟
☐ 五分熟
☐ 七分熟
☐ 全熟

---

im·per·a·tive [ɪmˋpɛrətɪv]

名 命令
形 絕對必要的、極重要的

英英 of vital importance or urgency; an order or a rule

例 It is **imperative** that students should have media literacy.
學生有媒體識讀的能力是很重要的。

☐ 三分熟
☐ 五分熟
☐ 七分熟
☐ 全熟

---

im·ple·ment [ˋɪmpləmənt]

名 工具
動 施行

英英 a tool or an equipment which is used for a particular purpose; to use a tool, utensil, or other piece of equipment for a particular purpose

例 The new traffic laws will be **implemented** next year.
新的交通法規明年會施行。

☐ 三分熟
☐ 五分熟
☐ 七分熟
☐ 全熟

---

im·pli·ca·tion [ˌɪmplɪˋkeʃən]

名 暗示、含意

英英 an implied conclusion that can be drawn from something

例 Her **implication** that our product has poor quality upset the manager.
她暗示我們產品有瑕疵的言論讓經理感到不滿。

☐ 三分熟
☐ 五分熟
☐ 七分熟
☐ 全熟

---

im·plic·it [ɪmˋplɪsɪt]

形 含蓄的、不表明的
反 explicit 明確的

英英 a thought that is not directly expressed

例 We failed to interpret the **implicit** message in the remarks of our Japanese client.
我們沒能夠理解日本客戶言論中隱含的訊息。

☐ 三分熟
☐ 五分熟
☐ 七分熟
☐ 全熟

---

im·pos·ing [ɪmˋpozɪŋ]

形 顯眼的

英英 having an impression that is grand and impressive

例 The singer is known for her **imposing** outfits in public occasions.
這位歌手以在公開場合搶眼的穿著著名。

☐ 三分熟
☐ 五分熟
☐ 七分熟
☐ 全熟

---

im·pris·on [ɪmˋprɪzn̩]

動 禁閉

英英 to put or keep in prison

例 The captive was **imprisoned** in the dungeon.
俘虜被監禁在地牢中。

☐ 三分熟
☐ 五分熟
☐ 七分熟
☐ 全熟

im·pris·on·ment

[ɪmˈprɪznɱmənt]

名 坐牢

英英 the act of putting or keeping in prison

例 The murderer was sentenced to life **imprisonment**.
殺人犯被判終身監禁。

☐三分熟
☐五分熟
☐七分熟
☐全熟

---

in·cen·tive

[ɪnˈsɛntɪv]

名 刺激、誘因
形 刺激的

英英 a thing that motivates or encourages someone to take faster action or increase effort; motivating someone to take faster action or increase effort

例 The children have no **incentive** to study.
小朋友缺乏學習的誘因。

☐三分熟
☐五分熟
☐七分熟
☐全熟

---

in·ci·den·tal

[ˌɪnsəˈdɛntl]

形 臨時發生的、偶然發生的

英英 something that is less important than the thing that is in connection with

例 The **incidental** meeting with my elementary school classmate made me recall some old anecdotes.
偶然遇到小學同學，讓我想到以前一些趣事。

☐三分熟
☐五分熟
☐七分熟
☐全熟

---

in·cline [ɪnˈklaɪn]

動 傾向
名 傾斜面

英英 to favor towards or willing to do; a surface which is inclined

例 The building **inclined** after the earthquake.
這棟大樓在地震之後傾斜了。

☐三分熟
☐五分熟
☐七分熟
☐全熟

---

in·clu·sive

[ɪnˈklusɪv]

形 包含在內的
反 exclusive 排外的

英英 including all the expected or required services or things

例 People of all ethnic groups should be welcomed in an **inclusive** society.
兼容並蓄的社會，應該要歡迎各個種族背景的人。

☐三分熟
☐五分熟
☐七分熟
☐全熟

---

in·dig·na·tion

[ˌɪndɪgˈneʃən]

名 憤怒
同 anger 憤怒

英英 anger or annoyance provoked by what is perceived as unfair treatment

例 The violence imposed on the demonstrators caused their **indignation**.
他們對加諸於抗爭者的暴力感到憤怒。

☐三分熟
☐五分熟
☐七分熟
☐全熟

---

in·ev·i·ta·ble

[ɪnˈɛvətəbl]

形 不可避免的

英英 absolutely certain to happen; unavoidable

例 The failure of the performance is **inevitable** for they didn't rehearse at all.
表演失敗是不可避免的，因為他們完全沒有排練。

☐三分熟
☐五分熟
☐七分熟
☐全熟

🎧 Track 221

in·fec·tious

[ɪnˋfɛkʃəs]

形 能傳染的

英英 able to be transmitted through the environment

例 Their passion for music is **infectious**; that's why people love to go to their concerts.

他們對音樂的熱情是有感染力的；這也是為什麼人們喜歡去他們的演唱會。

☐ 三分熟
☐ 五分熟
☐ 七分熟
☐ 全熟

in·fer [ɪnˋfɝ]

動 推斷、推理
同 suppose 假定、猜想

英英 to form an idea from evidence and reasoning rather than from explicit statements

例 The detective **inferred** that the murderer is an acquaintance of the victim.

偵探推斷兇手是受害者認識的人。

☐ 三分熟
☐ 五分熟
☐ 七分熟
☐ 全熟

in·fer·ence

[ˋɪnfərəns]

名 推理

英英 a conclusion reached on the basis of evidence and reasoning

例 I made an **inference** from the result of the experiment.

我由實驗結果做出了一個推論。

☐ 三分熟
☐ 五分熟
☐ 七分熟
☐ 全熟

in·gen·ious

[ɪnˋdʒinjəs]

形 巧妙的

英英 clever, skillful, original, and inventive

例 The **ingenious** stage design was impressive to the audience.

巧妙的舞台設計令觀眾印象深刻。

☐ 三分熟
☐ 五分熟
☐ 七分熟
☐ 全熟

in·ge·nu·i·ty

[ˌɪndʒəˋnuətɪ]

名 發明才能

英英 the ability to think of clever new ways to do things

例 Her **ingenuity** was discovered by the movie producer.

電影製作人發現了她的才能。

☐ 三分熟
☐ 五分熟
☐ 七分熟
☐ 全熟

in·hab·it [ɪnˋhæbɪt]

動 居住

英英 to live in or occupy

例 The cranes often **inhabit** near wetland.

鶴通常居住在溼地附近。

☐ 三分熟
☐ 五分熟
☐ 七分熟
☐ 全熟

in·hab·it·ant

[ɪnˋhæbətənt]

名 居民

英英 a person or animal that lives in or occupies a place

例 The **inhabitants** of the community have a consent to keep the surroundings clean.

社區的居民同意共同維護環境整潔。

☐ 三分熟
☐ 五分熟
☐ 七分熟
☐ 全熟

in·her·ent [ɪnˋhɪrənt]

形 天生的、內在的
同 internal 固有的、本質的

英英 existing in something as a permanent or essential characteristic

例 The problems you mention are **inherent** in the system.

你提及的那些問題是這一制度本身存在的。

☐ 三分熟
☐ 五分熟
☐ 七分熟
☐ 全熟

i·ni·ti·a·tive
[ɪ'nɪʃətɪv]

名 倡導
形 率先的
片 take the initiative
主動行動

英英 the ability to act independently and with a new approach to solve a problem; acting before others do

例 She took the **initiative** to send the product catalogue to the potential clients.
她主動寄送產品型錄給潛在的客戶。

☐ 三分熟 ☐ 五分熟 ☐ 七分熟 ☐ 全熟

in·ject [ɪn'dʒɛkt]

動 注入

英英 to use a needle and syringe to place drugs into a body

例 The diabetes patient **injects** insulin on the arm.
糖尿病患者在手臂上注射胰島素。

☐ 三分熟 ☐ 五分熟 ☐ 七分熟 ☐ 全熟

in·jec·tion
[ɪn'dʒɛkʃən]

名 注射

英英 introduce into the body with a needle and syringe

例 The children are taking the vaccine **injections** today.
小朋友們今天要注射疫苗。

☐ 三分熟 ☐ 五分熟 ☐ 七分熟 ☐ 全熟

in·jus·tice
[ɪn'dʒʌstɪs]

名 不公平
反 justice 公平

英英 without justice; an unjust act or occurrence

例 They protested the **injustice** in the salary system.
他們抗議薪資體系中的不公平。

☐ 三分熟 ☐ 五分熟 ☐ 七分熟 ☐ 全熟

in·no·va·tion
[ˌɪnə'veʃən]

名 革新
同 formation 公平

英英 the action or process of creating new ideas, methods, and products

例 **Innovation** is vital for a start-up company.
革新對新創公司是相當重要的。

☐ 三分熟 ☐ 五分熟 ☐ 七分熟 ☐ 全熟

in·no·va·tive
['ɪnoˌvetɪv]

形 創新的

英英 featuring new methods; advanced and original

例 The **innovative** ideas in his proposal was objected by some conservatives.
他提案當中的一些創新想法，遭到保守份子的反對。

☐ 三分熟 ☐ 五分熟 ☐ 七分熟 ☐ 全熟

in·quir·y [ɪn'kwaɪrɪ]

名 詢問、調查
同 research 調查

英英 the process of asking for information

例 The customer service representatives made proper response to all kinds of **inquiries**.
顧客服務代表對於各種詢問都能有適當的回應。

☐ 三分熟 ☐ 五分熟 ☐ 七分熟 ☐ 全熟

🎧 Track 223

in·sight [`ɪn͵saɪt]

名 洞察

英英 the ability to gain an accurate and intuitive understanding of something

例 A successful businessman has **insight** into the trend on the market.
成功的商人對於市場趨勢具有洞察力。

☐三分熟
☐五分熟
☐七分熟
☐全熟

---

in·sis·tence

[ɪn`sɪstəns]

名 堅持

英英 to be firm or very demanding

例 His **insistence** in the pursuit of his goal is the main reason for his success.
他堅持追求目標是成功的主因。

☐三分熟
☐五分熟
☐七分熟
☐全熟

---

in·stal·la·tion

[͵ɪnstə`leʃən]

名 就任、裝置

英英 the action furniture or equipment is put into position

例 The **installation** of the software took three minutes.
安裝軟體花了三分鐘的時間。

☐三分熟
☐五分熟
☐七分熟
☐全熟

---

in·stall·ment

[ɪn`stɔlmənt]

名 分期付款

英英 an amount of money due as one of several payments made over a period of time

例 He paid for his new car in **installments**.
他用分期付款買新車。

☐三分熟
☐五分熟
☐七分熟
☐全熟

---

in·sti·tu·tion

[͵ɪnstə`tjuʃən]

名 團體、機構、制度

英英 a large and important organization or public body, such as a university, bank, hospital, or church

例 The graduate **institution** is recruiting oversea students.
這個研究所正在招收海外學生。

☐三分熟
☐五分熟
☐七分熟
☐全熟

---

in·tact [ɪn`tækt]

形 原封不動的、完整無缺的

英英 not damaged or impaired

例 The antique vase remained **intact** when it arrived.
古董花瓶送到的時候完整無缺。

☐三分熟
☐五分熟
☐七分熟
☐全熟

---

in·te·grate

[`ɪntə͵gret]

動 整合、使合併

英英 to combine or be combined to form a whole

例 The public relation section will be **integrated** into the marking department.
公共關係部門將會整併至行銷部門。

☐三分熟
☐五分熟
☐七分熟
☐全熟

---

in·te·gra·tion

[͵ɪntə`greʃən]

名 統合、完成

英英 the action or process of integrating

例 The cultural **integration** process may take decades to complete.
文化整合的過程可能要好幾十年才能完成。

☐三分熟
☐五分熟
☐七分熟
☐全熟

in·teg·ri·ty

[ɪnˈtɛgrətɪ]

名 正直
同 honesty 正直

英英 the quality of being honest and having strong moral principles

例 The **integrity** of the candidate was questioned by his opponent.
這名候選人的正直遭到對手質疑。

□ 三分熟
□ 五分熟
□ 七分熟
□ 全熟

in·tel·lect

[ˈɪntḷɛkt]

名 理解力
片 superior intellect 理解力

英英 the ability reason and understand in an intelligent way

例 His superior **intellect** made it possible for him to skip a grade.
他高人一等的理解力，使他能夠跳級就讀。

□ 三分熟
□ 五分熟
□ 七分熟
□ 全熟

in·ter·sec·tion

[ˌɪntəˈsɛkʃən]

名 橫斷，交叉

英英 a point or line that intersect with another

例 The trucks crashed at the **intersection** of two highways.
卡車在兩條高速公路交叉處相撞。

□ 三分熟
□ 五分熟
□ 七分熟
□ 全熟

in·ter·val [ˈɪntəvḷ]

名 間隔、休息時間
同 break 休息

英英 a period or time or space between two points

例 The **interval** between buses running is about five minutes during the peak hours.
尖峰時間的公車間隔人約五分鐘。

□ 三分熟
□ 五分熟
□ 七分熟
□ 全熟

in·ter·vene

[ˌɪntəˈvin]

動 介入

英英 to intentionally come between so as to prevent or alter the result or course of events

例 The U.N. **intervened** to resolve the regional conflicts.
聯合國介入調停地區衝突。

□ 三分熟
□ 五分熟
□ 七分熟
□ 全熟

in·ter·ven·tion

[ˌɪntəˈvɛnʃən]

名 介入、調停、干預

英英 the action or process of intervening; interference by a state in another's affairs

例 The military **intervention** of the neighboring countries made the situation even more complicated.
鄰近國家軍事干涉，使該國的情勢更加複雜。

□ 三分熟
□ 五分熟
□ 七分熟
□ 全熟

in·ti·ma·cy

[ˈɪntəməsɪ]

名 親密

英英 close familiarity, relationship, or friendship

例 She felt a **intimacy** with her parents after the trip.
在這次旅行之後，她感覺與父母更加親近。

□ 三分熟
□ 五分熟
□ 七分熟
□ 全熟

🎧 Track 225

in·tim·i·date
[ɪnˈtɪməˌdet]

動 恐嚇

英英 to frighten or threaten, especially so as to coerce into doing something

例 The bandit **intimidated** the bank clerks to hand out the money.
搶匪恐嚇銀行行員要交出錢來。

☐ 三分熟
☐ 五分熟
☐ 七分熟
☐ 全熟

in·trude [ɪnˈtrud]

動 侵入、打擾、把……強加

同 interrupt 打擾、打斷

英英 to come into a place or situation where one is unwelcome nor invited

例 My parents like to **intrude** their opinions on me.
我父母喜歡把意見強加給我。

☐ 三分熟
☐ 五分熟
☐ 七分熟
☐ 全熟

in·trud·er
[ɪnˈtrudɚ]

名 侵入者

英英 a person who enters a place, especially into a building with criminal intent

例 The dog barked to alert its owner of the **intruder**.
狗狗吠叫來提醒主人有入侵者。

☐ 三分熟
☐ 五分熟
☐ 七分熟
☐ 全熟

in·val·u·a·ble
[ɪnˈvæljəbl̩]

形 無價的

英英 extremely useful

例 His advices were **invaluable** for they were derived from his life experience.
他的建議是無價的，因為是根據他的生活經驗得來的。

☐ 三分熟
☐ 五分熟
☐ 七分熟
☐ 全熟

in·ven·to·ry
[ˈɪnvənˌtori]

名 物品的清單、存貨
動 製作目錄

英英 complete list of items and products in stock or the contents of a building; to make a complete list of items and products in stock or the contents of a building

例 We checked the **inventory** right after the client placed an order.
顧客下訂單之後，我們馬上就檢查了庫存。

☐ 三分熟
☐ 五分熟
☐ 七分熟
☐ 全熟

in·ves·ti·ga·tor
[ɪnˈvɛstəˌgetɚ]

名 調查者、研究者

英英 carry out a systematic or formal inquiry into an incident or allegation so as to establish the truth

例 The **investigators** will ask the participants several questions regarding their shopping habits.
研究者會問參加者一些關於消費習慣的問題。

☐ 三分熟
☐ 五分熟
☐ 七分熟
☐ 全熟

IQ/in·tel·li·gence qu·o·ti·ent
[ɪnˈtɛlədʒəns ˈkwoʃənt]

名 智商

英英 a measure of someone's intelligence found from special tests

例 People with high **IQ** do not necessarily have a successful career.
有高智商的人不見得有成功的事業。

☐ 三分熟
☐ 五分熟
☐ 七分熟
☐ 全熟

i·ron·ic [aɪˈrɑnɪk]

形 譏諷的、愛挖苦人的

英英 interesting, strange, or funny because it is different from what is expected

例 The Net celebrity is known for his **ironic** comments on political events.
這位網路名人以諷刺政治事件而著名。

□ 三分熟
□ 五分熟
□ 七分熟
□ 全熟

---

i·ro·ny [ˈaɪrənɪ]

名 諷刺、反諷

英英 the expression of meaning through the use of language which normally signifies the opposite, typically for humorous effects

例 I like to read the **irony** cartoons in the newspaper.
我喜歡看報紙上面的諷刺漫畫。

□ 三分熟
□ 五分熟
□ 七分熟
□ 全熟

---

ir·ri·ta·ble [ˈɪrətəbl̩]

形 暴躁的、易怒的
同 mad 發狂

英英 easily annoyed or angered

例 Our boss tends to be **irritable** in the morning.
我們的老闆早上特別容易發脾氣。

□ 三分熟
□ 五分熟
□ 七分熟
□ 全熟

---

ir·ri·tate [ˈɪrəˌtet]

動 使生氣、刺激

英英 to make annoyed or angry

例 Your abrupt visit may **irritate** the manager.
你突然造訪，可能會讓經理生氣。

□ 三分熟
□ 五分熟
□ 七分熟
□ 全熟

---

ir·ri·ta·tion [ˌɪrəˈteʃən]

名 煩躁

英英 the act of making annoyed or angry

例 His apparent **irritation** made the other attendees of the meeting quite embarrassed.
他明顯的煩躁，讓其他與會者感到尷尬。

□ 三分熟
□ 五分熟
□ 七分熟
□ 全熟

Jj

joy·ous [ˈdʒɔɪəs]

形 歡喜的、高興的
同 cheerful 高興的

英英 full of happiness and joy

例 The **joyous** atmosphere in the parade made the child smile.
遊行歡樂的氣氛讓小孩微笑。

□ 三分熟
□ 五分熟
□ 七分熟
□ 全熟

Track 227

ker·nel [ˈkɚnl̩]

名 穀粒、籽、核心

英英 a softer part of a nut, seed, or fruit that is inside its hard shell

例 We haven't discussed about the true **kernel** of the matter.
我們還沒討論到這件事情的真正核心。

☐ 三分熟
☐ 五分熟
☐ 七分熟
☐ 全熟

kid·nap [ˈkɪdnæp]

動 綁架、勒索
同 snatch 搶奪、綁架

英英 to abduct and hold someone in captivity, typically to obtain a ransom

例 The billionaire's daughter was **kidnapped** on her way to school.
億萬富翁的女兒上學途中遭綁架。

☐ 三分熟
☐ 五分熟
☐ 七分熟
☐ 全熟

la·ment [ləˈmɛnt]

名 悲痛
動 哀悼
同 sorrow 悲痛

英英 to express grief or feeling sorry about something

例 The woman **lamented** for her son's death in the terrorist attack.
婦女悲嘆她的兒子死於恐怖攻擊。

☐ 三分熟
☐ 五分熟
☐ 七分熟
☐ 全熟

la·va [ˈlɑvə]

名 熔岩

英英 hot molten, liquid rock erupted from a volcano or fissure, or solid rock resulting from cooling of this

例 The **lava** flow burned the vegetation near the volcano.
熔岩將火山附近的植物都燒毀。

☐ 三分熟
☐ 五分熟
☐ 七分熟
☐ 全熟

lay·man [ˈlemən]

名 普通信徒、門外漢

英英 a person without professional, detailed, or specialized knowledge

例 He is a **layman** of the electronics industry.
他是電子產業的門外漢。

☐ 三分熟
☐ 五分熟
☐ 七分熟
☐ 全熟

lay·out [ˈleˌaʊt]

名 規劃、佈局、版面設計

英英 something set in a particular way

例 The real estate agent showed the interior **layout** of the apartment.
房地產銷售員給我們看公寓的室內平面圖。

☐ 三分熟
☐ 五分熟
☐ 七分熟
☐ 全熟

liq·uid crys·tal dis·play/LCD

[ˈlɪkwɪd ˈkrɪstl̩ dɪˈsple]/
[ˈɛlˈsiˈdi]

名 液晶顯示器

英英 electronics & computing liquid crystal display

例 The high resolution of the **LCD** makes better viewing experience.
液晶顯示器的高解析度會創造更好的觀看經驗。

□ 三分熟
□ 五分熟
□ 七分熟
□ 全熟

---

leg·end·ar·y

[ˈlɛdʒəndɛrɪ]

形 傳說的

英英 someone or something based on, or of legends

例 The knight claimed that he had slaughtered the **legendary** monster.
騎士宣稱他已經消滅傳說中的怪物。

□ 三分熟
□ 五分熟
□ 七分熟
□ 全熟

---

leg·is·la·tive

[ˈlɛdʒɪsˌletɪv]

形 立法的

英英 having the power to make laws

例 The congress of the country has the **legislative** power.
這個國家的國會有立法權。

□ 三分熟
□ 五分熟
□ 七分熟
□ 全熟

---

leg·is·la·tor

[ˈlɛdʒɪsˌletɚ]

名 立法者

英英 a person who makes laws; one member of a legislative body

例 The **legislator** is supposed to keep the constituents' opinions in mind.
立法者應該記得選民的意見。

□ 三分熟
□ 五分熟
□ 七分熟
□ 全熟

---

leg·is·la·ture

[ˈlɛdʒɪsˌletʃɚ]

名 立法院

英英 the legislative body of a state

例 We can now watch live streaming of the **Legislature** sessions.
我們現在可以看到立法院會的現場直播。

□ 三分熟
□ 五分熟
□ 七分熟
□ 全熟

---

le·git·i·mate

[lɪˈdʒɪtəˌmet]/
[lɪˈdʒɪtəmɪt]

動 使合法
形 合法的

英英 to make something legal; allowed by the law or rules

例 She claimed that she is the **legitimate** heir to the throne.
她宣稱自己是王位的合法繼承人。

□ 三分熟
□ 五分熟
□ 七分熟
□ 全熟

---

length·y [ˈlɛŋθɪ]

形 漫長的

英英 continuing for a considerable or unusual duration

例 Some students dozed off during his **lengthy** speech.
有些學生在他冗長乏味的演講中打瞌睡。

□ 三分熟
□ 五分熟
□ 七分熟
□ 全熟

Track 229

li·a·ble [ˈlaɪəbl̩]

形 可能的、易於……的、負法律責任的、應付稅的

同 probable 可能的

英英 having legal responsibility; legally answerable

例 The landlord is **liable** to pay taxes on the income earned from the lease.
房東需要繳納因為租約收入產生的稅金。

☐ 三分熟
☐ 五分熟
☐ 七分熟
☐ 全熟

---

lib·er·ate [ˈlɪbəˌret]

動 使自由、釋放

同 free 使自由

英英 to set free, especially from imprisonment or oppression

例 The political prisoner was **liberated**.
政治犯獲釋。

☐ 三分熟
☐ 五分熟
☐ 七分熟
☐ 全熟

---

lib·er·a·tion
[ˌlɪbəˈreʃən]

名 解放

英英 the act of setting free, especially from imprisonment or oppression

例 People gathered to celebrate the **liberation** of the slaves.
人們聚集慶祝奴隸的解放。

☐ 三分熟
☐ 五分熟
☐ 七分熟
☐ 全熟

---

like·wise
[ˈlaɪkˌwaɪz]

副 同樣地

英英 also; moreover

例 She told me to watch him carefully and do **likewise**.
她叫我仔細看她怎麼做並且重複同樣的動作。

☐ 三分熟
☐ 五分熟
☐ 七分熟
☐ 全熟

---

lim·ou·sine/ limo
[ˈlɪməˌzin]/[ˈlɪmo]

名 小客車

英英 a large, luxurious car of unusual length

例 He rented a **limousine** to pick up his prom date.
他租了一臺小客車去接他的畢業舞會舞伴。

☐ 三分熟
☐ 五分熟
☐ 七分熟
☐ 全熟

---

lin·er [ˈlaɪnɚ]

名 定期輪船（飛機）

英英 a large passenger ship (such a ship belonged to a line, or company, providing passenger ships on particular routes)

例 He worked as a sailor on an ocean **liner**.
他的工作是遠洋客輪上的水手。

☐ 三分熟
☐ 五分熟
☐ 七分熟
☐ 全熟

---

lin·guist [ˈlɪŋgwɪst]

名 語言學家

英英 a person who studies linguistics

例 The **linguist** devotes himself to preserving the languages of the minorities.
語言學家投入保存少數民族語言的工作中。

☐ 三分熟
☐ 五分熟
☐ 七分熟
☐ 全熟

---

li·ter [ˈlitɚ]

名 公升

英英 a metric unit of capacity, formerly the volume of one kilogram equal to 1,000 cubic centimeters (about 1.75 pints)

例 The capacity of the pot is five **liters**.
這個壺的容量是五公升。

☐ 三分熟
☐ 五分熟
☐ 七分熟
☐ 全熟

L

lit·er·a·cy
[ˈlɪtərəsɪ]

名 讀寫能力、知識

英英 the ability to read and write

例 Computer **literacy** is one of the requirements for the position.
電腦知識是這個職位的要求之一。

☐ 三分熟
☐ 五分熟
☐ 七分熟
☐ 全熟

lit·er·al [ˈlɪtərəl]

形 文字的

英英 using or interpreting words or meanings in their usual or most basic sense

例 You can check the dictionary for the **literal** meaning of the word.
你可以在字典中查到這個字的字面意義。

☐ 三分熟
☐ 五分熟
☐ 七分熟
☐ 全熟

lit·er·ate [ˈlɪtərɪt]

名 有學識的人
形 精通文學的、識字的
同 intellectual 知識分子

英英 a person who is knowledgeable in a particular field; being knowledgeable in a particular field

例 The old man asked someone **literate** to explain the terms in the contract for him.
老人請一位識字的人解釋合約的條款給他聽。

☐ 三分熟
☐ 五分熟
☐ 七分熟
☐ 全熟

lon·gev·i·ty
[lɑnˈdʒɛvətɪ]

名 長壽

英英 long life

例 Some people who live to 100 shared the secret to their **longevity** in the book.
有些百歲人瑞在這本書中分享他們長壽的祕訣。

☐ 三分熟
☐ 五分熟
☐ 七分熟
☐ 全熟

lounge [laʊndʒ]

名 交誼廳
動 閒逛

英英 a public sitting room in a hotel or theater; to walk in a relaxed way without a purpose

例 The tour guide waited for us at the hotel **lounge**.
導遊在旅館交誼廳等我們。

☐ 三分熟
☐ 五分熟
☐ 七分熟
☐ 全熟

lu·na·tic [ˈlunətɪk]

名 瘋子
形 瘋癲的
同 crazy 瘋的

英英 an extremely foolish or silly person; foolish or silly

例 Don't talk to the **lunatic**; his words wouldn't make any sense.
不要跟那個瘋子講話；他說的話完全沒意義。

☐ 三分熟
☐ 五分熟
☐ 七分熟
☐ 全熟

lure [lʊr]

名 誘餌
動 誘惑
同 attract 吸引

英英 a type of bait which is used in fishing or hunting; to tempt someone to do something or to go somewhere

例 The luxurious life in the cosmopolitan area is a great **lure** for many young people.
大都會的奢侈生活對很多年輕人來說是很大的誘惑。

☐ 三分熟
☐ 五分熟
☐ 七分熟
☐ 全熟

🎧 **Track 231**

lush [lʌʃ]

形 青翠的

英英 full of vegetation luxuriant

例 The cattle are grazing on the **lush** meadow.
牛隻在青翠的草原上面吃草。

☐ 三分熟
☐ 五分熟
☐ 七分熟
☐ 全熟

lyr·ic [ˈlɪrɪk]

名 抒情詩
形 抒情的

英英 the words of a song; expressing someone's emotions or feelings

例 He composed a **lyric** love poem for his lover on Valentine's Day.
情人節時，他為情人作了一首抒情詩。

☐ 三分熟
☐ 五分熟
☐ 七分熟
☐ 全熟

Mm

mag·ni·tude
[ˈmæɡnəˌtjud]

名 重大、強度

英英 of great size, extent, or importance

例 How is the **magnitude** of an earthquake calculated?
地震的強度是如何計算的？

☐ 三分熟
☐ 五分熟
☐ 七分熟
☐ 全熟

ma·lar·i·a
[məˈlɛrɪə]

名 瘧疾、瘴氣

英英 a disease transmitted from a certain type of mosquito which causes periods of fever and chills

例 The government takes some measures to prevent outbreak of **malaria**.
政府採取措施預防瘧疾爆發。

☐ 三分熟
☐ 五分熟
☐ 七分熟
☐ 全熟

ma·nip·u·late
[məˈnɪpjəˌlet]

動 巧妙操縱

英英 to handle or control something or someone to your advantage often in a dishonest or unfair way

例 It is said that the politician **manipulated** the media to gain popularity.
據說政治人物操縱媒體才能受歡迎。

☐ 三分熟
☐ 五分熟
☐ 七分熟
☐ 全熟

man·u·script
[ˈmænjəˌskrɪpt]

名 手稿、原稿

英英 the original copy of a book, document, or piece of music before it is printed

例 The **manuscript** of Einstein is exhibited in the museum.
愛因斯坦的手稿展示在博物館中。

☐ 三分熟
☐ 五分熟
☐ 七分熟
☐ 全熟

mar [mɑr]

動 毀損

英英 to spoil the appearance or quality of something

例 The statue of Venus was **marred** by the tourists.
維納斯的雕像遭到觀光客破壞。

☐ 三分熟
☐ 五分熟
☐ 七分熟
☐ 全熟

mas·sa·cre

[ˈmæsəkɚ]

名 大屠殺
動 屠殺
同 slaughter 屠殺

英英 mass killing of a large number of people; to kill brutally

例 We watched a documentary about Holocaust—the **massacre** of Jewish people.
我們看了一部關於猶太人大屠殺的紀錄片。

☐ 三分熟
☐ 五分熟
☐ 七分熟
☐ 全熟

mas·ter·y

[ˈmæstərɪ]

名 優勢、精通、掌握

英英 comprehensive knowledge or command of a subject or skill

例 She was admired for her **mastery** of AI technology.
她因為精通 AI 科技而受到尊敬。

☐ 三分熟
☐ 五分熟
☐ 七分熟
☐ 全熟

ma·te·ri·al(ism)

[məˈtɪrɪəl]/[məˈtɪrɪəˌlɪzm]

名 材質、材料、唯物論

英英 the belief that having money and things is the most important in life

例 The bag is made of waterproof **material**.
這個袋子是用防水材質做的。

☐ 三分熟
☐ 五分熟
☐ 七分熟
☐ 全熟

mat·tress

[ˈmætrɪs]

名 墊子

英英 a strong cover filled with soft, firm, or springy material used for sleeping on

例 She is used to sleeping on the soft **mattress**.
她習慣睡在軟的床墊上。

☐ 三分熟
☐ 五分熟
☐ 七分熟
☐ 全熟

mech·a·nism

[ˈmɛkəˌnɪzəm]

名 機械裝置
同 machine 機械

英英 a part of machinery; the way in which something works or is brought about

例 The graph illustrates the **mechanism** of an airplane engine.
這張圖片說明飛機引擎的機械裝置。

☐ 三分熟
☐ 五分熟
☐ 七分熟
☐ 全熟

med·i·ca·tion

[ˌmɛdɪˈkeʃən]

名 藥物治療

英英 a medicine or drug; treatment with medicines

例 She was taking **medication** to treat her depression.
她在服用抗憂鬱的藥物。

☐ 三分熟
☐ 五分熟
☐ 七分熟
☐ 全熟

me·di·e·val

[ˌmɪdɪˈivəl]

形 中世紀的

英英 in relation to the Middle Ages

例 The protagonist is a **medieval** knight.
故事主角是一個中世紀的騎士。

☐ 三分熟
☐ 五分熟
☐ 七分熟
☐ 全熟

🎧 **Track 233**

med·i·tate

[ˋmɛdə͵tet]

動 沉思

英英 to focus one's mind on calm thoughts for a time for spiritual purposes or for relaxation

例 She **meditated** on the choice of her career path.
她思考職業生涯的問題。

☐ 三分熟
☐ 五分熟
☐ 七分熟
☐ 全熟

---

med·i·ta·tion

[͵mɛdəˋteʃən]

名 熟慮

英英 the action or practice of meditating

例 The decision was made after much **meditation**.
這是深思熟慮過後的決定。

☐ 三分熟
☐ 五分熟
☐ 七分熟
☐ 全熟

---

mel·an·chol·y

[ˋmɛlən͵kɑlɪ]

名 悲傷、憂鬱
形 悲傷的
同 miserable 悲慘的

英英 deep and prolonged sadness; sad or depressed

例 The **melancholy** youngster recorded her miserable experience on her weblog.
憂鬱的年輕人在網誌上記錄她悲慘的境遇。

☐ 三分熟
☐ 五分熟
☐ 七分熟
☐ 全熟

---

mel·low [ˋmɛlo]

動 成熟、使圓熟
形 成熟的、圓潤的

英英 to become develop; pleasantly smooth, developed, or soft in sound, taste, or color

例 The old lady has a **mellow** attitude toward life.
老太太對人生有圓融的態度。

☐ 三分熟
☐ 五分熟
☐ 七分熟
☐ 全熟

---

men·tal·i·ty

[mɛnˋtælətɪ]

名 智力

英英 a certain way of thinking; the capacity for intelligent thought

例 The question is rather difficult to persons of average **mentality**.
這個問題對智力普通的人來說相當困難。

☐ 三分熟
☐ 五分熟
☐ 七分熟
☐ 全熟

---

mer·chan·dise

[ˋmɝtʃən͵daɪz]

名 商品
動 買賣
同 product 產品

英英 products for sale; to say and buy

例 The tax is applied to foreign **merchandise**.
這種稅是加諸在外國商品上。

☐ 三分熟
☐ 五分熟
☐ 七分熟
☐ 全熟

---

merge [mɝdʒ]

動 合併
同 blend 混合

英英 to combine parts or be combined into a whole

例 The two company will **merge** for greater business opportunity.
兩家公司即將為了更大的商機而合併。

☐ 三分熟
☐ 五分熟
☐ 七分熟
☐ 全熟

M

met·a·phor

[ˈmɛtəfə]

名 隱喻

英英 a figure of speech in which a word or phrase is applied to something with similar characteristics to the object or person described

例 He used **metaphors** and similes in his poem.
他在詩中使用暗喻和明喻。

☐ 三分熟
☐ 五分熟
☐ 七分熟
☐ 全熟

met·ro·pol·i·tan

[ˌmɛtrəˈpɑlətn̩]

名 都市人
形 大都市的
同 city 城市的

英英 relating to a metropolis; a person who is living in a city

例 The population of the **metropolitan** area keeps growing.
大都會區的人口持續增加中。

☐ 三分熟
☐ 五分熟
☐ 七分熟
☐ 全熟

mi·grate [ˈmaɪgret]

動 遷徙、移居

英英 to move from one place of living to another according to the seasons

例 Some Japanese people **migrated** to the Oceanian countries.
有些日本人移居到大洋洲的國家。

☐ 三分熟
☐ 五分熟
☐ 七分熟
☐ 全熟

mi·gra·tion

[maɪˈgreʃən]

名 遷移

英英 to move from one habitat to another according to the seasons

例 Religious persecution caused large-scale **migration** in Europe.
宗教迫害導致了在歐洲的大規模遷徙。

☐ 三分熟
☐ 五分熟
☐ 七分熟
☐ 全熟

mil·i·tant

[ˈmɪlətənt]

名 好戰份子
形 好戰的
同 hostile 懷敵意的

英英 a person who is aggressive in the support of a cause; to favor using confrontational methods in support of a cause

例 The **militant** monarch started wars on the neighboring countries.
好戰的君主對鄰國發動戰爭。

☐ 三分熟
☐ 五分熟
☐ 七分熟
☐ 全熟

mill·er [ˈmɪlə]

名 磨坊主人

英英 a person who owns or works in a grain mil

例 The **miller** sells flour to residents of the village.
磨坊主人賣麵粉給小鎮的居民。

☐ 三分熟
☐ 五分熟
☐ 七分熟
☐ 全熟

mim·ic [ˈmɪmɪk]

名 模仿者
動 模仿

英英 a person who imitates; to imitate in order to entertain or ridicule

例 The comedian is famous for **mimicking** the politicians.
這位喜劇演員以模仿政治人物出名。

☐ 三分熟
☐ 五分熟
☐ 七分熟
☐ 全熟

🎧 **Track 235**

min·i·a·ture

[`mɪnɪətʃɚ]

名 縮圖、縮印
形 小型的

英英 a thing that is much smaller than the usual size; to make a copy in a smaller size than normal; of a much smaller size than normal

例 The artist could assemble tiny **miniature** ship in a bottle.

這位藝術家可以在瓶子裡組裝小型的船隻模型。

☐ 三分熟
☐ 五分熟
☐ 七分熟
☐ 全熟

min·i·mize

[`mɪnəˌmaɪz]

動 減到最小

英英 to reduce to a smaller amount or degree

例 They tried to **minimize** the loss caused by their mistakes.

他們試圖將自己失誤造成的損失減到最低。

☐ 三分熟
☐ 五分熟
☐ 七分熟
☐ 全熟

mi·rac·u·lous

[məˋrækjələs]

形 奇蹟的

英英 very surprising, effective, difficult to believe, and welcome

例 It was **miraculous** that the girl survived the air crash.

那名女孩在空難中奇蹟生還。

☐ 三分熟
☐ 五分熟
☐ 七分熟
☐ 全熟

mis·chie·vous

[`mɪstʃɪvəs]

形 淘氣的、有害的

英英 causing or disposed to slightly bad behavior not intended to cause trouble

例 The **mischievous** child played a trick on his sister.

頑皮的孩子對他的妹妹惡作劇。

☐ 三分熟
☐ 五分熟
☐ 七分熟
☐ 全熟

mis·sion·ar·y

[`mɪʃənˌɛrɪ]

名 傳教士
形 傳教的

英英 a person sent on a religious mission; having the characteristic of a missionary or religious mission

例 The villagers were impressed with the sincerity of the **missionary**.

村民被傳教士的真誠感動。

☐ 三分熟
☐ 五分熟
☐ 七分熟
☐ 全熟

mo·bi·lize

[`mobəˌlaɪz]

動 動員

英英 to prepare and organize troops to be ready for active service

例 The school **mobilizes** the students to clean up the campus after the typhoon hit.

學校動員學生，在颱風過後清理校園。

☐ 三分熟
☐ 五分熟
☐ 七分熟
☐ 全熟

mod·er·ni·za·tion

[ˌmɑdɚnəˋzeʃən]

名 現代化

英英 adapting to current times; making modern

例 My grandparents were amazed by the **modernization** of the urban area.

我祖父母對都市區的現代化感到很驚訝。

☐ 三分熟
☐ 五分熟
☐ 七分熟
☐ 全熟

mold [mold]

名 鑄模
動 鑄造
同 shape 塑造

英英 a container in which hot liquid is poured into and gives shape when it cools and hardens; to make a container

例 The baker made a mooncake **mold** by himself.
烘焙師傅自己做了一個月餅的模型。

☐ 三分熟
☐ 五分熟
☐ 七分熟
☐ 全熟

mo·men·tum

[mo'mɛntəm]

名 動量、動力

英英 speed gained by movement or progress

例 The **momentum** of the crowd made him elected as the mayor.
群眾的力量使他當選市長。

☐ 三分熟
☐ 五分熟
☐ 七分熟
☐ 全熟

mo·nop·o·ly

[mə'nɑplɪ]

名 獨佔、壟斷

英英 the complete control of the supply of a commodity or service

例 Some experts worry about the potential risk in the **monopoly** of Android system.
有些專家擔心安卓系統壟斷有潛在風險。

☐ 三分熟
☐ 五分熟
☐ 七分熟
☐ 全熟

mo·not·o·nous

[mə'nɑtənəs]

形 單調的

英英 staying the same and not changing, therefore tedious

例 The **monotonous** life of preparing for the college entrance exam made some students feel depressed.
準備大學入學考試的單調生活，令一些高中生感到憂鬱。

☐ 三分熟
☐ 五分熟
☐ 七分熟
☐ 全熟

mo·not·o·ny

[mə'nɑtənɪ]

名 單調

英英 the act of staying the same and not changing, therefore tedious

例 The **monotony** in his work actually makes him feel secured.
工作的單調性質反而使他有安全感。

☐ 三分熟
☐ 五分熟
☐ 七分熟
☐ 全熟

mo·rale [mə'ræl]

名 士氣

英英 the amount of a person's or group's confidence and spirits

例 To boost **morale** of the staff, the boss decided to increase the year-end bonus.
為了提振員工士氣，老闆決定增加年終獎金。

☐ 三分熟
☐ 五分熟
☐ 七分熟
☐ 全熟

mo·ral·i·ty

[mɔ'rælətɪ]

名 道德、德行
同 character 高尚品德

英英 principles concerning the ability to distinct between right and wrong or good and bad behavior

例 The novice worker was unaware of some **morality** issues in the industry.
新進員工不曉得這個產業的道德議題。

☐ 三分熟
☐ 五分熟
☐ 十分熟
☐ 全熟

M

🎧 **Track 237**

---

mot·to [ˈmɑto]

名 座右銘
同 proverb 諺語

英英 a short sentence or phrase expressing a belief or ideal

例 My **motto** is "Love more, judge less."
我的座右銘是「多關愛、少批判」。

□ 三分熟
□ 五分熟
□ 七分熟
□ 全熟

---

mourn·ful

[ˈmɔrnfəl]

形 令人悲痛的

英英 very sad

例 The music creates the **mournful** atmosphere on the funeral.
音樂在喪禮上創造了悲傷的氣氛。

□ 三分熟
□ 五分熟
□ 七分熟
□ 全熟

---

mouth·piece

[ˈmaʊθ͵pis]

名 樂器吹口、代言人

英英 a part of a musical instrument, telephone, etc. that is designed to be put between, in, or against the mouth

例 The media company is a **mouthpiece** of certain politicians.
這家媒體公司是某些政治人物的代言人。

□ 三分熟
□ 五分熟
□ 七分熟
□ 全熟

---

mouth·piece/ spokes·per·son/ spokes·man/ spokes·wom·an

[ˈmaʊθ͵pis]/[ˈspoks͵pɝsn̩]/ [ˈspoksmən]/[ˈspokswʊmən]

名 發言人、代言人

英英 a person or newspaper that only expresses the opinions of one certain organization

例 The **spokesperson** of the company announced that they would recall the flawed products.
這家公司的代言人，宣布他們將回收有瑕疵的產品。

□ 三分熟
□ 五分熟
□ 七分熟
□ 全熟

---

mu·nic·i·pal

[mjuˈnɪsəpl̩]

形 內政的、市政的

英英 belonging to a city or town

例 She is going to attend a **municipal** high school.
她將要去就讀一間市立高中。

□ 三分熟
□ 五分熟
□ 七分熟
□ 全熟

---

mute [mjut]

名 啞巴
形 沉默的
同 silent 沉默的

英英 unable to form speech or temporarily speechless; a person who is unable to speak

例 I set the TV in **mute** mode.
我把電視設定在靜音模式。

□ 三分熟
□ 五分熟
□ 七分熟
□ 全熟

---

my·thol·o·gy

[mɪˈθɑlədʒɪ]

名 神話

英英 a set of popular beliefs which are not true or fictitious stories or beliefs

例 The story is a modern version of Greek **mythology**.
這個故事是現代版的希臘神話。

□ 三分熟
□ 五分熟
□ 七分熟
□ 全熟

Nn

N

nar·rate [næˋret]

動 敘述、講故事
同 report 報告

英英 to tell a story in a book, film, play, etc.; give an account of

例 We listened in full attention when she **narrated** the incident.
她描述這個事件的時候，我們全神貫注地聆聽。

- [ ] 三分熟
- [ ] 五分熟
- [ ] 七分熟
- [ ] 全熟

nar·ra·tive

[ˋnærətɪv]

名 敘述、故事
形 敘事的

英英 an account of a series of events; a story

例 Students are learning how to write a creative personal narrative.
學生在學習如何撰寫有創意的個人故事。

- [ ] 三分熟
- [ ] 五分熟
- [ ] 七分熟
- [ ] 全熟

nar·ra·tor

[næˋretɚ]

名 敘述者、講述者

英英 a person who tells a story from a book, play, film, or gives an account of

例 The first-person **narrator** makes the story appear more intimate to the audience.
第一人稱的敘事者，使故事對觀眾來說更有親切感。

- [ ] 三分熟
- [ ] 五分熟
- [ ] 七分熟
- [ ] 全熟

na·tion·al·ism

[ˋnæʃənḷɪzəm]

名 民族主義、國家主義

英英 belief and advocacy in political independence for a particular country

例 She studies how the **nationalism** is represented in the literary works.
她研究國家主義如何表現在文學作品裡面。

- [ ] 三分熟
- [ ] 五分熟
- [ ] 七分熟
- [ ] 全熟

nat·u·ral·ist

[ˋnætʃərəlɪst]

名 自然主義者

英英 an expert in or student of plants and animals

例 Thoreau is a poet and a **naturalist**.
梭羅是一位詩人兼自然主義者。

- [ ] 三分熟
- [ ] 五分熟
- [ ] 七分熟
- [ ] 全熟

na·val [ˋnevḷ]

形 有關海運的、海軍的

英英 of or relating to a navy or navies

例 He attended the **Naval** Academy in his teens.
他十幾歲的時候去念海軍學校。

- [ ] 三分熟
- [ ] 五分熟
- [ ] 七分熟
- [ ] 全熟

na·vel [ˋnevḷ]

名 中心點、肚臍

英英 the small hollow in the center of a person's belly due to the detachment of the umbilical cord at birth

例 She had a **navel** piercing at the age of eighteen.
她十八歲的時候去將肚臍穿洞。

- [ ] 三分熟
- [ ] 五分熟
- [ ] 七分熟
- [ ] 全熟

🎧 **Track 239**

nav·i·ga·tion

[ˌnævəˈgeʃən]

名 航海、航空

英英 the process or activity of finding the right direction using maps

例 The glitches in the **navigation** system were considered the main cause of the air crash.
導航系統出錯，被認為是導致空難的主因。

☐三分熟
☐五分熟
☐七分熟
☐全熟

ne·go·ti·a·tion

[nɪˌgoʃɪˈeʃən]

名 協商、協議

英英 try to reach an agreement, change, or compromise by discussion

例 The **negotiation** between the U.S. and North Korea broke down.
美國和北韓的協商破裂了。

☐三分熟
☐五分熟
☐七分熟
☐全熟

ne·on [ˈniˌɑn]

名 霓虹燈

英英 an gas that produces an orange glow when electricity is passed through it, used in fluorescent lighting

例 I was amazed by the **neon** lights on the street of Seoul.
我對首爾街頭的霓虹燈感到很驚訝。

☐三分熟
☐五分熟
☐七分熟
☐全熟

neu·tral [ˈnjutrəl]

名 中立國
形 中立的、中立國的
同 independent 無黨派的

英英 independent, not supporting any side, impartial or unbiased; a country which is independent and not supporting any side

例 Swiss remains a **neutral** country for years.
瑞士多年來都保持中立國的立場。

☐三分熟
☐五分熟
☐七分熟
☐全熟

new·ly·wed

[ˈnjulɪˌwɛd]

名 新婚夫婦

英英 someone who has recently gotten married

例 The **newlyweds** will go for the honeymoon in the Scandinavian countries.
這對新婚夫妻會去北歐地區度蜜月。

☐三分熟
☐五分熟
☐七分熟
☐全熟

news·cast·er/ an·chor·man/ an·chor·wom·an

[ˈnuzˌkæstɚ]/[ˈæŋkɚˌmæn]

/[ˈæŋkɚˌwʊmən]

名 新聞播報員

英英 a person who's profession is reading the news

例 The **newscaster** had a slip of tongue, and the clip went viral in the Internet.
這位新聞播報員口誤的影片在網路上被瘋傳。

☐三分熟
☐五分熟
☐七分熟
☐全熟

nom·i·na·tion
[ˌnɑməˈneʃən]

名 提名、任命
同 selection
　　被挑選出的人或物

英英 the act of putting someone forward as a candidate for election or for an honor or award

例 The **nomination** for Best Actress at Oscar was considered a great honor.
被提名奧斯卡最佳女主角獎被認是很高的榮譽。

☐三分熟
☐五分熟
☐七分熟
☐全熟

nom·i·nee
[ˌnɑməˈni]

名 被提名的人

英英 a person who is nominated for something

例 Tom was the **nominee** for the best employee of the year.
湯姆是本年度最佳員工的被提名人。

☐三分熟
☐五分熟
☐七分熟
☐全熟

norm [nɔrm]
名 基準、規範
同 criterion 準則

英英 the usual or standard way that something happens

例 Those who do not follow the **norms** will be punished.
不遵守規則的人會受到懲罰。

☐三分熟
☐五分熟
☐七分熟
☐全熟

no·to·ri·ous
[noˈtorɪəs]

形 聲名狼藉的

英英 famous for something bad, a bad quality, or bad deed

例 He is **notorious** for his offensive remarks.
他因為冒犯人的言論而惡名昭彰。

☐三分熟
☐五分熟
☐七分熟
☐全熟

nour·ish [ˈnɝɪʃ]
動 滋養

英英 to provide living things with the food or other substances necessary for growth and health

例 We should **nourish** our spirits with positive thoughts.
我們可以用正面的思想來滋養心靈。

☐三分熟
☐五分熟
☐七分熟
☐全熟

nour·ish·ment
[ˈnɝɪʃmənt]

名 營養

英英 the food or other substances necessary for growth, health to maintain in good condition

例 Her inspiring talk was a **nourishment** of my soul.
她激勵人心的談話是滋養我靈魂的養分。

☐三分熟
☐五分熟
☐七分熟
☐全熟

nui·sance
[ˈnjusn̩s]

名 討厭的人、麻煩事

英英 a disruptive person or thing causing inconvenience or annoyance

例 I tried not to be upset about the **nuisances.**
我嘗試不要因為麻煩事情而覺得難過。

☐三分熟
☐五分熟
☐七分熟
☐全熟

nur·ture [ˈnɝtʃɚ]
名 養育、培育
動 培育、養育

英英 to rear, support, and encourage the development of something or someone (a child)

例 Nature and **nurture** are both important for the mental development of a child.
天性和教養，對一個孩子的心理發展都是很重要的。

☐三分熟
☐五分熟
☐七分熟
☐全熟

🎧 **Track 241**

nu·tri·ent
[`njutrɪənt]

名 營養物
形 有養分的、滋養的

英英 a substance that provides nourishment essential for life and growth; having nourishment essential for life and growth

例 The dietician will plan for meals that contain all essential **nutrients**.
營養師會規劃含有所有重要養分的餐點。

☐三分熟
☐五分熟
☐七分熟
☐全熟

nu·tri·tion
[nju`trɪʃən]

名 營養物、營養
同 nourishment 營養

英英 the process of taking in and assimilating nutrients

例 Poor **nutrition** may cause health problems.
營養不良會導致健康的問題。

☐三分熟
☐五分熟
☐七分熟
☐全熟

nu·tri·tious
[nju`trɪʃəs]

形 有養分的、滋養的

英英 food or plants that are full of nutrients; nourishing

例 Sweet potato is considered one of the most **nutritious** foods.
甘藷被視為是最具營養價值的食物之一。

☐三分熟
☐五分熟
☐七分熟
☐全熟

Oo

ob·li·ga·tion
[ˌɑbləˈgeʃən]

名 責任、義務

英英 an act or course of action to which a person is morally or legally tied to

例 We are under the **obligation** to get rid of the glitches in the machine for our clients.
我們有義務為顧客排除機器的故障。

☐三分熟
☐五分熟
☐七分熟
☐全熟

o·blige [əˈblaɪdʒ]

動 使不得不、強迫

英英 to be compelled to either legally or morally

例 He is **obliged** to compensate for his mistakes.
他不得不彌補自己的錯誤。

☐三分熟
☐五分熟
☐七分熟
☐全熟

ob·scure [əbˈskjʊr]

動 使陰暗
形 陰暗的、晦澀的、模糊的

英英 to become unknown or uncertain; not discovered or known about; uncertain

例 I had difficulty reading the note in the **obscure** room.
我在晦暗的房間裡看不到字條上的字。

☐三分熟
☐五分熟
☐七分熟
☐全熟

of·fer·ing [ˈɔfərɪŋ]

名 供給、提供

英英 a small gift or donation

例 She didn't accept the **offering** from the philanthropic organization.
她沒有接受慈善機構提供的援助。

☐三分熟
☐五分熟
☐七分熟
☐全熟

off·spring

[ˈɔfsprɪŋ]

名 子孫、後裔
同 descendant 子孫、後裔

英英 a person's child or children, or the young of an animal

例 Princess Diana left a good model for her **offspring**.
黛安娜王妃為後代留下好的模範。

☐ 三分熟
☐ 五分熟
☐ 七分熟
☐ 全熟

op·er·a·tion·al

[ˌɑpəˈreʃənl̩]

形 操作的、經營上的

英英 orking or ready for use

例 The plant is fully **operational** after the new machine is installed.
新機器裝設好之後，工廠就全面投入營運。

☐ 三分熟
☐ 五分熟
☐ 七分熟
☐ 全熟

op·po·si·tion

[ˌɑpəˈzɪʃən]

名 反對的態度
同 disagreement 反對

英英 strong disagreement, resistance, or dissent

例 The implementation of new laws was faced with **opposition**.
新法施行遭到反對。

☐ 三分熟
☐ 五分熟
☐ 七分熟
☐ 全熟

op·press [əˈprɛs]

動 壓迫、威迫

英英 to limit freedom, keep in subjection and hardship; cause to feel distressed or anxious

例 Some employees were **oppressed** for their ethnic background.
有些員工因為他們的種族背景受到壓迫。

☐ 三分熟
☐ 五分熟
☐ 七分熟
☐ 全熟

op·pres·sion

[əˈprɛʃən]

名 壓迫、壓制

英英 when people are treated in an unfair and cruel way and prevented from having opportunities and freedom

例 The record of political **oppression** was eliminated from history.
政治壓迫的紀錄被從歷史中刪去。

☐ 三分熟
☐ 五分熟
☐ 七分熟
☐ 全熟

op·tion [ˈɑpʃən]

名 選擇、取捨
同 choice 選擇

英英 thing that is or may be chosen; the freedom or right to choose

例 There are four **options** in the multiple-choice question.
選擇題當中有四個選項。

☐ 三分熟
☐ 五分熟
☐ 七分熟
☐ 全熟

op·tion·al [ˈɑpʃənl̩]

形 非強制性的、非必要性的、可選擇的

英英 available to be chosen from, but not obligatory

例 She registered in three **optional** courses in her junior year.
她大三的時候上了三門選修課。

☐ 三分熟
☐ 五分熟
☐ 七分熟
☐ 全熟

O

Track 243

or·deal [ɔrˈdiəl]

名 嚴酷的考驗

英英 a prolonged painful, tiring, or horrific experience

例 Writing the project report was an **ordeal** for Mike.
寫專案報告對麥可來說是個嚴酷的考驗。

□三分熟
□五分熟
□七分熟
□全熟

or·der·ly [ˈɔrdəlɪ]

名 勤務兵
形 整潔的、有秩序的

英英 a soldier who carries orders for an officer; neatly arranged in an organized way

例 She gave a presentation in a **orderly** manner.
她做了一次條理分明的報告。

□三分熟
□五分熟
□七分熟
□全熟

or·gan·ism

[ˈɔrgənɪzəm]

名 有機體、生物體
同 organization 有機體

英英 a living thing, or single-celled life form

例 The biologist claimed that he found the trace extraterrestrial **organism** in the mountain.
生物學家宣稱在山上找到外星生物體的足跡。

□三分熟
□五分熟
□七分熟
□全熟

o·rig·i·nal·i·ty

[əˌrɪdʒəˈnælətɪ]

名 獨創力、創舉
同 style 風格

英英 the quality of being able to think independently or creatively

例 Juming showed great **originality** in his sculptures.
朱銘在雕刻作品中表現出獨創風格。

□三分熟
□五分熟
□七分熟
□全熟

o·rig·i·nate

[əˈrɪdʒəˌnet]

動 創造、發源

英英 to have a specified beginning; create or initiate

例 It is generally believed that pizzas **originated** from Italy.
一般相信披薩源自義大利。

□三分熟
□五分熟
□七分熟
□全熟

out·break

[ˈaʊtˌbrek]

名 爆發、突然發生

英英 a sudden, difficult to control, or violent occurrence of war, or disease

例 The measles **outbreak** in the U.S. raised public concern.
美國麻疹爆發引起大眾擔憂。

□三分熟
□五分熟
□七分熟
□全熟

out·fit [ˈaʊtˌfɪt]

名 裝備
動 提供必需的裝備

英英 a set of clothes worn for a particular activity or event; to provide equipments or devices which is required

例 The store sells mountain hiking **outfit**.
這家店賣登山裝備。

□三分熟
□五分熟
□七分熟
□全熟

out·ing [ˈaʊtɪŋ]

名 郊遊、遠足

英英 short trip taken for pleasure

例 The kids look forward to going for an **outing** during the spring break.
小朋友期待春假時去郊遊。

□三分熟
□五分熟
□七分熟
□全熟

O

---

out·law [ˋautˌlɔ]

名 逃犯
動 禁止

英英 a fugitive running from the law; to forbid something

例 Accommodating the **outlaw** will make you the accessory of a crime.
收容逃犯會使你成為犯罪的幫兇。

☐ 三分熟
☐ 五分熟
☐ 七分熟
☐ 全熟

---

out·let [ˋautˌlɛt]

名 逃離的出口、出路、銷路

英英 a pipe or hole through you can connect a wire on a piece of electronic equipment

例 She used painting as an **outlet** for emotions.
她用繪畫當作情緒的出口。

☐ 三分熟
☐ 五分熟
☐ 七分熟
☐ 全熟

---

out·look [ˋautˌluk]

名 觀點、態度
同 attitude 態度

英英 person's point of view or attitude about life; a view

例 The book has changed my **outlook** on life.
這本書改變我對人生的態度。

☐ 三分熟
☐ 五分熟
☐ 七分熟
☐ 全熟

---

out·num·ber

[ˌautˋnʌmbɚ]

動 數目勝過
同 exceed 超過

英英 to be more numerous than

例 In my class the girls **outnumber** the boys two to one.
我班上女生比男生多，比例為二比一。

☐ 三分熟
☐ 五分熟
☐ 七分熟
☐ 全熟

---

out·rage

[ˋautˌredʒ]

名 暴力、暴行、憤怒
動 施暴

英英 n extremely strong reaction of anger, shock, or indignation; to make an extremely strong reaction of anger, shock, or indignation

例 Some public figures expressed **outrage** at the under-the-table deal.
有些公眾人物對這次黑箱作業的協定表達憤怒。

☐ 三分熟
☐ 五分熟
☐ 七分熟
☐ 全熟

---

out·ra·geous

[autˋredʒəs]

形 暴力的、蠻橫的

英英 shockingly bad or extreme

例 Many people were astonished by the **outrageous** remarks of the politician.
許多人對這個政治人物蠻橫的言論感到震驚。

☐ 三分熟
☐ 五分熟
☐ 七分熟
☐ 全熟

---

out·right [ˋautˌrait]

形 毫無保留的、全部的
副 無保留地、公然地

英英 altogether; openly; being open and direct

例 There is an **outright** contradiction between his words and his deeds.
他的言行完全是相反的。

☐ 三分熟
☐ 五分熟
☐ 七分熟
☐ 全熟

---

out·set [ˋautˌsɛt]

名 開始、開頭

英英 from the start or beginning of something

例 There has been a problem with the project from the **outset**.
這個計畫一開始就有問題了。

☐ 三分熟
☐ 五分熟
☐ 七分熟
☐ 全熟

🎧 Track 245

o·ver·head

[`ovɚ͵hɛd]

形 頭頂上的、位於上方的
副 在上方地、在頭頂上地
同 above 在上方

英英 to be above one's head; in the sky

例 The **overhead** projector was not working normally.
投影機無法正常運作。

☐ 三分熟
☐ 五分熟
☐ 七分熟
☐ 全熟

o·ver·lap

[͵ovɚ`læp]

名 重疊的部份
動 重疊

英英 a part of extending over and covered; to extend over and partly cover

例 His duties **overlap** with mine.
他的職務和我的職務相重疊。

☐ 三分熟
☐ 五分熟
☐ 七分熟
☐ 全熟

o·ver·turn

[`ovɚ͵tɝn]/[͵ovɚ`tɝn]

名 顛覆
動 顛倒、弄翻

英英 to turn over onto its side or top; to turn upside down

例 The tyrant was **overturned** by the oppressed people.
暴君被受到壓迫的人們推翻了。

☐ 三分熟
☐ 五分熟
☐ 七分熟
☐ 全熟

Pp

pact [pækt]

名 契約

英英 a formal agreement between a group of people or individuals

例 The two countries signed a non-aggression **pact**.
兩國簽訂和平契約。

☐ 三分熟
☐ 五分熟
☐ 七分熟
☐ 全熟

pam·phlet

[`pæmflɪt]

名 小冊子
同 brochure 小冊子

英英 a small booklet or leaflet containing information about something

例 The travel agent offered a **pamphlet** which contains details of the itinerary.
旅行社提供一本包含行程細節的小冊子。

☐ 三分熟
☐ 五分熟
☐ 七分熟
☐ 全熟

par·a·lyze

[`pærə͵laɪz]

動 麻痺、使癱瘓

英英 to cause a person to be partly or wholly incapable of movement

例 He was **paralyzed** from the waist down after the car accident.
車禍之後，他腰部以下癱瘓。

☐ 三分熟
☐ 五分熟
☐ 七分熟
☐ 全熟

P

par·lia·ment

[`pɑrləmənt]

名 議會
同 congress 美國國會

英英 the highest legislature, consisting of the Sovereign, the House of Lords, and the House of Commons

例 The British **parliament** is made up of two chambers.
英國國會是由上下兩個議院組成。

☐ 三分熟
☐ 五分熟
☐ 七分熟
☐ 全熟

pa·thet·ic

[pə`ðɛtɪk]

形 悲慘的

英英 itiful; miserably inadequate

例 The **pathetic** stories of the orphan arouse sympathy of many people.
孤兒的悲慘經驗引起許多人的同情。

☐ 三分熟
☐ 五分熟
☐ 七分熟
☐ 全熟

pa·tri·ot·ic

[ˌpetrɪ`ɑtɪk]

形 愛國的
同 loyal 忠誠的

英英 pitiful; miserably inadequate

例 They boost the morale of the soldiers by playing **patriotic** songs.
他們藉由播放愛國歌曲提振軍人的士氣。

☐ 三分熟
☐ 五分熟
☐ 七分熟
☐ 全熟

PDA [`pi`di`e]

名 個人數位祕書、
掌上型電腦

英英 a small handheld computer that can be carried on the go

例 He updated the contact information on his **PDA**.
他更新了掌上型電腦裡面的聯絡資訊。

☐ 三分熟
☐ 五分熟
☐ 七分熟
☐ 全熟

ped·dle [`pɛdl]

動 叫賣、兜售
同 sell 銷售

英英 to sell goods by going from place to place on foot

例 The girl **peddled** her home-made cookies on the street.
那個女生在街道上兜售手工餅乾。

☐ 三分熟
☐ 五分熟
☐ 七分熟
☐ 全熟

pe·des·tri·an

[pə`dɛstrɪən]

名 行人
形 徒步的
片 pedestrian crossing 行人穿越道

英英 person traveling on foot rather than travelling in a vehicle; to travel on foot

例 The **pedestrian** crossing is decorated with LED lights.
這個行人穿越道有 LED 燈裝飾。

☐ 三分熟
☐ 五分熟
☐ 七分熟
☐ 全熟

pen·in·su·la

[pə`nɪnsələ]

名 半島

英英 a long, narrow piece of land extending out into a sea or lake

例 The DMZ on Korean **peninsula** was open to tourists.
朝鮮半島的非武裝地區開放給觀光客參觀。

☐ 三分熟
☐ 五分熟
☐ 七分熟
☐ 全熟

🎧 Track 247

pen·sion [ˈpɛnʃən]

名 退休金
動 給予退休金
同 allowance
　 津貼、發津貼

英英 a regular payment made people in retirement and to some widows and disabled people, either by the state or from an investment fund; to pay a pension

例 The **pension** reform was objected by the labors.
年金改革遭到勞工反對。

☐ 三分熟　☐ 五分熟　☐ 七分熟　☐ 全熟

per·cep·tion [pəˈsɛpʃən]

名 感覺、察覺
同 sense 感覺

英英 the ability to see, hear, or become aware of something from the senses

例 His **perception** of the issue is quite different from mine.
他對問題的感知和我很不相同。

☐ 三分熟　☐ 五分熟　☐ 七分熟　☐ 全熟

per·se·ver·ance [ˌpɝsəˈvɪrəns]

名 堅忍、堅持

英英 to continue to try in a course of action in spite of difficulty or lack of success

例 He showed persistence and **perseverance** in the pursuit of his goal.
他追求目標時表現出毅力和堅持不懈。

☐ 三分熟　☐ 五分熟　☐ 七分熟　☐ 全熟

per·se·vere [ˌpɝsəˈvɪr]

動 堅持

英英 to try to do or continue doing something in a determined way, despite having problems

例 He **persevered** with his research despite shortage of the financial support.
儘管缺乏金錢援助，他還是堅持進行研究。

☐ 三分熟　☐ 五分熟　☐ 七分熟　☐ 全熟

per·sis·tence [pəˈsɪstəns]

名 固執、堅持
同 maintenance 維持

英英 when someone or something persists

例 When you run a marathon, **persistence** is more important than speed.
跑馬拉松的時候，堅持比速度更重要。

☐ 三分熟　☐ 五分熟　☐ 七分熟　☐ 全熟

per·sist·ent [pəˈsɪstənt]

形 固執的、堅持不懈的

英英 persisting or having a tendency to persist

例 The old man is **persistent** in his political stance.
老先生堅持他的政治立場。

☐ 三分熟　☐ 五分熟　☐ 七分熟　☐ 全熟

per·spec·tive [pəˈspɛktɪv]

名 透視、觀點
形 透視的
同 position 立場

英英 a certain view or prospect; a particular way of regarding something; seeing something through

例 The floor plan of the museum was presented in 3D **perspective**.
博物館的平面圖是用 3D 透視的方式呈現。

☐ 三分熟　☐ 五分熟　☐ 七分熟　☐ 全熟

P

pes·ti·cide
[`pɛstɪˌsaɪd]

名 農藥、殺蟲劑

英英 a substance used for destroying insects or other pests

例 They did not use **pesticide** on the crops.
他們沒有在作物上面使用殺蟲劑。

☐ 三分熟
☐ 五分熟
☐ 七分熟
☐ 全熟

pe·tro·le·um
[pə`trolɪəm]

名 石油

英英 il or petrol

例 Saudi Arabia has great revenue from exporting crude **petroleum**.
沙烏地阿拉伯靠著出口原油獲得收益。

☐ 三分熟
☐ 五分熟
☐ 七分熟
☐ 全熟

pet·ty [`pɛtɪ]

形 瑣碎的、小的
同 small 小的
片 petty things
不重要的小事

英英 unimportant, trivial

例 Don't worry about those **petty** things.
別擔心那些不重要的小事了。

☐ 三分熟
☐ 五分熟
☐ 七分熟
☐ 全熟

phar·ma·cist
[`fɑrməsɪst]

名 藥劑師

英英 a person qualified to prepare and sell medicinal drugs

例 He is a licensed **pharmacist**.
他是一位有證照的藥劑師。

☐ 三分熟
☐ 五分熟
☐ 十分熟
☐ 全熟

phar·ma·cy
[`fɑrməsɪ]

名 藥劑學、藥局

英英 n area where medicinal drugs are prepared or sold

例 You can fill the prescription in the **pharmacy** in your neighborhood.
你可在附近的藥局配藥。

☐ 三分熟
☐ 五分熟
☐ 七分熟
☐ 全熟

phase [fez]

名 階段
動 分段實行
同 stage 階段

英英 a distinct period of time or stage in a process of change or development; to carry out in gradual stages

例 Consumers' need is our focus in the first **phase** of the project.
客戶需求是我們計劃地第一階段的重點。

☐ 三分熟
☐ 五分熟
☐ 七分熟
☐ 全熟

pho·to·graph·ic
[ˌfotə`græfɪk]

形 攝影的

英英 a picture made with a camera, in which an image is focused on to film and then made visible and permanent through chemical treatment

例 The photographer shares some **photographic** tips on his weblog.
這名攝影師會在自己的部落格上分享攝影的技巧。

☐ 三分熟
☐ 五分熟
☐ 七分熟
☐ 全熟

🎧 **Track 249**

pic·tur·esque

[ˌpɪktʃəˈrɛsk]

形 如畫的

英英 visually attractive in a quaint or charming manner

例 They were awed by the **picturesque** scenery in Alaska.
阿拉斯加如畫的景色之美，令他們驚艷。

□三分熟
□五分熟
□七分熟
□全熟

pierce [pɪrs]

動 刺穿

英英 to make a hole in or through using a sharp object

例 The sunlight **pierced** through the fog, so we could see the path ahead.
陽光穿過迷霧，我們看到前方的道路。

□三分熟
□五分熟
□七分熟
□全熟

pi·e·ty [ˈpaɪətɪ]

名 虔敬

英英 the quality of having strong religious morals or reverent

例 The pilgrims showed the **piety** to the Goddess Matsu.
朝聖者表示對女神媽祖的虔敬。

□三分熟
□五分熟
□七分熟
□全熟

pi·ous [ˈpaɪəs]

形 虔誠的
同 faithful 忠誠的

英英 devoutly religious, having strong religious beliefs

例 The **pious** devotees bent down to pass under Goddess Matsu's palanquin.
虔誠的信徒彎下從媽祖鑾轎底下穿過。

□三分熟
□五分熟
□七分熟
□全熟

pipe·line

[ˈpaɪpˌlaɪn]

名 管線

英英 a long pipe for carrying oil, gas, etc. over a distance

例 There is a fracture on the **pipeline**.
管線上面有裂縫。

□三分熟
□五分熟
□七分熟
□全熟

pitch·er [ˈpɪtʃɚ]

名 投手

英英 the player who throws the ball at the batter

例 The **pitcher** stepped on the mound and stretched a little.
投手站上投手丘，稍微伸展了一下。

□三分熟
□五分熟
□七分熟
□全熟

plight [plaɪt]

名 誓約、婚約、困境

英英 an unpleasant and often times difficult situation

例 He showed pity when seeing the **plight** of the refugees.
他看到難民的困境，表示同情。

□三分熟
□五分熟
□七分熟
□全熟

pneu·mo·nia

[njuˈmonjə]

名 肺炎

英英 a lung infection making a person difficult to breathe

例 The doctor diagnosed that the old man contracted **pneumonia**.
醫生診斷老人是得到了肺炎。

□三分熟
□五分熟
□七分熟
□全熟

poach [potʃ]

動 偷獵、水煮

英英 to cook by gently boiling in a small amount of liquid

例 She had some **poached** eggs and beans for dinner.
她晚餐吃水煮雞蛋和豆子。

☐三分熟
☐五分熟
☐七分熟
☐全熟

---

poach·er [`potʃə]

名 偷獵者

英英 a pan for poaching foods and eggs

例 Those rhino **poachers** got arrested.
犀牛盜獵者已被逮捕。

☐三分熟
☐五分熟
☐七分熟
☐全熟

---

pol·lu·tant

[pə`lutənt]

名 污染物
形 污染物的

英英 harmful or poisonous substances that contaminate something or the environment; having harmful or poisonous substances

例 Because of the food chain, the **pollutant** in the ocean may be consumed by human beings.
因為食物鏈的關係，海洋中的污染物可能會被人類食用。

☐三分熟
☐五分熟
☐七分熟
☐全熟

---

pon·der [`pandə]

動 仔細考慮
同 consider 考慮

英英 to consider carefully

例 We have to **ponder** over the long-term consequences when making a decision.
我們做決定的時候要考慮長期的影響。

☐三分熟
☐五分熟
☐七分熟
☐全熟

---

pop·u·late

[`papjə‚let]

動 居住

英英 to form the population of an area, country

例 The area is **populated** by both aborigines and immigrants.
有原住民和外來移民者居住在這個地區。

☐三分熟
☐五分熟
☐七分熟
☐全熟

---

pos·ture [`pastʃə]

名 態度、姿勢
動 擺姿勢

英英 a particular position of the body; to behave in a particular way

例 He adjusted his sitting **posture** before taking the picture.
他在拍照前調整了一下坐姿。

☐三分熟
☐五分熟
☐七分熟
☐全熟

---

pre·cede [pri`sid]

動 在前
同 lead 走在最前方

英英 to happen or exist before in time, order, or position

例 She **preceded** me as the Chief Financing Officer.
她是在我之前擔任財務長的人。

☐三分熟
☐五分熟
☐七分熟
☐全熟

🔊 **Track 251**

---

pre·ce·dent

[ˋprɛsədənt]

名 前例、判例

英英 an earlier event or action acting as an example or guide

例 There is no **precedent** for such criminal case.
沒有這種犯罪案件的判例。

☐ 三分熟
☐ 五分熟
☐ 七分熟
☐ 全熟

---

pre·ci·sion

[prɪˋsɪʒən]

名 精準
同 accuracy 準確

英英 the quality or condition of being exact

例 The **precision** of the weather forecast has been questioned.
這個氣象預報的準確性遭到質疑。

☐ 三分熟
☐ 五分熟
☐ 七分熟
☐ 全熟

---

pred·e·ces·sor

[ˏprɛdɪˋsɛsɚ]

名 祖先、前輩

英英 a person who held a job or office before the one currently holding the position

例 The **predecessors** have established the conventions.
前輩們已經建立了常規。

☐ 三分熟
☐ 五分熟
☐ 七分熟
☐ 全熟

---

pre·dic·tion

[prɪˋdɪkʃən]

名 預言

英英 a forecast of something to happen

例 His **prediction** about the catastrophe was taken seriously by some people.
有些人把他的災難預言當真了。

☐ 三分熟
☐ 五分熟
☐ 七分熟
☐ 全熟

---

pref·ace [ˋprɛfɪs]

名 序言
同 introduction 序言

英英 n piece of writing at the beginning of a book, stating its subject, scope, or aims

例 The author stated his motivation for compiling the book in the **preface**.
作者在序言中提到他寫這本書的動機。

☐ 三分熟
☐ 五分熟
☐ 七分熟
☐ 全熟

---

prej·u·dice

[ˋprɛdʒədɪs]

名 偏見
動 使存有偏見

英英 preconceived opinion or assumption that is not based on reason or experience; to give rise to prejudice in someone

例 Sometimes **prejudice** derives from ideologies.
有時候偏見是由意識形態產生的。

☐ 三分熟
☐ 五分熟
☐ 七分熟
☐ 全熟

---

pre·lim·i·nar·y

[prɪˋlɪməˏnɛrɪ]

名 初步
形 初步的

英英 done in order to prepare for something fuller or more important; a preliminary action or event

例 We could come up with a **preliminary** conclusion from the medical research.
我們可以由這個醫學研究得出一個初步的結論。

☐ 三分熟
☐ 五分熟
☐ 七分熟
☐ 全熟

P

pre·ma·ture
[ˌprimə`tjʊr]

形 過早的、未成熟的

英英 occurring or done before the proper or expected time

例 The information is not verified yet; it's a **premature** conclusion.
這項資訊還未獲得證實；下結論還太早。

☐ 三分熟
☐ 五分熟
☐ 七分熟
☐ 全熟

pre·mier [`primɪɚ]

名 首長
形 首要的
同 prime 首要的

英英 he leader, first in importance, order, or position.; Prime Minister or other head of government

例 The provincial **premiers** will gather for an annual meeting.
省長們會聚在一起開年度會議。

☐ 三分熟
☐ 五分熟
☐ 七分熟
☐ 全熟

pre·scribe
[prɪ`skraɪb]

動 規定、開藥方

英英 to recommend and authorize the use of medical treatment

例 Doctors are not allowed to **prescribe** opiates for patients.
醫師不能開鴉片類藥物處方。

☐ 三分熟
☐ 五分熟
☐ 七分熟
☐ 全熟

pre·scrip·tion
[prɪ`skrɪpʃən]

名 指示、處方

英英 an instruction written by a medical practitioner authorizing the issuance of a medicine or treatment for a patient

例 You can request a **prescription** refill in the local pharmacy.
你可以在本地的藥局要求重新配處方藥。

☐ 三分熟
☐ 五分熟
☐ 七分熟
☐ 全熟

pre·side [prɪ`zaɪd]

動 主持

英英 to be in the authoritative position in a meeting, court, etc.

例 He was designated to **preside** the opening ceremony.
他被指定要來主持開幕典禮。

☐ 三分熟
☐ 五分熟
☐ 七分熟
☐ 全熟

pres·i·den·cy
[`prɛzədənsɪ]

名 總統的職位

英英 he period of time when someone is in the office or status of president

例 She is devoted to pension reform during her **presidency**.
她於總統任期當中，致力推動退休金改革。

☐ 三分熟
☐ 五分熟
☐ 七分熟
☐ 全熟

pres·i·den·tial
[ˌprɛzə`dɛnʃəl]

形 總統的

英英 relating to the elected head of a republican state; the head of a society, council, or other organization

例 He announced to run for the next **presidential** campaign.
他宣布要參加下一屆總統選舉。

☐ 三分熟
☐ 五分熟
☐ 七分熟
☐ 全熟

🎧 **Track 253**

pres·tige [prɛsˈtiʒ]

名 聲望

英英 respect and admiration attracted through a perception of success, high achievements, or quality

例 The **prestige** of the institute is a merit for the graduates.
這個研究所的聲望對畢業生來說是種優勢。

☐ 三分熟
☐ 五分熟
☐ 七分熟
☐ 全熟

---

pre·sume

[prɪˈzum]

動 假設
同 guess 推測

英英 to think that something is probably the case; take for granted

例 Don't just **presume** that everyone on the meeting can get the gist of the presentation.
不要假設會議上面所有人都抓得到報告的重點。

☐ 三分熟
☐ 五分熟
☐ 七分熟
☐ 全熟

---

pre·ven·tive

[prɪˈvɛntɪv]

名 預防物
形 預防的

英英 designed to prevent something from happening, especially an unwanted result; a preventive medicine or treatment

例 The government took **preventive** measures of the typhoon.
政府進行颱風的預防措施。

☐ 三分熟
☐ 五分熟
☐ 七分熟
☐ 全熟

---

pro·duc·tiv·i·ty

[ˌprodʌkˈtɪvətɪ]

名 生產力

英英 the rate at which goods are being produced, the state or quality of being productive

例 The writer has better **productivity** when he composes in the library.
作家在圖書館寫作時，會有比較好的生產力。

☐ 三分熟
☐ 五分熟
☐ 七分熟
☐ 全熟

---

pro·fi·cien·cy

[prəˈfɪʃənsɪ]

名 熟練、精通

英英 ompetent; skilled

例 A certificate of language **proficiency** is required for applicants of this position.
語言能力證明是求職者必備的條件。

☐ 三分熟
☐ 五分熟
☐ 七分熟
☐ 全熟

---

pro·found

[prəˈfaʊnd]

形 極深的、深奧的

英英 extreme or intense

例 His words has **profound** influence on me.
他說的話對我有很深的影響。

☐ 三分熟
☐ 五分熟
☐ 七分熟
☐ 全熟

---

pro·gres·sive

[prəˈgrɛsɪv]

形 前進的

英英 developing or proceeding gradually or in stages

例 There is **progressive** advance in the country's democratic system.
這個國家的民主制度有漸進的進展。

☐ 三分熟
☐ 五分熟
☐ 七分熟
☐ 全熟

pro·hi·bit

[prəˋhɪbɪt]

動 制止、禁止

英英 to officially forbid by law, rule, etc.

例 Smoking in public places is **prohibited**.
禁止在公共場所吸菸。

☐ 三分熟
☐ 五分熟
☐ 七分熟
☐ 全熟

---

pro·hi·bi·tion

[ˌproəˋbɪʃən]

名 禁令、禁止

英英 the action of prohibiting

例 The **prohibition** has been lifted.
這項禁令已被解除。

☐ 三分熟
☐ 五分熟
☐ 七分熟
☐ 全熟

---

pro·jec·tion

[prəˋdʒɛkʃən]

名 計畫、預估

英英 an estimate or forecast based on the trends that are present

例 Some experts made a **projection** that population on the island will start to decline within a decade.
有些專家預測本島人口十年內會開始減少。

☐ 三分熟
☐ 五分熟
☐ 七分熟
☐ 全熟

---

prone [pron]

形 俯臥的、易於……的

英英 likely or liable to suffer from, do, or experience something unfortunate

例 Teenagers are **prone** to be addicted to social media.
青少年容易對社群媒體上癮。

☐ 三分熟
☐ 五分熟
☐ 七分熟
☐ 全熟

---

prop·a·gan·da

[ˌprɑpəˋgændə]

名 宣傳活動
同 promotion 促銷活動

英英 often biased and misleading information, used to promote a political cause or point of view

例 They have a **propaganda** campaign for raising environmental awareness.
他們有一個提升環保意識的宣傳活動。

☐ 三分熟
☐ 五分熟
☐ 七分熟
☐ 全熟

---

pro·pel [prəˋpɛl]

動 推動

英英 to drive or push forwards with a lot of force

例 They invented a new type of mechanically **propelled** vehicle.
他們發明了一個新型的機械推動車。

☐ 三分熟
☐ 五分熟
☐ 七分熟
☐ 全熟

---

pro·pel·ler

[prəˋpɛlɚ]

名 推進器

英英 a revolving shaft with two or more angled blades, for propelling a ship or aircraft

例 The **propeller** is not functionally normal.
推進器沒有正常運作。

☐ 三分熟
☐ 五分熟
☐ 七分熟
☐ 全熟

---

prose [proz]

名 散文

英英 ordinary written or spoken language that is not poetry

例 We studied the **prose** works of William Wordsworth in English class.
我們英文課時，研讀了華滋華斯的散文。

☐ 三分熟
☐ 五分熟
☐ 七分熟
☐ 全熟

P

🎧 Track 255

pros·e·cute

[`prasɪˌkjut]

動 檢舉、告發

英英 to institute legal proceedings against the accused someone or with reference to a crime

例 He was **prosecuted** for embezzling.
他被告發盜用公款。

☐ 三分熟
☐ 五分熟
☐ 七分熟
☐ 全熟

pros·e·cu·tion

[ˌprasɪ`kjuʃən]

名 告發

英英 he prosecuting of someone in respect to a criminal charge

例 He has brought a **prosecution** against the politicians who took bribes.
他已經將收賄政客告發。

☐ 三分熟
☐ 五分熟
☐ 七分熟
☐ 全熟

pro·spec·tive

[prə`spɛktɪv]

形 將來的、預期的
同 future 未來的

英英 expected or possible to happen or be in the future

例 He gave some advices to his **prospective** son-in-law.
他給準女婿一些建議。

☐ 三分熟
☐ 五分熟
☐ 七分熟
☐ 全熟

pro·vin·cial

[prə`vɪnʃəl]

名 省民
形 省的

英英 relating to a province or the provinces; a person of a province

例 The **provincial** government will move its office to a new building.
省政府將要把辦公室遷到新大樓。

☐ 三分熟
☐ 五分熟
☐ 七分熟
☐ 全熟

pro·voke [prə`vok]

動 激起

英英 to stimulate or cause a strong or unwelcome reaction or emotion in someone

例 The controversial editorial article has **provoked** much discussion.
爭議的社論文章引起很多討論。

☐ 三分熟
☐ 五分熟
☐ 七分熟
☐ 全熟

prowl [praʊl]

名 徘徊
動 潛行

英英 an act of prowling; to move about stealthily or slowly as if in search of prey

例 The leopard cat **prowls** at night, looking for prey.
石虎夜間伏行，尋找獵物。

☐ 三分熟
☐ 五分熟
☐ 七分熟
☐ 全熟

punc·tu·al

[`pʌŋktʃʊəl]

形 準時的

英英 happening or keeping to the appointed time

例 The professor is always **punctual** for the seminars.
教授總是準時參加座談。

☐ 三分熟
☐ 五分熟
☐ 七分熟
☐ 全熟

pu·ri·fy [`pjʊrəˌfaɪ]

動 淨化
同 cleanse 淨化

英英 to remove contaminants from something polluted; to make pure

例 The gadget is used to **purify** water for drinking.
這個工具是用來將水淨化以供飲用。

☐ 三分熟
☐ 五分熟
☐ 七分熟
☐ 全熟

pu·ri·ty [`pjʊrətɪ]

名 純粹

英英 the state of being pure

例 The **purity** of gold is expressed in carats.
黃金的純度是用克拉計算的。

☐ 三分熟
☐ 五分熟
☐ 七分熟
☐ 全熟

Qq

qual·i·fi·ca·tion(s)
[ˌkwɑləfəˈkeʃən(z)]

名 賦予資格、證照
同 competence 勝任

英英 the action of receiving training and obtaining an official record of having finished a training course; becoming qualified

例 She passed her **qualification** for the Olympic gymnastic competition.
她獲得了奧林匹克體操比賽的資格。

☐ 三分熟
☐ 五分熟
☐ 七分熟
☐ 全熟

quar·rel·some
[`kwɔrəlsəm]

形 愛爭吵的

英英 characterized by repeated arguments

例 The **quarrelsome** kids made their parents rather upset.
這些愛爭吵的小孩，讓他們父母很頭痛。

☐ 三分熟
☐ 五分熟
☐ 十分熟
☐ 全熟

quench [kwɛntʃ]

動 弄熄、解渴

英英 to satisfy by drinking a beverage or water; satisfy a desire

例 Nothing can **quench** my passion for art.
什麼也無法澆熄我對藝術的熱情。

☐ 三分熟
☐ 五分熟
☐ 七分熟
☐ 全熟

que·ry [`kwɪrɪ]

名 問題
動 質疑
同 inquire 詢問

英英 question, often one expressing doubt; a question mark; to question something or someone

例 We have **query** for his innocence.
我們對他的清白存疑。

☐ 三分熟
☐ 五分熟
☐ 七分熟
☐ 全熟

ques·tion·naire
[ˌkwɛstʃənˈɛr]

名 問卷、調查表

英英 a set of printed questions, usually of multiple choice answers, devised for a survey or statistical study

例 It takes about three minutes to finish the **questionnaire**.
完成這份問卷大約需要三分鐘。

☐ 三分熟
☐ 五分熟
☐ 七分熟
☐ 全熟

Rr

rac·ism [ˋresɪzəm]

名 種族、差別主義

英英 the belief that they are characteristics, abilities, or qualities or people are specific to each race

例 They boycotted the ad which has implication of **racism**.
他們抵制這個有種族歧視意涵的廣告。

☐ 三分熟
☐ 五分熟
☐ 七分熟
☐ 全熟

---

ra·di·ant [ˋredjənt]

名 發光體
形 發光的、輻射的、洋溢著幸福的

英英 shining subject; shining or glowing brightly; emanating great joy, love, or health

例 The bride wears a **radiant** smile on her face.
新娘臉上帶著幸福的微笑。

☐ 三分熟
☐ 五分熟
☐ 七分熟
☐ 全熟

---

ra·di·ate [ˋredɪˬet]

動 放射、流露
形 放射狀的

英英 to emit or be emitted in the form of beams, rays, noises, or waves

例 He **radiated** confidence as he delivered his speech.
他演講時流露出自信。

☐ 三分熟
☐ 五分熟
☐ 七分熟
☐ 全熟

---

ra·di·a·tion
[ˌredɪˋeʃən]

名 放射、發光、輻射

英英 the action or process of radiating; energy emitted as electromagnetic waves or subatomic particles

例 The suit can protect you from **radiation**.
這套衣服可以防輻射。

☐ 三分熟
☐ 五分熟
☐ 七分熟
☐ 全熟

---

ra·di·a·tor
[ˋredɪˬetɚ]

名 發光體、暖房裝置、散熱器、輻射體

英英 a thing that emits light, heat, or sound

例 The **radiators** in the room is not functioning normally.
這個房間的暖氣機沒有正常運作。

☐ 三分熟
☐ 五分熟
☐ 七分熟
☐ 全熟

---

rad·i·cal [ˋrædɪkl̩]

名 根本
形 根源的、激進的

英英 a unit in a number of compounds; believing or expressing belief that there should be an extreme or dramatic change to the fundamental nature of something

例 He has a **radical** political stance.
他抱持激進的政治立場。

☐ 三分熟
☐ 五分熟
☐ 七分熟
☐ 全熟

---

raft [ræft]

名 筏、救生艇
動 乘筏

英英 a flat floating structure made of timber or other materials fastened together, used as a boat or floating platform; to take a raft

例 Put on a life vest before you get on the **raft**.
先穿上救生衣再乘坐救生艇。

☐ 三分熟
☐ 五分熟
☐ 七分熟
☐ 全熟

raid [red]

名 突擊
動 襲擊

英英 a quick surprise attack on an enemy or on the premises to commit a crime; to give a quick surprise attack on an enemy

例 The police made a **raid** on the illegal casino.
警方突襲非法賭場。

☐ 三分熟
☐ 五分熟
☐ 七分熟
☐ 全熟

---

ran·dom [ˈrændəm]

形 隨意的、隨機的
反 deliberate 蓄意的

英英 ade, done, or happening by chance, without plan, or conscious decision

例 Several people were injured in the incident of **random** attack.
好幾個人在這次隨機攻擊事件中受傷。

☐ 三分熟
☐ 五分熟
☐ 七分熟
☐ 全熟

---

ran·som [ˈrænsəm]

名 贖金
動 贖回

英英 a sum of money demanded or paid in exchange for the release of a captive; to get the release of someone by paying a ransom

例 The abductor requested a large sum of **ransom**.
綁匪要求一大筆贖金。

☐ 三分熟
☐ 五分熟
☐ 七分熟
☐ 全熟

---

rash [ræʃ]

名 疹子
形 輕率的

英英 an area of reddening of a person's skin; acting or done hastily, without careful consideration

例 She has a **rash** whenever she takes in alcohol.
她只要一喝酒就會起疹子。

☐ 三分熟
☐ 五分熟
☐ 七分熟
☐ 全熟

---

ra·tion·al [ˈræʃənl]

形 理性的
反 absurd 不合理的

英英 based on or in accordance within reason or logic

例 To make a **rational** decision, you should verify the information first.
為了做出理性的決定，你應該要先證實這項資訊。

☐ 三分熟
☐ 五分熟
☐ 七分熟
☐ 全熟

---

rav·age [ˈrævɪdʒ]

名 毀壞
動 破壞

英英 devastate; to cause extensive damage to

例 The wooden house was **ravaged** by the tornado.
木造房子被龍捲風摧毀。

☐ 三分熟
☐ 五分熟
☐ 七分熟
☐ 全熟

---

re·al·ism

[ˈriəlɪzəm]

名 現實主義

英英 he practice of accepting a situation as is, and dealing with it accordingly

例 The artist shifted from **realism** to surrealism later.
藝術家從寫實主義轉向超現實主義。

☐ 三分熟
☐ 五分熟
☐ 七分熟
☐ 全熟

🎧 Track 259

re·al·i·za·tion
[ˌrɪələˋzeʃən]

名 現實、領悟

英英 when one starts to understand a situation, especially suddenly

例 He has a growing **realization** that health is invaluable.
他逐漸領悟到健康是無價的。

☐三分熟
☐五分熟
☐七分熟
☐全熟

re·bel·lion
[rɪˋbɛljən]

名 叛亂

英英 acting against an established government or ruler

例 The **rebellion** of the warlord was suppressed in a week.
軍閥的叛亂在一星期之內被鎮壓。

☐三分熟
☐五分熟
☐七分熟
☐全熟

re·ces·sion
[rɪˋsɛʃən]

名 衰退

英英 a temporary economic decline in which trade and industrial activity are reduced

例 The economic **recession** has made many people sent to unpaid leave.
經濟衰退讓很多人被放無薪價。

☐三分熟
☐五分熟
☐七分熟
☐全熟

re·cip·i·ent
[rɪˋsɪpɪənt]

名 接受者、接受的
同 receiver 接受者

英英 a person who receives something; able to receive or accept

例 The **recipient** of the financial aid expressed his gratitude to the donor.
財務援助的接受者對捐贈者表達感謝。

☐三分熟
☐五分熟
☐七分熟
☐全熟

rec·om·men·da·tion
[ˌrɛkəmɛnˋdeʃən]

名 推薦
同 reference 推薦

英英 to give with approval as being suitable for a purpose or role

例 Professor wrote a **recommendation** letter for me.
教授為我寫了一封推薦信。

☐三分熟
☐五分熟
☐七分熟
☐全熟

rec·on·cile
[ˋrɛkənˌsaɪl]

動 調停、和解

英英 to restore friendly relations between two sides; make or show to be compatible

例 The official **reconciled** the dispute between the local organizations.
官員調解了兩個當地組織之間的紛爭。

☐三分熟
☐五分熟
☐七分熟
☐全熟

rec·re·a·tion·al
[ˌrɛkrɪˋeʃənl̩]

形 娛樂的、消遣的

英英 enjoyable leisure activity

例 Do you do **recreational** activities with your family?
你會和家人一起從事休閒活動嗎？

☐三分熟
☐五分熟
☐七分熟
☐全熟

re·cruit [rɪˋkrut]

動 徵募
名 新兵
同 draft 徵兵

英英 to enlist someone in the armed forces; enroll someone as a student, member, or worker in an organization; a person who enrolls as a new member

例 The company is **recruiting** customer representatives.
這家公司在招募客戶服務代表。

R

---

re·cur [rɪˋkɜ]

動 重現、再發現、復發

英英 to occur again; something such as a thought comes back to one's mind

例 There is chance that the disease will **recur**.
這個疾病有復發的可能。

---

re·dun·dant

[rɪˋdʌndənt]

形 過剩的、冗長的、多餘的
反 concise 簡要的

英英 not or no longer needed or useful; extra, more than needed

例 The **redundant** words in the script should be omitted.
稿子上面多餘的字應該要刪除。

---

re·fine [rɪˋfaɪn]

動 精鍊、提煉
同 improve 改善

英英 to make a substance pure by removing impurities or unwanted elements from it

例 The crude oil is **refined** at the plant.
原油在這間工廠裡面提煉。

---

re·fine·ment

[rɪˋfaɪnmənt]

名 精良

英英 the process of refining; an improvement or clarification brought about by the making of small changes

例 He was praised for the **refinement** of his final report.
他因為期末報告品質精良而受到表揚。

---

re·flec·tive

[rɪˋflɛktɪv]

形 反射的

英英 providing or produced by sending back light in reflection

例 This dress is made of **reflective** fabric.
這件洋裝是反光布料作成的。

---

re·fresh·ment(s)

[rɪˋfrɛʃmənt(s)]

名 清爽、提神之物、茶點

英英 small amounts of snacks or drinks

例 Let's take a break and have some **refreshments**.
我們休息一下、吃些點心吧。

🎧 **Track 261**

re·fund
[rɪˋfʌnd]/[ˋrɪfʌnd]

名 償還、退款
動 償還

英英 refunded sum of money; to pay back money to

例 He asked for a **refund** of the flawed product.
他要求退還這個有瑕疵的商品。

☐ 三分熟
☐ 五分熟
☐ 七分熟
☐ 全熟

re·gard·less
[rɪˋgɑrdlɪs]

形 不關心的
副 不關心地、無論如何、不顧一切地
同 despite 儘管

英英 not caring; despite

例 He pursued a career in art **regardless** of his parents' objection.
他不顧父母的反對，走上藝術這一行。

☐ 三分熟
☐ 五分熟
☐ 七分熟
☐ 全熟

re·gime [rɪˋʒim]

名 政權
片 regardless of 不顧、不管

英英 a government, especially an authoritarian one

例 The authoritarian **regime** was overthrown by the people.
威權政體被人民推翻。

☐ 三分熟
☐ 五分熟
☐ 七分熟
☐ 全熟

re·hears·al
[rɪˋhɝsl̩]

名 排演
同 practice 練習

英英 a practice performance of a play or other work for later public performance

例 The actor spent weeks on the **rehearsal** for the stage play.
演員花了好幾個星期在排練舞臺劇。

☐ 三分熟
☐ 五分熟
☐ 七分熟
☐ 全熟

re·hearse [rɪˋhɝs]

動 預演

英英 to practice for later public performance

例 She is **rehearsing** for the commencement speech.
她在預演畢業典禮的演講。

☐ 三分熟
☐ 五分熟
☐ 七分熟
☐ 全熟

rein [ren]

名 箝制
動 控制
片 rein in 控制

英英 long, narrow strap attached at one end to a horse's bit, used in pairs to direct, guide, or check a horse; to take control

例 He was told by his wife to **rein** in his temper.
他太太提醒他要控制脾氣。

☐ 三分熟
☐ 五分熟
☐ 七分熟
☐ 全熟

re·in·force
[ˌriɪnˋfors]

動 增強、使更結實、加強
同 intensify 增強

英英 to make stronger a military force with additional personnel or material

例 The negative remarks **reinforced** the public's dislike of the politician.
負面言論，讓大眾更不喜歡這位政治人物。

☐ 三分熟
☐ 五分熟
☐ 七分熟
☐ 全熟

R

re·lay

[ˋrɪle]/[rɪˋle]

名 接力（賽）
動 傳達

英英 a group of people or animals engaged in a task for a period of time and then replaced by a similar group to continue the task

例 The runner dropped the baton by accident in the **relay** race.
接力賽時，跑者不小心弄掉了接力棒。

☐ 三分熟
☐ 五分熟
☐ 七分熟
☐ 全熟

rel·e·vant

[ˋrɛləvənt]

形 相關的

英英 closely connected with the matter in hand

例 His professional competence is not necessarily **relevant** to his educational background.
他的專業能力不一定是跟他的教育背景相關。

☐ 三分熟
☐ 五分熟
☐ 七分熟
☐ 全熟

re·li·ance

[rɪˋlaɪəns]

名 信賴、依賴

英英 to depend on or trust in someone or something

例 We placed complete **reliance** on our consultant.
我們完全信任我們的顧問。

☐ 三分熟
☐ 五分熟
☐ 七分熟
☐ 全熟

rel·ish [ˋrɛlɪʃ]

名 嗜好、美味、調味
動 愛好、品味

英英 to like or have great enjoyment

例 She shared some homemade sweet pickle **relish** with me.
她給我一些自製的甜味醃漬開胃菜。

☐ 三分熟
☐ 五分熟
☐ 七分熟
☐ 全熟

re·main·der

[rɪˋmendɚ]

名 剩餘
同 remain 殘留

英英 a leftover part, number, or quantity

例 The **remainder** steak can be made into delicious dishes.
剩餘的牛排可以做成美味的菜餚。

☐ 三分熟
☐ 五分熟
☐ 七分熟
☐ 全熟

re·mov·al [rɪˋmuvl̩]

名 移動、移除、清除

英英 the action of taking away or abolishing something unwanted; the transfer of furniture and other contents when moving house

例 The detergent is very effective in stain **removal**.
這種清潔劑對於移除髒污相當有效。

☐ 三分熟
☐ 五分熟
☐ 七分熟
☐ 全熟

re·nais·sance

[ˏrəˋnesn̩s]

名 再生、文藝復興

英英 the revival of art and literature under the influence of classical models in the 14th-16th centuries

例 The **Renaissance** in Europe happened between the 14th and 17th centuries.
歐洲的文藝復興發生在 14 世紀至 17 世紀之間。

☐ 三分熟
☐ 五分熟
☐ 七分熟
☐ 全熟

🎧 **Track 263**

ren·der [ˈrɛndɚ]

動 給予、讓與

英英 to cause someone or something to be in a certain state

例 The residents had to **render** part of their income to the landlord.
居民必須要將一部分的收入讓給地主。

☐ 三分熟
☐ 五分熟
☐ 七分熟
☐ 全熟

---

re·nowned

[rɪˈnaʊnd]

形 著名的
同 famous 著名的

英英 in the state of being famous

例 You will know more **renowned** pianists other than Beethoven and Mozart after taking the course.
上完這堂課之後，你就會認識貝多芬和莫札特以外其他的著名鋼琴家。

☐ 三分熟
☐ 五分熟
☐ 七分熟
☐ 全熟

---

rent·al [ˈrɛntl̩]

名 租用物、租金
形 租賃的、供出租的

英英 an amount of money paid or received as rent to occupy a place

例 We can negotiate about the month **rental** with the landlord.
我們可以和地主商量每月的租金。

☐ 三分熟
☐ 五分熟
☐ 七分熟
☐ 全熟

---

re·press [rɪˈprɛs]

動 抑制

英英 to subdue using force

例 She **repressed** her anger for she wouldn't embarrass other participants of the occasion.
她為了不要讓其他參加這個場合的人尷尬，壓抑著自己的怒氣。

☐ 三分熟
☐ 五分熟
☐ 七分熟
☐ 全熟

---

re·sem·blance

[rɪˈzɛmbləns]

名 類似
同 similarity 類似

英英 when two things or people are similar or look like each other

例 The **resemblance** between these two research articles aroused suspicion of plagiarism.
這兩篇研究文章之間相似之處引發瓢竊的嫌疑。

☐ 三分熟
☐ 五分熟
☐ 七分熟
☐ 全熟

---

res·er·voir

[ˈrɛzɚˌvɔr]

名 儲水池、倉庫
同 warehouse 倉庫

英英 a large natural or artificial lake used as a source to store water supply

例 They cleaned the **reservoir** every year.
他們每年清理這個儲水池。

☐ 三分熟
☐ 五分熟
☐ 七分熟
☐ 全熟

---

res·i·den·tial

[ˌrɛzəˈdɛnʃəl]

形 居住的

英英 designed for or relating to a place of living

例 Factories are not allowed in the **residential** area.
居住區是不可以蓋工廠的。

☐ 三分熟
☐ 五分熟
☐ 七分熟
☐ 全熟

R

re·si·stant
[rɪˈzɪstənt]

形 抵抗的、反抗的

英英 to fight against someone or something

例 Many people were **resistant** to the new law.
許多人反對這項新法律。

☐ 三分熟
☐ 五分熟
☐ 七分熟
☐ 全熟

res·o·lute
[ˈrɛzəˌlut]

形 堅決的

英英 determined in actions, ideas, or character; unwavering

例 He is **resolute** in opposing the construction of the incinerator.
他堅決反對建造這座焚化爐。

☐ 三分熟
☐ 五分熟
☐ 七分熟
☐ 全熟

re·spec·tive
[rɪˈspɛktɪv]

形 個別的
同 individual 個別的

英英 belonging or relating separately to each of two or more people or things

例 They have to report to their **respective** supervisors.
他們必須各自向主管戶匯報。

☐ 三分熟
☐ 五分熟
☐ 七分熟
☐ 全熟

res·to·ra·tion
[ˌrɛstəˈreʃən]

名 恢復、重建

英英 the action of returning something to its former condition, place, or owner

例 The **restoration** of the regime was objected by many citizens.
復辟政權受到許多公民反對。

☐ 三分熟
☐ 五分熟
☐ 七分熟
☐ 全熟

re·straint
[rɪˈstrent]

名 抑制

英英 something which limits the action or growth of someone or something

例 The government took necessary measures to **restrain** smuggling cigarettes.
政府採必要措施抑制菸品走私。

☐ 三分熟
☐ 五分熟
☐ 七分熟
☐ 全熟

re·tail [ˈritel]

名 零售
動 零售
形 零售的
副 零售地
反 wholesale 批發

英英 the sale of goods to the general public in small quantities selling goods to the general public in small quantities

例 The **retail** price is usually higher than the wholesale price.
零售價通常比批發價高。

☐ 三分熟
☐ 五分熟
☐ 七分熟
☐ 全熟

re·tal·i·ate
[rɪˈtælɪˌet]

動 報復

英英 to make an attack or assault in return for a similar attack previously committed

例 The gangsters **retaliated** by vandalizing the police station.
幫派份子破壞當地警察局作為報復。

☐ 三分熟
☐ 五分熟
☐ 七分熟
☐ 全熟

Track 265

---

re·trieve [rɪˈtriv]

動 取回、（獵犬）銜回

英英 to get or bring something back

例 The hound helped its owner **retrieve** a lost wallet.
獵犬幫主人銜回弄丟的錢包。

□ 三分熟
□ 五分熟
□ 七分熟
□ 全熟

---

rev·e·la·tion

[ˌrɛvəˈleʃən]

名 揭發
同 disclosure 揭發

英英 the revealing of new information previously unknown

例 The prime minister resigned after the **revelation** of the scandal.
醜聞被揭發後，首相便辭職。

□ 三分熟
□ 五分熟
□ 七分熟
□ 全熟

---

rev·e·nue

[ˈrɛvəˌnju]

名 收入

英英 the income received by an organization, company, or government on a regular basis

例 They develop a variety of products, hoping to increase the **revenue**.
他們發展各種產品，希望可以增加收入。

□ 三分熟
□ 五分熟
□ 七分熟
□ 全熟

---

re·viv·al [rɪˈvaɪvl̩]

名 復甦、恢復

英英 when something has improved condition, strength, or popularity of something

例 The medical staff were surprised by the patient's speedy **revival**.
醫療團隊對這個病人快速恢復感到驚訝。

□ 三分熟
□ 五分熟
□ 七分熟
□ 全熟

---

rhet·o·ric

[ˈrɛtərɪk]

名 修辭（學）、辯才、花言巧語

英英 the art of effective or persuasive speaking or writing

例 She would not be persuaded by your **rhetoric** language.
她不會被你的花言巧語給說服的。

□ 三分熟
□ 五分熟
□ 七分熟
□ 全熟

---

rhyth·mic

[ˈrɪðmɪk]

形 有節奏的

英英 having or relating to rhythm

例 They danced to the **rhythmic** music.
他們隨著有節奏的音樂起舞。

□ 三分熟
□ 五分熟
□ 七分熟
□ 全熟

---

rid·i·cule [ˈrɪdɪkjul]

名 嘲笑
動 嘲笑

英英 unkind words or actions of mockery or derision; to make fun of; mock

例 He was **ridiculed** because of his strong accent.
他因為口音很重而被嘲笑。

□ 三分熟
□ 五分熟
□ 七分熟
□ 全熟

---

rig·or·ous [ˈrɪgərəs]

形 嚴格的

英英 extremely strict, severe, thorough, or accurate

例 Few people survived the **rigorous** training for pilots.
很少人能撐過嚴格的飛行員訓練。

□ 三分熟
□ 五分熟
□ 七分熟
□ 全熟

---

ri·ot [ˈraɪət]

名 暴動
動 騷動、放縱

英英 a violent disturbance of the peace by a rowdy crowd; to make violent disturbance of the peace by a crowd

例 The prison **riot** in Brazil left dozens of inmates injured.
巴西的監獄暴動，造成數十名受刑人受傷。

☐ 三分熟
☐ 五分熟
☐ 七分熟
☐ 全熟

ri·te [raɪt]

名 儀式、典禮

英英 a religious or ceremonious act

例 The **rite** of marriage began with an opening prayer by the priest.
這場結婚典禮由牧師進行開場禱告。

☐ 三分熟
☐ 五分熟
☐ 七分熟
☐ 全熟

rit·u·al [ˈrɪtʃʊəl]

名 （宗教）儀式
形 儀式的
同 ceremony 儀式

英英 a religious or solemn ceremony involving a set series of actions performed; relating to a religious or solemn ceremony involving a set series of actions performed

例 The witch live streamed a special blessing **ritual** on the Internet.
女巫在網路上直播特殊的祈福儀式。

☐ 三分熟
☐ 五分熟
☐ 十分熟
☐ 全熟

ri·val·ry [ˈraɪvəlrɪ]

名 競爭

英英 a person, company, or thing competing with another for the same objective

例 There is fierce **rivalry** for the chance to join the delegation.
參加代表團的機會競爭激烈。

☐ 三分熟
☐ 五分熟
☐ 七分熟
☐ 全熟

ro·tate [roˈtet]

動 旋轉

英英 to move in a circle round a central axis

例 The Earth **rotates** around its own axis.
地球以地軸旋轉。

☐ 三分熟
☐ 五分熟
☐ 七分熟
☐ 全熟

ro·ta·tion [roˈteʃən]

名 旋轉、輪替

英英 when something revolves around a fixed point

例 The **rotation** of the Sun is not easily detected.
太陽的輪替不容易觀察。

☐ 三分熟
☐ 五分熟
☐ 七分熟
☐ 全熟

roy·al·ty [ˈrɔɪəltɪ]

名 貴族、王權、權利金、版稅
同 commission 職權

英英 people of royal blood or status

例 She claimed that she is related to **royalty**.
她宣稱和王室有關聯。

☐ 三分熟
☐ 五分熟
☐ 七分熟
☐ 全熟

279

🎧 Track 267

ru·by [ˋrubɪ]

名 紅寶石
形 紅寶石色的

英英 a precious stone in color varieties varying from deep crimson or purple to pale rose; of a color between crimson and pale red

例 She bought a **ruby** ring for herself.
她買了一個紅寶石戒指給自己。

☐ 三分熟
☐ 五分熟
☐ 七分熟
☐ 全熟

Ss

safe·guard

[ˋsef͵gɑrd]

名 保護者、警衛
動 保護

英英 a measure taken to protect; to make something safe, or prevent something; a guard who works to protect somebody or something safe

例 Several police officers **safeguarded** the minister's residence.
數名員警在部長的住宅外面守衛。

☐ 三分熟
☐ 五分熟
☐ 七分熟
☐ 全熟

sa·loon [səˋlun]

名 酒店、酒吧

英英 a place where alcoholic drinks are served over a counter

例 He hung out with his friends at the **saloon** overnight.
他徹夜和朋友待在酒吧。

☐ 三分熟
☐ 五分熟
☐ 七分熟
☐ 全熟

sal·va·tion

[sælˋveʃən]

名 救助、拯救

英英 being saved from sin and its consequences, believed by Christians to be brought about by faith in Christ

例 The infrastructure project was considered a **salvation** of the high unemployment rate.
建設工程被視為是高失業率的救星。

☐ 三分熟
☐ 五分熟
☐ 七分熟
☐ 全熟

sanc·tion

[ˋsæŋkʃən]

名 批准、認可
動 批准、認可
同 permit 准許

英英 a potential penalty for disobeying a law or rule

例 They did not apply for official **sanction** to this demonstration campaign.
他們並未申請這次示威活動的許可。

☐ 三分熟
☐ 五分熟
☐ 七分熟
☐ 全熟

sanc·tu·ar·y

[ˋsæŋktʃʊ͵ɛrɪ]

名 聖所、聖堂、庇護所
同 refuge 庇護所

英英 a place of refuge or safety; a nature reserve

例 We were asked to remain solemn in the **sanctuary**.
我們在聖殿裡被要求要維持莊嚴的態度。

☐ 三分熟
☐ 五分熟
☐ 七分熟
☐ 全熟

sane [sen]

形 神智穩健的

英英 of a healthy mind; not mentally ill; reasonable; sensible

例 She has a **sane** attitude toward investing in the stock market.
她對於投資股市有很神智穩健的態度。

☐ 三分熟
☐ 五分熟
☐ 七分熟
☐ 全熟

---

san·i·ta·tion [ˌsænəˈteʃən]

名 公共衛生

英英 the systems for taking away waste and sewage for the sanitary health of people

例 Good public **sanitation** system is fundamental for preventing epidemic diseases.
好的公共衛生系統對防治流行病來說是很重要的。

☐ 三分熟
☐ 五分熟
☐ 七分熟
☐ 全熟

---

sce·nic [ˈsinɪk]

形 無喜的、佈景的、風景的

英英 in relevance to impressive or beautiful natural scenery

例 Enoshima is a **scenic** spot in Tokyo.
江之島是東京的一處景點。

☐ 三分熟
☐ 五分熟
☐ 七分熟
☐ 全熟

---

scope [skop]

名 範圍、領域
同 range 範圍

英英 the extent of the area or subject matter that something deals with or to which it is relevant

例 This question is beyond his **scope** of expertise.
這個問題超出他的專業領域了。

☐ 三分熟
☐ 五分熟
☐ 七分熟
☐ 全熟

---

script [skrɪpt]

名 原稿、劇本
動 編寫

英英 the written text of a play, film, or television broadcast; to write a script

例 The actor took the role after he read the **script**.
演員讀過腳本後，決定接下這個角色。

☐ 三分熟
☐ 五分熟
☐ 七分熟
☐ 全熟

---

sec·tor [ˈsɛktɚ]

名 扇形、部門

英英 an area or portion that stands out from the other areas

例 The government offers emergency bailout package for private **sectors**.
政府提供緊急救助金給民營部門。

☐ 三分熟
☐ 五分熟
☐ 七分熟
☐ 全熟

---

se·duce [sɪˈdjus]

動 引誘、慫恿
同 tempt 引誘

英英 to persuade someone to do something inadvisable

例 They **seduced** me into making investment in the start-up company.
他們慫恿我投資那家新創公司。

☐ 三分熟
☐ 五分熟
☐ 七分熟
☐ 全熟

---

se·lec·tive [səˈlɛktɪv]

形 有選擇性的、對……很挑剔

英英 to choose something over others intentionally

例 He is **selective** about the people he associates with.
他對來往的對象很挑剔。

☐ 三分熟
☐ 五分熟
☐ 七分熟
☐ 全熟

🎧 **Track 269**

---

sem·i·nar

[ˈsɛmənɑr]

名 研討會、講習會

英英 a conference or other meeting for discussion or for training purposes

例 Professor Krashen will attend the **seminar** of second language acquisition.
卡森教授會出席有關第二語言習得的研討會。

☐ 三分熟
☐ 五分熟
☐ 七分熟
☐ 全熟

---

sen·a·tor [ˈsɛnətɚ]

名 參議員、上議員

英英 a member of a senate

例 The **senator** announced that he would run for the next presidential campaign.
這位參議員宣布他會參加下次總統競選。

☐ 三分熟
☐ 五分熟
☐ 七分熟
☐ 全熟

---

sen·ti·men·tal

[ˌsɛntəˈmɛntl̩]

形 受情緒影響的、多情的
同 emotional 情緒的

英英 deriving from or prone to sensitive feelings of tenderness, sadness, or nostalgia

例 She chose to start a business in her hometown for **sentimental** reasons.
她因為重感情的關係，選擇在家鄉創業。

☐ 三分熟
☐ 五分熟
☐ 七分熟
☐ 全熟

---

se·quence

[ˈsikwəns]

名 順序、連續
動 按順序排好
同 succession 連續

英英 a particular order in which related things follow each other in sequence; to arrange something in order

例 She put the files in alphabetical **sequence**.
她把這些檔案依照字母順序排列好。

☐ 三分熟
☐ 五分熟
☐ 七分熟
☐ 全熟

---

se·rene [səˈrin]

形 寧靜的、安祥的
反 furious 狂暴的

英英 calm, peaceful, and without worry

例 The **serene** atmosphere in the small town makes me feel calm.
小鎮的寧靜氣氛讓我覺得平靜。

☐ 三分熟
☐ 五分熟
☐ 七分熟
☐ 全熟

---

se·ren·i·ty

[səˈrɛnɪtɪ]

名 晴朗、和煦、平靜
同 peace 平靜

英英 peaceful and calm; worried by nothing

例 We admired the **serenity** of the sea.
我們欣賞海洋的靜謐氣氛。

☐ 三分熟
☐ 五分熟
☐ 七分熟
☐ 全熟

---

serv·ing [ˈsɝvɪŋ]

名 服務、服侍、侍候、一份（食物、飲料等）

英英 the amount of food suitable for or served to one person

例 Check the label on the package for the calories in a **serving**.
看一下包裝上面説每份含有的熱量是多少。

☐ 三分熟
☐ 五分熟
☐ 七分熟
☐ 全熟

---

ses·sion [ˈsɛʃən]

名 開庭、會議
同 conference 會議

英英 a period of time devoted to a certain activity
例 The afternoon **session** will begin at 2 P.M.
下午的會議在兩點開始。

☐ 三分熟
☐ 五分熟
☐ 七分熟
☐ 全熟

---

set·back

[ˈsɛtˌbæk]

名 逆流、逆轉、逆行、
挫折

英英 a reversal or delay in the progress of something
例 He didn't give up pursuing his career despite the **setbacks**.
儘管有挫折，他還是沒有放棄追求事業。

☐ 三分熟
☐ 五分熟
☐ 十分熟
☐ 全熟

---

sew·er [ˈsuə]

名 縫製者、裁縫師、下
水道

英英 a person who sews
例 The **sewer** of the gown will come to the wedding.
禮服的裁縫師會來參加婚禮。

☐ 三分熟
☐ 五分熟
☐ 七分熟
☐ 全熟

---

shed [ʃɛd]

動 流出、發射出

英英 to pour out, pour forth
例 She **shed** tears of happiness.
她喜極而泣。

☐ 三分熟
☐ 五分熟
☐ 七分熟
☐ 全熟

---

sheer [ʃɪr]

形 垂直的、絕對的、
純粹的
副 完全地
動 急轉彎

英英 used to emphasize how great, nothing but; to change course quickly
例 It was a **sheer** accident that he ran into his ex-girlfriend.
他遇見前女友純粹是巧合。

☐ 三分熟
☐ 五分熟
☐ 七分熟
☐ 全熟

---

shil·ling [ˈʃɪlɪŋ]

名 （英國幣名）先令

英英 a former British coin and monetary unit equal to one twentieth of a pound or twelve pence
例 He sold the bottle of wine for 40 **shillings**.
他用 40 先令的價格將這瓶酒賣出。

☐ 三分熟
☐ 五分熟
☐ 七分熟
☐ 全熟

---

shop·lift [ˈʃɑpˌlɪft]

動 逛商店時行竊
同 pirate 掠奪

英英 to steal goods from a shop by someone pretending to be a customer
例 He was arrested for **shoplifting**.
他因為在商店行竊而被逮捕。

☐ 三分熟
☐ 五分熟
☐ 七分熟
☐ 全熟

---

shrewd [ʃrud]

形 敏捷的、精明的

英英 having or showing sharp powers of good judgment of a situation
例 The **shrewd** businessman would never make a deal unfavorable to him.
精明的商人不會做出對自己不利的交易。

☐ 三分熟
☐ 五分熟
☐ 七分熟
☐ 全熟

S

shun [ʃʌn]

動 避開、躲避

英英 to persistently avoid, ignore, or reject

例 She **shunned** the question about the controversial issue.
她迴避了與爭議相關的問題。

☐ 三分熟
☐ 五分熟
☐ 七分熟
☐ 全熟

---

siege [sidʒ]

名 包圍、圍攻
同 surround 包圍

英英 a military operation in which enemy forces surround a town or building, by cutting off essential supplies, with the goal of forcing those inside to surrender

例 The city was under **siege** of the rebellion army.
這個城市遭到反叛軍包圍。

☐ 三分熟
☐ 五分熟
☐ 七分熟
☐ 全熟

---

sig·ni·fy [ˈsɪgnəˌfaɪ]

動 表示

英英 to be a symbol or indication of something

例 The commander **signified** the soldiers to retrieve.
指揮官示意士兵要撤退。

☐ 三分熟
☐ 五分熟
☐ 七分熟
☐ 全熟

---

sil·i·con [ˈsɪlɪkən]

名 矽

英英 a grey element with semiconducting properties, used in making electronic circuits

例 A special **silicon** material is used in the wafer.
這種晶片使用了一種特殊的矽膠材質。

☐ 三分熟
☐ 五分熟
☐ 七分熟
☐ 全熟

---

sim·plic·i·ty [sɪmˈplɪsətɪ]

名 簡單、單純

英英 the quality or condition of being simple

例 **Simplicity** in the design of the exterior is a feature of the mobile gadget.
外殼的簡約設計，是這種行動裝置的特色。

☐ 三分熟
☐ 五分熟
☐ 七分熟
☐ 全熟

---

sim·pli·fy [ˈsɪmpləˌfaɪ]

動 使……簡易、使……單純
反 complicate 使複雜

英英 to make something more simple

例 The children are reading a **simplified** version of Shakespeare scripts.
小朋友在讀簡化版的莎士比亞劇本。

☐ 三分熟
☐ 五分熟
☐ 七分熟
☐ 全熟

---

si·mul·ta·ne·ous [ˌsaɪmlˈtenɪəs]

形 同時發生的

英英 occurring, operating, or done at the same time

例 Special equipment is needed for the **simultaneous** interpretation.
同步口譯需要應用特殊的設備。

☐ 三分熟
☐ 五分熟
☐ 七分熟
☐ 全熟

---

skep·ti·cal [ˈskɛptɪkl̩]

形 懷疑的

英英 to doubt the truth about something

例 I was **skeptical** about his proposition.
我對他的主張存疑。

☐ 三分熟
☐ 五分熟
☐ 七分熟
☐ 全熟

S

skim [skɪm]

動 掠去、去除、略讀
名 脫脂乳品

英英 to remove a solid substance from the surface of a liquid; milk from which the cream has been removed

例 She **skimmed** through the applicants' resumes.
她快速略讀過求職者的履歷。

□ 三分熟
□ 五分熟
□ 七分熟
□ 全熟

---

slang [slæŋ]

名 俚語
動 謾罵、說俚語

英英 informal language that is more common in speaking rather than writing and is typically restricted to a particular context or within a group; to use a slang

例 The Urban Dictionary collects the meaning of colloquial **slang**.
都會字典收錄口語中俚語的意思。

□ 三分熟
□ 五分熟
□ 七分熟
□ 全熟

---

slash [slæʃ]

名 刀痕、裂縫
動 亂砍、鞭打
同 cut 砍

英英 a cut made with a wide stroke; to cut with a violent sweeping movement

例 The slave was **slashed** by the brutal master for no reason.
奴隸被無情的主人鞭打。

□ 三分熟
□ 五分熟
□ 七分熟
□ 全熟

---

slav·er·y [ˈslevərɪ]

名 奴隸制度
反 liberty 自由

英英 the state of being enslaved

例 The modern-day **slavery** is an issue that deserves more concern.
現代的奴隸制度是需要更多關注的議題。

□ 三分熟
□ 五分熟
□ 七分熟
□ 全熟

---

slot [slɑt]

名 狹槽、職位、電視或廣播的時段
動 在⋯⋯開一狹槽、把⋯⋯塞進

英英 a given place in an arrangement or scheme; to place into a slot

例 He inserted a coin into the **slot** of the vending machine.
他把硬幣投入販賣機的投幣孔中。

□ 二分熟
□ 五分熟
□ 七分熟
□ 全熟

---

slum [slʌm]

名 貧民區
動 進入貧民區

英英 a run down and overcrowded urban area inhabited by very poor people; to move in an area of a lower social level

例 Some children from the **slum** peddled their handcrafts to the tourists.
有些來自貧民區的孩童向觀光客兜售手工藝品。

□ 三分熟
□ 五分熟
□ 七分熟
□ 全熟

---

smack [smæk]

動 拍擊、甩打
同 slap 拍擊

英英 to blow with the palm of the hand

例 His supervisor **smacked** him on the shoulder.
主管拍打了他的肩膀一下。

□ 三分熟
□ 五分熟
□ 七分熟
□ 全熟

🎧 **Track 273**

small·pox

[ˋsmɔlˏpɑks]

名 天花

英英 an acute contagious disease spread by a virus, with fever and pustules usually leaving permanent scars

例 The child undertook the **smallpox** vaccine.
小孩接種天花疫苗。

□三分熟
□五分熟
□七分熟
□全熟

smoth·er [ˋsmʌðɚ]

動 使窒息、掩飾
名 使窒息之物

英英 to suffocate by covering the nose and mouth; extinguish a fire by covering it; a device which cause to suffocate

例 The city is **smothered** in smog.
城市被煙霧所籠罩。

□三分熟
□五分熟
□七分熟
□全熟

smug·gle [ˋsmʌgl̩]

動 走私

英英 to shift something illegally into or out of a country; convey secretly and illicitly

例 The man tried to **smuggle** a tiger cub to Mexico.
這名男子企圖走私幼虎到墨西哥。

□三分熟
□五分熟
□七分熟
□全熟

snare [snɛr]

名 陷阱、羅網
動 誘惑、捕捉

英英 a trap for catching small animals, consisting of a loop of wire or cord that pulls tightly around the prey; to catch with a snare

例 The hunter laid a **snare** for the boar.
獵人設下捕山豬的陷阱。

□三分熟
□五分熟
□七分熟
□全熟

sneak·y [ˋsnikɪ]

形 鬼鬼祟祟的

英英 secretive or sly

例 The **sneaky** shoplifter tried to steal some valuable items but got caught on the spot.
鬼鬼祟祟的小偷想要從店裡偷值錢的物品，但是被當場抓到了。

□三分熟
□五分熟
□七分熟
□全熟

sneer [snɪr]

名 冷笑
動 嘲笑地説
片 sneer at 嘲笑

英英 a contemptuous look or mocking smile, remark, or tone; to talk in a mocking way

例 Nobody **sneered** at him for his blunder.
沒有人嘲笑他的錯誤。

□三分熟
□五分熟
□七分熟
□全熟

soar [sor]

動 上升、往上飛、上漲

英英 to fly or rise high into the air; maintain height in the air by gliding

例 The price of houses continues to **soar**.
房價持續上漲。

□三分熟
□五分熟
□七分熟
□全熟

S

so·cia·ble
[`soʃəbl̩]

形 愛交際的、社交的

英英 having the ability to willingly talk and engage in activities with others

例 The director at the sector of public relation is a **sociable** person.
公關部門的主任是個善於社交的人。

☐ 三分熟
☐ 五分熟
☐ 七分熟
☐ 全熟

so·cial·ism
[`soʃəlɪzm̩]

名 社會主義

英英 a political and economic theory of social organization which advocates that the means of production, distribution, and exchange should be agreed or regulated by the community as a whole

例 The book is about the pros and cons of **socialism**.
這本書是關於社會主義的優、缺點。

☐ 三分熟
☐ 五分熟
☐ 七分熟
☐ 全熟

so·cial·ist
[`soʃəlɪst]

名 社會主義者

英英 a person who is an advocate of political and economic theory of social organization which advocates that the means of production, distribution, and exchange should be owned or regulated by the community as a whole

例 Lenin, the leader of the Soviet Union, is a **socialist**.
蘇聯的領導者列寧，是一位社會主義者。

☐ 三分熟
☐ 五分熟
☐ 七分熟
☐ 全熟

so·cial·ize
[`soʃəlɪaɪz]

動 使社會化、交際
同 civilize
使文明、使開化

英英 to socially mix with others; make someone behave in a way that is socially acceptable

例 Children learn to **socialize** with others when they go to the kindergarten.
小孩上幼稚園的時候學習和他人交際。

☐ 三分熟
☐ 五分熟
☐ 七分熟
☐ 全熟

so·ci·ol·o·gy
[ˌsoʃɪ`ɑlədʒɪ]

名 社會學

英英 the study of social development, structure, and functioning of human society

例 We watched a documentary on the **sociology** class.
我們在社會學課堂上看了一部紀錄片。

☐ 三分熟
☐ 五分熟
☐ 七分熟
☐ 全熟

so·di·um [`sodɪəm]

名 鈉

英英 a soft silver-white reactive metallic chemical element of which common salt and soda are compounds

例 Overconsumption of **sodium** may lead to high blood pressure.
過度攝取鈉可能導致高血壓。

☐ 三分熟
☐ 五分熟
☐ 七分熟
☐ 全熟

🎧 Track 275

---

sol·i·dar·i·ty

[ˌsɑləˋdærətɪ]

名 團結、休戚相關

英英 a group unifying as a result of common interests, feelings, or sympathies

例 She sought cross partisan **solidarity** to resolve the issue.
她尋求跨黨派的團結來解決這個問題。

☐ 三分熟
☐ 五分熟
☐ 七分熟
☐ 全熟

---

sol·i·tude

[ˋsɑləˌtjud]

名 獨處、獨居

英英 the state of being alone

例 The volunteer pays regular visit to the old lady who lives in **solitude**.
志工固定去拜訪獨居的老太太。

☐ 三分熟
☐ 五分熟
☐ 七分熟
☐ 全熟

---

soothe [suð]

動 安慰、撫慰

同 comfort 安慰

英英 to give moral strength to; cause to feel better

例 His words **soothed** those grieving the loss of a loved one.
他的話安慰了那些因失去摯愛而哀痛的人們。

☐ 三分熟
☐ 五分熟
☐ 七分熟
☐ 全熟

---

so·phis·ti·cat·ed

[səˋfɪstɪˌketɪd]

形 世故的

英英 highly developed and complex

例 The **sophisticated** woman would never fall victim to a scam.
世故的女子不會淪為詐騙的受害者。

☐ 三分熟
☐ 五分熟
☐ 七分熟
☐ 全熟

---

sov·er·eign·ty

[ˋsɑvrɪntɪ]

名 主權

英英 the power of a country to have supreme power or authority of its own government

例 The **sovereignty** of Senkaku Islands remains a controversial issue.
釣魚臺的主權仍是一項爭議。

☐ 三分熟
☐ 五分熟
☐ 七分熟
☐ 全熟

---

spa·cious

[ˋspeʃəs]

形 寬敞的、寬廣的

英英 having plenty of space

例 She wants to have a car with **spacious** trunk.
她想要有寬敞車廂的車子。

☐ 三分熟
☐ 五分熟
☐ 七分熟
☐ 全熟

---

span [spæn]

名 跨距

動 橫跨、展延

英英 the full extent of something from one end to the other; the amount of space covered; to extend across or over

例 She accumulated a fortune of three million dollars over a short **span** of two months.
她在短短兩個月內累積了三百萬財富。

☐ 三分熟
☐ 五分熟
☐ 七分熟
☐ 全熟

---

spe·cial·ize

[ˋspɛʃəlˌaɪz]

動 專長於

英英 to emphasize on and become expert in a particular skill or area

例 Mr. White **specializes** in marketing strategy.
懷特先生專攻行銷策略。

☐ 三分熟
☐ 五分熟
☐ 七分熟
☐ 全熟

S

spe·cial·ty

[ˈspɛʃəltɪ]

名 專門職業、本行

英英 a pursuit, area of study, or skill to which someone has devoted themselves to become an expert

例 She is advised to pursue a career according to her **specialty**.
她被建議要找本行的工作。

☐ 三分熟
☐ 五分熟
☐ 七分熟
☐ 全熟

---

spec·i·fy

[ˈspɛsəˌfaɪ]

動 詳述、詳載

英英 to make specific; state or identify clearly and definitely

例 The ingredients of the processed food are **specified** on the label of the package.
這種加工食品的成份詳細標註在包裝的標籤上。

☐ 三分熟
☐ 五分熟
☐ 七分熟
☐ 全熟

---

spec·tac·u·lar

[spɛkˈtækjələ]

名 大場面
形 可觀的，壯觀的
同 dramatic 引人注目的

英英 a performance or event produced on a large scale and with awesome effects; very large and impressive

例 The audience applauded for the **spectacular** performance.
觀眾為精彩的表演喝采。

☐ 三分熟
☐ 五分熟
☐ 七分熟
☐ 全熟

---

spec·trum

[ˈspɛktrəm]

名 光譜

英英 a band of colors produced by separation of the components of light by their different degrees of refraction, e.g. in a rainbow

例 They showed a color **spectrum** on the screen.
他們在螢幕上呈現出一個顏色的光譜。

☐ 三分熟
☐ 五分熟
☐ 七分熟
☐ 全熟

---

spec·u·late

[ˈspɛkjəˌlet]

動 沉思

英英 to form a theory or view without firm evidence

例 She **speculated** about the implications in his words.
她思考他話中的隱含意義。

☐ 三分熟
☐ 五分熟
☐ 七分熟
☐ 全熟

---

sphere [sfɪr]

名 球、天體、範圍、領域、圈子

英英 a round solid figure in which every point on the surface is equidistant from the centre

例 NASA found that sun is not a perfect **sphere**.
美國國家太空總署發現太陽不是完整的球體。

☐ 三分熟
☐ 五分熟
☐ 七分熟
☐ 全熟

---

spike [spaɪk]

名 長釘、釘尖
動 以尖釘刺、
把烈酒攙入……

英英 a thin, pointed piece of metal or wood; to impale with a spike

例 The runner wears **spike** shoes during the race.
跑者在賽跑期間穿著釘鞋。

☐ 三分熟
☐ 五分熟
☐ 七分熟
☐ 全熟

🎧 **Track 277**

---

spi·ral [ˋspaɪrəl]

名 螺旋
動 急遽上升
形 螺旋的
同 twist 旋轉

英英 a spiral curve, shape, or pattern; to show a dramatic increase

例 The man installed a **spiral** ladder in his house.
男子在自己家中裝設了螺旋梯。

☐ 三分熟
☐ 五分熟
☐ 七分熟
☐ 全熟

---

spire [spaɪr]

名 尖塔、尖頂
動 螺旋形上升、發芽

英英 a tall pointed or pyramidal structure on the top of a building, especially a church tower; to furnish with a spire

例 He had the photo of a church **spire** as his computer screensaver.
他電腦螢幕保護程式設定成一張教堂尖塔的照片。

☐ 三分熟
☐ 五分熟
☐ 七分熟
☐ 全熟

---

spokes·per·son/ spokes·man/ spokes·wom·an

[ˋspoks͵pɝsn̩]/[ˋspoksmən] /[͵ˋspoks͵wʊmən]

名 發言人

英英 a person who speaks on behalf of a group or an organization

例 The chief party **spokesperson** resigned after the scandal broke out.
政黨發言人在醜聞爆發後辭職。

☐ 三分熟
☐ 五分熟
☐ 七分熟
☐ 全熟

---

spon·sor [ˋspɑnsɚ]

名 贊助者
動 贊助、資助

英英 a person or organization that pays for or contributes to the costs of a sporting or artistic event or a radio or television program in exchange for advertising; to pay for or contributes to the costs of a sporting or artistic event or a radio or television program in exchange for advertising

例 The beer brewing company is a **sponsor** of the football game.
這家啤酒釀造公司是足球比賽的贊助商之一。

☐ 三分熟
☐ 五分熟
☐ 七分熟
☐ 全熟

---

spon·ta·ne·ous

[spɑnˋtenɪəs]

形 同時發生的、自發的、不由自主的

英英 an impulsive performance or occurrence without external stimulus

例 The **spontaneous** smile of the infant may indicate that she is drowsy.
寶寶自發的微笑可能代表她很睏。

☐ 三分熟
☐ 五分熟
☐ 七分熟
☐ 全熟

---

spouse [spaʊz]

名 配偶、夫妻
同 mate 配偶

英英 a husband or wife

例 Being married to a **spouse** with a different nationality may be very challenging.
和不同國籍的配偶結婚可是一件具有挑戰性的事。

☐ 三分熟
☐ 五分熟
☐ 七分熟
☐ 全熟

S

sprawl [sprɔl]

名／動 任意伸展

英英 to sit, lie, or fall with one's limbs spread out from the center of the body

例 Some sea lions **sprawled** on the beach.
有些海獅在海灘任意伸展。

□三分熟
□五分熟
□七分熟
□全熟

---

squad [skwɑd]

名 小隊、班

英英 a small number of soldiers assembled for drill or assigned to a certain task

例 A **squad** of soldiers was sent to rescue the hostages.
一小隊軍人被派去救援人質。

□三分熟
□五分熟
□七分熟
□全熟

---

squash [skwɑʃ]

名 壓擠
動 壓擠

英英 to crush or squeeze something so that it becomes flat, soft, or out of shape

例 The tomatoes on the ground were **squashed** by passing cars.
地上的番茄被來往的車輛壓爛了。

□三分熟
□五分熟
□七分熟
□全熟

---

sta·bil·i·ty

[stə`bɪlətɪ]

名 穩定、穩固

英英 the state of being stable

例 **Stability** in power supply is important for the manufacturing plant.
電力供應的穩定對於製造工廠來說很重要。

□三分熟
□五分熟
□七分熟
□全熟

---

sta·bi·lize

[`stebl͵aɪz]

動 保持安定、使穩定

英英 to make something or become stable

例 The managerial team took some measures to **stabilize** the finances of the company.
管理團隊採取了一些措施來穩定公司的財務狀況。

□三分熟
□五分熟
□七分熟
□全熟

---

stalk [stɔk]

名 軸、莖
動 蔓延、追蹤

英英 the main stem of a herbaceous plant; to illegally follow

例 She called for help when realizing that she was **stalked**.
她發現自己被跟蹤的時候，就開始呼救。

□三分熟
□五分熟
□七分熟
□全熟

---

stam·mer

[`stæmɚ]

名 口吃
動 結結巴巴地說

英英 a tendency to say something with unusual pauses and stops; to speak with sudden pauses

例 The presenter **stammered** for he was unfamiliar with the content.
講者因為對內容不熟悉而說話結巴。

□三分熟
□五分熟
□七分熟
□全熟

🎧 **Track 279**

---

sta·ple [ˋstepl̩]

名 釘書針、主要產物
動 用釘書針釘住、
　分類、選擇
同 attach 貼上

英英 a small flattened U-shaped piece of wire pushed through to fasten papers together; to fasten papers with a staple

例 An announcement of office renovation was **stapled** on the bulletin board.
辦公室整修的公告被釘在公告欄上。

☐ 三分熟
☐ 五分熟
☐ 七分熟
☐ 全熟

---

sta·pler [ˋsteplɚ]

名 釘書機

英英 an equipment used for fastening papers together with staples

例 I purchased some office supplies like copy paper and **staplers**.
我買了一些影印紙和釘書機之類的辦公室用品。

☐ 三分熟
☐ 五分熟
☐ 七分熟
☐ 全熟

---

starch [stɑrtʃ]

名 澱粉
動 上漿

英英 an odorless, tasteless carbohydrate which is obtained chiefly from cereals and potatoes and is an important part of the human diet; to stiffen with starch

例 Foods that are rich in refined **starches** may cause obesity.
富含精緻澱粉的食品可能會導致肥胖。

☐ 三分熟
☐ 五分熟
☐ 七分熟
☐ 全熟

---

star·va·tion

[stɑrˋveʃən]

名 饑餓、餓死
同 famine 饑餓

英英 the state of not having food for a long period, often causing death

例 Some children died of **starvation** in the drought-stricken area.
乾旱地區有些小孩死於饑餓。

☐ 三分熟
☐ 五分熟
☐ 七分熟
☐ 全熟

---

sta·tion·ar·y

[ˋsteʃənˌɛrɪ]

形 不動的

英英 not moving, or not changing

例 The captivated soldiers were asked to remain **stationary**.
遭俘虜的軍人被要求保持不動。

☐ 三分熟
☐ 五分熟
☐ 七分熟
☐ 全熟

---

sta·tion·er·y

[ˋsteʃənˌɛrɪ]

名 文具

英英 paper and other materials intended for writing purposes

例 What is your monthly expense on **stationery**?
你每個月花多少錢買文具呢？

☐ 三分熟
☐ 五分熟
☐ 七分熟
☐ 全熟

---

stat·ure [ˋstætʃɚ]

名 身高、身長

英英 a person's natural height when standing

例 The basketball player is a man of large **stature**.
這名籃球選手的身材高大。

☐ 三分熟
☐ 五分熟
☐ 七分熟
☐ 全熟

---

steam·er [ˈstimɚ]

名 汽船、輪船

英英 a ship or boat powered by steam

例 They boarded a **steamer** bound for Kyushu, Japan.
他們搭上一艘前往日本九州的汽船。

□ 三分熟
□ 五分熟
□ 七分熟
□ 全熟

stim·u·late [ˈstɪmjəˌlet]

動 刺激、激勵
同 motivate 刺激

英英 to encourage something to act, become active, or grow

例 The government issues consumer voucher to **stimulate** economy.
政府發行消費券來刺激經濟。

□ 三分熟
□ 五分熟
□ 七分熟
□ 全熟

stim·u·la·tion [ˌstɪmjəˈleʃən]

名 刺激、興奮

英英 when something causes someone or something to become more active or enthusiastic, or to grow or operate

例 Extroverts tend to pursue **stimulations**.
外向者喜歡追求刺激。

□ 三分熟
□ 五分熟
□ 七分熟
□ 全熟

stim·u·lus [ˈstɪmjələs]

名 刺激、激勵

英英 something that evokes a specific reaction in an organ or tissue

例 The insect reacts to **stimulus** of light.
昆蟲對光刺激有反應。

□ 三分熟
□ 五分熟
□ 七分熟
□ 全熟

stock [stɑk]

名 庫存
動 庫存、進貨

英英 a supply of products or materials available for sale or use; to keep a supply of products or materials available for sale or use

例 Do we have enough packaged food in **stock**?
我們有足夠庫存的包裝食品嗎？

□ 三分熟
□ 五分熟
□ 七分熟
□ 全熟

stran·gle [ˈstræŋgl̩]

動 勒死、絞死

英英 to squeeze or constrict the neck causing inability to breathe, especially so as to cause death

例 A white dolphin was **strangled** to death by fishnet.
一隻白海豚被漁網勒斃。

□ 三分熟
□ 五分熟
□ 七分熟
□ 全熟

stra·te·gic [strəˈtidʒɪk]

形 戰略的

英英 forming part of a long-term plan or aim to achieve a specific goal or purpose

例 The country has the **strategic** superiority for its special landscape.
該國因為地形的關係而擁有戰略優勢。

□ 三分熟
□ 五分熟
□ 七分熟
□ 全熟

S

🎧 Track 281

stunt [stʌnt]

名 特技、表演
動 阻礙
同 performance 表演

英英 an exciting action, usually in a film, that is dangerous or appears dangerous and usually needs to be done by someone skilled; to regard the growth or movement

例 Circus performers often do risky **stunts**.
馬戲團表演者常表演危險特技。

☐ 三分熟
☐ 五分熟
☐ 七分熟
☐ 全熟

---

sub·jec·tive
[səbˋdʒɛktɪv]

形 主觀的
同 internal
　　內心的、固有的

英英 a decision that is influenced by personal feelings, tastes, or opinions

例 Give objective reasoning instead of **subjective** opinions in your essay.
在你的文章裡要寫客觀的推論而不是主觀意見。

☐ 三分熟
☐ 五分熟
☐ 七分熟
☐ 全熟

---

sub·or·di·nate
[səˋbɔrdṇɪt]

名 附屬物
形 從屬的、下級的
同 secondary 從屬的

英英 a person working under the authority or control of another; lower in rank

例 Our company offers bailout for our **subordinates**.
我們公司提供援助給子公司。

☐ 三分熟
☐ 五分熟
☐ 七分熟
☐ 全熟

---

sub·scribe
[səbˋskraɪb]

動 捐助、訂閱、簽署
同 contribute 捐助

英英 to arrange to receive something, especially a periodical regularly by advanced payment

例 She **subscribed** the newsletter of her favorite brand company.
她訂閱喜愛品牌公司的通訊刊物。

☐ 三分熟
☐ 五分熟
☐ 七分熟
☐ 全熟

---

sub·scrip·tion
[səbˋskrɪpʃən]

名 訂閱、簽署、捐款

英英 the action or fact of subscribing

例 Our **subscription** to the magazine expires this December.
我們訂閱這個雜誌到今年十二月為止。

☐ 三分熟
☐ 五分熟
☐ 七分熟
☐ 全熟

---

sub·se·quent
[ˋsʌbsɪ.kwɛnt]

形 伴隨發生的、隨後的

英英 happening after something in time

例 The **subsequent** episode surprised all of the audience.
接下來的那一集令所有觀眾驚訝。

☐ 三分熟
☐ 五分熟
☐ 七分熟
☐ 全熟

---

sub·sti·tu·tion
[.sʌbstəˋtjuʃən]

名 代理、代替
同 relief 接替

英英 a person or thing acting or serving as deputy, or in place of another

例 She used tofu in **substitution** of rice in the Oyakodon.
她用豆腐取代親子丼的飯。

☐ 三分熟
☐ 五分熟
☐ 七分熟
☐ 全熟

S

sub·tle [ˈsʌtl̩]

形 微妙的
同 delicate 微妙的

英英 small yet important

例 The psychiatrist detected the **subtle** change in his client's emotions.
精神科醫師察覺到病人情緒的微小變化。

☐ 三分熟
☐ 五分熟
☐ 七分熟
☐ 全熟

---

sub·ur·ban

[səˈbɝbən]

形 郊外的、市郊的

英英 an outlying residential area of a city

例 He lives in a mansion in the **suburban** area.
他住在郊區的豪宅。

☐ 三分熟
☐ 五分熟
☐ 七分熟
☐ 全熟

---

suc·ces·sion

[səkˈsɛʃən]

名 連續

英英 a number of people or things following one after the other

例 The economy has been growing four quarters in **succession**.
經濟連續四季成長。

☐ 三分熟
☐ 五分熟
☐ 七分熟
☐ 全熟

---

suc·ces·sive

[səkˈsɛsɪv]

形 連續的、繼續的
同 continuous 繼續的

英英 following one another or following others

例 The company has increased its investment in South East Asian countries for three **successive** years.
這間公司連續三年增加對東南亞國家的投資。

☐ 三分熟
☐ 五分熟
☐ 七分熟
☐ 全熟

---

suc·ces·sor

[səkˈsɛsɚ]

名 後繼者、繼承人
同 substitute 代替者

英英 a person or thing that succeeds another

例 The **successor** of the Theresa May as the Prime Minister of U.K. is Boris Johnson.
鮑里斯・強森繼任德雷莎・梅伊成為英國總理。

☐ 三分熟
☐ 五分熟
☐ 七分熟
☐ 全熟

---

suf·fo·cate

[ˈsʌfəˌket]

動 使窒息
同 choke 使窒息

英英 to die or cause to die due to lack of air or inability to breathe

例 Several victims **suffocated** in the fumes during the big fire.
大火中有數名罹難者是被煙嗆窒息的。

☐ 三分熟
☐ 五分熟
☐ 七分熟
☐ 全熟

---

suite [swit]

名 隨員、套房

英英 a set of connected rooms for one person's or family's use or for a particular purpose

例 The singer stayed in the penthouse **suite** of the luxurious hotel.
歌手住在這間飯店的頂樓套房。

☐ 三分熟
☐ 五分熟
☐ 七分熟
☐ 全熟

su·perb [suˋpɝb]

形 極好的、超群的
同 excellent 出色的

英英 excellent, magnificent or splendid

例 The child has a **superb** talent in singing.
這個小孩有超群的歌唱才華。

☐ 三分熟
☐ 五分熟
☐ 七分熟
☐ 全熟

---

su·pe·ri·or·i·ty

[səˌpɪrɪˋɔrətɪ]

名 優越、卓越

英英 the state of being superior

例 We all agree to the **superiority** of the new project over the old one.
我們都同意新的計劃比舊的計劃好。

☐ 三分熟
☐ 五分熟
☐ 七分熟
☐ 全熟

---

su·per·son·ic

[ˌsupɚˋsɑnɪk]

形 超音波的、超音速的

英英 involving or referring to a speed traveling faster than that of sound

例 What does it feel like to fly at **supersonic** speed?
以超音速飛行是什麼感覺？

☐ 三分熟
☐ 五分熟
☐ 七分熟
☐ 全熟

---

su·per·sti·tious

[ˌsupɚˋstɪʃəs]

形 迷信的

英英 characterized or influenced by certain cultural beliefs

例 The **superstitious** woman hung a Taoist charm at her door.
這名迷信的婦女在門上貼了一張符咒。

☐ 三分熟
☐ 五分熟
☐ 七分熟
☐ 全熟

---

su·per·vi·sion

[ˌsupɚˋvɪʒən]

名 監督、管理
同 leadership 領導

英英 when someone watches a person or activity and to be certain that everything is done correctly, safely, etc.

例 She finished the thesis under the **supervision** of the Professor.
她在教授監督下完成這篇論文。

☐ 三分熟
☐ 五分熟
☐ 七分熟
☐ 全熟

---

sup·ple·ment

[ˋsʌpləmənt]/[ˋsʌpləˌmɛnt]

名 副刊、補充
動 補充、增加

英英 something added to something else to enhance or complete it; to add something to something else

例 She offered some **supplement** materials for students.
她提供一些補充教材給學生。

☐ 三分熟
☐ 五分熟
☐ 七分熟
☐ 全熟

---

sur·pass [sɚˋpæs]

動 超過、超越
同 exceed 超過

英英 to be greater or better than

例 Don't work hard to please others; do it to **surpass** yourself.
不要為了討好別人而努力；要為了超越自己而奮鬥。

☐ 三分熟
☐ 五分熟
☐ 七分熟
☐ 全熟

S

sur·plus [ˈsɝˈplʌs]

名 過剩、盈餘
形 過剩的、過多的
同 extra 額外的

英英 an amount left over, or that is more than needed when requirements have been met; more than what is needed

例 How will they deal with the **surplus** inventory?
他們要如何處埋剩餘的庫存呢？

☐三分熟
☐五分熟
☐七分熟
☐全熟

sus·pense

[səˈspɛns]

名 懸而未決、擔心
同 concern 擔心、掛念

英英 a state or feeling of excited or anxious uncertainty about what may happen

例 The viewers were left in **suspense** when they finished the episode.
觀眾看完這一集之後留下懸念。

☐三分熟
☐五分熟
☐七分熟
☐全熟

sus·pen·sion

[səˈspɛnʃən]

名 暫停、懸掛

英英 the action of hanging in midair or the condition of being suspended

例 His was kept in **suspension** from the school team because of his misbehavior.
他因為不當行為而被暫停參加校隊活動。

☐三分熟
☐五分熟
☐七分熟
☐全熟

swap [swɑp]

名 交換
動 交換
同 exchange 交換

英英 an act of exchanging one thing for another

例 The twin sisters played a prank on their parents by **swapping** their identities.
這對雙胞胎姊妹交換身份，對他們的父母惡作劇。

☐三分熟
☐五分熟
☐七分熟
☐全熟

sym·bol·ic

[sɪmˈbɑlɪk]

形 象徵的

英英 acting as a symbol

例 These **symbolic** icons can be understood by most people regardless of their cultural backgrounds.
這些象徵符號可以跨越文化背景，被大多數的人理解。

☐三分熟
☐五分熟
☐七分熟
☐全熟

sym·bol·ize

[ˈsɪmbəˌlaɪz]

動 作為……象徵

英英 to be a symbol of

例 A yellow rose **symbolizes** friendship, joy, and caring.
黃玫瑰代表友情、歡樂、和關懷。

☐三分熟
☐五分熟
☐七分熟
☐全熟

sym·me·try

[ˈsɪmɪtrɪ]

名 對稱、相稱
同 harmony 和諧

英英 the quality of being made up of exactly similar parts facing each other or around a fixed point

例 The **symmetry** in the arrangement of the painting is pleasing.
這幅畫中對稱的安排令人感到愉悅。

☐三分熟
☐五分熟
☐七分熟
☐全熟

🎧 Track 285

symp·tom

[ˋsɪmptəm]

名 症狀、徵兆

英英 a feature which indicates a condition of illness, in particular one apparent to the patient

例 The medicine could only alleviate the **symptoms**.
這種藥只能夠緩解症狀。

☐ 三分熟
☐ 五分熟
☐ 七分熟
☐ 全熟

syn·o·nym

[ˋsɪnəˏnɪm]

名 同義字
反 antonym 反義字

英英 a word or phrase that means the same as another word or phrase in the same language

例 Can you think of a **synonym** of "honesty"?
你可以想到「誠實」這個字的同義詞嗎？

☐ 三分熟
☐ 五分熟
☐ 七分熟
☐ 全熟

syn·thet·ic

[sɪnˋθɛtɪk]

名 合成物
形 綜合性的、人造的
同 artificial 人造的

英英 a material made of artificial substances, especially a textile fiber; not nature, made of artificial substances

例 The **synthetic** fabric is effective in heat dissipation.
這個合成織品有好的散熱效果。

☐ 三分熟
☐ 五分熟
☐ 七分熟
☐ 全熟

Tt

tact [tækt]

名 圓滑
同 diplomacy 圓滑

英英 skill at not offending people or at at gaining good will by saying or doing the right thing

例 The veteran manager has diplomacy and **tact**.
資深經理有外交手腕又有圓滑的處事方式。

☐ 三分熟
☐ 五分熟
☐ 七分熟
☐ 全熟

tac·tic(s)

[ˋtæktɪk(s)]

名 戰術、策略

英英 an action or strategy planned to achieve a specific goal

例 They adopted the shock **tactic** on the battle.
他們在戰場上採用突襲戰術。

☐ 三分熟
☐ 五分熟
☐ 七分熟
☐ 全熟

tar·iff [ˋtærɪf]

名 關稅、關稅率
同 duty 稅

英英 a tax or duty to be paid on a particular section of imports or exports

例 The U.S. president announced to impose 25% **tariff** on goods imported from China.
美國總統宣布將對中國進口商品課徵百分之二十五的關稅。

☐ 三分熟
☐ 五分熟
☐ 七分熟
☐ 全熟

te·di·ous [ˈtidɪəs]

形 沉悶的

英英 too long, slow, or boring

例 He thought life of an accountant would be **tedious**.
他認為會計的生活會十分沉悶。

☐ 三分熟
☐ 五分熟
☐ 七分熟
☐ 全熟

---

tem·per·a·ment

[ˈtɛmprəmənt]

名 氣質、性情
同 character 性格

英英 a person's nature with regard to the effect it has on their behavior

例 The pianist has a romantic **temperament**.
鋼琴家有浪漫的氣質。

☐ 三分熟
☐ 五分熟
☐ 七分熟
☐ 全熟

---

tem·pest

[ˈtɛmpɪst]

名 大風暴、暴風雨
同 storm 暴風雨

英英 a violent windy storm

例 The vessel sailed in **tempest**.
船隻在暴風雨中航行。

☐ 三分熟
☐ 五分熟
☐ 七分熟
☐ 全熟

---

ter·mi·nate

[ˈtɝməˌnet]

動 終止、中斷
同 conclude 結束

英英 to bring something to an end

例 They should inform the other party if they intend to **terminate** the contract.
他們如果要終止合約，要先通知另一方。

☐ 三分熟
☐ 五分熟
☐ 七分熟
☐ 全熟

---

tex·tile [ˈtɛkstaɪl]

名 織布
形 紡織成的
同 material 織物

英英 a type of cloth or woven fabric with or without design; relating to fabric or weaving

例 It is a leading company of the **textile** industry.
它是紡織產業的龍頭。

☐ 三分熟
☐ 五分熟
☐ 七分熟
☐ 全熟

---

tex·ture [ˈtɛkstʃɚ]

名 質地、結構
動 使具有某種結構、特徵
同 structure 結構

英英 the feel, appearance, or consistency of a surface, substance, or fabric decided by touch; to give a rough texture

例 I was amazed by the melt-in-the-mouth **texture** of the cake.
這個蛋糕入口即化的質地令我驚訝。

☐ 三分熟
☐ 五分熟
☐ 七分熟
☐ 全熟

---

the·at·ri·cal

[θɪˈætrɪkl̩]

形 戲劇的

英英 of, for, or relating to acting, actors, or the theater

例 The **theatrical** props were all designed by the performers.
劇場的道具都是表演者自己設計的。

☐ 三分熟
☐ 五分熟
☐ 七分熟
☐ 全熟

Track 287

theft [θɛft]

名 竊盜
同 steal 偷竊
片 identity theft 身份盜用

英英 the action or crime of stealing from a place or person

例 A potential consequence of trusting a phishing email is identity **theft**.
信任釣魚信件內容的可能結果就是身份遭到盜用。

□三分熟
□五分熟
□七分熟
□全熟

the·o·ret·i·cal

[ˌθiəˈrɛtɪkl]

形 理論上的

英英 concerned with or involving theory over its practical application

例 The scholar proposed a **theoretical** framework in his thesis.
學者在論文中提出一個理論架構。

□三分熟
□五分熟
□七分熟
□全熟

ther·a·pist

[ˈθɛrəpɪst]

名 治療學家、物理治療師

英英 someone whose job is to treat a particular type of mental or physical illness or disability, usually with a specific type of therapy

例 She arranged an appointment to her son to meet with the language **therapist**.
她替兒子安排了一次和語言治療師的會面。

□三分熟
□五分熟
□七分熟
□全熟

ther·a·py [ˈθɛrəpɪ]

名 療法、治療
同 treatment 治療

英英 treatment intended to relieve or overcome a disorder

例 Taking Chinese herbs is a traditional **therapy**.
吃中藥是一種傳統的治療方法。

□三分熟
□五分熟
□七分熟
□全熟

there·af·ter

[ðɛrˈæftɚ]

副 此後、以後
同 afterward 以後

英英 after that time

例 The couple lived happily **thereafter**.
這對夫妻從此過著幸福快樂的日子。

□三分熟
□五分熟
□七分熟
□全熟

there·by [ðɛrˈbaɪ]

副 藉以、因此

英英 by that means; as a result of that

例 He plans to interview some villagers and **thereby** understand the local culture.
他計畫要訪問村民來了解本地文化。

□三分熟
□五分熟
□七分熟
□全熟

ther·mom·e·ter

[θəˈmɑmətɚ]

名 溫度計

英英 an instrument used for measuring and indicating temperature, typically consisting of a graduated glass tube containing mercury or alcohol which expands when heated

例 The automatic digital **thermometer** can be used to measure baby temperature.
自動數位溫度計可以用來測量寶寶的體溫。

□三分熟
□五分熟
□七分熟
□全熟

thresh·old
[ˈθrɛʃold]
名 門口、入口、門檻

英英 a strip of wood or stone forming the bottom of a doorway and crossed on entering a house or room

例 His test scores are below the **threshold** of admission to the prestigious high school.
他的考試成績未達明星高中的入學門檻。

☐ 三分熟
☐ 五分熟
☐ 七分熟
☐ 全熟

thrift [θrɪft]
名 節約、節儉
同 economy 節約

英英 carefulness and frugality in the use of money and other resources

例 **Thrift** was considered as a virtue in Chinese society.
節約在中國社會中被當成是一種美德。

☐ 三分熟
☐ 五分熟
☐ 七分熟
☐ 全熟

thrift·y [ˈθrɪftɪ]
形 節儉的
同 economical 節約的

英英 careful and frugal with money

例 She is **thrifty** in her daily expenses.
她對於日常花費很節約。

☐ 三分熟
☐ 五分熟
☐ 七分熟
☐ 全熟

thrive [θraɪv]
動 繁茂

英英 to grow or develop well or vigorously

例 The pop music industry continues to **thrive**.
流行音樂產業持續繁榮。

☐ 三分熟
☐ 五分熟
☐ 七分熟
☐ 全熟

throb [θrɑb]
名 脈搏、抽痛
動 悸動、跳動
同 beat 跳動

英英 a strong regular beat or sound; to beat with a regular rhythm

例 His heart **throbbed** when the plane flew through an air turbulence.
飛機經過空中亂流的時候，他的心跳加速。

☐ 三分熟
☐ 五分熟
☐ 七分熟
☐ 全熟

toll [tol]
名 裝貨、費用、通行稅
動 徵收、繳費
同 fare 車費

英英 a charge to use a bridge or road or for a long-distance telephone call; to charge the fee

例 The electronic system has been installed to collect the highway **toll**.
已經裝設電子系統來收取高速公路過路費。

☐ 三分熟
☐ 五分熟
☐ 七分熟
☐ 全熟

top·ple [ˈtɑpl̩]
動 推倒、推翻
同 tumble 顛覆

英英 unbalanced causing something to fall or push over

例 The truck **toppled** over for the driver was speeding.
卡車因為司機超速而翻覆。

☐ 三分熟
☐ 五分熟
☐ 七分熟
☐ 全熟

tor·na·do
[tɔrˈnedo]
名 龍捲風

英英 violently rotating wind storm having the appearance of a funnel-shaped cloud

例 A damaging **tornado** hit Luxembourg last month.
破壞力強的龍捲風上個月侵襲盧森堡。

☐ 三分熟
☐ 五分熟
☐ 七分熟
☐ 全熟

T

🎧 Track 289

trait [tret]

名 特色、特性
同 characteristic 特性

英英 a distinguishable quality or characteristic

例 Generosity is a popular personality **trait**.
慷慨是一個受歡迎的人格特質。

☐ 三分熟
☐ 五分熟
☐ 七分熟
☐ 全熟

---

tran·quil

[ˋtræŋkwɪl]

形 安靜的、寧靜的
同 peaceful 寧靜的

英英 peaceful, undisturbed; calm

例 We felt rather relaxed because of the **tranquil** atmosphere of the camp site.
我們因為營區的寧靜氣氛過到很放鬆。

☐ 三分熟
☐ 五分熟
☐ 七分熟
☐ 全熟

---

tran·quil·iz·er

[ˋtræŋkwɪˏlaɪzɚ]

名 鎮靜劑

英英 a medicinal drug taken to reduce tension or anxiety

例 The zookeepers injected tranquilizer on the escaped chimpanzee.
動物園管理員對逃脱的黑猩猩注射鎮定劑。

☐ 三分熟
☐ 五分熟
☐ 七分熟
☐ 全熟

---

trans·ac·tion

[trænˋsækʃən]

名 處理、辦理、交易
同 deal 交易

英英 the act of buying or selling; the action of conducting business

例 The electronic **transaction** was not completed yet.
電子交易還未完成。

☐ 三分熟
☐ 五分熟
☐ 七分熟
☐ 全熟

---

tran·script

[ˋtrænˏskrɪpt]

名 抄本、副本
片 academic transcript 成績單

英英 a written or printed version of material originally presented in another situation

例 He printed a copy of academic **transcript** for the last semester.
他印了上學期的成績單。

☐ 三分熟
☐ 五分熟
☐ 七分熟
☐ 全熟

---

trans·for·ma·tion

[ˏtrænsfɚˋmeʃən]

名 變形、轉變

英英 an obvious change in nature, form, or appearance

例 She went through a spiritual **transformation** because of the major changes in her life.
她因為生活的改變而經歷了心靈的改變。

☐ 三分熟
☐ 五分熟
☐ 七分熟
☐ 全熟

---

tran·sis·tor

[trænˋzɪstɚ]

名 電晶體

英英 a semiconductor device with three connections, capable of amplification and rectification

例 The manufacturer of **transistor** plays an important role in the semiconductor industry.
電晶體製造商在半導體產業中扮演重要的角色。

☐ 三分熟
☐ 五分熟
☐ 七分熟
☐ 全熟

tran·sit [ˈtrænsɪt]

名 通過、過境
動 通過

英英 something that carries of people or things from one place to another; to pass through

例 The **transit** passengers had to go through the security check.
過境的旅客也需要經過安檢。

☐三分熟
☐五分熟
☐七分熟
☐全熟

T

tran·si·tion

[trænˈzɪʃən]

名 轉移、變遷

英英 a change from one form or type to another, or the process by which this happens

例 The **transition** words play an important role in the coherence of a composition.
轉承詞在作文的連貫性當中扮演重要角色。

☐三分熟
☐五分熟
☐七分熟
☐全熟

trans·mis·sion

[trænsˈmɪʃən]

名 傳達

英英 the action or process of being moved

例 Electronic **transmission** of information has made cross-region communication much easier.
電子傳輸資訊使跨域的溝通更容易。

☐三分熟
☐五分熟
☐七分熟
☐全熟

trans·mit

[trænsˈmɪt]

動 寄送、傳播
同 forward 發送

英英 cause to pass on from one place or person to another

例 The broadcast satellite could **transmit** the signals from the TV station to the TV viewers.
廣播衛星可以將電視臺的信號傳送給觀眾。

☐三分熟
☐五分熟
☐七分熟
☐全熟

trans·plant

[ˈtrænsplænt]/[trænsˈplænt]

名 移植手術
動 移植

英英 act of transplanting; to transfer from one place in the body to another or from one body to another

例 The kidney **transplant** surgery may last for three hours.
腎臟移植手術大約需要三小時。

☐三分熟
☐五分熟
☐七分熟
☐全熟

trau·ma [ˈtrɔmə]

名 外傷、損傷、
心理創傷

英英 a severe emotional shock or strain caused by a deeply distressing experience

例 The childhood emotional **trauma** may impact a person even until the adulthood.
兒童時期的創傷會影響一個人直到成年。

☐三分熟
☐五分熟
☐七分熟
☐全熟

tread [trɛd]

名 腳步
動 踩、踏、走
同 walk 走

英英 a walking step; to walk in a specified way

例 Don't **tread** on the grass.
不要踩草皮。

☐三分熟
☐五分熟
☐七分熟
☐全熟

🎧 Track 291

trea·son [ˋtrizn̩]

名 叛逆、謀反
同 betray 背叛

英英 the crime of betraying one's country, especially by attempting to kill or overthrow the sovereign or government

例 The soldier was convicted **treason** for revealing confidential information to the enemy.
軍人因為洩漏機密資訊給敵國而被判定為叛國罪。

☐ 三分熟
☐ 五分熟
☐ 七分熟
☐ 全熟

---

trek [trɛk]

名 移居
動 長途跋涉

英英 a long and difficult journey, especially one made on foot; to move to another place

例 The hikers **trekked** for 8 consecutive hours yesterday.
登山者昨天連續跋涉八個小時。

☐ 三分熟
☐ 五分熟
☐ 七分熟
☐ 全熟

---

trem·or [ˋtrɛmɚ]

名 震動
同 shake 震動

英英 an involuntary shaking movement

例 The **tremor** of the building astonished all the hotel guests.
大樓震動嚇到旅館住客。

☐ 三分熟
☐ 五分熟
☐ 七分熟
☐ 全熟

---

tres·pass [ˋtrɛspəs]

名 犯罪、非法侵入
動 踰越、侵害

英英 a person who enter the land or property of someone without their permission; to enter the land or property of someone without their permission

例 The man who **trespassed** the office of Ministry of Foreign Affairs was arrested.
非法侵入外交部辦公室的男子被逮捕。

☐ 三分熟
☐ 五分熟
☐ 七分熟
☐ 全熟

---

trig·ger [ˋtrɪgɚ]

名 扳機
動 觸發

英英 a device that releases a spring or catch and so sets off a mechanism, especially in order to fire a gun; to cause to function

例 The leader's provocative remarks **triggered** conflicts between the country and its neighboring nations.
領導者煽動的言論引發該國於鄰國之間的衝突。

☐ 三分熟
☐ 五分熟
☐ 七分熟
☐ 全熟

---

tri·um·phant [traɪˋʌmfənt]

形 勝利的、成功的
同 successful 成功的

英英 having won a battle or contest; victorious

例 The winner of the game wore a **triumphant** smile on his face.
比賽優勝者臉上帶著勝利的微笑。

☐ 三分熟
☐ 五分熟
☐ 七分熟
☐ 全熟

triv·i·al [ˈtrɪvɪəl]

形 平凡的、淺薄的、不重要的
同 superficial 淺薄的

英英 small, mundane, unimportant details or pieces of information
例 He likes to make a big fuss over **trivial** things.
他喜歡因為無關緊要的事而大做文章。

☐ 三分熟
☐ 五分熟
☐ 七分熟
☐ 全熟

---

tro·phy [ˈtrofɪ]

名 戰利品、獎品

英英 a cup or other decorative object awarded as a prize or encouragement for a victory or success
例 The champion of the swimming contest could have the **trophy**.
游泳比賽的冠軍可以得到這個獎盃。

☐ 三分熟
☐ 五分熟
☐ 七分熟
☐ 全熟

---

trop·ic [ˈtrɑpɪk]

名 回歸線
形 熱帶的

英英 north or south of the equator; torrid
例 The **Tropic** of Cancer passes through Taiwan.
北回歸線經過臺灣。

☐ 三分熟
☐ 五分熟
☐ 七分熟
☐ 全熟

---

tru·ant [ˈtruənt]

名 曠課者、逃學者
形 曠課的、曉課的
同 absent 缺席的

英英 a pupil who does not go to school without permission or explanation, not going to school without permission or explanation
例 The **truants** were often recruited by the local sinister gangs.
逃學者常常被當地黑幫吸收。

☐ 三分熟
☐ 五分熟
☐ 七分熟
☐ 全熟

---

truce [trus]

名 停戰、休戰、暫停
同 pause 暫停

英英 an agreement between enemies to stop fighting for a certain time
例 The two countries are currently in the state of **truce**.
這兩國目前在停戰的狀態。

☐ 三分熟
☐ 五分熟
☐ 七分熟
☐ 全熟

---

tu·ber·cu·lo·sis
[tjuˌbɝkjəˈlosɪs]

名 肺結核

英英 an infectious bacterial disease characterized by the growth of tubercles in the tissues, especially the lungs
例 The patient of **tuberculosis** was kept in quarantine.
肺結核的病人被隔離。

☐ 三分熟
☐ 五分熟
☐ 七分熟
☐ 全熟

---

tu·mor [ˈtjumɚ]

名 腫瘤、瘤

英英 a swelling of a part of the body caused by an abnormal growth of tissue, whether benign or malignant
例 She underwent a surgery to remove the brain **tumor**.
她接受手術移除腦瘤。

☐ 三分熟
☐ 五分熟
☐ 七分熟
☐ 全熟

T

🎧 Track 293

tur·moil [ˈtɝmɔɪl]

名 騷擾、騷動
同 noise 喧鬧

英英 a state of disturbance, confusion, or uncertainty

例 The country is in a **turmoil** as heated protests against the legal pact continued.
隨著反對法案的激烈抗爭行動持續進行，國家處於混亂中。

☐ 三分熟
☐ 五分熟
☐ 七分熟
☐ 全熟

---

twi·light [ˈtwaɪˌlaɪt]

名 黎明、黃昏
同 dusk 黃昏

英英 the soft glowing light from the sky when the sun is just below the horizon

例 The traveler set off in the **twilight** of dawn.
旅人在黎明微光中踏上旅程。

☐ 三分熟
☐ 五分熟
☐ 七分熟
☐ 全熟

---

tyr·an·ny [ˈtɪrənɪ]

名 殘暴、專橫

英英 a small group of people who have unlimited power over the state or country and use it cruelly towards the people; cruel and oppressive government or rule; a state under such rule

例 The documentary is about the **tyranny** of an ancient emperor.
這部紀錄片是關於古代帝王的暴政。

☐ 三分熟
☐ 五分熟
☐ 七分熟
☐ 全熟

Uu

ul·cer [ˈʌlsɚ]

名 潰瘍、弊病

英英 an open sore on the body, caused by a break in the skin or mucous membrane failing to heal

例 Mr. White suffered stomach **ulcers** in his late fifties.
懷特先生快六十歲的時候受到胃潰瘍所苦。

☐ 三分熟
☐ 五分熟
☐ 七分熟
☐ 全熟

---

ul·ti·mate

[ˈʌltəmɪt]

名 基本原則
形 最後的、最終的
同 final 最後的

英英 most extreme or important, being or happening at the end of a process; a basic principle

例 The Constitutional law is the **ultimate** reference of all legal regulations.
憲法是所有法規的最終依據。

☐ 三分熟
☐ 五分熟
☐ 七分熟
☐ 全熟

---

u·nan·i·mous

[jʊˈnænəməs]

形 一致的、和諧的

英英 fully in agreement; of an opinion, decision, or vote held or carried by everyone involved

例 We had a **unanimous** agreement on this issue.
我們對這個議題有一致的看法。

☐ 三分熟
☐ 五分熟
☐ 七分熟
☐ 全熟

un·cov·er
[ʌnˈkʌvɚ]

動 掀開、揭露
同 expose 揭露

英英 to remove a cover or covering from something

例 The prosecutor **uncovered** the truth behind the bribery scandal.
檢察官揭露收賄弊案背後的真相。

☐ 三分熟
☐ 五分熟
☐ 七分熟
☐ 全熟

un·der·es·ti·mate
[ˌʌndɚˈɛstəmɪt]/
[ˌʌndɚˈɛstəˌmet]

動 低估

英英 to estimate something to be smaller or less important than it really is

例 Don't **underestimate** your opponent.
不要低估你的對手。

☐ 三分熟
☐ 五分熟
☐ 七分熟
☐ 全熟

un·der·go
[ˌʌndɚˈgo]

動 廣禍、經歷

英英 to experience or be subjected to something unpleasant or arduous

例 The victim of racism talked about the plight he **underwent**.
種族歧視受害者，描述他經歷過的苦難。

☐ 三分熟
☐ 五分熟
☐ 七分熟
☐ 全熟

un·der·mine
[ˌʌndɚˈmaɪn]

動 削弱基礎、逐漸損害
同 destroy 破壞

英英 erode the base or foundation something

例 The construction of the dam may **undermine** the ecosystem.
建設水壩可能會破壞生態環境。

☐ 三分熟
☐ 五分熟
☐ 七分熟
☐ 全熟

un·der·take
[ˌʌndɚˈtek]

動 承擔、擔保、試圖
同 attempt 試圖

英英 to commit oneself to and begin a responsibility; to take on a large responsibility

例 He **undertook** the enormous responsibility of reorganizing the company.
他承擔整頓公司的重任。

☐ 三分熟
☐ 五分熟
☐ 七分熟
☐ 全熟

un·do [ʌnˈdu]

動 消除、取消、解開
反 bind 捆綁

英英 to unfasten or loosen; cancel or reverse the effects of

例 What is done cannot be **undone**.
覆水難收。

☐ 三分熟
☐ 五分熟
☐ 七分熟
☐ 全熟

un·em·ploy·ment
[ˌʌnɪmˈplɔɪmənt]

名 失業、失業率

英英 the state of being without employment; the number or proportion of unemployed people

例 The government took measures to lower **unemployment** rate.
政府採取措施以降低失業率。

☐ 三分熟
☐ 五分熟
☐ 七分熟
☐ 全熟

🎧 **Track 295**

un·fold [ʌn`fold]

動 攤開、打開
同 reveal 揭示

英英 to open or spread out from a folded position

例 As the plot **unfolds**, the viewers came to realize the intricate relationship between the characters.
隨著劇情展開，觀眾漸漸了解角色之間的複雜關係。

☐三分熟
☐五分熟
☐七分熟
☐全熟

---

u·ni·fy [`junə͵faɪ]

動 使一致、聯合
同 combine 聯合

英英 to come together

例 The small companies were **unified** into an enterprise.
這些小公司被聯合成為一個企業。

☐三分熟
☐五分熟
☐七分熟
☐全熟

---

un·lock [ʌn`lɑk]

動 開鎖、揭開

英英 to undo the lock of something with a key

例 The secret in her mind was **unlocked** during the appointment with the consultant.
她心中的祕密，在與諮商師的會談中被揭露出來。

☐三分熟
☐五分熟
☐七分熟
☐全熟

---

un·pack [ʌn`pæk]

動 解開、卸下
同 discharge 卸下

英英 to open and take out the contents of a suitcase or container

例 We **unpacked** our luggage as soon as we checked in the hotel.
我們一到達旅館就打開行李。

☐三分熟
☐五分熟
☐七分熟
☐全熟

---

up·bring·ing [`ʌp͵brɪŋɪŋ]

名 養育、教養

英英 the treatment and instruction received throughout one's childhood to adulthood

例 His good **upbringing** is the foundation of his success.
好的教養是他成功的基礎。

☐三分熟
☐五分熟
☐七分熟
☐全熟

---

up·grade [`ʌp͵gred]/[͵ʌp`gred]

名 增加、向上、升級
動 改進、提高、升級
同 promote 升級

英英 to an act of upgrading or an upgraded version; to raise to a higher standard or class

例 The budget will be used to **upgrade** the computers in the office.
這筆預算將會用在升級辦公室的電腦。

☐三分熟
☐五分熟
☐七分熟
☐全熟

---

up·hold [ʌp`hold]

動 支持、支撐

英英 to confirm or support; maintain a custom or practice

例 All the committee members **upheld** the decision.
所有的委員會成員都支持這項決定。

☐三分熟
☐五分熟
☐七分熟
☐全熟

U

u·ra·ni·um
[jʊˋrenɪəm]
名 鈾

英英 a grey heavy radioactive metallic chemical element used as a fuel in nuclear reactors

例 The **uranium** has become one of the world's most important energy minerals.
鈾已經成為最重要的能源礦物。

□ 三分熟
□ 五分熟
□ 七分熟
□ 全熟

ur·gen·cy
[ˋɝdʒənsɪ]
名 迫切、急迫

英英 requiring immediate action or attention

例 This is not a matter of some **urgency**.
這是相當緊急的事情。

□ 三分熟
□ 五分熟
□ 七分熟
□ 全熟

u·rine [ˋjʊrɪn]
名 尿、小便

英英 a pale yellowish fluid stored in the bladder and discharged through the urethra, consisting of excess water and waste substances removed from the blood by the kidneys

例 The **urine** sample will be tested to see whether the athlete took illegal drugs.
尿液檢體會被檢驗來查明運動員是否有使用禁藥。

□ 三分熟
□ 五分熟
□ 七分熟
□ 全熟

ush·er [ˋʌʃɚ]
名 引導員
動 招待、護送

英英 a person who shows people in the audience to their seats in a theater or cinema or in church; to show someone somewhere

例 The guard **ushered** the customer to the parking lot.
警衛護送客人到停車場。

□ 三分熟
□ 五分熟
□ 七分熟
□ 全熟

u·ten·sil [juˋtɛnsl]
名 用具、器皿
同 implement 用具

英英 a household tool or container

例 They had a sale on cooking **utensils**.
他們辦了餐具的拍賣會。

□ 三分熟
□ 五分熟
□ 七分熟
□ 全熟

u·til·i·ty [juˋtɪlətɪ]
名 效用、有用
片 utility bill 水電費單

英英 the state of being useful, profitable, or beneficial

例 The payment of **utility** bill can be made by Internet Banking.
水電費帳單可以用網路銀行繳納。

□ 三分熟
□ 五分熟
□ 七分熟
□ 全熟

u·ti·lize [ˋjutl͵aɪz]
動 利用、派上用場

英英 to make practical and effective use of

例 The ingredients for the cuisine were fully **utilized**.
這道菜的食材全都被充分應用。

□ 三分熟
□ 五分熟
□ 七分熟
□ 全熟

🎧 **Track 297**

ut·most [`ʌtˌmost]

名 最大可能、極度
形 極端的
同 extreme 極端的

英英 the most extreme; greatest; greatest possibility or limit

例 He does his **utmost** in whatever he is assigned to do.
他不管分派到什麼工作，都會全力以赴。

□ 三分熟
□ 五分熟
□ 七分熟
□ 全熟

Vv

vac·cine [`væksin]

名 疫苗

英英 a substance used to stimulate the production of antibodies and provide immunity against one or several diseases, prepared from the causative agent of a disease or a synthetic substitute

例 The medical scientists were developing a **vaccine** for Ebola virus.
這些醫藥學家在發展伊波拉病毒的疫苗。

□ 三分熟
□ 五分熟
□ 七分熟
□ 全熟

val·iant [`væljənt]

形 勇敢的
名 勇士
同 brave 勇敢的

英英 showing bravery or determination

例 They made a **valiant** attempt to swim across the English Channel.
他們進行勇敢的嘗試，泳渡英吉利海峽。

□ 三分熟
□ 五分熟
□ 七分熟
□ 全熟

val·id [`vælɪd]

形 有根據的、有效的

英英 well based or logical; legally binding or acceptable

例 She gave a **valid** argument in the debate.
她在辯論當中給出有利的論證。

□ 三分熟
□ 五分熟
□ 七分熟
□ 全熟

va·lid·i·ty

[və`lɪdətɪ]

名 正當、正確
同 justice 正義

英英 based on truth or reason; able to be accepted

例 The lawyer of the defendant questioned the **validity** of the evidence.
被告的律師質疑證據的正當性。

□ 三分熟
□ 五分熟
□ 七分熟
□ 全熟

va·ni·lla [və`nɪlə]

名 香草

英英 a substance obtained from the pods of a tropical climbing orchid or produced artificially, used as a flavoring and in the manufacture of cosmetics

例 She made **vanilla** pudding for her kids.
她做香草布丁給小孩吃。

□ 三分熟
□ 五分熟
□ 七分熟
□ 全熟

var·i·a·ble

[ˈvɛrɪəbl]

形 不定的、易變的

> 英英 inconsistent or without a fixed pattern; liable to vary
>
> 例 His monthly budget consists of fixed and **variable** expenses.
> 他的當月預算包含固定支出和變動支出。

☐ 三分熟
☐ 五分熟
☐ 七分熟
☐ 全熟

var·i·a·tion

[ˌvɛrɪˈeʃən]

名 變動

> 英英 a change or slight difference in condition, amount, or level
>
> 例 The **variation** in the price is determined by the condition of supply-demand balancing.
> 價格的變動是由供需平衡狀況所決定的。

☐ 三分熟
☐ 五分熟
☐ 七分熟
☐ 全熟

vend [vɛnd]

動 叫賣、販賣

> 英英 to offer small items for sale; sell
>
> 例 The local farmer **vended** his produces in the marketplace.
> 本地農夫在市場叫賣自己的農產品。

☐ 三分熟
☐ 五分熟
☐ 七分熟
☐ 全熟

ven·dor [ˈvɛndɚ]

名 攤販、小販

> 英英 a person or company offering selling something
>
> 例 Authorities urged that street **vendors** should be given a place to peddle their goods.
> 當局呼籲街道小販應該要有一個地方可以兜售他們的貨品。

☐ 三分熟
☐ 五分熟
☐ 七分熟
☐ 全熟

verge [vɝdʒ]

名 邊際、邊
動 接近、逼近
同 edge 邊緣

> 英英 an edge or border; a grass edging by the side of a road or path; to be near or close
>
> 例 He was on the **verge** of emotional breakdown after working a consecutive session of 12 hours.
> 他連續工作十二個小時之後，在精神崩潰的邊緣。

☐ 三分熟
☐ 五分熟
☐ 七分熟
☐ 全熟

ver·sa·tile

[ˈvɝsətl]

形 多才的、多用途的
同 competent 能幹的

> 英英 able to adapt or be adapted to many different situations, functions, or activities
>
> 例 The **versatile** actor made his debut in a TV commercial.
> 這位多才多藝的演員是在電視廣告中首次亮相。

☐ 三分熟
☐ 五分熟
☐ 七分熟
☐ 全熟

ver·sion [ˈvɝʒən]

名 說法、版本
同 edition 版本

> 英英 a particular form of something differing in certain respects from other forms of the same type
>
> 例 The students read a simplified **version** of the New Testament.
> 學生讀的是簡化版的新約聖經。

☐ 三分熟
☐ 五分熟
☐ 七分熟
☐ 全熟

V

🎧 Track 299

vet·er·an
[ˈvɛtərən]

名 老手、老練者
同 specialist 專家

英英 a person who has had long experience in a certain field

例 The **veteran** soldier suffered from post-traumatic stress.
這名資深軍人受創傷後壓力症候群所苦。

☐三分熟
☐五分熟
☐七分熟
☐全熟

vet·er·i·nar·i·an /vet
[ˌvɛtərəˈnɛrɪən]/[vɛt]

名 獸醫

英英 a person qualified to treat diseased or injured animals

例 He makes sure that his pet receives good medical care by a certified **veterinarian**.
他確保他的寵物可以獲得合格獸醫的醫療照護。

☐三分熟
☐五分熟
☐七分熟
☐全熟

vi·bra·tion
[vaɪˈbreʃən]

名 震動

英英 an instance of quick, shaking movement

例 The baby was petrified by the **vibration** of the floor.
寶寶被地板的震動嚇到。

☐三分熟
☐五分熟
☐七分熟
☐全熟

vice [vaɪs]

名 不道德的行為
形 副的、代替的
反 virtue 美德

英英 immoral or wicked behavior; criminal activities involving prostitution, pornography, or drugs

例 The **vice** minister will give a speech on the conference.
副部長會在研討會上致詞。

☐三分熟
☐五分熟
☐七分熟
☐全熟

vi·cious [ˈvɪʃəs]

形 邪惡的、不道德的
片 vicious cycle 惡性循環

英英 cruel or violent; wild and dangerous

例 The procrastinators are in the **vicious** cycle of putting off tasks and catching up with the schedule.
拖延者陷入拖延事務以及趕上時程的惡性循環。

☐三分熟
☐五分熟
☐七分熟
☐全熟

vic·tim·ize
[ˈvɪktɪmˌaɪz]

動 使受騙、使受苦

英英 to single out a person for cruel or unjust treatment

例 The teenager was **victimized** in the phishing scam.
這名青少年是網路釣魚的受害者。

☐三分熟
☐五分熟
☐七分熟
☐全熟

vic·tor [ˈvɪktə]

名 勝利者、戰勝者
同 winner 勝利者

英英 the winner of a game, a person who defeats an opponent in a battle, game, or competition

例 The **victor** in the contest will have a golden trophy.
比賽的勝利者可以得到金色的獎盃。

☐三分熟
☐五分熟
☐七分熟
☐全熟

vic·to·ri·ous

[vɪkˋtorɪəs]

形 得勝的、凱旋的

英英 winning a victory; triumphant

例 The representative of Japan emerged **victorious** after the three-hour game.
三個小時的比賽之後，日本的代表選手勝出。

□三分熟
□五分熟
□七分熟
□全熟

---

vil·la [ˋvɪlə]

名 別墅

英英 a large country home in its own grounds; a detached or semi-detached house in a residential district

例 The billionaire lived a luxury **villa**.
億萬富翁住在豪華別墅裡。

□三分熟
□五分熟
□七分熟
□全熟

---

vine·yard [ˋvɪnjəd]

名 葡萄園

英英 a plantation of grapevines, typically producing winemaking grapes

例 These wine grapes were from a local **vineyard**.
這些釀酒用的葡萄是來自本地的葡萄園。

□三分熟
□五分熟
□七分熟
□全熟

---

vir·tu·al [ˋvɝtʃʊəl]

形 事實上的、實質上的
同 actual 事實上的

英英 practically as described, but not completely or according to strict definition

例 The **virtual** reality technology has been applied in military training.
虛擬實境的科技已被應用在軍事訓練上。

□三分熟
□五分熟
□七分熟
□全熟

---

vi·su·al·ize

[ˋvɪʒʊəˌlaɪz]

動 使可見、使具形象
同 fancy 想像

英英 to form a mental image of something; imagine

例 He **visualized** the city to be underdeveloped, but it turned out to be rather modernized.
他想像這個城市很落後，但其實它很現代化。

□三分熟
□五分熟
□七分熟
□全熟

---

vi·tal·i·ty

[vaɪˋtælətɪ]

名 生命力、活力

英英 the state of being strong, lively, and active

例 The dolphin in the sea that we saw during the voyage were full of **vitality**.
我們在航行期間看過的海豚充滿活力。

□三分熟
□五分熟
□七分熟
□全熟

---

vo·cal [ˋvokl̩]

名 母音
形 聲音的

英英 of the human voice; expressing opinions or feelings freely or loudly; vowels

例 The teacher suffered from **vocal** cord paralysis symptoms after teaching for 25 years.
這名老師教書 25 年之後，受到聲帶麻痺症狀之苦。

□三分熟
□五分熟
□七分熟
□全熟

🎧 Track 301

vo·ca·tion [voˈkeʃən] 名 職業 同 occupation 職業	英英 a particular career or occupation 例 He chose computer engineering as his **vocation**. 他選擇電腦工程作為自己的職業。	☐三分熟 ☐五分熟 ☐七分熟 ☐全熟
vo·ca·tion·al [voˈkeʃənḷ] 形 職業上的、業務的 同 professional 專業的、職業上的	英英 relating to an occupation or employment 例 Students of the **vocational** high school are expected to take an internship before graduation. 職業學校的學生需要在畢業之前去實習。	☐三分熟 ☐五分熟 ☐七分熟 ☐全熟
vogue [vog] 名 時尚、流行物 同 fashion 時尚	英英 the temporary fashion or style at a particular time 例 According to the fashion magazine editor, hoop earnings are in **vogue**. 時尚雜誌的編輯表示，大耳環是很時尚的。	☐三分熟 ☐五分熟 ☐七分熟 ☐全熟
vom·it [ˈvɑmɪt] 名 嘔吐、催嘔藥 動 嘔吐、噴出	英英 to empty the contents of stomach matter through the mouth 例 The drunk man **vomited** by the street. 醉漢在街上嘔吐。	☐三分熟 ☐五分熟 ☐七分熟 ☐全熟
vul·gar [ˈvʌlgɚ] 形 粗糙的、一般的 反 decent 體面的	英英 lacking cultivation or taste 例 The slang words and **vulgar** terms are usually not included in the dictionary. 俚語和粗俗的話通常不會收錄在字典裡。	☐三分熟 ☐五分熟 ☐七分熟 ☐全熟
vul·ner·a·ble [ˈvʌlnərəbl̩] 形 易受傷害的、脆弱的 同 sensitive 易受傷害的 片 vulnerable to 易受影響	英英 weak, and liable to being attacked or harmed 例 The president of the company is in a position **vulnerable** to criticism. 公司總裁的地位容易受到批評。	☐三分熟 ☐五分熟 ☐七分熟 ☐全熟

Ww

W

ward·robe
['wɔrdˌrob]

名 衣櫃、衣櫥
同 closet 衣櫥

英英 a large, tall storage unit in which clothes may be hung or stored

例 She thought the fur coat would not fit in her **wardrobe**.
她認為這件毛皮大衣不適合放在自己的衣櫃中。

☐ 三分熟
☐ 五分熟
☐ 七分熟
☐ 全熟

war·fare ['wɔrˌfɛr]

名 戰爭、競爭

英英 engaged in war or the state of war

例 The record of the **warfare** between the two countries was erased.
兩國之間戰爭的紀錄被抹滅了。

☐ 三分熟
☐ 五分熟
☐ 七分熟
☐ 全熟

war·ran·ty
['wɔrəntɪ]

名 依據、正當的理由
保證、擔保

英英 a written guarantee promising repair or replacement of an article if necessary within a specified period

例 The **warranty** period of the air conditioner is one year.
冷氣機的保固期是一年。

☐ 三分熟
☐ 五分熟
☐ 七分熟
☐ 全熟

wa·ter·proof/
wa·ter·tight
['wɔtɚˌpruf]/['wɔtɚˌtait]

形 防水的
同 resistant 防……的

英英 not allowing water to go through, impervious to water

例 The **waterproof** coating spray can be applied to your shoes.
這種防水保護層噴霧可以用在你的鞋子上面。

☐ 三分熟
☐ 五分熟
☐ 七分熟
☐ 全熟

what·so·ev·er
[ˌhwɑtso'ɛvɚ]

形 任何的、不論什麼
同 however 無論如何

英英 at all, whatever

例 Her parents pampered her by offering **whatsoever** she wanted.
她的父母給她任何他想要的東西，把她寵壞了。

☐ 三分熟
☐ 五分熟
☐ 七分熟
☐ 全熟

wind·shield
['windˌʃild]

名 擋風玻璃

英英 a large window on the front of a vehicle

例 It is necessary to clean the **windshield** before driving.
開車之前，清理擋風玻璃是必要的。

☐ 三分熟
☐ 五分熟
☐ 七分熟
☐ 全熟

with·stand
[wiθ'stænd]

動 耐得住、經得起
同 resist 忍耐

英英 to remain undamaged or unaffected by

例 The needle-leaved trees could **withstand** the cold weather.
針葉樹可以耐得住寒冷的氣候。

☐ 三分熟
☐ 五分熟
☐ 七分熟
☐ 全熟

🎧 Track 303

wit·ty [ˈwɪtɪ]

形 機智的、詼諧的
同 clever 機敏的

英英 talking in a funny, clever or inventive way

例 We were inspired by the old man's **witty** words.
我們受到老人機智話語的啟發。

☐ 三分熟
☐ 五分熟
☐ 七分熟
☐ 全熟

woo [wu]

動 求婚、求愛、
　　爭取……的支持

英英 to try to influence and gain the love of a woman

例 What did the gentleman say to **woo** her?
那位紳士說了什麼向她求愛呢？

☐ 三分熟
☐ 五分熟
☐ 七分熟
☐ 全熟

wrench [rɛntʃ]

名 扭轉
動 猛扭
同 wring 擰、扭斷

英英 to pull or twist something suddenly and violently

例 He **wrenched** the door-knob, only to realize that it was locked.
他扭動門把，卻發現門鎖著。

☐ 三分熟
☐ 五分熟
☐ 七分熟
☐ 全熟

wres·tle [ˈrɛsl̩]

動 角力、搏鬥
同 struggle 奮鬥

英英 take part in a fight or contest that involves closely grappling with one's opponent and throwing them to the groun

例 The shopkeeper was **wrestling** with the robber when the police arrived.
警方趕到時，店老闆正在跟搶匪搏鬥。

☐ 三分熟
☐ 五分熟
☐ 七分熟
☐ 全熟

Xx

Xe·rox/xe·rox

[ˈzɪrɑks]

名 全錄影印
動 以全錄影印法影印
片 Xerox machine
　　影印機

英英 a xerographic copying process; to copy by a xerographic copying process

例 Do you know how to repair the **Xerox** machine?
你知道如何修理影印機嗎？

☐ 三分熟
☐ 五分熟
☐ 七分熟
☐ 全熟

Yy

X
Y
Z

yearn [jɜn]

動 懷念、想念、渴望

英英 to have an intense feeling of loss and longing for something or someone

例 She **yearned** for a chance to study abroad.
她渴望有機會出國唸書。

☐ 三分熟
☐ 五分熟
☐ 七分熟
☐ 全熟

Zz

zeal [zil]

名 熱誠、熱忱

英英 great energy, eagerness, or enthusiasm for something

例 She has the **zeal** to promote the welfare of stray animals.
她有熱忱推動流浪動物的福祉。

☐ 三分熟
☐ 五分熟
☐ 七分熟
☐ 全熟

語研力 **E073**

精準7000單字滿分版：
中高級程度 Level 5 & Level 6

更短時間，更高效率，完勝7000單字！

作　　者	Michael Yang、Tong Weng ◎合著
顧　　問	曾文旭
出版總監	陳逸祺、耿文國
主　　編	陳蕙芳
執行編輯	翁芯俐
文字校對	莊詠翔
美術編輯	李依靜
法律顧問	北辰著作權事務所

印　　製	世和印製企業有限公司
初　　版	2022 年 11 月
出　　版	凱信企業集團 - 凱信企業管理顧問有限公司
電　　話	（02）2773-6566
傳　　真	（02）2778-1033
地　　址	106 台北市大安區忠孝東路四段 218 之 4 號 12 樓
信　　箱	kaihsinbooks@gmail.com

定　　價	新台幣 360 元 / 港幣 120 元
產品內容	1 書

總 經 銷	采舍國際有限公司
地　　址	235 新北市中和區中山路二段 366 巷 10 號 3 樓
電　　話	（02）8245-8786
傳　　真	（02）8245-8718

國家圖書館出版品預行編目資料

精準 7000 單字滿分版：中高級程度 Level 5 & Level
6／Michael Yang & Tong Weng◎合著. – 初版. –
臺北市：凱信企業集團凱信企業管理顧問有限公
司, 2022.11
　面；　公分
ISBN 978-626-7097-26-7(平裝)

1.CST: 英語 2.CST: 詞彙
805.12　　　　　　　　　　　111012530